The
Devil's
Work

The Devil's Work

ED MULLINS

SIMON & SCHUSTER

LONDON · SYDNEY · NEW YORK · TOKYO · SINGAPORE · TORONTO

First published in Great Britain by Simon & Schuster Ltd, 1996
A Viacom Company

Simon & Schuster Ltd
West Garden Place
Kendal Street
London W2 2AQ

Simon & Schuster of Australia Pty Ltd
Sydney

A CIP catalogue record for this book is available from the
British Library

ISBN 0-684-81646-6

Typeset in Palatino 11.5/13pt by
Palimpsest Book Production Limited, Polmont, Stirlingshire
Printed and bound in Great Britain by
Butler & Tanner, Frome

To all the Devil's disciples.

'Don't you see I have grown up outside the pale of duty and "oughts"? Love me as I am, sweet one, for I shall never be better.'

(Elizabeth Gaskell, *Wives and Daughters*)

One

On the first day of what David insisted on calling 'our trial separation' I got drunk. Maybe I'd have been less drunk if it hadn't been for Caroline, who decided to celebrate my 'Liberation Day', as she put it, by dragging me to Langan's Brasserie for a lunch which stretched further and deeper into the afternoon as neither of us felt confident of making a straight line to the door.

'God, you're lucky, Claudia, having a divorce to look forward to,' she said loudly, pouring out the first bottle. 'What's it feel like?' Then, without waiting for an answer she went on in the same penetrating voice, 'I've always imagined divorce must be one of those things that make marriage worth while. Perhaps I should suggest it to Patrick. God knows, we need something to make our marriage worth while.' Her blue eyes were sharp with mischief and she gave one of her rippling laughs, quite unconcerned by how far across the restaurant her remarks had carried. 'But at least you managed to escape without having children,' she added.

Caroline could never quite believe that I would have loved to have children. Or she pretended not to, just as she pretended that her own had arrived with special instructions from the Devil. She supposed she quite liked them really, she would confess sometimes, looking thoughtful, provided she didn't have to see them too often: now she was waiting for them to grow old enough to rebel so she could see them even less. Meanwhile they were safely parked in distant boarding-schools, which allowed her to wax indignant about the fees. The more expensive the school the longer the holidays, she'd noticed. Why on earth couldn't the state provide boarding-schools like they provided Borstals? There wasn't a great deal of difference anyway, as far as she could see.

Charitable views of this nature had been aired frequently

during the two years I'd known Caroline, and they were resistant to all argument. Usually they'd be dropped into some quite different conversation and then, when it suited her, dismissed again so she could return to the discussion she'd already wrecked.

'Go on, then, tell me,' she asked again as though I'd been the one to create the diversion. 'What *does* it feel like?'

Since I'd only moved into my own little rented flat that morning, I hadn't had a lot of time to think about it.

'Exhausting,' I found myself saying. 'I feel I want at least a year to recover.'

She said nothing for a few seconds, and began to gaze at me quizzically. There was always something on Caroline's mind when she looked at people like that, and it was usually dangerous.

'Well, I've got an idea,' she announced. 'A brilliant idea. I've been thinking about it for weeks while you've been dithering, and I want you to say "Yes"!'

My heart sank at what might be coming next.

'Am I allowed to say "No"?' I asked, laughing.

As usual when asked a direct question, Caroline was no longer listening. She was casting an eye over the restaurant just to check that she was the most glamorous woman here, and certainly the only real blonde. Then, having satisfied herself that this was so, she looked back at me. This time she was frowning.

'God, you're pretty,' she said, having already forgotten my question. 'I'm getting old and frumpy, and look at you. What *are* you, thirty-one, thirty-two? Gorgeous – *and* divorced. Well, nearly divorced. Free! Those cheek-bones. And that incredible skin. I suppose it's all that Italian blood. I'm just English and blotchy. The sun looks at me and laughs, and I can see why. And I bet you don't even wear a bra.'

A waiter serving three tables away looked up expectantly. Caroline caught his eye and waved the empty wine-bottle at him.

Then she turned back to me.

'Now. My idea. Listen, you know my father died, don't you? Well, he finally did, the old bastard.'

This was another of Caroline's games. Her father had been dying ever since I'd known her, and Caroline had devotedly rushed down to Devon to look after him each time he phoned to announce he was at death's door. He invariably chose to be dying at strategic moments. Only last winter she'd cut the family Christmas lunch and driven flat out down the motorway to Norton Abbas praying she wouldn't arrive too late, only to find him energetically in bed with his mistress. Then a few months later – perhaps during a repeat performance – he really did have a heart attack, whereupon Caroline dashed down to Norton Abbas again, this time too late. None of his other children had been able to stand him, but Caroline had enjoyed a special relationship with her father, based as far as I could tell on mutual bloody-mindedness.

'Well, he's left me the house,' she went on. 'It's the only kind thing he ever did. Most unlike him; I thought the mistress might get it. But no, it's mine.'

The second bottle of wine arrived. Caroline tasted it, and sent it back.

'Nothing wrong with it really,' she assured me, tucking into her pheasant. 'It's a matter of principle. Otherwise they don't respect you.'

From the look on the waiter's face as he brought the replacement bottle, he already didn't. I looked down in embarrassment. This time she just sniffed it.

'Yes, it's fine,' she said with her most winning smile. 'And thank-you for taking so much trouble.' The waiter's expression changed instantly to one of grovelling pleasure.

This was how Caroline always conquered men: she clobbered them first, then poured on the charm. And she didn't always bother about the charm.

'Now,' she continued, placing her elbows on the table and gazing at me while she tugged at a pheasant leg with her teeth. 'The other thing that's happened in my life since I saw you last is that Patrick's gone bust, the silly bugger. I always told him not to put his money into Lloyd's. Just at the wrong time – of course. He would. Every time an oil tanker goes down, so does he. Mind you he goes down all the time; that's just the trouble.' Caroline gave a raunchy laugh that turned several heads. 'I keep telling him it's symbolic, but instead of listening to me he goes off to some sex therapist. He came back after the first session saying it was all much better now, and "Look." Well, I did look. I told him I honestly couldn't tell the difference, which didn't please him at all. That was when he started putting Growmore on it, until I refused to do fellatio because it tasted so disgusting; besides I thought it might give me throat cancer. You never know, do you?'

The restaurant was riveted by this time, and the service was clearly declining at the far end of the room as waiters found it necessary to refill glasses at the tables nearest to us. Caroline's laughter was the only sound audible in the place. I tried to remind myself that this was the day of my separation, which was why Caroline had insisted on bringing me here – 'to celebrate,' she said, 'and to hear you tell me what a total louse David has been'. As it was I'd managed to say half a dozen words at most, and didn't get the feeling I'd be invited to say many more. It was as well that I loved Caroline. What was extraordinary was how many other people did too. But then in the end her nuisance value had always been overshadowed by her entertainment value, and I supposed that somewhere beneath those impeccable designer clothes a heart of gold lay buried. At least I chose to think so.

'Well, the point of all this is' – Caroline paused to wipe her fingers on the napkin and reach for the menu – 'the house in London is a "collateral" – I think that's what the lawyers called it. Which means that the next time a bloody oil tanker goes down we may lose it.' I was beginning to feel quite horrified by this story, but Caroline seemed unperturbed by this collapse of the family fortunes, and was already summoning lemon sorbets for us both and pouring out yet more glasses of wine.

'So, Claudia, maybe it's good-bye London,' she said with the broadest smile. 'And you know, I really don't give a fuck. I never liked the house much anyway. Gloomy great hulk. Patrick bought it to make up for the size of his willy. I think we'll just sell it anyway – the house, I mean. And now I've got Priory Hall, who cares? Besides' – Caroline raised her wine-glass in front of her face and gazed at me over it – 'it's where I was born, Priory Hall. And I *love* it. I really love it. I want to return to the womb.'

I blinked at so uncomfortable a thought.

'But what about Patrick?' I asked. 'He can't exactly commute from Devon.'

Patrick did something gilt-edged in the City. I never knew what, and I suspected Caroline didn't either. Though she cared for him a great deal more than she ever let on, this never extended to what he did for a living.

'Patrick,' she exclaimed, looking surprised. 'Oh, he'll come down for the odd weekend, I suppose. He'll get himself a small pad in town. He'll like that, and then he won't have to lie to me about his little infidelities. All the secretaries fall for him; it must be those pretty curls. Now he won't need to tell them he's about to leave me, and they won't need to ring up sobbing. You know, I used to answer the phone and laugh. After I'd put the receiver down I'd say to Patrick terribly cheerfully, "Darling, if that's what you want, you'd better have it," then he'd go pale and rush off to give her the boot. I did wonder though what on earth they'd discovered about him that I hadn't. After all, it's the same cock.' She gave a sigh. 'Just think of being married to a man called Uppingham. I always tell people he should be called Halfwayuppingham.'

The couple at the next table rose and walked out without paying the bill. Caroline didn't seem to notice. The *maître d'* did, and glared at us.

'Now, you won't let me get to the real point,' she went on, digging into her sorbet. 'I'm going to be a country mouse. And I'm going to be almost as free as you. So why don't you come down too?' She raised a hand to stop me answering. 'Listen, Claudia, I've thought it all out, and it's perfectly simple. Since you walked out on David and you've got no dependants, and he's a mean bastard anyway, you're only going to be able to afford some miserable hutch in Tooting, or wherever, and why the hell should you want to live in London anyway? Here's the answer. Priory Hall has a gatehouse – terribly old, part of the former priory. And it's empty.'

To my surprise Caroline reached across the table and grasped my arm.

'And it's yours. No rent. There are the old priory ruins if you should feel maudlin and nun-like, with its own shrine to some female saint in the Dark Ages – miracle hunters are a bit of a pest in the summer – and there are thirty-five acres of land to play around with which my father never bothered with. You always said you wanted a large garden so you could grow all those things you're so brilliant at cooking. So you can do what you like with it. Create a Versailles, well, a small Versailles. And think of the fun we can have. Parties. Picnics. Lovers. We can spread our wings. Mayhem! Claudia, we can *live*!'

I felt stunned. I'd expected some entirely lunatic scheme from Caroline. But this! To my astonishment it suddenly seemed exactly the sort of break I needed after the long grey days of my marriage. A year to do nothing in, or everything in, whatever I chose. I tried to imagine what it would be like. The country. Walks. The sea. That huge garden. Caroline nearby but not too near. Time to think. Time to heal the bruises. And space. I could have a dog. I could write maybe. Read a lot. Invite friends. Reassemble my life.

And most of all I'd be far, far away from the suffocating world of being a loyal MP's wife, always smiling, always gracious, always caring, always waking in the pit of the night wondering if I'd ever manage to get out of it, and would it be this darkness of the soul for ever and ever and ever? And David in pyjamas with his back to me, snoring.

After all the decisions I hadn't been able to make for so long, this one hardly needed to be made.

'You're on,' I said, feeling intensely happy. 'I think I'd love it.'

She gave a whoop. Then another raunchy laugh.

'Tremendous!' And she washed down the last of her sorbet with the last of her wine. 'Christ, we'll wake the place up, Claudia. It could do with it. Sleepy old Devon. They'll all think you're some Italian film star, and perhaps I'll tell them you are. Of course Norton Abbas is terribly ancient and pretty and all that. You'll love it. It's just that the people . . .' Caroline's voice rose again, and her eyes grew wide. 'Mirrors of each other, most of them. The same voices. The same clothes. The same opinions. The same friends. I tell you, it's like living in a mail-order catalogue. And as for sex!' She gave out another of her rippling laughs. 'It's so dirty a word it doesn't even feature in the local graffiti.'

The laugh died away and she looked at me anxiously for a moment.

'Jesus, now I've probably put you off. Have I?'

It was my turn to laugh.

'I can always leave, Caroline. I don't have to take on a lease for fifty years, do I? And frankly,' I said, 'right now I don't think I care a damn what the town's like. Or the people. I'd just love to give it a go.'

Caroline looked relieved, and then mischievous.

'Actually there *are* a few human beings around. There's Megan who's huge and Welsh and a portrait painter. She also paints cabbages, I'm told, but I suspect that's only because her bosom gets in the way. You'll like her. You might also like Joan, who's my doctor's wife. Waspish and wicked: always trying to get Patrick into bed, the poor misguided soul. Gets terribly cross when you tell her that, and goes off in a sulk to her bees. Keeps millions of them in the priory grounds. A strange displacement activity, I think, but maybe there's something I don't know about bees. Wasn't Cupid stung by them, or was that somebody else? Anyway, that's two people who'll help keep you sane, even if I don't. Does that make the place sound better?'

Perhaps it was the wine, but I leaned over and gave her a kiss on both cheeks. A couple passing our table glanced at us. The man was gross and middle-aged, with a sweaty forehead and sweaty hair sprouting from an open-necked shirt.

'Couple of bloody dykes,' he said in a nasal voice loud enough to make sure we heard.

Perhaps it was the wine too, but I got up from my chair, scooped up the remains of my lemon sorbet in one hand, and tipped it down the inside of his shirt. Then with the other hand I squashed it.

'Cool it,' I said, smiling. 'And have a nice day.'

I sat down feeling exhilarated while the man bustled away from the laughter in the restaurant. Caroline's face was radiant.

'Wow! Terrific!' she said. 'Why don't we just pretend you're divorced, then we can call it D-Day?'

David rang to ask if I was absolutely sure I was doing the right thing. I said I was quite sure. In the silence I could hear him thinking, and knew exactly *what* he was thinking. I'd heard it all before, dozens and dozens of times. The thoughts always came in layers. The top layer was the plea for reason. He was convinced we could work it out. Our differences were small (first mistake), and we were both of us civilised people, weren't we? (Second mistake.) Of course some breathing-space was an excellent thing; he was glad we'd agreed to it. (We hadn't . . . I'd walked out.) When I felt calmer we should get together and talk. (When had we ever done anything else?) It wasn't as though he didn't understand me. (Third mistake.) But all marriages required accommodation, didn't they? (Yes, of me to him.)

Then there was the second layer. First the softening of the voice, followed by – he loved me, he'd always loved me. (Definition please.) He couldn't imagine himself ever living with anyone else. (Frankly, nor could I.) I'd given him so much in his life. (Possibly.) We'd fought so many battles together. (His battles. Mine were placated as tantrums.) And then, in case I'd forgotten, he loved me.

The third layer was invariably well hidden among the other two, but by now I'd learnt to read the small print. It was phrased as gently as possible, but once extracted from the undergrowth it went something like this: I do need to think of my career (when did he not?); as a QC I am an advocate of marital fidelity (yes, on and on and on, in every newspaper that would print it); as a parliamentarian I have always championed old-fashioned family values (boss-man rules); as a member of the government I'm a merciless critic of Commons immorality and double standards; I'm Mr Squeaky-Clean (the morning shower and clean pyjamas, that *cordon sanitaire* around him); it mustn't be known that my wife left me; please let us be discreet. (OK, buster, you can have that bit. I'd like my privacy too.)

This evening's phone call had one more layer. David's voice sounded agitated. The press had somehow got hold of our separation, he explained. They didn't know where I was, so he'd taken it upon himself to answer for me, but only in the *Telegraph* 'exclusively'. He'd refused to discuss it with the others: they would only have twisted what he said. I knew what the press was like, didn't I? So, please would I not talk to them. That would be a kindness. He hoped I was looking after myself.

I was, thank-you.

Intrigued by what the papers would have to say tomorrow morning, I began to cook myself some supper. I'd bought basil and pine nuts from the deli I'd discovered round the corner, and made a pesto sauce. David always hated garlic – I always suspected it reminded him of body odours – so the smell of it as I ground in the basil, nuts, oil and grated Parmesan made me feel specially separated and happy.

That was when I realised what it was that so attracted me to Norton Abbas, apart, that is, from Caroline (who might in any case prove a mixed blessing). It was the savour of things that had been grown. In a flat I couldn't grow anything. In the little weekend cottage in Kent which David and I used to have, there'd been only the tiniest garden; what was more, as if by some projection of my mood – or my marriage – it had managed to grow only the most spartan things. Nothing you could possibly eat, or smell, nothing luxuriant, nothing that made you want to linger barefoot in the magic hour with a low blouse and a glass of wine, holding hands. But then David and I didn't. David's magic hour was preparing legal briefs or studying government white papers.

Yes, it was the basil and the garlic that did it, and that lovely rich, dark olive oil. Thirty-five acres, Caroline had said. An absurd quantity of course; one could get lost in it. But I could cultivate it, some of it at least. The climate of South Devon was warm, wasn't it? Well, warm*ish*. And the soil rich. Red soil rich as wine.

It was strange being alone. Not lonely, which pleased me. I was far lonelier when David was with me. That already seemed quite another life. In fact everything that had happened in that other life felt entirely detached from what I was now. It was a chain of muddled events which ended abruptly *there*, just a few feet from me, and I was free to walk away from it, leaving it to rust, letting other lives and other miseries entwine themselves among it.

I boiled and drained the spaghetti, and mixed in the pesto sauce. It was late, a summer dusk. Swifts were screaming round the rooftops. There was a police siren somewhere. Sounds of a piano drifted up from the pub on the corner. Someone's telephone rang downstairs.

So, it was the end of the first day of my separation. And what would I remember of it? I laughed. Perhaps I would remember it as the day I poured lemon sorbet over some smartarse in a restaurant. Perhaps I would remember it as the first day of my life.

Men always fell in love with my eyes. It was as if they saw their own dreams and longings reflected in them – dark pools beckoning Narcissus to plunge in and drown. It always mystified me, and sometimes excited me, how a meeting of eyes can feel like a meeting of bodies; and my eyes invariably seemed to transmit that message whether I wished to or not.

I could only think this must have been why I married David: he didn't fall in love with my eyes. It was a long time before I came to understand why he didn't, but at the time I felt intrigued, even flattered. At first I was vain enough to imagine there must be something wrong with me. Then it dawned on me that here perhaps was a man who'd fallen in love with what lay behind my eyes: my mind, my soul, my private mystery. The real stuff. The real me.

And, oh dear God, what an appalling mistake that was.

In the midst of these reflections the phone went. I was in the bath (the first deprivation, no hand-phone). I clutched a towel round me and glanced at my watch on the way to the sitting-room, hair dripping, hoping there was no voyeur across the street. It was nine o'clock. Christ, I'd slept late. It was just the sort of hour David might choose to ring, no doubt with some further 'thoughts'.

But it was Caroline. She was in high spirits. Had I seen the papers? Why not? They were full of me, she said. She'd gone out and bought the lot, including the tabloids – especially the tabloids. She laughed. 'You wait.' Why didn't I come over immediately, and we'd go through them? She'd have some coffee ready. 'You may need it. Hurry.'

Caroline lived just over the river, in a large gloomy house on the common that Patrick had bought to make his willy feel bigger, so Caroline claimed. What she didn't know was that a friend of mine had had a brief affair with Patrick, and his willy was perfectly normal, she assured me. Unless of course the Growmore had worked by then. But perhaps Caroline simply had extravagant tastes. One day I would ask her, but not today. I wanted to see what David had chosen to tell – and *not* to tell – the press about me.

I dried my hair, slipped into a T-shirt and jeans, and drove my baby Fiat (loyalty to Italy dies hard) down the Fulham Palace Road and over the river against the late rush-hour traffic. A flock of Canadian geese was planing down on to the low tide, and the sun was dabbing silver brushstrokes on the water. I envied Caroline living here. I'd been to the house often enough, pouring my heart out to her over an evening bottle of wine in the garden while David was inevitably at the House of Commons, or on some important committee or other. 'I hope you've got a lover,' she'd say inevitably, stretching herself lazily on a garden chair. 'But of course you have, just look at you,' she'd go on. 'And he's obviously good at it.' It was true on only one occasion, and I had to be very careful not to tell her who it was, or she'd certainly claim to have had him too – and she'd probably have been right, MPs being what they are.

The front door was open, and there were sounds from within of Caroline giving hell to some builder on the telephone. I found her draped across the sofa with one extremely shapely leg crooked over the back of it. Her shirt was unbuttoned almost to the waist to prove that at thirty-eight (thirty-nine would have been too obvious a lie) she still had wonderful breasts. Caroline was always highly competitive about such things, assuring me that even though I was quite a few years younger, mine would certainly droop long before hers, the price I had to pay for being half-Italian and having that dusky peasant complexion and those disgracefully bedroom eyes. She always had to talk her way into bed, she complained; I only had to look at a man, 'damn you'.

She gave me a nod without bothering to smile, and went on with her phone call.

'Well, just build me one; you're supposed to be a builder, for Christ's sake.'

The voice was jagged with irritation. She gave a final grunt and switched off the hand-phone.

'Can you believe it?' she grumbled. 'I only want the man to run me up a simple drinks cabinet.'

'Perhaps you should try a carpenter,' I suggested.

Caroline looked at me witheringly, and changed the subject.

'Well, there they are. Look.'

The glass table in the centre of the sitting-room was scattered with newspapers which looked as though they'd been hastily ransacked. Caroline swung herself languidly to her feet and wandered over to the sideboard, where she poured out two cups of coffee and handed me one of them. Then she strode over to the table and picked up one of the newspapers. It was the *Daily Telegraph*.

'Right,' she said. 'This is going to be fun. Let's have a little character profile, shall we? See if anything here rings a bell with you.' There was a pause as she flicked over several pages. I was dreading this: I wanted to grab all the papers and run away, but this was going to be another Caroline performance. 'Here we are. Now, I want you to tell me who this Claudia Hazlitt person is who seems to be staying temporarily with friends in the country because, and I quote, "She has been under severe strain due to excessive work in her husband's constituency," explained junior government minister David Hazlitt at his home in Leatherhead yesterday. "It's nothing at all serious," Mr Hazlitt added. "She just needs a bit of a break, that's all."' Caroline laughed, and threw me the *Telegraph*. 'Oh, and there's more to come. Read it.'

I did. David was quoted at tedious length. Methinks my husband doth protest too much. It was like reading the school report of the class goodie-goodie. I was a loyal and diligent person. I had a powerful sense of duty. I never spared myself. I shared his commitment to family values. No, there was no disharmony between us whatsoever: we were the happiest couple imaginable. He couldn't ask for a better wife, or a greater support in his career. No, she had chosen not to make a statement because really there was no statement to make. She would soon be home again after her rest. Tum-ti-tum-ti-tum-ti-tum.

'Recognise yourself, do you?' asked Caroline, settling in to enjoy herself. 'Well, try this.'

She picked up the *Daily Mail*.

'Here's a pithy little piece, on the gossip page: you probably know the man, don't you? Everybody does. "Is the party over?" the headline goes. Now, "Would-be environment secretary David Hazlitt's bright prospects may have dimmed with the departure of his beautiful, gifted wife Claudia. Party pressures have proved too much and the ten-year marriage is cracking up. Many saw her as the dour Hazlitt's greatest political asset. Glittering hostess and *cordon bleu* cook, whom he first met at the exclusive Hurlingham Club, she smoothed his path to the top with her famously elegant dinner parties. Others think he may do better without her. Half-Italian and with a temperament to match, she's a bit of a loose cannon. As I revealed at the time, at a Mansion House dinner she once referred to the Prime Minister all too audibly as 'Mr Minor'. Claudia's present whereabouts are unknown, but local constituency chairperson Hilda Gobbit informed me yesterday, 'The dear girl just needs a rest. I can assure you there's no question of a divorce. No, no, no!' And when Hilda Gobbit says no, she means no, as Mr Hazlitt's predecessor once famously discovered."'

Caroline looked up at me with a gleeful expression.

'That's getting a bit nearer it, wouldn't you say? Want some more?' And she reached down for the *Daily Mirror*. 'Well, you've made the headline here, my darling. "Claudia's Haddit with Hazlitt." Not bad, that.' She laughed and read on. '"Italian beauty Claudia Hazlitt has found out what *Mirror* readers have known for years. That her husband, MP for Box Hill David Hazlitt, is a pompous fart. She moved out yesterday after a mega-row. 'She's a lovely girl,' a neighbour said. 'He's just a self-righteous prat.' So, good on you, bellissima! Now let's boot the rest of them out."'

If I was looking bewildered Caroline didn't seem to notice. She picked up the *Daily Express*.

'And another headline. "Claudia's Tory is Truly Blue." Now, you'll love this, darling. "David Hazlitt's chances of being the next environment secretary may have taken a knock with the news that he can't even keep his own environment in order. The loveliest lady ever to bedeck a Tory party conference has left the elegant Surrey house she and David bought together in happier times. Readers of this column will recall that there was an earlier rift after Claudia hired a fire-eating Kissogram to liven up David's fortieth birthday party. The young lady unfortunately set fire to her pubic hair and had to be rushed to the local hospital. Hazlitt couldn't see the funny side of it, and his career-conscious attempts at a cover-up cost him friends. A wife too? Sources close to the couple say David's very blue. Will she come back? He says so . . . but then he would, wouldn't he?"'

Caroline chuckled, and poured out more coffee.

'There are quite a few things I'm beginning to learn about you, Claudia,' she said wryly. 'You've been bloody guarded about your past, haven't you? And here's a bit more of it. You must tell me about that too.'

With that she picked up *Today*, then spread out one of the centre pages on the table. Right across half of one page was a photograph of David and me. I didn't remember ever having seen it before, and at first I couldn't even place it. We were in a garden. There were a number of people all with glasses in their hands except for David who was looking glum. Next to him was me looking anything but glum; in fact, I was looking extremely animated. I also seemed to be revealing a generous amount of myself, not only by what I was wearing (or not wearing), but from the look on my face. My eyes were doing it again. Thank heavens the man on the receiving end was hidden by another figure, because as I gazed at the photograph I suddenly remembered exactly where and when it had been taken, two years ago, and that the invisible man was very soon to become my first and only extra-marital lover. It was as if the photographer, whoever it was, had spotted that this was the moment when I knew that my fidelity to David was over.

I was shaken. It was uncanny, creepy, seeing it there. It stared out of the page at me like a prophesy. It was a photograph of the end of a marriage.

I glanced hastily at the short piece that ran beside the photo, horrified lest the truth of the picture was spelt out in print. Caroline read the look on my face, and laughed.

'It's all right, my darling. Nothing incriminating. Go on, read it out.'

The headline was 'Arrividerci Davie!' I gulped and read on. '"The likely next environment secretary David Hazlitt may be a clear winner for the Tories, but his marriage is looking distinctly marginal. Luscious Claudia Hazlitt has moved out of the matrimonial home. It's believed she may have fled to Italy, where her aristocratic mother Anna-Maria comes from an old Bologna family. Husband David refused to comment yesterday, but friends reveal that Claudia has grown tired of coffee parties for the chattering classes. Nor have her to-die-for looks made her a favourite with the tweedy frumps who put David into Westminster. The family solicitor denied rumours that the rift has been caused by Claudia saying 'Yes' to a modelling job. Our photograph certainly reveals why she might do so. Oh, those Italian curves!"' There followed a little postcript in italics. '"*Morally upright David may simply not be up to it.*"'

Caroline gave a bellow of laughter.

'Wow! That was a low blow. Morally upright, but otherwise not. D'you remember telling me the only time David got a real erection was when he heard he'd been made PPS to the home secretary. Is that true?'

I wished I'd never told Caroline that, though it made a good story at the time. It was poetically true at least. What was undeniably true about David was that he found power much more of a turn-on than sex. In the days when I believed he loved me for what lay behind my eyes, I never realised that he never really looked at me at all.

'He's never liked bodies much, except when they form committees,' I said. 'It's amazing, isn't it? Just about every member of the House of Commons is having it off like a rabbit, except one. And he's the one I married. You know I had to show him where to put it on our wedding night.'

Caroline looked at me wide-eyed.

'So that's what they mean by a "Tory wet"! Jesus, he makes Patrick seem like Don Juan.' She went on gazing at me, shaking her head. 'Claudia! Why . . . did . . . you . . . do . . . it?' she asked very slowly. 'You of all people? I've never understood. You're sexy. You're gorgeous. You're bright. You could have had any man you wanted. So, why?'

'I *did* have one man I wanted, very briefly,' I said. 'The trouble was, I was married by then, so it was even briefer.'

Caroline made a face.

'That doesn't answer my question.' Her voice had a petulant edge. 'Why did you marry him, for Christ's sake?'

We'd had this conversation so many times before, and I'd never got very far, perhaps because I never really knew the answer. Why does one agree to marry someone? Isn't it much more chancy than people think? After all, one doesn't exactly get practice at it. Marriage had seemed quite different from having an affair, and I'd only had one of those at that time. I only knew that I was young, I was a foreigner, I had no father, no brothers or sisters, my mother was half a continent away, and I was swept up by this incredibly clever lawyer who seemed to know absolutely everything, who was so self-assured, who knew exactly where he was going and who was determined that I was the perfect woman to accompany him there. He would share everything with me, he said. I was his ideal partner. I'd never met a man like that before. I assumed that since he had everything, it would *be* everything. Nothing would be left out. I was Italian; I didn't know about puritans then.

'You have to understand the power of people who know exactly what they want,' I said.

I thought perhaps Caroline *would* understand, being that sort of person herself, but she was still shaking her head.

'But why you?' She swept a hand in the direction of the papers scattered on the table. 'All those things they say there. You come from an old Italian family. You had a terrific social life. Looks that could kill. Men were falling over themselves. All that stuff about the Hurlingham Club, for Christ's sake.'

Perhaps it was because Caroline was so grand, because she was 'the Hon', had been Deb of the Year, was married in the chapel of the House of Lords, and all that; perhaps that was why I'd never told her where I really did come from. Inverse snobbery on my part, maybe. Cowardice. Who knows? None the less I never had told her.

Suddenly I decided I would.

'Caroline,' I said. 'All that's a load of rubbish. It's true I met David in the Hurlingham Club. I was a waitress there. He often used to turn up for lunch, always on his own. He'd sit reading a book while he ate his lamb cutlets. Never took any notice of me at all. But then to my amazement one day he followed me into the kitchen and asked me if I'd have dinner with him. He was so old-fashioned and sweet about it, and terribly presentable. And I said "Yes". He was the first really intelligent man I'd ever met. I was only twenty.'

Caroline was looking puzzled.

'And what was someone from an aristocratic Italian family doing waitressing in London, I'd like to know?'

It was my turn to laugh.

'Caroline, d'you think I could have a drink?'

She gave a jolt as if surprised she hadn't thought of it first.

'Of course. What? Vodka-and-tonic?'

'Wine? White wine?'

'One second.'

She was out of the room in four or five quick strides. I could hear the the fridge door being closed; then 'Fuck it! Patrick's finished the Montrachet, the bastard. Australian all right?' she called out. There was the sound of a cork being drawn and the clink of glasses. Caroline re-emerged with that hip-swinging gait of hers. She put down the glasses and poured out the wine.

'Thank God you asked,' she said. 'It must be at least eleven o'clock. I don't usually wait this long. There you go.' And she threw herself back on the sofa and kicked off her shoes. 'So . . . rich and beautiful Italian girl becomes a waitress. Why?'

'Well,' I began cautiously, looking Caroline firmly in the eye.

'For a start my mother's actually a baker's daughter, and I'm illegitimate.'

I waited for the reaction on Caroline's face. She just smiled rather sweetly.

'Funny you should say that,' she said. 'So am I. My mother was too. It runs in the family.' There was a pause while she let me take in this unlikely information. 'Mind you,' she went on, 'my father did marry her in the end. I think he'd sort of forgotten: he was a bit like that. And she wasn't a baker's daughter, I admit. Her father was said to be the Archbishop of Canterbury, but I think it's much more likely to have been Lloyd George. Who was yours?'

'I don't know,' I said.

Caroline frowned.

'What d'you mean, you don't know? You must have some idea, surely. There are always a few likely candidates around. Hangers-on. Men with guilty faces bearing unexpected gifts. That's how you usually tell. What does your mother say?'

'She lies.'

'Oh, but mothers always do. I do.'

'Not like mine,' I said.

No one could have told lies like mine. They must have started nine months before I was born. I'd often tried to imagine that conceptual moment, but Anna-Maria had mythologised it so long ago in order to placate her family in Bologna that I'd been compelled to reconstruct it from my knowledge of her. The tearful version I was brought up with was of a love-match made in heaven between this magnificently handsome English gentleman who died tragically only months after falling for (and presumably into bed with) the lovely and shy Anna-Maria Foscari, whom he'd met improving her culture one summer afternoon in the National Gallery. The reality, as I learnt piecemeal over the years, was of an accommodating Italian *au pair* girl in Wimbledon who divested herself of her Catholicism and her virginity on the master of the house, only to be hustled back to Italy by the tight-lipped mistress once the consequences of the girl failing to take the *pilola* became all too evident.

'My mother was only eighteen when I was born,' I explained, 'appropriately enough in the Hospital of the Immaculate

Conception. At least I think she was eighteen: it's hard to be sure with Anna-Maria. What I do know is that if she insists on being forty-nine for many more years she'll soon qualify as the youngest mother in the Guinness Book of Records.'

Caroline sipped her wine happily, and gazed up at me from the sofa.

'Goodness. Think of never having known one's father. Mind you, there were many years when I wished I'd never known mine.' She looked reflective for a moment. 'But then I suppose I'd never have inherited Priory Hall, would I? God, I can't wait to go and live there, away from this dump.' She raised herself up on one elbow and began to coil strands of blonde hair idly round one finger. 'So there you were, a squalling illegitimate brat in the Hospital of the Immaculate Conception. What happened then? I love all this.'

I told her I was brought up in Bologna, the city of towers, which Anna-Maria dreamed of, and of sausage, which she consumed – although unlike most Italian women she'd always been fortunate where she put it on. My mother's claim to be only forty-nine had often been understood by my less kind friends to refer to her bust.

'Oh, this is wonderful,' exclaimed Caroline, refilling her glass. 'This is getting better and better. Go on, go on.'

I decided to make it as brief as I could. My mind was running on what David would have made of the morning papers. He was probably blowing a gasket right now and trying to phone me every five minutes. I could hear the cool indignation in his lawyer's voice, with renewed pleas for me to return 'and put an end to all this nonsense'. The only nonsense I was determined to put an end to was my marriage.

'Well, I left,' I said. 'I always do things on impulse. You know that. Like the affair I had. Like leaving David. Like saying "Yes" to your offer of the gatehouse. If I start thinking, I have doubts, and the doubts are always wrong. So I left. Maybe because I was half-English I began to feel a terrific urge to go to the country which was half-me, and which I'd never set eyes on.'

'How old were you then?' Caroline asked, beginning to look bored.

'Sixteen.'

That woke her up.

'Sixteen! And you left home? What did your mother think?'

She was appalled, I explained. But by this time I'd pieced together the secret of my existence. And so I teased her: I reminded her of all that uplifting culture she'd once imbibed in London, those wonderful pictures in the National Gallery, and all those elegant English gentlemen who surely wouldn't all of them die after the first embrace, 'Would they mother, eh?' In the end, with many tears and much heaving of the bosom she let me go. It brought out the best in her. She revealed the existence of a cousin who'd married a policeman in Raynes Park, and I could stay with them. There was good state education in England, she'd been assured. And when I came back I'd be even more eligible to marry some pasta-maker she had her eye on for me. She never admitted as much, but I knew that the moment I left she'd be preparing the ground.

Caroline was looking bored again.

'And then what?'

'I went to Raynes Park Comprehensive School.'

That made her laugh. She'd probably never met anyone who'd been to a state school before.

'A comprehensive. Really? How extraordinary. And what did you learn about there?'

'Domestic science. And boys.'

Caroline gave another laugh.

'I never learnt about either of those at Benenden. Only about being a lady, which is the one thing in the world I'm absolutely no good at, as you know.'

It wasn't true. Being a lady, as I'd learnt from Caroline, was being free to act as though you had no breeding when you were actually steeped in it. I had none at all. And perhaps that's what brought us together: Caroline forever cocking a snook at what I'd never had. Perhaps, too, this was what had attracted David to me. He wanted to be Professor Higgins, and I was his Eliza Doolittle. And it worked. I learnt to be gracious, wear good clothes, make the most of my figure – not that David took much notice of that, though his colleagues in the House most certainly did. Jesus, the propositions: they were thrust at me like trading stamps. Party loyalty, I soon came to understand, might be loudly trumpeted along the corridors but was firmly locked out of the bedroom. Certainly there was no lack of offers from party colleagues to replace the member for Box Hill with their own.

Caroline's voice cut through my drift of thought.

'Why didn't you return to Italy?'

'Oh, I did,' I said. 'After leaving school I studied for a year at a domestic science college, learning all the usual womanly things, and then I went back. It was dreadful. Anna-Maria started hoovering up young men for me the instant I stepped off the plane. And I'd been absolutely right: they were all eligible pasta-makers or sausage-makers who'd heard so much about me, *o cara mia*. Anyway, within a week I was suffocated. In England all men had ever wanted to do was to fuck me; in Italy all they ever wanted to do was marry me.'

That produced a chuckle from Caroline.

'So you came back to be a waitress in London and marry morally upright David.'

'Yes. And found myself still being a waitress, entertaining David's cronies,' I said. 'The only difference was that instead of getting tips *and* propositions, now I just got propositions.'

Caroline reached out for her glass of wine and looked surprised to find it empty.

'Well, you're not likely to get either in Norton Abbas, I can tell you. We'll have to import our pleasures. God, won't that be wonderful. So, when will you come? Tomorrow? Next week? It's there. Just say.'

Yes, I thought, it would be wonderful. Not to be a waitress for the first time in my life. Not to have to serve anybody. Not to have to be polite. Not to be a career support. Not to be a government minister's hostess. Not to be a wife. And never, never again to wear powder-blue. A year! A whole year to be myself. And then? Who knows? Something would turn up that would be actually mine.

Caroline saw I wanted to leave, and got up, giving her hair a lazy flick.

'You still haven't told me what the "mega-row" was that

made you finally walk out. You've got to give me the best bit before you go.'

I hesitated by the door.

'It wasn't actually a row at all,' I said. 'Just a brief exchange.'

'And . . . ?'

It was such a very small 'and' that I didn't feel like telling her. David had just made a 'major' speech in the House, and afterwards there was a party. He was drinking in the applause. Most of the other MPs were just drinking, when they weren't peering at my breasts. I was feeling rather sexy, and in the taxi home David took my hand, said he loved me, said I was beautiful. I thought, 'Well, maybe it's actually going to work out at last.' He hadn't touched me for three months. No one had touched me for three months. I put on my Janet Reger nightdress and dabbed vital places with Giorgio. Then I stretched myself across the bed with my hair loose on the pillow and watched him undress, folding his clothes as he did so, neatly placing his shoes side by side. As he removed his pants I noticed that his prick looked quite a lot less wrinkly than usual, and I told myself it was because of me, not his speech in the House. As he approached the bed I took it in my mouth while he stood there silently, making indeterminate noises. It grew sort of half-mast as I kept working at it with my lips, until finally I pulled him down on me and tried to squeeze it inside. But it kept bending, and David did nothing, made no movement at all, and no sound. My muscles kept trying to draw it in, but it gradually shrivelled away and finally lay there limp against me. Perhaps I would have been understanding had he not rolled away and announced almost proudly – as though he were addressing me across the teacups – 'Sex isn't everything, darling.' I knew then that I was going. And I did.

Caroline was still looking at me expectantly.

'And . . . ?'

I made a face.

'Let's just say it was a small anti-climax. One too many.'

For once Caroline didn't click her tongue and say, 'Christ, how boring.' Instead she just gazed at me, and I could see she was reading in my face everything I hadn't said to her.

'Poor you,' she murmured, shaking her head.

Then her expression suddenly became fierce.

'So what the hell are you grinning about, then?'

I just looked at her and grinned even more.

'Because, Caroline, I feel gloriously and gorgeously free,' I said.

Two

It felt right that the weather should be perfect, and that it should be Midsummer's Day. The sun was in his heaven, and I was in mine. It was my high summer, driving westwards with everything I owned squeezed into the tiny Fiat. At least, everything I valued most: other bulkier possessions would be following by van in a day or so – a few pieces of furniture, kitchen stuff, blankets, winter clothes, bric-a-brac. David had been entirely reasonable about parting with items I was attached to. But then he *would* be; David could always be relied upon to be that. He'd even managed to sound reasonable saying I was making a terrible mistake; he was reasonable about the cruel things the press had written about him ('politicians are used to that'), and reasonable about my monthly allowance during our 'trial separation'. I felt bad about taking it, but resolved that after this year, or maybe sooner, I'd find a way of being totally independent, even if I had to go back to being a waitress; though I had a feeling I was going to do rather better for myself than that.

And yes of course I'd let him have my address and phone number, I said, just as soon as I knew what they were, though the phone might take a little time to get installed, this being Devon, not Westminster. I didn't tell him there was already a phone in the gatehouse, so Caroline had assured me, just as there was hot water, central heating, a well-equipped kitchen and a double bed. The gatehouse had not exactly been unoccupied, she explained. For years the gardener and his family had lived there; more recently, when companionship became more important to her father than a garden, the regular mistress of the moment had been installed there – the *'maîtresse en titre'*, as he referred to her – which left the big house free to accommodate more temporary visitors of the night. The admiral had always been democratic with his favours. 'But at least he left me the house,' Caroline said again with some relief, 'the old bastard.'

The car windows were open and my hair flailed about my face. Classic FM was playing an aria from *Rigoletto* on the radio, *La donna è mobile*. Yes, that was me, I thought. *Mobile*. This little lady was on the move, here in a little box of a Fiat, and here in my head and in my heart. I was all in one piece; I could do with myself as I wished, give myself to whatsoever and whomsoever I wished; and I was going to a place where I'd never been, and where nobody knew a single thing about me, except of course Caroline, who regrettably was beginning to know rather too much. I resolved to drink less in her company.

This afternoon, I remembered, David would be standing up in the House to defend the government's re-routing of the Channel Tunnel link, explaining why it was unfortunately necessary to destroy five Kent villages (packed with Tory voters – until now). Only this time I wouldn't be lying in bed at eleven o'clock listening to him being reasonable about it while he clambered into his pyjamas.

Good-bye, David.

Another thought came to me. What would I call myself in Norton Abbas? Mrs Claudia Hazlitt? That might provoke enquiries, given David's high profile. Then I'd be pestered, whispered about, country towns being the same the world over; and should some man I fancied be spotted departing in the morning with a smile on his face, what would be said then? I could imagine only too well. So perhaps I should be what I once was, Claudia Foscari. Unmarried? Widow? Divorcee? But then what would happen when the press found out – which they surely would? Or when David turned up – which he surely would? No, if there were to be scandals, let them be of my own making: I must be Mrs Claudia Hazlitt, separated wife of that moral paragon who was always rabbiting on about old-fashioned values on television. And let the locals think what they like – which they surely would.

The summer green of Devon woods was still fresh and damp, laundered by overnight rain. I pulled the car off the road to stretch my legs. In the shadow of the trees a stream tumbled over red rocks, and I kicked off my shoes and stepped into a pool where bubbles of foam clung to my ankles. Dappled sunlight was flickering through the branches as I tossed back my hair and splashed water from the cup of my hands over my face and neck. I shivered as it trickled down inside my shirt over my breasts. I felt alive. I felt young. I wanted to plunge into that purple-green water. I wanted to laugh. I wished at that moment I could be here with a lover, sharing this place, sharing our bodies in the cold water.

I found myself smiling. I'd only ever had one lover since marrying David, and I'd said good-bye to him more than a year ago. It had been a wrench, but I had to do it. There'd been so much need, and so much guilt, and the guilt had won. Then just a week ago I'd telephoned him on a sudden impulse. Looking back, it seemed absurd. But I was free of a husband, free of guilt, I felt starved, and what I wanted at that moment was a tremendous fuck.

And suddenly it was all different. I suppose I made it embarrassingly clear why I'd rung. And of course he obliged. He paraded his prick at me, almost with a smirk, then got on with it. He fucked me as though he hadn't much time. He was excavating: it was the gold-rush. Afterwards he didn't exactly say, 'Do you a favour any time, darling,' but that's what his face said. Lying there I realised he'd touched me everywhere, and touched me nowhere.

And, like David, I never gave him my phone number.

My shirt was drying chill on my body. My feet ached in the cold stream. I clambered on to the bank. So here I was, no husband, and no lover. Just a small car packed with all I possessed, bound for somewhere I'd never been.

Round the next bend in the road I caught sight of the first signpost to Norton Abbas. Five miles. So it really did exist.

And suddenly I was frightened. Seriously frightened. What on earth did I imagine I was doing here? Instant solutions jumped into my brain. I'd ring David this evening and say, yes, he was right, I'd come to my senses, it was all a big mistake; then I'd set about finding another lover and this time smother the guilt.

That solution jumped out again extremely fast, accompanied by a shudder.

Next one. I'd remind myself that for Christ's sake I was Italian really. I'd never quite understood about England and the English: I'd cut my losses, go back where I belonged and marry the pasta-maker Anna-Maria would certainly have earmarked for me, whereupon with a taste of Italian passion I'd discover I could have children after all, one a year for five years, put on a stone in weight for every child, and waddle along to join the mamma-gossips in the piazza after Sunday Mass.

That solution jumped out even faster.

The signpost said Norton Abbas, 1½ miles. Now I could see a distant church tower. It must be the church of the former priory, whose gatehouse I was to occupy. Perhaps it would have a portcullis – at least that would keep David out; and me safely locked inside with my thirty-five acres to play with. I remembered Caroline's voice in the restaurant. 'Think of the fun we can have. Parties. Picnics. Lovers. We can spread our wings. Mayhem! Claudia, we can *live!*'

It was about time I learnt to do that. The fear had gone.

I gazed at it for a long time. I knew nothing about medieval gatehouses, or what they were built for, but the longer I gazed the more I became convinced that whatever their functions comfortable living was most unlikely to be one of them. It had the air of a place to be tortured in, incarcerated in, go mad in, or from which to cast a malevolent eye on the world beyond. That gaping maw of an entrance was so obviously designed never to let you out again; a traitors' gate, a mouth of hell. The windows were mean slits in the stone whose only possible use was for launching arrows or tipping noxious fluids over passers-by. I could just imagine myself waiting expectantly for my weekend lover, only to see him take one look at my love-nest, clutch his genitals, leap back into his car and speed away.

Oh well, I thought, the gate appeared to be open, I might as well pluck up courage and drive in. Then, as I was about to close the car door a large woman with a froth of dark hair bustled across the road towards me, waving her arms.

'You must be Claudia,' she called out.

I smiled and got out of the car. We shook hands. Hers was large and damp.

'I'm Megan,' she explained. 'Caroline said you'd be arriving about now. She's told me a lot about you. And I dare say she told you a few things about me, which I'd rather you didn't repeat. She asked me to look after you because she's none too well this morning, I'm afraid.'

I laughed.

'You mean she's got a hangover.'

Megan's eyes crinkled.

'How did you guess? Now, I'm to show you everything. Caroline insists.' And she squeezed herself into the passenger seat, first removing two suitcases, then cushioning them on her lap with a grunt. 'Drive in. Drive in.'

There was an attractive Welsh lilt in Megan's voice, and between my suitcases the large, handsome face seemed to be thrusting itself at the outside world with an expression of permanent amusement. Her skin was very pink and glowing, and she wore no make-up. She had a bosom worthy of Harvest Thanksgiving. I guessed she must be around fifty, though a larding of flesh disguised any tell-tale signs of age.

'I can see from your face you think the place must be a dungeon,' she announced as I drove suspiciously under the crumbled archway. 'But you wait. The admiral liked to make sure his ladies enjoyed their comforts.' Megan chuckled. 'Just as he liked to enjoy the comfort of his ladies . . . Well, here we are. Welcome to the *parc aux cerfs*.'

She thrust the two suitcases out of the car door and clambered after them. I got out and looked about. It was hard to believe it was the same place I'd seen from the road. Large areas of the rear wall had been torn away and replaced by spacious glass windows which, under the medieval battlements, looked decidedly odd. But the sun poured through them to reveal elegantly furnished rooms, and the promise of further comfort on the floor above.

I commented that the admiral didn't seem to have had much respect for history. Megan gave a chuckle.

'I think he respected other things more.' She gave another chuckle. 'Yes, I think you could have called him a philistine, except when it came to women. There he was a connoisseur. Surprising for a naval man. Always at sea. But I suppose it was all those foreign ports. Must have given him a broader view. A certain Catholic taste. They were certainly all sorts, his women. I'll show you. I'm a painter, you see. He always got me to paint them, nude of course. Didn't think much of clothes, the admiral. Trouble was, when a new lady arrived – took up residence, you might say – the picture of the last one had to come down right away. He had nowhere to put it. Couldn't exactly hang it in Priory Hall among the ancestral portraits, could he? So I'd store it for him. Oh, I must have a dozen. My husband's a bit uneasy about them: he's a church warden by the way. I'll introduce you to the vicar when you're settled in. Pype, his name is. An old-fashioned man – I think that would be the polite way of putting it. But a great fisherman. Suppose it's all part of the calling.' She giggled. 'And now I must stop prattling; you'll want to get yourself organised. I've prepared you some lunch. Wine in the fridge. I'll call in later and show you the rest. Oh, by the way, Caroline says will you phone her this afternoon? She's in a rotten mood: one of her children is home. Samantha. Such a pretty girl. Bye bye now.'

The large rear view of Megan disappeared into the gloom of the archway.

I took a deep breath. So this was it. I unloaded the car and began to lug my possessions into the house. The living-room was eccentrically furnished – an old steamer chair, a round brass table supported on four wooden elephants, a large Turkish kelim rug in rich browns and reds, an oriental-looking mirror with golden dragons grinning around it, several gaudy Guatemalan wall-hangings, and in the centre of the room a very suburban G-plan sofa in screaming mauve. It was as though each of his women had left behind some ethnic item from her native heath, whether Singapore or Sidcup – so many wreaths decorating a memorial to past loves. (Remember me. Remember me.) I stood there feeling like the new mistress of the admiral's ghost.

A door at the far end of the room led me back into the Middle Ages. The kitchen was on the north side of the gatehouse facing the road, stone-flagged and dank, with a single slotted window and a narrow view of the priory church, now the parish church I imagined, domain of the Rev Pype, fisher of men. There appeared to be no entrance to it. I wondered why. Perhaps no one went to church in Norton Abbas any longer, which was why Mr Pype could devote his spiritual life to the rod and line.

Laid out on the kitchen table was the lunch Megan had prepared for me. Smoked trout (the vicar again?), salad, blue cheese, biscuits and a bowl of cherries. Bless her, I thought. Perhaps I was going to like the people in this place. And there protruding from under the fruit-bowl I caught sight of a note on which Megan had scrawled 'Wine', with an arrow pointing to the fridge. Beneath the arrow she'd added, 'Cheers!' Yes, I was going to enjoy Megan.

I dragged a couple of suitcases up the stone staircase to what I guessed must be the bedroom. A door opened into a single huge room, medieval on the north side, glass modernist on the south. By contrast to the living-room the furnishings seemed entirely conventional, with a single exception, the bedhead. I looked at it, and I looked again. It was about three feet high and considerably more than the width of the double bed, all in a reddish carved wood. At first the carvings appeared to be just a mass of figures, twenty or thirty of them. Peering closer I could see that they were a good deal more than a mass of figures. I was quite startled. Stretched across the entire width of the bedhead was a demonstration of the most gymnastic contortions of love-making imaginable. How did people ever manage to bend like that, or keep it in if they did? I imagined the admiral emulating them on this very bed, perhaps glancing up from time to time to make sure he'd got it right. No wonder he died of a heart attack.

My first reaction was, can I really sleep here, alone or not?

My second reaction was, how utterly appalled David would be.

My third reaction was, perhaps if he'd had an instruction manual like this to stir his libido I might never have left him.

I came to the conclusion that I'd probably cover the thing up for the sake of my peace of mind, unveiling it only on very special occasions, should they occur. But then my eye caught a neat typewritten notice on the wall to one side, the kind of yellowing label one sees next to exhibits in a rural museum. I leaned closer. Amid a few dark stains the notice read, 'Replica of a carved panel from the Visvanatha temple, Khajuraho, India. Presented as a token of gratitude to Admiral Sir Howard Romsey from the Ladies' Bridge Club of Bombay, December 1974. *Per ardua ad astra.*'

What, I wondered, would Caroline have to say about all this? I thought of her being Deb of the Year while her father dallied with the grateful ladies of the Bombay Bridge Club. But at least she'd had a father, I didn't even know who mine was.

I decided to leave the altarpiece to Eros unshrouded for the time being and tackle Megan's lunch. The wine I'd leave for this evening: there was far too much to do today to fall drowsy in the afternoon. After the initial shock of arrival I felt excited, bewildered and a bit lost, all at the same time. The question 'What am I doing here?' kept playing in my head, and no answer came. For the moment I didn't care: today was today, and a great deal had happened in it already. I put the smoked trout, salad, cheese, biscuits and bowl of cherries on a tray and carried it on to the small terrace where I'd noticed there was a wrought-iron garden table with chairs. On the way I caught sight of a hand-phone near the door, and added it to the tray.

First I'd have lunch, I decided. Then I'd phone Caroline.

The sky was cloudless. The gods were smiling on me. And the trout was delicious. I began to feel relaxed, almost at home, as if I could actually belong here. I gazed around at my borrowed acres: they seemed to stretch everywhere. Over to the left, close to the high wall separating the garden from the church, I could make out what I imagined to be the ruins of the former priory: not much more than a pattern of crumbled walls and grassy humps, with just a single rounded arch rising out of the thick vegetation. A large bird of prey took off from it as I looked, and I followed its swift flight across the open grassland until it disappeared into a copse two or three hundred yards away. Beyond the trees the land dipped out of sight, until far away a shimmer of light on the water reminded me that Caroline had explained how the garden ran down to an expanse of marsh and a tidal estuary.

I sat there in the sun eating Megan's cherries while my eyes continued to take in this strange, deserted place that had suddenly become mine. The muffled sound of traffic was the only indication that I was a mere stone's throw from a busy market town; it was as if I'd passed through a magic door into some timeless country whose existence no one beyond those high walls was even aware of. It was my lost world, and I was free to make of it whatever I wished. It was like a blank canvas on which I was about to paint my own portrait. The new Claudia.

The expanse of grassland must once have been a lawn, I assumed. Tennis courts probably. Croquet. Garden parties. Now it was a rich and uncut hayfield, bright with poppies, marguerites and swathes of purple clover over which butter-flies danced like scraps of coloured tissue paper tossed in the wind. And there were bees, huge droning bumble-bees that bent the flowerheads as they settled on them; and among them, fussing from flower to flower, scores of smaller, golden honey-bees. These puzzled me: I'd always thought honey-bees were dark. They certainly had been in our cottage garden in Kent, but then everything had been dark there, so perhaps they'd merely caught the mood of the place, whereas here they were as golden as the sun. That seemed to make a kind of poetic sense. I laughed, and spat cherry stones in their direction.

I noticed too that the honey-bees clearly belonged somewhere else. There was a regular flight-path of heavily laden creatures in the direction of what I took to be an old orchard far away to my right. I found it hard to imagine the admiral taking time off for apiculture, and Caroline wouldn't have known a bee from a mosquito; so I wondered who tended the hives. Come to think of it, Caroline had mentioned someone called Joan.

It was intriguing sitting here, too lazy to move, trying to work out what 'my' vast garden consisted of, knowing that tomorrow, or whenever I'd unpacked and settled in, I'd explore the entire place. I was excited by that thought. But for now I was content to munch cherries, gaze about, and speculate.

What, for example, was the enormous barn partly hidden by

an untrimmed beech-hedge a short distance beyond the ruins of the old priory? OK, I told myself, it's a barn. But what was a barn doing here, let alone one of such a size? Again, from what I'd come to know of him it didn't seem likely that the admiral was one to dabble in farming.

Another puzzle: the cluster of amazingly ancient-looking yew-trees which blocked the view of the estuary to the left of the wood where the bird of prey had flown. Yew-trees I associated with churchyards, yet these weren't anywhere near the church. Besides they weren't large single trees but appeared to form some sort of geometrical pattern, with here and there a specimen which looked as though it had been deliberately shaped at some much earlier time.

And where was the big house? Priory Hall. Where the admiral had officially lived, and where Caroline was at this very moment nursing her hangover. I could see no sign of it.

I glanced at my watch. It was two-thirty in the afternoon. I'd finished the cherries, and decided to ring her.

It rang and rang. I was about to switch it off when there was a click, followed by a loud thump. I heard a distant voice.

'Oh, fuck it! Now I've dropped the thing. Why do people always phone me when I'm in the loo?' There was a pause. Suddenly the voice bellowed in my ear – more a challenge than a greeting – 'Yes?' Megan had said Caroline was in a rotten mood, and she was clearly right.

'It's me, Claudia,' I said. I could hear the laughter in my voice, which was a mistake.

'What d'you want?' she said sharply.

'You asked me to phone. I'm here.'

There was another pause.

'Where?'

'In the gatehouse.'

'Well, I'm in the loo.'

I didn't quite know how to follow this.

'Would you rather I phoned you later, Caroline?' I suggested.

'No.' A further pause. Then the voice changed. 'Oh God! Claudia, of course. I'm really sorry. I was miles away – well, in the loo anyway.' There was a hint of a laugh. 'You've arrived.

That's terrific. Come round.' Another hesitation, followed by a sigh. 'Come to think of it, don't come round. Not just yet. I can't cope. Bloody children. Samantha's got a friend. Dreadful girl. She stinks. Look darling' – again the sigh – 'Christ, I want to see you. Come to supper. Please. You must. And you know what I'd really *love*? I've bought a salmon. Would you cook it? Claudia, you know how hopeless I am, and I'll only ruin it. Please, will you? I've got some champagne.'

I said of course I would, conscious that everyone always said yes to Caroline, however inconvenient the demand. Here I was: I'd just driven two hundred miles; many of my life's possessions were still unpacked; and she expected me to go and cook for her.

The large bird of prey had settled once again on the stone arch. I wondered if the spirit of Caroline inhabited it.

'And how do I find you?' I asked.

She sounded surprised that I didn't know. It was easy, she explained. I just followed the wall round to the left after leaving the gatehouse. Her voice was now that of the lady of the manor. 'You can't miss it. The gates should be open. If they're not, hoot.' And no doubt some aged retainer would shuffle out to open them, I imagined. 'About seven,' she added commandingly; then with a sudden gust of warmth, 'God, I'm pleased you're here.'

All in all, so was I, even though it seemed that I'd given up serving David only to find myself serving Caroline. At the moment, however, this struck me as the better bargain. Yes, I *was* glad I was here.

Everything I did triggered off the same question in my head, 'What would David have thought?' This had the effect of adding an unexpected gloss of pleasure to quite minor events, besides making me understand just how much I'd instinctively censored my life all these years, suppressing my needs, accommodating his disapprovals and learning how not to arouse them. They were the smallest things, like leaving my hair loose, which had always disquieted David, who liked order and who kept two monogrammed hairbrushes of his own neatly side by side on the dressing-table. I used to disturb them surreptitiously, but by the evening there they were again in their appointed places, a little apart, like his shoes, and like us in bed.

Late that first afternoon at the gatehouse I met Joan. I was busy unpacking, trying to make the place look as though it actually belonged to me rather than to assorted ladies hijacked from various naval ports of call. I'd begun by draping a rug over the illustrated version of *The Kama Sutra* by my bed, and removing from the wall the touching tribute from the Ladies' Bridge Club of Bombay.

That done, I caught sight of a figure strolling across my hayfield towards the gatehouse. She had bright-red hair and was carrying over one arm a garment that appeared to be a diving-suit, while from the other hand dangled what I took to be a shrimping-net. Since we were some considerable distance from the open sea I was more than a little puzzled, and hurried downstairs to greet her.

She smiled as she saw me, and stopped. She was tiny, forty-ish I imagined, and dressed in a faded blue shirt and equally faded jeans that were tucked into incongruously smart leather boots.

'I'm Joan,' she said, dropping the shrimping-net and thrusting out a hand. 'You must be Claudia. Megan told me you'd arrived. I hope you don't mind; I was just seeing to the bees. It's the lime-flow season and I needed to put on an extra super.'

I had no idea what she was talking about, but there was something bubbly and sharp about her which I liked immediately, and an impish smile that flicked on and off as she talked. It occurred to me that the outfit she was carrying must presumably be a bee-suit, and the shrimping-net a bee-keeper's hat and veil.

I said of course I didn't mind at all, and that I'd been wondering who it was that kept bees. Why were they golden, not dark?

'Ah, you've noticed,' Joan said, looking pleased. 'Because they're Italian bees. Very gentle. Lovely creatures. You're Italian, aren't you?'

I was taken aback. Was there anyone in Norton Abbas Caroline hadn't been talking to about me?

'Half,' I said.

'And the other half?'

'Presumed English.'

'I see.' She laughed, and gave me one of her flickering smiles. 'He presumed a bit too much, then, did he?'

That made me laugh too.

'I'm afraid so.'

She shook her head and raised her eyes in a gesture of mock disapproval.

'Not much of that round here, I may tell you. Far too stuffy. All church and family values, like that prat in the government who's always sounding off on television. What his name? Hazlitt. Can't stand the man, can you?'

I blinked. This was a rich moment. Should I or should I not tell her?

'No,' I said, keeping a straight face. 'Nor can I much.'

'I'd better be off,' Joan went on, picking up her bee-keeping hat. 'I'm so glad to have met you. And I hope you don't mind my trespassing from time to time. I'll bring you some honey.'

I thanked her.

'And next time stay for tea or a drink,' I suggested.

'I'd like that, especially the drink,' she said with another quick flicker of a smile.

Well, I decided, any enemy of David's has to be a friend of mine. I was rather ashamed of that thought, but perhaps it was all part of the liberating process, like letting my hair loose. I went back to my unpacking.

By about five o'clock I was as organised as ever I intended to be, and again I couldn't help thinking how restless David would have been at the profligate scatter of my belongings: piles of things everywhere; all the cupboards open; the floor a camp-site. I felt a twinge of guilt that I hadn't phoned him; then I remembered gratefully that he'd be at the House of Commons being reasonable about the destruction of Kent villages. Why should I phone him anyway? Patience was one of David's interminable virtues after all, so I would take full advantage of it.

Instead I decided to explore my wonderful thirty-five acres in the evening sun. I began with the ruins. Apart from the single elegant arch where the bird of prey had perched, these were as dull as most ruins, with no information provided as to what pile of stones was supposed to be what. A large rectangular area I guessed must have been the cloisters, and a row of extremely small rectangles might, I imagined, have been the miserable cells where the inmates snatched a few hours' sleep between the tinkling of bells for prayers.

Then, close to the cloister-patch a semi-circular wall suggested itself as the east end of a church. It must have been a small private chapel of some kind since I knew that the main one – the huge hulk of stone that towered over where I was standing – was now the Norton Abbas parish church. Why had the monks needed a place that large? And why had they also needed a place this small? I pondered on the difference between large and small prayers, and knew that David would have looked at me rather stonily for that thought. He was about as low a churchman as you could get – loathed all forms of what he called 'churchianity' – yet his private cell of virtue demanded respect for the humble institution of prayer, even if he'd never been known to practise it.

I was about to leave the ruins to their timeless slumber when my eye was taken by a small typewritten notice encased in plastic and raised on what looked like a music stand just to one side of the chapel. My first thought was that it might be another tender missive from the Ladies' Bridge Club of Bombay, but then I saw that next to it lay a stone grave, and that wreaths of flowers had been laid beside it, some of them fading. I clambered over the low wall to read the notice, and as I did so I remembered Caroline saying dismissively how there was some sort of shrine here where a female saint called 'St Something-or-other-burga' was buried in the Dark Ages, and how miracle hunters flocked into the garden during the summer and made the souvenir shops in the town stinking rich.

So this was it. I was now the guardian of a saintly shrine. The notice read very simply, 'Tomb of St Cuthburga, sister of King Ina of Wessex, died c. AD 725'. No flourishes. The admiral obviously hadn't been into lauding women who sought blissful union with any male except himself.

I would ask the vicar about St Cuthburga, when he wasn't fishing.

It was half past five. I had an hour and a half before kitchen duty with Caroline. I made my way past the uncut beech-hedge and through the thick grass towards the enormous barn I'd noticed earlier. A stone wall rose to about head-height, and from here a tiled roof, buckled with age, soared up to a ridge far above, patterned with coloured lichens and alive with sparrows which exploded out of invisible spaces between the tiles as I drew near. There was no door, merely a huge black entrance. I gazed at it for a while, then I stepped inside. Everything was just as black, except that above me hundreds of tiny points of light like stars seemed to pierce their way into the darkness, until gradually – as my eyes grew accustomed – the blackness of the place began to melt into the softest grey. And out of that greyness emerged the structure of a roof so hugely and intricately beamed that suddenly I had the sensation of looking, not up, but far down into the belly of some gigantic ship.

I felt overawed. The place appeared to be quite empty. The only sound was the deafening cacophony of sparrows. Well, I thought, so I'm the guardian of this too. A medieval gatehouse. A Dark Ages shrine. And now an even darker barn.

I wandered on. Ahead of me lay the strange complex of yew-trees I'd caught sight of from the terrace. As I approached it I realised I was right. There had been some sort of pattern in the way they were planted, some in double rows to form a path, others in clumps and semi-circles, some stubby, some tall, except heaven knows how many years it was since they'd last been clipped. Centuries even. I looked about me, wondering what might possibly have been intended. All I could think of was the word 'topiary'. Wasn't that what they called the carving of trees into shapes, animals, birds, classical urns, castles, whatever? But why? And why here?

Then, right in the centre of this forgotten jungle I came across one of the single tall yew-trees I'd picked out from a distance. Like the others it seemed of quite extraordinary age: its peeling, reddish trunk was as thick as a church column. It must be centuries old. Out of curiosity I fought my way through the tangle of leaves and stood right in the centre of it. I gazed upwards. Clearly all the main branches had been systematically severed except for this central trunk, which rose up absolutely straight until some twenty feet above my head where it changed shape quite perceptibly, narrowing as though it had been squeezed or clamped. After this the trunk had been allowed to spread again to form a thick rim before tapering upwards to a blunted point. None of this had been in the least visible from the outside, but from here it was quite distinct, so distinct that I suddenly had no doubt at all what I was looking at. It couldn't be anything else. I was standing at the foot of a colossal penis.

After the first shock of surprise I began to giggle. This was ridiculous. It couldn't possibly be. It was my imagination; my fancies had been let loose; this was all to do with my having left David. After years of straining to accommodate a more or less limp six inches, now everything thrusting vigorously upwards was becoming the prick of my dreams. Probably if I looked around I'd see rampant penises everywhere. What about the church spire? Or the offices of the Cheltenham & Gloucester Building Society? Really Claudia! Besides, this had been a priory. Holy ground. My childhood Catholicism admonished me. Nuns didn't do things like that, did they? *That* size! Anyway, you'd have to be a giantess.

David's face cut across my obscene speculations, lips pursed in disapproval. And for once I agreed with him: I ought to be ashamed of myself.

All the same it *was* a penis. I knew that.

It was a quarter past six. From far across my summer hayfield I could make out the large form of Megan standing in the archway, gazing about her. She was carrying a bunch of flowers. I waved to her. She waved back, then gestured to me not to hurry and seated herself on one of the garden chairs. I saw her lay the flowers on the table, and realised she must have brought them for me. I felt touched, and quickened my step. I would have preferred to make a detour through the wood to where the garden ran down to the marsh and the tidal estuary beyond. But that would have to wait. I skirted the trees and headed for the gatehouse. The sun had dipped below the level of the beech-trees, casting broken patterns of light across the floor of last year's leaves. And as I passed I noticed that much of the bare ground close to the trees to my left was carpeted with a strange plant, greenish and dull red, the flowers curiously lobed like heavy sacks with smaller sacks on either side as if they were stubby arms. I'd never seen them before. Caroline wouldn't have the faintest idea what they were, but somebody would, Joan perhaps. Maybe her bees fed off them. I would ask her.

As I drew close I hailed Megan. She rose heavily from the garden chair and held out the flowers with a smile.

'You've been exploring,' she said. 'Are you a gardener?'

I explained that the English bit of me would like to be but was entirely ignorant, while the Italian bit understood only plants you could eat. Megan laughed.

'Well, I'm afraid the Welsh are ignorant of both, but my husband's a fanatic and he gave me these for you. I know just about enough to recognise them as roses. Sorry about the greenfly.' And she shook the bunch of roses vigorously, scattering small bugs across the garden table. 'There, that's better. Now, are you all right?'

I assured her I was very much all right, and that I'd been summoned to dinner by Caroline.

'Oh, you poor thing!' Megan exclaimed. 'Prepare for salmonella poisoning.'

'*I'm* the cook,' I said.

She laughed, shaking a great deal of flesh.

'Ah, that's Caroline. Well, at least you won't need an ambulance. You must come and have dinner with us in a day or two. My husband's an ace cook, and I promise you won't get any greenfly.'

She waved a heavy hand and departed, chuckling.

Half an hour later I clambered into the Fiat and followed Caroline's directions to Priory Hall. The gates were open, just as she'd said, yet I still half-expected a lackey in a peasant smock to emerge from the lodge and doff his sweaty cap as I drove in. Stretching ahead of me was a gravel drive between tall lime-trees (I remembered Joan mentioning the 'lime-flow'), and finally one of those lordly circuits like a long curtsy in front of the house to ensure that visitors appreciate the full grandeur of the place, and their own relative insignificance. I parked my Fiat modestly to one side in case some neighbouring Rolls-Royce was expected.

It was a handsome, classical-looking house with a spread of stone steps leading up to a magnificent door with an intricate fan-light above. I remembered Caroline explaining how the place had been built for the wife of a wealthy merchant who'd managed to acquire the entire estate following the destruction of the priory – by whom, and when, she was entirely vague, though with my ignorance of English history it wouldn't have meant anything even if she'd been able to tell me. What interested Caroline much more was that the merchant, as soon as the house was complete, had found urgent and permanent business abroad, his place in the marital bed being taken by the gentleman who had paid for the house, namely King Charles II, to whom the lady bore a son, Caroline's distant ancestor, or so she claimed.

At any rate the house was extremely large: God knows what she intended to do with that all these rooms. As for the admiral, I felt sure he could have kept an entire harem here without the lady of the house being even aware of it.

I rang the bell, which clanked and clattered deep within the house, on and on, gradually dying away into silence. Eventually I heard small footsteps and the door swung open to reveal a slim blonde child with bare feet, whom I recognised as Caroline's ten-year-old Samantha, her youngest. She was a miniature Caroline, only with a smile.

'Hello,' she said brightly. 'Mum's in the pool.'

Caroline wasn't in the pool. She was seated on the edge of it with her feet dangling in the water and a tall glass of what I took to be vodka-and-tonic in one hand. Her bikini top lay beside her, and she made a half-hearted move to grasp it until she saw it was me. To judge from her sun-tan she hadn't worn it much.

'For a moment I thought it might be my solicitor,' she said languidly, continuing to dabble her toes in the water. 'He seems to think my father's will must be in the house somewhere. As if it matters: we all know what's in it.' She tossed back her hair, swung her legs out of the pool and got to her feet. Leaving her bikini top where it lay and dragging a towel nonchalantly behind her she began to wander in the direction of the house. 'I'll find you a drink,' she said as though it was a tedious obligation. Then suddenly she paused, gazed back at me, and for the first time smiled. 'God, it's good to see you. We must open that champagne. Would you like that?'

I said I would very much, and followed her indoors. Next to Caroline I felt overdressed in my shirt and jeans as we wandered through the enormous drawing-room lined with portraits of bewhiskered ancestors and their tight-lipped wives staring fiercely from above diamond chokers and bulging corsets.

'That was my grandmother,' she said, pausing to indicate a particularly fierce-looking matron. 'I'm supposed to look like her. Do you think so?'

It was impossible not to smile. There above us was this pinned and primped matriarch all but throttled by clothing, and standing beneath her Caroline within a polite wisp of being entirely naked. Again my thoughts wandered to David, who had met Caroline only once and had thoroughly disapproved of her clothed; my mind went blank trying to imagine what he would have thought of her now.

'Can't see much similarity, I'm afraid, Caroline,' I said, trying not to smile too obviously.

She glanced at me as if I were severely unperceptive and moved on, still dragging her towel. We came to a smaller room where a marble table was laden with bottles of all descriptions, and next to it a fridge, which Caroline opened. She pulled out a bottle of champagne, closed the fridge, and called out, 'Carmen!' As we walked back through the drawing-room a dark-haired Spanish girl hurried up to us, far too shy to look surprised at her employer's nakedness – or maybe she was used to Caroline by now.

'Carmen, bring this out to us with a couple of glasses, will you? And by the way this is Claudia who's sweetly offered to cook the salmon. You might care to give her a hand with the vegetables.'

We sat by the pool and watched the sun go down, Caroline

silent, leaning back in her deck-chair with her towel draped round her shoulders, eyes half-closed, sipping her champagne.

'I love it here,' she said eventually. 'Don't you?'

It wasn't exactly difficult to see why. However many oil tankers went down – even if Lloyd's itself went down – I felt sure she would always have this. There are some privileges the privileged never lose, I decided. The English upper-class mafia would always be there to throw a protective cordon round people like Caroline. She would always manage to swim in champagne and sunshine.

After a while she seemed to come to life again.

'So, Claudia, your first day,' she announced. 'Tell me – I want to know – what have you done? Are you pleased you've come? I want to know everything.'

I watched her refill her glass and settle back into the deck-chair.

'Well,' I said. 'Let me think what I've done. I've sort of unpacked. I've met Megan, who's a delight. I've met Joan, who's another delight. I've met her bees. I've discovered the shrine of St Cuthburga. And some weird flowers. I've explored the great barn. Oh, and I've found the largest penis in England.'

Caroline put down her glass of champagne very carefully, then looked at me with just the hint of a smile.

'It's the country air, darling,' she said. 'Most uplifting.'

I'd only ever lived in cities, first in Bologna where everyone knew everyone, then in London where no one knew anybody. Neither was any kind of preparation for an English country town, and I felt doubly a foreigner. How could I ever really belong?

Joan helped during those first weeks, exploding into the gatehouse every so often like a small firework, each time with a different member of her family in tow: first her taciturn husband Geoff, a doctor, who was instructed by Joan to register me as one of his NHS patients; then a nine-year-old daughter who was an even smaller firework than her mother; and finally two teenage sons who were identical twins, redheads like Joan, and whom she referred to affectionately as 'the flame-throwers', These invasions were swift and unannounced; the invaders tended the bees, consumed my cakes, eyed me with amused curiosity and departed, leaving numerous pots of honey.

Megan helped too, sweeping me off on shopping expeditions and introducing me to whomever we happened to encounter in the street. 'This is *our* Claudia,' she'd announce possessively, sometimes adding with a laugh, 'She's living in the harem,' which embarrassed me until it became clear that the whole of Norton Abbas had been familiar with the admiral's indulgent lifestyle whether they approved of it or – more often – not. Megan took great care to avoid the latter, dragging me across the road with a heavy whisper, 'Oh God, not her!' It was after one such moment that I told her Caroline's remark about sex being such a dirty word in Norton Abbas it didn't even feature in the local graffiti, which pleased her hugely. 'I must tell Glyn that,' she said, Glyn being presumably her husband, the church warden. I wondered how he'd take it.

I very soon found out. I was invited to dinner, as Megan had promised. And, as Megan had also promised, Glyn was indeed an ace cook. He was a quiet, confidential man, and serving his guests with exquisite food appeared to be his way of drawing close to them. I noticed that he had a private remark for each guest as he moved round the table to refill the plates, and I watched as one after the other they smiled at something they were clearly not expected to repeat. His own lips would give a little twitch, and he'd pass silently on to the next guest as though he were the butler. When it came to my turn the remark was 'It's not true, my dear, that sex is a dirty word in Norton Abbas. It's a word that simply doesn't exist.'

He was a silver-haired, scholarly-looking man. After dinner he drew up a chair next to me and began to talk very softly as though what he had to say was for my ears only. I learnt that he kept a small local bookshop, having taken early retirement from the civil service. The bookshop was largely a hobby, he explained, which was just as well, he added, since he cared to stock only books on subjects which interested him. These were scarcely universal in appeal. His shelves positively bulged with volumes on church architecture, dinghy-sailing, wild-flowers, cooking of course, and – to please the vicar – fly-fishing. But little else. Accordingly, as he admitted a little sadly, most people in Norton Abbas who read anything at all made their purchases across the road at W. H. Smith's. Glyn Davies Books remained the quiet and learned haven of men whom Glyn could actually talk to, which it soon became clear was the principal reason he kept the place. It was his social club; he liked most of all to gather 'like minds' around him, he explained carefully. I wasn't sure whether he thought of me as a 'like mind' or not. But then suddenly he announced that he had no intention of boring me any further with his own eccentric interests, so please would I tell him all about myself?

Flattery, I felt, didn't come much more appealing than that.

It was something of a shock to realise this was the first dinner party for ten years when I wasn't being treated as the wife and property of David Hazlitt. I wasn't sure if Glyn had even heard of David Hazlitt, newspapers and TV not being among his declared interests. I thought how dismayed David would have been to know that there were people alive in this land who were entirely unaware of his existence, people for whom his moral crusade had managed to pass unnoticed. Perhaps someone should tell him that what this place urgently needed was an *im*moral crusade.

Not knowing what I was free to say and what I wasn't, I merely explained to my host that I was separated from my husband and was spending some time at the priory gatehouse trying to sort my life out, courtesy of Caroline Uppingham.

Glyn's face brightened.

'Lovely lady,' he said. Then he gave me a shy little smile. 'But I'm not sure I'd like to be Mr Uppingham. And you?' he went on. 'You're not lonely there?'

I shook my head, and he looked relieved.

'Well, in any case you must call on me in my shop. I don't often have beautiful visitors. Please, will you?'

I felt pleased. There was such a gentle air of courtesy about Glyn, flirtatious and avuncular at the same time. However grey his life in the civil service might have been, I imagined him to have deliberately chosen it that way so as never to erode the energies he needed for his private pleasures. He was a happy man.

'Of course I shall do that,' I said.

And the following morning I took myself there, wondering what we might find to talk about.

The shop was empty apart from one mystified visitor, who took some time realising that whatever book he was searching for was most unlikely to be there. He wandered from fly-fishing to church architecture to dinghy-sailing before heading for the door and W. H. Smith's across the road.

'Good riddance,' said Glyn, half to himself as if anyone not interested in dinghy-sailing, church architecture or fly-fishing had no business reading books at all. Then he came up to me with a smile. 'I'm most honoured,' he announced. 'And now you shall have some coffee. How's the nunnery, and all its secrets?'

The question made me feel uneasy. What secrets? Could he possibly mean the topiary? I didn't feel too happy about discussing giant phalluses with this avuncular man I scarcely knew. So I answered cautiously that I assumed he meant the old priory.

'Ah yes, your splendid ruins,' he went on. 'Your shrine of the great St Cuthburga. How fortunate you are, my dear, to have so much history on your own back-doorstep.'

I felt relieved, as well as intrigued, and urged him to tell me more. His face lit up.

'Oh my goodness, yes! Norton Abbey, a most famous establishment. Declined a bit after the Black Death of course, became just a priory.' He hurried over to one of the shelves, reached up for a book and began to flick through the pages. 'Yes, here you are, you see. Norton Abbey, sister house of Wimborne Abbey in Dorset, which as you are probably aware was also founded by St Cuthburga, a little earlier in my view, though some scholars disagree. She was a missionary, you know. A most courageous lady. But of course,' he went on, closing the book and turning to me with boyish enthusiasm, 'Norton really owes its fame to King Edward the Elder, son of Alfred the Great, you'll remember. It was Edward who endowed the nunnery most handsomely and placed it under the Rule of St Benedict. Needless to say that was much later, as recently as AD 907, though personally I think it more likely to have been 908: that would fit the Chronicles better.'

I was far too polite to enquire how he expected a girl from Bologna, Raynes Park Comprehensive School and Surbiton Domestic Science College to know what the hell he was talking about. But I smiled, and Glyn seemed to take this for scholarly agreement. Besides, I was genuinely interested to learn more about this unlikely place in which fate (or, rather, Caroline) had dumped me.

'You can tell how it grew, of course, from the size of the present parish church,' Glyn went on. 'Just as you can tell it was a nunnery church by the fact that it has no western door, in order to keep the laity out, naturally. You'll have noticed that, I'm sure.' (To my relief, I had). 'But have you noticed the corbels round the roof above the apse? Extremely rude, some of them.' He laughed, then looked as though perhaps he shouldn't have done. 'But of course they were frank about things in those days. Not like today, oh dear no! Good thing most of our parishioners are shortsighted, or they'd have quite a shock. Do them good in my view. The vicar too, blind as a bat, the Reverend Pype. The truth is, you see' – and Glyn drew a little closer – 'the nuns were all from the ruling classes, royalty even, and they were quite unfit for hard labour, or study, or any of the things St Benedict insisted on, prayer included. They were just bored out of their pretty little minds. They kept pets, went to taverns, wore extravagent dresses, heaven knows what else they got up to, or one rather hopes for their sake heaven didn't. D'you know' – Glyn leaned towards me even closer and his voice became conspiratorial – 'Pope Boniface VIII was compelled to issue a bull known as the *Periculoso* commanding all nuns to remain enclosed within their monasteries.' He gave a laugh. 'Had no effect at all, of course.'

I was delighted by all this, and perfectly happy for Glyn to go on as long as he liked. But at that moment a customer wandered into the shop, and he went over to speak to her. He listened, then drew back sharply. 'No, most definitely not. Try W. H. Smith's,' I heard him say. He returned shaking his head.

'Do I stock Jilly Cooper, indeed? What will people ask for next? Now, where was I?'

'The nunnery,' I reminded him. 'Of which all that seems to remain is my gatehouse and the parish church,' I said. 'And you're a church warden, Megan tells me.'

Glyn made a face.

'For my sins, yes. I'm afraid vicars can be a severe trial to men of reason. I often wish Jonathan would stick to fly-fishing.'

I laughed, and asked why.

'Well,' he went on, shaking his head, 'he was almost sane, our vicar, until this women priests business. Now he can't talk about anything else. Every sermon. Every telephone call. Real bee in his bonnet about it, he has. You'd think every woman was Mary Magdalen. Ridiculous, seeing as he's got a nunnery church. He doesn't wish to be reminded of that. Frankly we've rather been hoping he'd be driven into the Church of Rome.' Suddenly there was a glint in his eye, and Glyn gave a little laugh. 'You wouldn't be thinking of taking holy orders by any chance, would you, my dear? Because that would do the trick most wonderfully. He'd be off like a shot and you'd be doing us all such a service. You might even get canonised.'

He went on smiling at the idea for quite a time.

Before I left he imparted a few more intriguing pieces of information. Had I noticed the quince orchard? he asked. I said I had, and how amazed I'd been by how ancient the trees were. Yes, he explained, there had always been quince-trees here, dating back to monastic days. The nuns had always grown things, like herb gardens – there would certainly have been one of those; perhaps I might find the site of it. And bees. Joan – I'd met Joan, hadn't I? Well, she was merely carrying on an ancient tradition. No sugar of course in those days. People used honey. And this was why there were honey buzzards here. Had I seen them yet? Beautiful creatures. Very rare. Bird watchers were always hanging around the place – what did they call themselves? Twitchers, that was it. And what about the orchids? Had I come across them? They were even rarer of course.

I looked mystified, and Glyn strode over to the wild-flower shelves and pulled down a book.

'There, that's the one. See? The Hooded Orchis. Only place in England you'll find it. Native of the Middle East; God knows how it got here.'

I peered down at the open page. There was no doubt about it: the illustration in the book was exactly the strange reddish flower I'd noticed growing in profusion near the beech-wood on my first afternoon.

'Thank heaven not many people know about it,' Glyn was saying, 'or they'd all be along with their horrible little trowels, and you'd get no peace at all. So for your own sake don't go talking about it.'

I told him I certainly wouldn't, and that I was sorry but I also had no intention of taking holy orders. Besides, as a lapsed Catholic who'd just walked out on her husband, I mightn't be entirely welcome, I suggested.

Glyn gazed at me rather shyly.

'But you'll always be welcome here, my dear. I promise you that.'

Another customer came into the shop, and before I waved Glyn good-bye I just had time to explain that although I wasn't quite in his league as a chef I did make a mean *osso buco*; would he and Megan please come and sample it one evening? He looked delighted, and nodded vigorously. Then as I was about to close the shop door I heard him explain that no, he most certainly didn't stock Jeffrey Archer. I felt Glyn should be getting a commission from W. H. Smith's.

That evening I was due to have a drink with Caroline, whom I hadn't seen for almost a week. Before undertaking that assault course I plucked up courage to make two long-delayed phone calls. The longer I'd left them the harder they'd become.

'David, it's me,' I said warily. 'I have an address to give you now if you'd like it. And a phone number.'

He sounded surprised, then pleased, and then patient.

'When can I see you?' he said once he'd taken down what I'd told him. 'We do need to talk.'

I felt immediately defensive.

'What about?'

'Us. Our future.'

Irritation began to rise in me.

'David, we don't have a future,' I said sharply. 'And we've done nothing but talk for ten years.'

That was a little unkind, but I felt unkind. There was a pause. I could hear David thinking of the next move. The lawyer's mind.

'Then I'll write,' he said quietly. 'I'd like to visit you, but it sounds as though you'd rather I didn't just yet.'

There was David being reasonable again. How I hated that calm 'defence counsel' voice. 'Or, frankly, ever,' I felt like saying. But that would have been cruel, and not entirely true. In six months' time I could imagine we might well find things to talk about – such as the divorce.

'I need space,' I said. Particularly between him and me, I thought. Lots of it. Infinite space. Space to breathe. Space to obliterate the thought of being Mrs David Hazlitt.

Why was I so angry with him? Perhaps it was a way of not being angry with myself for having married him when I should have known better. Even at twenty-one I should have known. There was a lesson which should be engraved on all our hearts. 'It will *never* get better.'

'Yes, I understand,' he was saying. He didn't understand. There were things David could never understand: he wasn't built that way. Then he added almost pleadingly, 'I do wish we could get this separation over soon. It's getting terribly embarrassing having to answer for you. Television. The tabloids.'

That made me angry again. Christ, who was it who chose to be the high-profile moral guardian of the nation?

'Then *don't* answer for me,' I said. 'Just tell the truth. The nation will stand the shock.'

After I put down the phone I gave myself a quarter of an hour and a glass of Frascati to calm down: then I phoned Anna-Maria. Phoning mothers requires quite different lessons, even more difficult in my case because Italian is a language so much harder to hide behind. It's a language of emotions, and Anna-Maria was never short of those.

'Mother, I've left David,' I announced. I decided to let her have it straight before her sentiments began to coil themselves around me.

There was a muffled shriek down the phone. I had to say it
again. There followed a longer shriek. Then the gush and the
tears began, and various saints were evoked.

'I'm perfectly all right,' I assured her during a brief pause in
the aria. No, I wasn't proposing to rush out to Bologna and be
comforted. Yes, of course her prayers would be most welcome.
No, I didn't believe her cousin in Raynes Park would be able
to offer useful advice. And no, I hadn't been to confession:
that wasn't the sort of thing I did much these days. Well, yes,
it might possibly all have something to do with my having
married a Protestant. But no, David wasn't actually a wicked
and adulterous blasphemer, indeed things might have turned
out better if he had been. She didn't understand that. No,
Mamma, I really wasn't planning to live in mortal sin with
another man, at least not just yet; in fact I was staying in the
country in an old nunnery.

There was another pause. Then a long sigh of relief carried
along the wires like a song.

'Oh, heaven be praised,' she said. 'The good nuns will take
care of you, my poor darling.'

I found myself agreeing. Suddenly Anna-Maria's misunder-
standing seemed like a heaven-sent barrier against her flying
over to look after me. I was safe in a nunnery, my virtue
guarded by the saints: that thought would keep Anna-Maria
quiet for a long while.

A few more tears, and plentiful blessings, and we managed
to say good-bye.

It was early evening. I'd been here almost two weeks. The
place was beginning to seem like my own. Strangely I couldn't
help feeling that, even in their absence, the nuns *were* somehow
watching over me; not themselves perhaps, because I doubted
if they would have approved of me much, but the spirit of
what they'd left behind. It was the fact that the place seemed
to have remained untouched since they departed. So much of
it would have been the same. The shrine. The bees. The quince
orchard. The view over the tidal marsh which I was gazing at
now. Maybe even the honey buzzards, as I now knew from
Glyn that was what they must be; indeed there was one of
them now, hunting along the verges of the beech-wood, its

pale striped wings tilting gracefully on the wind. And the strange orchids, all but vanished in the undergrowth now, might they have been here too?

And what about the topiary? A thought came into my head. That yew-tree shaped into a colossal penis. Was it perhaps conceivable after all that nuns might have created such a thing? Glyn had explained that the nuns in those days were noble ladies bored out of their pretty little minds. Admittedly a giant tree-phallus didn't sound an awful lot like boredom. And those carved corbels round the church, which the Reverend Pype was too short-sighted to notice, what might they have to do with it? I definitely needed to go and look at them.

I was also determined that very soon I'd start doing something with this place. Perhaps not Caroline's 'little Versailles', but at least a vegetable garden before the season became too late. Salads. Herbs. I might even recreate the monastery herb garden. Glyn Davies Books would at least have something on that.

Yes, my year of rebirth would be given over to green things.

The heatwave had broken that morning, and now thin rain was spitting through the beech-trees. It was almost time for me to drive up to see the lady of the manor. I assumed she wouldn't be naked by the pool this evening.

When I reached Priory Hall I found the front door open, and there was an unfamiliar stillness about the place. I came across Caroline in the huge drawing-room, seated at a small table by the window. She didn't look up. Her hair, normally glossy and immaculate, was dishevelled. Even more unusual, there was no sign of a drink. Caroline sober was a dangerous animal at any hour; at seven in the evening I could only fear the worst.

After a moment she raised her eyes. Then without any form of greeting she let out a laugh, and began to drum her fingers on a piece of paper that was lying on the table in front of her.

'D'you want to hear a joke, Claudia?' she announced. 'A really good joke. I've been laughing my bloody head off all afternoon.' I stood there, waiting. This was clearly going to be a five-star Caroline performance. 'Well, this is how it goes – are you ready? My father, right? My beloved father. Whom

I nursed. Changed his bed-linen. Paid his bills. Put up with his temper. And his mistresses. In return for which, in the one moment of affection he ever showed me in my entire life, he left me this house. Got the story so far? Am I making myself clear?'

I nodded rather vaguely.

'OK,' she went on, rising to her feet and picking up the piece of paper from the table. 'This pompous little missive is from our dear family solicitor. And d'you know what? He's found the will. And d'you know what my beloved father did shortly before he died?' I waited while Caroline glared; then she tossed the letter on the floor and aimed a kick at it. 'Well, in a moment of unique generosity he decided to leave the place, not to me, not to my family, not to the Naval Widows' and Orphans' Benevolent Society, not to the Jehovah's Witnesses, not to Battersea Dogs' Home. No, nothing like that. He's left the whole lot TO THE BLOODY NATION! The National Fucking Trust!'

Three

It had never occurred to me that one day I'd be compelled to feel sorry for Caroline. True, her life had always bumped from catastrophe to catastrophe, but these had invariably been of her own manufacture; they offset boredom, added agreeable drama to the day, ensured that she remained the star of the show, and that the show would never close. Besides, it intrigued me to watch how these catastrophes would vanish into thin air the moment they'd fulfilled their function: one wave of the wand of privilege and they'd be gone.

But this was quite different. Privilege was suddenly no use at all. The combination of Patrick's disastrous flutter with Lloyd's and her own father's deathbed patriotism was a body-blow against which Caroline had no defence: nothing in her expensive upbringing had equipped her to deal with anything quite as lowly as poverty. In her experience the word 'broke' applied only to what the servants sometimes did to the Royal Doulton china.

The silence that filled the house was like shellshock, and Caroline's face during the days following the solicitor's bomb-shell was a study in helpless bewilderment. It was like watching someone being plunged into a cold sea without ever having been taught how to swim. And other than be with her, cook for her, pour out her drinks and offer comforting platitudes there was little I could usefully do.

It also occurred to me that my own tenancy of the gatehouse was now likely to be extremely brief, and my year of liberation be snuffed out almost as soon as it had begun.

Then on the third day Caroline rallied. Characteristically it took even worse news to rouse her. Patrick had hurried down from London to announce that things at Lloyd's were even more dire than he'd imagined, and he was definitely being forced to put the London house on the market.

This was just the fuel Caroline needed. Now she had a target. She rang me late one morning to announce that she intended to kill Patrick just as soon as she'd poured herself the next vodka-and-tonic, and I'd better come over quickly before a charge of murder was added to bankruptcy.

'I'm perfectly serious,' she yelled down the phone. 'I've had enough. He's lousy in bed. He's lousy with money. I'm going to kill him and disappear to South America.'

'Caroline, please don't,' I said cautiously. 'Only Nazi war criminals do that.'

She ignored the remark.

'*And* the National bloody Trust are sending someone over to see me this afternoon to talk about my "rights". The cheek of it. "Rights" in my own house!' Suddenly her voice became soft and helpless. 'Oh, please do come over, Claudia, and hold my hand. I hate all this. I hate it.'

There was real distress in her voice, though the clink of vodka-and-tonic did make the sob less convincing.

'I will, I promise,' I said. 'The moment I've cleaned up. I'm covered in earth at the moment, but I'll be as quick as I can.'

It was midday. All morning I'd been digging and planting out a small herb garden on the edge of my hayfield close to the terrace. To my joy I'd found that the local Waitrose sold pots of broad-leaved basil, and I'd been carefully pricking these out in the red soil, together with clumps of sage, thyme, dill and oregano. My favourite smells rose from my hands, and I thought of all the dishes I'd soon enjoy making – if, if, *if* I was going to be able to stay here at all.

The threat of losing this place made it suddenly appear extraordinarily precious. Precious and rather romantic. Here were my vast acres where I could do exactly as I wished. Dress as I chose – or not if I chose. I could read, wander, garden, gaze at the estuary, watch the honey buzzards, discover that being alone wasn't necessarily to feel lonely – and if I did then there was always Joan, or Megan, or Caroline to share an hour with. I'd never known an idyll before except in my dreams. Already in a few weeks it was as if my marriage had never existed: it was a long sleep from which I'd finally been able to wake. Every morning I laughed with pleasure at being free of it; at not having to be what I was not. And gazing in the mirror was like meeting myself for the first time.

And on particularly soft evenings I'd catch myself imagining how I might share this place with someone I fancied – someone who I sincerely hoped would fancy a share of me too; eating and drinking wine on my terrace as the sun went down; wandering through the summer grass in the dusk to where the estuary glistened; making love under the sighing beech-trees. And I'd give a friendly nod towards the shrine of St Cuthburga, and hope she'd understand. Women's solidarity after all, even if she were a nun.

These were disconcerting and unexpected things to be discovering about myself. Was it the country air? Was it the proximity of Caroline? Or the effect of having an illustrated *Kama Sutra* above my bed? Or maybe just liberation at last from David in his striped pyjamas and his brotherly 'Good-night'.

And now? Was my idyll really all going to end?

I drove up the long avenue of lime-trees and parked behind Patrick's BMW. The silence in the house suggested that either the murder was already committed or it hadn't yet begun.

Carmen opened the door. She looked alarmed; then on seeing me, a little less alarmed.

'The lady is in the garden; she is not good,' she said nervously.

That seemed a fair description of Caroline at the best of times. I nodded a thank-you and walked past.

'Mr Uppingham, he not very good either,' came Carmen's voice from behind me. 'He blooding.'

Oh God! I hurried through the drawing-room towards the French windows. At first I could see only Caroline: she was seated at the garden table brandishing a large kitchen knife and staring fiercely in the direction of the swimming-pool. By now I was the one feeling alarmed.

A glance at the pool revealed no body, 'blooding' or other-wise. Then I caught sight of a figure in swimming-trunks bending over the garden tap and dabbing his forehead with a towel streaked with blood.

'Can you believe it?' said Caroline as she saw me. 'The stupid idiot decides to take a dip and dives in at the shallow end. As if all those oil tankers going down wasn't enough.' She craned her neck in Patrick's direction. 'Are you all right?' she called out somewhat carelessly. 'Go and lie down and I'll come and dress it for you just as soon as I've finished these beans.' Then she looked up at me and shook her head. 'Silly bugger.'

'Why don't *I* do it?' I suggested.

Caroline laid down the kitchen knife, and got up.

'No, I suppose I'd better not let him bleed to death, had I?'

As she strode off into the house, Patrick looked up at me from his bloodstained towel.

'Oh Jesus, no! Don't let her, Claudia.'

From the look of alarm on his face I decided the wound probably wasn't life-threatening, and as I walked up to him he began to dab it with an air of heroic self-pity.

'*You* do it, for God's sake. Will you? Please,' he went on, stretching himself languidly on a poolside chair and gazing up at me. 'The last time I hurt myself Caroline became pregnant.'

'She did?' I said, grasping the towel from his hand and taking a close look at the gash on his head which by now had stopped bleeding. Patrick lifted one hand and began to touch his scalp gingerly with his fingertips; already he seemed more concerned about his precious curls. He was loving all this, I realised as I bent over him: the wounded warrior submitting to the healing touch of female hands. Had I been one of his secretaries I was sure he'd have reached up and stroked my breasts. I was glad he didn't, though I couldn't help acknowledging that his body was only a little less perfect than he himself believed it to be. His appearance was his pride and joy. Patrick was the most vain Peter Pan I knew, and much of Caroline's declared contempt for him was exasperation at how effortlessly the aura of youth still clung to him. I suspected that the day Patrick grew old his sun would set for ever.

'Go on, then,' I said, wiping the last of the blood from his pretty hair. 'Tell me how she became pregnant.'

He laughed. It was when he'd cut his hand on a carving-knife once, he explained. There was no disinfectant in the house, but Caroline had heard that alcohol would do. Her idea of alcohol turned out to be a bottle of fifty-year-old Napoleon brandy he'd been keeping for some special occasion; and when she poured it on the wound it stung so much he almost fainted. In order to relieve the pain he'd then drunk it, or, rather, they'd drunk it between them, until midway through the bottle they both felt so randy they made love on the kitchen floor.

'The result was Samantha,' he explained.

Not bad for Halfwayuppingham, I thought. And the next time Caroline complained about how lousy Patrick was in bed, I would answer, 'Never mind, Caroline, I understand he's wonderful on the floor.'

She returned at that moment with a tube of Dettol cream, a bandage and a safety-pin which she threatened to stick in his balls. Patrick flung both hands across his bathing trunks and pleaded that he needed both of them and please would she let me finish the job.

'Claudia's got such gentle hands,' he added. 'Besides, Caroline darling, you'll be needing yours for throttling the lady from the National Trust. Remember?'

Mention of the National Trust sent Caroline flouncing away in a sulk, leaving me to my angel-of-mercy act.

Patrick was now in heaven, allowing me to lift his head as I wound the bandage round the precious curls.

'Beautiful eyes you've got,' he said with a slightly mocking smile.

I ignored the remark and went on with the bandage.

'And wonderful skin.'

I said nothing.

'And a great body.'

Resisting the temptation to do with the safety-pin what Caroline had threatened, I secured the bandage and stood up. Patrick gave a sigh.

'Oh, those legs.'

I tried to frown.

'Any more clichés, Patrick?'

There was another sigh.

'Only one,' he said. 'Why don't we go and make love and leave the National Trust to Caroline?'

I made a face.

'And what would you do if I said yes?'

A look of surprise came over his face. Then he let out a laugh.

'God, I'd be absolutely terrified.'

That was when I finally decided to like Patrick. I gave his chest hairs a tweak.

'What a pity,' I said. 'And I've got the brandy. And the kitchen floor. Ah well!' Then, as we started to walk towards the house I put my hand affectionately on his arm. 'Tell me, Patrick. Is it really as bad as Caroline makes out?'

He stopped, and looked at me.

'Yes,' he said thoughtfully. 'And no. It's true we *have* lost just about everything . . . except my salary. And for anyone but Caroline that would be more than enough. It's a lot more than most people ever have. But Caroline's not most people, is she? And this is the place she was born in, and she loves it. She really loves it.'

And from his face I realised that he really loved *her*.

Touching his bandaged head to make sure his curls were still intact, he strolled away to get dressed, and I found myself pondering on the strangeness of marriages. Patrick's and Caroline's seemed like a permanent civil war, yet they could make love on the kitchen floor. David and I, on the other hand, had scarcely ever raised our voices in anger, yet in bed it had been as though an iceberg floated between us. Our marriage could have lasted for ever if peace had been the only requirement. Caroline's would die of boredom if peace were ever to settle on it.

The lady from the National Trust announced herself warmly as Pamela Leggatt. Patrick had wisely gone to the front door: had it been Caroline she might have got no further.

He led her into the drawing-room where she glanced about her with a practised eye, accompanied by a crisp smile. She was a smartly dressed, handsome woman of perhaps fifty, with a well-boned face which I suspected had been lifted, and which Caroline was probably quite certain had been lifted – I could see a little weapon was already being sharpened there.

Carmen produced coffee, and Caroline ostentatiously served herself first.

'Well,' she said, reclining in her chair and glaring at the woman. It was the first word Caroline had uttered, and it was a shot across the bows.

This was clearly going to be a spectator sport, and I had a ringside view. I wondered if Ms Leggatt had met the likes of Caroline before in her professional life. If so, it soon became clear that she'd learnt dangerously little. Her first mistake was to smile.

'I should like to say,' she began, as I imagined she always began, 'how deeply the Trust appreciates Admiral Romsey's generosity.'

As she opened her mouth to continue Caroline jerked forward in her chair.

'Generosity!' she spat. 'My father was never generous to anyone in his life. He was an uncaring bastard.'

I could see Patrick's left foot begin to drum uneasily against the table-leg. But Ms Leggatt's smile showed no sign of wilting.

'Of course we understand how hard it must be to relinquish ownership of a place one has loved and cherished,' she continued. 'We all of us at the Trust appreciate that. Which is why your father's most gracious endowment—'

There was no question of her finishing the sentence. Caroline was on her feet.

'His *what*?' Her mouth remained open. Patrick made a peace-keeping gesture, which Caroline ignored. 'Did you say "endowment"? Are you telling me he actually left you money? Money as well as the house, and the estate, and, and . . .' Caroline waved her arms about as if to suggest the very air she breathed was about to be stolen from her. 'Endowment!' she repeated. 'Endowment for what, for Christ's sake, Ms Leggatt? For what?'

The smile withered a little, but only a little. She coughed politely, and the face recomposed itself.

'The Trust rarely accepts a property without an endowment, Mrs Uppingham. The expense—'

Caroline gave a snort.

'You mean, you're prepared to accept a free gift only if a second free gift is attached to it. But that's quite outrageous.

It's criminal. This is *my* house. I was born here. I live here. And I intend to go on living here.'

For a moment there was a meeting of eyes. I began to have some respect for our visitor as a gentle expression spread over her face.

'And so you shall, Mrs Uppingham. So you shall. You and your family, in perpetuity. That has always been our policy. And by the way my name is Pamela.'

Caroline was looking mystified. She gazed at me. Then at Patrick. Then back at me. And finally at Pamela Leggatt. After a moment or two she ran both hands through her hair and let out a strange laugh.

'I have to tell you, Mrs Leggatt,' she began, ignoring the woman's plea for intimacy, 'I may not possess a Nobel Prize-winning brain. In fact I have precisely one more O-Level than Princess Di. So you must bear with me. Are you seriously trying to tell me my beloved father left *you* a sum of money in order to allow *me* to live in my own house? Is that what you're saying?'

Ms Leggatt tried an uneasy laugh, doing her best to remain calm.

'It's not quite like that, Mrs Uppingham,' she said. 'What it means, you see, is that you'll never have to pay any rent.'

I saw Caroline swallow hard. Then her eyes widened.

'Rent.' The word came out in a half-croak. 'Rent!' she said again.

Before Caroline could recover, the woman recomposed her smile and continued.

'As I explained, Mrs Uppingham, it's the policy of the Trust always to offer right of free occupation to the family. We feel it's only just in view of the generosity of the gift. Besides, our members like to feel that a great house is lived in when they come to visit it.'

I was finding it increasingly hard to decide whether Ms Leggatt was being deliberately provocative or hopelessly naive. By now Caroline was gazing at the woman in pure amazement.

'*Visit* it,' she exclaimed. 'What on earth d'you mean, visit it?'

Patrick was looking even more uneasy. Again he tried to say something, but Pamela was in full stride. Clearly she'd come here to explain the situation and was determined to do precisely that. The whole purpose of National Trust properties, she said, was that they should be preserved and made available to the public. Not all the time of course: perhaps two or three days a week during the spring, summer and autumn. And on those occasions it was always felt to be a privilege to be taken round a noble house such as this one by the occupant of the place – unless of course Mrs Uppingham should wish to employ someone else as guide, but this would be a purely private arrangement. She rather hoped Mrs Uppingham would be prepared to undertake it herself: this would save extra expense on her part, and in fact many former owners had found the experience richly rewarding, meeting so many people of varying interests and nationalities. The Americans, in particular, always asked the most unexpected questions, besides very often leaving the most handsome tokens of their gratitude. Of course large parties were to be discouraged – theft and damage had to be taken into consideration – but groups of, say, fifteen or twenty at a time were quite manageable, each tour to take perhaps an hour, after which visitors were free to wander in the grounds, enjoy a picnic on fine days, make purchases at the shop. This would mean of course that extra toilet facilities would need to be provided, as well as facilities for the disabled – many elderly and retired folk enjoyed these visits, as Mrs Uppingham would discover; and one of the first things she, Pamela, would need to do on her next visit was to inspect such facilities in order to recommend whatever plumbing and structural alterations would be necessary. Naturally the Trust would meet all costs of this nature, leaving the occupant with merely the annual running costs, which would be unlikely to exceed £20,000 for a property of this size, she imagined.

She paused.

'Well, that in a nutshell is how it works, Mrs Uppingham,' she added cheerfully. 'You know, I'm quite sure you'll enjoy it once you get used to the idea. And we're always available to offer advice should you need it.'

Her business concluded, Ms Leggatt was obviously pleased with herself, and sat comfortably back in her chair.

There was a long silence. Then I saw Caroline begin to move her head very slowly. She took in the whole room, fixing her gaze on ancestor after ancestor, and as she did so they seemed to gaze disdainfully back at her from their lofty portraits. I felt entirely wretched. I was looking at a woman who sensed that she had lost everything. She was betrayed, mortally wounded. Even the grandmother who was supposed to look so much like her seemed to wear a look of special disapproval.

Finally Caroline got up, placed her coffee-cup carefully on the table, and walked towards the door. Reaching it she looked back and gazed at Pamela Leggatt. Her eyes began to make a careful inspection of the well-corseted body of her visitor, and for a moment or two she said nothing. Then an icy smile formed on her lips, and she gave a litle laugh.

'Tell me, Mrs Leggatt – it is *Mrs*, is it?' she said quietly. 'My father never in his whole life gave anything away for nothing. So . . . what exactly did he get in return for this place?'

And she turned and left.

There was something about Pamela Leggatt that was deeply dislikeable. I kept trying to think who she reminded me of. Various memories floated before my eyes. There'd been the mother of one of Anna-Maria's pasta-makers who'd spoken in much the same patronising way with the same aggressive smile: she'd evidently concluded that I was the best available match for her son – rather as she might have settled for the best available leg of veal from the butcher's – and was now privately deciding when the marriage was to take place, where the honeymoon was to be, what I should wear, what I should cook for my husband, how often I was expected to satisfy his desires, which of his fads I must learn to respect, how many children I should bear, and what saints' names they should be given. Her charm in never acknowledging any of these things was like soft moss on a rock of granite.

Then there'd been my headmistress at Raynes Park Comprehensive. 'Ah, Miss Foscari,' she announced one morning, having called me into her office after assembly. 'I imagine in Italy they may do things rather differently, my dear, but I need to explain to you that in this country a cross worn round the neck is intended to draw attention to one's faith, not one's bosom. There is an excellent underwear department at British Home Stores: kindly avail yourself of it.' She herself clearly did so: her own bra would have withstood the siege of Mafeking.

My third memory was of the lady chairperson of the Box Hill Conservative Party. She'd expressed a desire to meet the young wife of their new parliamentary candidate. I duly wore powder-blue and invited her to tea, where she ate cakes and interrogated me with her steel-grey eyes. It was refreshing, she said (she meant 'dangerous'), to have a foreign wife accompanying 'our' candidate on the hustings, especially one who – following Mrs Thatcher's splendid example – dressed so elegantly (she meant my skirt was disgustingly short), and who would bring to 'our' staid meetings a breath of Latin warmth (she meant I seemed a flighty little piece who'd have to be kept under strict surveillance). And no doubt, she went on, the Hazlitt family would soon be blessed with offspring – 'our' party was of course the party of family values (in other words, we like nothing better than a little Tory breeder), and children were such invaluable anchors to a busy political life (keep the young trollop safely at home changing nappies). 'David is very lucky,' she added as she departed, still smiling. 'And so of course are we.'

Pamela Leggatt reminded me of all three of these creatures – a hybrid version of women whose knives are sheathed in a smile.

Caroline, on the other hand, was possessed by a single thought. She had made up her mind that her father had somehow been seduced by 'that Legover woman' into parting with the house. She couldn't imagine what amazing talents in bed the old bag could possibly possess, but none the less she could obviously do something wonderfully restorative to eighty-year-olds, and exact a high price for it.

But Patrick was shaking his head.

'Come on, darling, you've got absolutely no evidence for that at all.'

'Evidence,' Caroline snorted, wrinkling up her nose as though evidence was a particularly foul dog-turd. 'Evidence! My father was all the evidence I need. He was a man who'd have sold his soul for a last fuck; only I don't imagine his soul was worth very much, so he had to produce something else. For Christ's sake, Patrick, he wouldn't have known what the National Trust was: he'd probably have thought you said "Truss". No, that bitch screwed it out of him.'

Patrick was still shaking his head.

'Come on, Caroline. Your father screwed like other men use dental floss, something hygienic which helps put a brilliant smile on your face. He wouldn't have handed over this place for a bonk with anyone, not even a nubile twenty-year-old, let alone some grey-haired matron.'

Caroline merely clicked her tongue dismissively, and stalked off.

Earlier that afternoon Patrick and I had been left to 'clear up a few other matters in Mrs Uppingham's absense, if we'd be so kind,' Ms Leggatt explained, smiling. She made no mention of Caroline's parting shot, and I wondered if it was all part of the normal working day for her, and if dispossessed owners regularly implied she enjoyed bonking for Britain, or at least for the National Trust.

'The "few other matters" mostly related to such things as insurance, the need for a structural survey of Priory Hall, for an inventory of the entire contents of the house (both personal and Trust property), and the provision of gardeners. Ms Leggatt noted, with an attempt at tact, that the estate hadn't exactly been well-maintained by the late admiral during his advanced years. I was tempted to point out that advanced years had in no way prevented the admiral from maintaining his mistresses in fine style; but I restrained myself, and merely exchanged a knowing glance with Patrick, who was looking bemused.

Then there was the matter of the gatehouse, she continued. I drew breath and waited anxiously. This was the crunch. Was it to be good-bye? There seemed an interminable pause before Ms Leggatt put me out of my misery. Under the terms of the admiral's bequest, she explained, occupancy of the gatehouse was to be entirely at the discretion of the family. I suggested that discretion was hardly Mrs Uppingham's strongest point, as Ms Leggatt might well have noticed (she ignored the remark); none the less I was living there at the moment by her invitation, and might I therefore assume that I'd be permitted to stay? My habits were quite clean, I added (she chose to ignore this too).

'There will of course be a requirement to pay the Trust rent,' she went on. Auxiliary buildings, she emphasised, were normally used to house gardeners or caretakers, who would now need to be lodged elsewhere at the Trust's expense.

I asked nervously how much the rent might be. Ms Leggatt looked at me challengingly.

'I'm afraid that's not for me to decide, Mrs . . . um,' she said. 'I would have to let you know. But I should imagine it to be in the nature of four or five hundred pounds a month. Plus all running costs of course.'

I did my best not to look alarmed. But even as the tedious woman droned on about parking and toilet facilities my mental arithmetic was hard at work on how I could possibly afford to live here without going cap-in-hand to David, a thought which filled me with the deepest dismay. My year was to have been a year of freedom, freedom from David, freedom from allowances paid into the account of 'Mrs David Hazlitt'. I'd already accepted from him what amounted to little more than pocket-money on the understanding that I was to live here as Caroline's guest. Somehow the very smallness of my demand had helped give me my sense of freedom. David, reasonable as ever, had offered so much more, along with all the unspoken ties that went with it. One of my greatest pleasures had been in saying 'No'.

Then, even as Pamela Leggatt was moving into her party piece about conserving the nation's rich heritage, it came to me that Caroline and I were now in precisely the same boat. In order that the nation's rich heritage should be enjoyed to the full, we would need – somehow – to make this place pay.

The prospect was laid out before me. A mansion. A gate-house. A ruin. A shrine. A barn. Plus thirty-five acres of Devonshire hayfield, orchard and woodland. What could we possibly do with all this in order to be able to stay here? That was the challenge and for the moment it had to be the key issue in both our lives. I vowed to offer the most earnest prayer to St Cuthburga; even coming from a severely lapsed Catholic it would be worth a try.

'There is just one thing more,' Ms Leggatt was saying, 'before I leave.' Patrick and I looked anxiously at one another. 'Since the priory estate is of the greatest historical importance we shall be arranging for our expert on the medieval period to visit you. A most eminent historian, Dr Fergus Corrigan of the University of Exeter, you may well have heard of him; I'm told he's often to be seen on the television, though I don't possess such a thing myself,' she added proudly. 'May I give him your phone number, Mr Uppingham?'

Patrick gave me another anxious look.

'Perhaps it might be better if *I* dealt with your Dr Corrigan,' I suggested. 'Mr Uppingham isn't always here. Would that be all right, Mrs Leggatt?'

I smiled in imitation of her smile, and handed her my phone number. She gazed at it suspiciously, and then took it.

Finally she got up to leave. Caroline was nowhere to be seen, which was just as well, and Patrick was already glancing at his watch. He needed to get back to London, he explained unconvincingly. I felt sure that another angel of mercy would be patiently waiting to tend his terrible wound. As if the same thought were in his head, he tenderly fingered his curls.

After both of them had gone I found Caroline in bed, her eyes wide open and her body curled into a foetal position. She looked so small and vulnerable. All the arrogance had melted away. Even the frown. I took her hand, and she squeezed mine.

'Thank-you,' she said very quietly. Then she uncurled her body and raised herself on to one elbow. 'Tell me, Claudia,' she went on, 'how easy d'you think it would be to poison that Legover woman?'

I laughed.

'Almost as easy as getting caught for it,' I suggested.

She looked thoughtful for a moment.

'Might be worth it though, don't you think? A few moments of pure pleasure, rather like an orgasm.' With the switch of subject her face visibly brightened, and she sat up. 'D'you have orgasms easily, Claudia? I've never asked you.'

I tried not to look surprised. I burbled something, then confessed that I'd never managed to have an orgasm at all with David, and that for a long time I'd assumed it was all my fault. This was the sort of thing women were conditioned to believe, wasn't it?

But Caroline wasn't listening. Her eyes were wide with amazement.

'Never!' she exclaimed. 'Not once! Good God! Well, all I can say is you must be terribly good at masturbating. Are you?'

I said I didn't really know how one judged that sort of thing. One either did, or one didn't, I thought.

Caroline gave a sigh of irritation.

'Christ, how boring you can be, Claudia. We get on to something interesting for once, and you shut up like a clam. What's the use of having friends?' She composed herself in bed, looking quite sprightly now. 'Well, I can tell you, from my experience a well-conducted masturbation is a great improvement on a bungled coitus. And being married to Patrick, I should know. Now, I need a drink. God, I do.'

Caroline was on the road to recovery. She reached for the bottle of wine I'd brought up.

After a couple of drinks her recovery seemed buoyant enough for me to risk mentioning the question of fund-raising. I explained as gently as I could that it was no good just fulminating against the National Trust, Pamela Leggatt, her dead father, Patrick or anyone else for that matter. The fact remained that she had no money, any more than I did; and unfamiliar though that situation might be, it had to be tackled. We needed to come up with some ideas.

Caroline gave me a po-faced look, then broke into a grin.

'Well, I've got an idea,' she said. 'Two ideas in fact. One is that I need another drink.' With that, she reached for the winebottle and refilled her glass. 'And the other is that I'm going to have a swim. I'm going to wash that Legover woman out of my hair.'

Wine-bottle in one hand, glass in the other, she kicked off

the bedclothes and wandered towards the door. She was completely naked.

'Come on, Claudia. Join me,' she called out as she began to stomp down the regal staircase. Then, swigging alternately from the glass and the bottle she began to giggle. 'Didn't that Legover woman say I'd enjoy taking guided tours round the house? Well, here I am, Claudia. This is how it's going to go.' She stumbled against the wrought-iron banister, recovered her balance and gave a bow to an imaginary party of tourists in the hall below. 'Welcome, dear friends,' she called out. 'Welcome to Priory Hall. This is an informal establishment, as you can see. We've never gone for dressing up in my family, for very good reason, let me tell you: the house was built for one of King Charles II's mistresses, my esteemed ancestor; and by loyal tradition – which I know all you Americans love – each owner of Priory Hall has kept a mistress here ever since, except my father who kept a dozen or so. And there he is, the old bugger.' Caroline had reached the drawing-room by now, and was gesticulating at the portraits with the aid of her wine-bottle. 'A total bastard, he was. Died of syphilis. And that old fart up there is my grandfather, who strangled his wife. And there, down at the end of the room, is my great-great-great-grandfather, who made a fortune in the slave trade. I can't remember who all the others are, but that's the end of the tour; that'll be five pounds each, and any of you who wish are welcome to join me for a dip in the pool, where I hope the whole fucking lot of you will drown.'

Caroline had veered out of the French windows by this time, and was negotiating the steps towards the swimming-pool. Then, watched by me and a totally expressionless Carmen, she stepped into the deep end, her head disappearing below the surface of the water followed by two arms and finally the winebottle and the glass. A red stain of wine slowly spreading was all that remained visible.

Concerned that this might be the last I ever saw of her, I hurried to the edge of the pool in time to see her head re-emerge, followed by two arms still holding the bottle and glass. She blew out a mouthful of water, tossed back her hair and gave out a laugh.

'Wonderful,' she called out. 'Take these, Claudia, and join me. Come on.'

And so I did.

I couldn't help thinking as I jumped in that this wasn't quite the kind of freedom I had had in mind when I left David. And once again I found myself conjuring up a picture of his face as he gazed at his loyal wife and parliamentary support – stark naked with another naked woman in a pool owned by the very nation whose moral rectitude he championed.

'Hey, Caroline,' I called out. 'How about this for a headline in the *News of the World*? "Government Minister's Wife in Lesbian Pool Romp."'

She laughed.

'Well, if Carmen's got a camera, we could oblige and send it to them.'

I looked up and saw the Spanish girl standing motionless on the terrace, her face entirely blank. Her forearms were extended horizontally in front of her like a pair of hand-rails, and over each rail rested a neatly folded towel. What tales, I wondered, was she storing up behind that curtain of silence to tell her family back in Salamanca about the habits of the staid British?

It was almost six o'clock when I left. After the events of the past hour there was absolutely no point mentioning anything as serious as fund-raising to Caroline, and I decided I'd ring her in the morning, provided she hadn't returned to her foetal position by then. Meanwhile I'd have a word with Megan and Joan, to see what useful ideas they might possibly have.

My hair still damp, I drove back towards the gatehouse. I was struck suddenly by how the evening sun seemed to gather up the compact little town and draw it towards the old priory wall as if for protection. Most of the warm brick houses looked too recent to have witnessed the to-ing and fro-ing of nuns, or to have heard the endless tinkling of bells for prayers, though here and there a half-timbered building, lopsided and squeezed among the others, might perhaps have done so, I imagined. One of them carried a sign saying Priory Tavern, and I wondered if centuries ago it had opened its doors surreptitiously to those high-born ladies Glyn had talked about, 'bored out of their pretty little minds', as he'd described them, with their pets, extravagant dresses and 'heaven knows what else they got up to'. Perhaps medieval nuns had all been rather like Caroline, privileged, then dumped, as it were, with nothing left to do with their lives except cause mayhem. If so, no wonder the place had to be destroyed. I rather liked the idea of a nunnery full of Carolines, and decided I must ask Glyn a bit more about them. After all, I was now the guardian of the patron saint of the place: I needed to know what sort of ghosts I was guarding.

Even as I thought of Glyn I realised that his shop was still open; and as I drove past I caught sight of him, re-arranging books in the window, no doubt removing any volume which might conceivably sell and replacing it with the latest tome on Norman fonts. Suddenly it occurred to me that Glyn might also know about the National Trust's medieval expert who was about to be thrust upon me. I pulled the car over to the kerb, and got out.

Glyn saw me, and waved. The shop-window, I noticed, was entirely taken up with books on fly-fishing, with Izaak Walton's *The Compleat Angler* prominently displayed as if it had been published yesterday rather than in 1653. It had been one of the books David had insisted on reading aloud to me in the early days when he still believed my mind worth improving, which is why the date – even if nothing else about it – was indelibly stamped on my brain.

'The things I do for the vicar,' Glyn moaned, welcoming me into the shop. 'He's in a particularly tiresome mood. Women priests again, I'm afraid. Even the ladies who do the flower arrangements he's beginning to view with suspicion. This is the only way to divert his attention. Get him on to fishing.'

And he gestured towards the window display.

'It puzzles me, you know,' he went on, closing the door behind me and clasping his hands neatly, 'that so many Protestant clergymen, who are permitted to marry, hate women, whereas Roman Catholics, who are supposed to be celibate, revere them.' I said my only experience of Catholic reverence was being goosed outside a confession-box and then propositioned inside it. Glyn raised his eyes in mock horror. 'Oh, my dear,' he said gravely, 'I can assure you there's no danger of anything like that with the Reverend Pype. Perhaps if you were a choirboy . . . No, no, no, I should never have said that, and I have no reason whatever for believing it. Absolutely none, I assure you.'

I was laughing. And he began to laugh too.

'Of course,' he went on, 'if it were true it would be one way of getting rid of him, wouldn't it? Perhaps I should be putting books on child-molesting in the window instead of fly-fishing.'

Suddenly he looked at me with the most gentle expression.

'Oh, my dear, it really is so very nice to see you. What a truly beautiful woman you are, if you don't mind my saying so.' Then a smile broke over his face. 'But I don't imagine for a moment that you dropped in to see me. Is there perhaps some book I can help you find?'

I told him I wanted to pick his brains. Glyn looked bashful and flattered. Did he, I asked, know of a medieval scholar by the name of Corrigan? He brightened immediately.

'Oh indeed,' he answered. 'Of course' – as though how could anyone not have done?

I explained about the meeting with the National Trust lady that afternoon, and the visit I was threatened with from this fearfully distinguished man. I couldn't help rather dreading it. What did Glyn know about him, I was keen to know? Was he some dry old fart?

Glyn's eyes widened in surprise.

'Oh no, no, no,' he said. 'Goodness me, I don't imagine so. A very fine scholar, Dr Corrigan. Might that make him an old fart, as you put it? I suppose it might. I really wouldn't know.' With that, he hurried over to a far shelf, ran his thin fingers along it, muttering as he did so, then pulled down a thick volume, which he held out towards me as if it were a communion plate. 'There. This is his most celebrated work. A quite masterly study. You'll enjoy it.'

My heart sank. I took the volume from him and glanced at the title. It was *The Dissolution of the English Monasteries*. I flicked through it. There were more than seven hundred pages. The notes alone must have accounted for a fair slice of

Amazonian rain-forest. Oh Lord, I thought. Does Glyn really expect me to buy this? Does he expect me to read it? Nothing at Raynes Park Comprehensive had prepared me for a task like this.

'Do please borrow it,' Glyn insisted. 'You'll find many references to Norton Abbey there. Something of a mystery, Dr Corrigan seems to think.'

Intrigued, I opened the book again. Thank God for the man who invented the index, I thought. Another slice of Amazonian rain-forest opened up before me. And there was Norton Abbey: at least twenty entries.

I smiled, and assured Glyn I was most grateful. At least I'd now be able to do a little homework before meeting this formidable sage.

'But you must wait just another minute,' Glyn was saying as I was about to leave.

Again he bustled across the shop, this time to a circular table which displayed a haphazard pile of books which the general public might actually want to buy. It was Glyn's one small concession to business – though of course there was no Jilly Cooper or Jeffrey Archer. He picked up another hefty volume, and turned towards me.

'Now, I don't believe I'm giving away any secrets. No, I'm sure I'm not: it's been in all the papers, I'm told.' He handed me the book. I recognised it immediately. *Cardinal Error* was the historical novel that had been high in the best-seller lists for months. Even David, who never read anything as flippant as a novel, had been aware of it. 'A freak,' I remembered him calling it. 'Who could have imagined a book about Cardinal Wolsey being read all over the world?' Even Anna-Maria, who never read anything at all, had rung me up about it: it was being published in Italy, she claimed, solely in order to show how wicked and corrupt the English church had always been. She hoped I wouldn't read it. Well, I hadn't, though the cardinal-red – blood-red – jacket had jumped out at me from every bookstore window for the past six months. And the author's name had become familiar through sheer repetition. Carl Magnus.

'That's Dr Corrigan,' Glyn was saying. 'A very clever man.'

Then he added wistfully, 'And a rather rich man now, I imagine. I don't suppose the halls of academe will hold him much longer, more's the pity.'

With any luck, I thought, the National Trust wouldn't be able to hold him either; then I might be spared this terrifying encounter.

'Take it,' Glyn insisted. 'Take them both.'

I promised to come back and at least pay for *Cardinal Error*. But Glyn waved his hands dismissively.

'Just do me one favour, my dear,' he said. 'Ask Dr Corrigan when you meet him if he'd do me the honour of a visit to sign a copy or two. And please tell him not to be put off by the fly-fishing.'

I thanked Glyn warmly, asked him to give my love to Megan, and left the shop burdened by my two tomes which I might, or might not, display prominently when the great man honoured me with his presence. As I drove under the arch of the gatehouse I wished there was a portcullis I could lower.

During the week following the visit of 'that Legover woman', Caroline's mood swung dramatically. In the mornings she was angry, in the afternoons maudlin, and in the evenings drunk. None of these conditions seemed conducive to planning our survival, and the chief problem of arranging a practical meeting was choosing the moment when Caroline was least likely to disrupt it.

Megan, who'd once painted Caroline's portrait, swore that the only way to ensure a reasonable spell of normality was to catch her just as the anger was beginning to subside, then to hold her attention with delicious gossip. I pointed out that this was all very well if you were just painting Caroline, but gossip wasn't exactly going to help Priory Hall pay its way, was it? Megan said cheerfully that she supposed this was so.

Joan favoured a meeting late in the afternoon. Caroline could always be lifted out of her maudlin state with the promise of a drink, she suggested brightly. The secret, she'd always found, was to delay the arrival of that drink until whatever business you wanted had been completed. I said that in my experience Caroline's patience, especially when a drink was in prospect, had a duration of roughly three minutes, and I didn't see how we could expect to plan the future of Priory Hall and the entire estate in that time. Joan also said she supposed this was so.

Having run out of ideas, both of them then left it to me. I came to the conclusion that Caroline with a glass in her hand was invariably more civilised than when she was without one, and opted for the early evening. So I rang her and proposed a meeting in a week's time, which would give all of us time to come up with some ideas. Please would she put some thoughts together: it really was very important, I insisted. I then told Megan and Joan the same, and they promised to come along to the meeting bursting with projects.

That afternoon I was filled with dark premonitions. Neither Megan nor Joan, after all, had any vested interest in the future of Priory Hall. Joan would always be able to find somewhere else to put her bee-hives, and no doubt Megan's nude portraits of the admiral's mistresses could stay where they were indefinitely. Caroline, what was more, seemed the least likely person in the world to run any kind of profitable venture.

And that left me and the gatehouse.

I searched my brain for any way I might possibly use the resources of this place to pay the rent. Summer pilgrims had started to arrive in numbers to genuflect at the shrine of St Cuthburga, but their tearful piety never seemed to spill over into largesse, and the box I'd put up in the entrance arch announcing 'St Cuthburga Fund' attracted little more than a few prayers eagerly scrawled on scraps of paper, plus a quantity of miserable foreign coins, gathered no doubt during visits to similar shrines abroad. How was it, then, that souvenir shops managed to grow rich on such people, and not me? Perhaps I could bring out a little brochure, I thought. So I looked up my Dark Ages saint in Dr Corrigan's seven-hundred-page tome for useful biographical material, but the learned doctor had little to add to what Glyn had already told me, other than the fact that Cuthburga had married someone called Aldrid of Northumbria who'd promptly allowed his wife to enter a nunnery at Barking. This seemed to me an odd reaction to conjugal bliss, even in the Dark Ages, unless of course Aldrid had been rather like David, in which case perhaps I was rather like St Cuthburga.

That was when I hit on an idea. Supposing I *had* been St Cuthburga, walled up here after fleeing my husband, how would I usefully have spent my time? Prayer? Well, I could rule that out for myself: Anna-Maria already bent the ear of the Good Lord quite enough for one family. Reading holy texts? Even Glyn Davies Books was unlikely to stock many of those, and in any case Cuthburga would have been illiterate, wouldn't she? So, what else would she have done? The answer came to me from the herb book I'd been using for my new garden. The introduction, on the history of herbs, described how early monasteries would supply the entire district with plants for every possible culinary and medicinal purpose. It was God's cottage industry: the Church possessed the skills, and the fact that the plants came from a holy place was said to give them a special potency and flavour.

So, why shouldn't I do the same? Instead of footling around with my little strips of broad-leaved basil to make pesto sauce for myself, why didn't I grow great quantities of herbs of all possible kinds and market them under the holy banner of St Cuthburga? Here was a perfect mixture of food and faith. What's more I was part-Italian; I was reared to these things, both how to grow them and how to cook with them. Anna-Maria had seen to that, if not much else. Her brother's garden outside Bologna was always crammed with foodstuffs which Anna-Maria would lovingly tend, and later eat, with me in obedient attendance. In this way I'd acquired her knowledge, if not thankfully her shape.

Then the idea began to expand. I could group the herbs in pots, and label them 'Herbs for fish', 'Herbs for casseroles', 'Herbs for roasts', 'Herbs for salads', and so on; then perhaps throw in more exotic offerings like 'The Italian collection', 'Herbs of Greece', even 'Herbs from the Bible Lands' or 'Herbs of the Old Testament'. (I didn't think the New Testament paid much attention to food, apart from the Last Supper in which I seemed to remember herbs played no part.) And with my pilgrims specially in mind, what about 'The St Cuthburga collection', or 'The healing herbs of St Cuthburga'? (I ruled out 'Healing herbs from the Dark Ages' as sounding a bit sinister: I didn't wish to be branded a witch.)

What was more, if I could scrape up the money for a small greenhouse with a paraffin heater I could continue to grow plants right through the winter. There was plenty of room by the gatehouse arch for a daily stall: this was right on a bend in the main road in full view of the town; and, what with visiting pilgrims, local custom and passing trade, I could see myself being busy seven days a week if I chose.

And it wouldn't even have to be only herbs. Because we'd lived in a flat in the heart of Bologna, Anna-Maria used to fill every room with all kinds of fruit and vegetables which she grew in pots, tubs, hanging baskets, olive-oil cans, anything in fact that could be made to hold a few handfuls of earth. Everywhere you moved there'd be sweet peppers, minia-ture tomatoes, strawberries, kumquats, aubergines, zucchinis, cucumbers, heaven knows what else. The whole place had been like a food jungle.

Well, the British were supposed to be a nation of gardeners: surely they'd love all that. *And* – for those who wanted it – with the added blessing of God. Surely I was on to a winner.

By now I was so excited I decided I had to ring Glyn. He was the ace chef after all; he might know cheap sources of supply to get me started.

It was dinnertime. He would certainly be in the kitchen; and I was right. I could hear, almost smell, his cooking down the tele-phone. No, of course he had time to talk, he assured me. Had I devoured Dr Corrigan's books already and was coming back for more? Gentle laughter penetrated the sound of sizzling.

I told him my idea, and he made appreciative noises. Well, I might just be in luck, he said. It so happened that a garden centre he knew some ten miles away had recently gone bust. The place was firmly padlocked at present against looters, but he was quite sure the bank responsible for the foreclosure would be only too glad to sell off for a song whatever I might want. He could say this with confidence, he added, since he knew the manager well. They often played golf together. In fact they were due to have a round this weekend. He would certainly enquire on my behalf.

'Then maybe, my dear, you'd allow me to accompany you,' he added. 'Apart from the great pleasure of your company I might find something for my own garden too.'

I felt an altogether different woman that evening. I was no longer trapped. The summer was my own again. Even when David phoned there was no edge in my voice as I parried yet another bid for reconciliation. We should seek professional help, he said: marriage-guidance counsellors were estimable people, he assured me as if I weren't already aware of it. The differences between us were so very small, after all. He was sure I would agree.

Perhaps it would have been easier had I felt angry. I could have said that the main difference between us was that we were two entirely different people, and there was nothing small about that. I could have said that I didn't want my marriage guided by anyone; I wanted it ended. And if I'd really felt cruel I could have said that no amount of professional help could possibly turn a capon into a cockerel.

'David,' I said calmly, 'I just want to lead my own life.'

There was the usual thoughtful pause.

'Then, can I come and see you?'

Now it was more difficult to keep calm.

'No, David. Please, no.'

Another pause.

'I miss you,' he said plaintively, then waited for me to say the same. I could feel my jaw muscles tighten, and I said nothing. And then he spoilt it. 'The local committee are most understanding, Claudia, but I have to say that it *is* becoming rather embarrassing. What with the press and—'

That was when I lost my cool.

'David,' I broke in, 'I do *not* belong to your local committee. I do *not* belong to you. I do *not* belong to your precious career. If that's embarrassing for you, then tough. My life is my own, and as far as I'm concerned you can all go and FUCK YOURSELVES.'

So much for my new calm self. It wasn't elegant, but it did put an end to the phone call.

I poured myself a glass of wine and went and sat on the terrace to simmer down. Why did talking to David always do that to me? It was like being in an airless room and having to force open the windows to breathe.

It was a soft summer evening. The honey buzzard was perched on the arch of the ruined abbey. As I watched, it took off and flapped lazily across the hayfield towards the old orchard, heading for Joan's bee-hives perhaps. And at that moment I caught sight of her, a tiny red-headed figure bobbing between the trees. She was lugging various pieces of bee paraphernalia, and heading towards me. The familiar faded jeans were tucked into her smart leather boots. She saw me and waved.

I felt relieved. There was something comfortingly normal about these encounters. It was the kind of easygoing life I'd never known. In Italy there'd never been enough space: one encountered everyone all the time – that constant jostle of family and community. And with David I never encountered anybody at all except by careful and polite arrangement. The constituency had been a kind of open-air prison; one was only let out on parole for good behaviour, and my behaviour was often well short of that.

Joan didn't need to be invited. She sat down and waited while I fetched another glass and set the wine-bottle on the table between us. Then she glanced at me with that impish flicker of a smile with which she liked to greet the daily comedy of life.

'What's new then?' she asked briskly.

'Everything,' I said. 'Just about everything.' I told her my plans for survival, and she gave an excited little bob in her chair, like a squirrel.

'Terrific! You could sell some of my honey if you like. And what about help with the stall? The flame-throwers would be good at that. Get them out of the house. I'll ask them. No I won't, I'll *tell* them. Do something useful for once. Bloody teenagers. Did you never want children?'

'It never happened,' I said. I didn't add that the chances of it ever happening with David had been pretty small.

Joan gazed at me.

'Sad. For me it happened all too quickly, I can tell you. What's it like to be on your own? I've quite forgotten.'

It was a question everyone asked, and I never knew quite how to answer since I'd scarcely known anything else. In Bologna I was alone in a crowd. With David I was just alone.

'I've got quite good at it,' I said. 'Lots of practice.'

Joan looked puzzled.

'And marriage?'

'The loneliest institution I know.'

There was another flicker of a smile.

'Sometimes I could do without it too, just to feel what it's like. But what about him, now that you've left?'

I was about to say he was a total pain in the arse. But then the phone rang. I was sure it would be David again, and I couldn't bear it.

'Joan, do me a favour and answer it,' I said. 'Please. Just say I'm out, will you? Anything. Say anything you like.'

Joan hurried into the house, and I saw her pick up the phone. There was a moment's silence, then she started making faces through the open French windows. Oh God, what was David asking her? 'Yes, I can understand you perfectly,' I heard her say. There was a longish silence, followed by 'What?' A look of wide-eyed mischief began to spread over Joan's face, and I saw her raise her eyes to the ceiling. 'Yes, this is St Cuthburga's Nunnery,' she announced loudly. I gave a jolt. There was another short pause, then, 'This *is* the Mother Superior,' Joan went on, 'Your daughter Claudia? You mean Sister Claudia. Yes, she's perfectly well . . . No, at prayers. In the chapel . . . Oh yes, spends a lot of time praying. Always on her knees . . . Yes, *we're* very glad too . . . No, we don't actually encourage visitors – we're a silent order, you see. She's only allowed to speak between six and seven, and usually she chooses not to . . . Yes, we all pray for her too, signora . . . Yes, of course marriage is a sacred institution, but so is a nunnery, I'm sure you'd agree . . . Absolutely. Your daughter is in God's hands, signora . . . I will tell her. *Buona notte.*'

Joan emerged, both hands pressed to her face, her eyes peeping through.

'You did tell me to say "anything", didn't you? Well, I did. Was that all right?'

I nodded helplessly.

'Of course, Joan,' I said. 'Just one thing, though. If my mother does turn up, you must promise me you'll play the part. I want the full outfit right down to the black stockings . . . Now, would Mother Superior care for another glass of wine?'

And we subsided into helpless laughter.

I could scarcely believe it.

'As far as the bank's concerned you can take more or less whatever you like.' Glyn's friend produced a bunch of keys like a jailer from his pocket, and swung open the gates. 'You'll need to arrange any transport, of course,' he added. 'Oh, and there'll be a nominal charge for anything like a greenhouse, or a cultivator, I imagine. But the plants – well, they'll be going to waste anyway, so you might as well help yourself.'

Glyn was whispering that the bank manager had come over specially from Exeter.

'Mind you, I did tell him you were extremely beautiful and half-Italian. I hope you don't mind. That was on the sixteenth tee, and do you know, he did an air-shot. I'm afraid I laughed. He spends his holidays in Italy apparently. D'you bank with the NatWest, by the way? It might be a nice gesture.'

I nearly said I'd not only bank with them I'd almost be prepared to bonk with them after this.

'Of course,' I said. 'Anything. It's just incredible.'

The bank manager waited by the gates idly jangling his keys while Glyn and I hurriedly scoured the place. I felt like a child in a toyshop with a rich uncle.

I worked feverishly, aware that the man was anxious to get back to Exeter. Each time I glanced up I could see him gazing at me. I gave him a reassuring smile just in case he should change his mind.

I piled boxes of plants on to barrows.

I lugged sacks of potting soil on to further barrows.

I stacked up quantities of little plastic pots, and larger earthenware ones.

I grabbed armfuls of white labels.

I crammed my pockets with packets of seeds.

I made a small mountain of cloches and cultivator boxes.

I filled a black plastic bag with trowels, forks, dibblers, pruning shears, gardening knives and wire ties.

I found a paraffin heater and added that to my collection.

Finally I took a deep breath and decided on a twenty-foot greenhouse, equipped with shelving, ventilated windows and sun-blinds. I prayed that when the bank manager had said 'nominal charge' he'd really meant it.

'I can't tell you how grateful I am,' I said when I'd finished, shamelessly turning my eyes on him.

'It's my pleasure,' he replied, smiling. 'We shall enjoy handling your account when your business is set up.' From his expression it was clear that he'd very much rather handle me. 'You must promise to have lunch with me when you do.'

And he handed me his card.

'Of course,' I said keenly. 'I'd enjoy that.'

I felt ashamed of myself, but only a little. Business was business, and a lunch and one pair of flirtatious eyes seemed a small price to pay for a coup like this.

As he locked the gates behind us we arranged that I'd fix the transport as soon as possible, and he offered to lend me the key if I'd collect and return it on whatever day it was.

'I look forward to seeing you again, Miss Foscari,' he said as he shook my hand. He stressed the 'Miss'. Then he turned as he walked away. '*Ciao*.'

He made it sound like something you might buy in a pet-shop. Glyn had a twinkle in his eye as I glanced at him.

'There'll be plenty of air-shots next time, I should imagine,' he said in a low voice as we made our way to my little Fiat. 'Which means I might actually win,' he added with a chuckle.

We watched as the bank manager drove away throatily in his Volvo.

'Terrible one for the ladies,' announced Glyn very seriously.

'Oh really?' I said innocently. 'But then I imagine bank managers have to be good with figures.'

Glyn glanced at me again, and gave a nervous laugh.

It was midday when I dropped him at his home, then drove on towards the gatehouse. A wedding party was issuing from the side door of the church, and I caught sight of the papery figure of the Reverend Pype, whom I'd so far scrupulously managed to avoid. I had no appetite for vicars, least of all misogynist vicars; and I sincerely hoped that his mistrust of women would embrace me, and spare me an unctious visitation. After all, not only was I a woman, but I was separated from my husband, and I was the guardian of a Catholic shrine: that ought to ensure that I was anathema three times over.

It was Saturday in Norton Abbas. Ancient walls and church bells. Cobblestones. Blue sky. Cats. The smell of beer and lunch. On this July day it all felt like a paradigm of rural England. And my year – my free year – was gradually edging itself into place. I felt I was *doing* something for the first time in my life. I was making things happen, rather than waiting for them to happen to me. On Monday I'd arrange the transport for my wonderful loot. And later today was to be our policy meeting with Caroline. In fact everything was happening, even in a place where nothing ever seemed to happen.

I thought about our meeting. I was to pick up Megan and Joan around six; then we'd descend on Caroline and cross our fingers she'd be in a mood to be serious. And what if she weren't? Now I was putting my own house in order, Caroline's plight seemed altogether less threatening. And yet at the same time it was more worrying. How could she ever cope? Money, to Caroline, was something you always had – like a social position, like knowing the right people – and if you suddenly hadn't then you were the victim of some divine injustice, and you could only rage. And rage was something Caroline understood only too well. It was wonderful if it could be effective. But impotent rage; that was entirely different. Now she had only herself to destroy. I felt uneasy.

And I felt restless. There was so much I was itching to do, and nothing I *could* do until Monday.

I spent the afternoon wandering. The sight of confetti strewn along the path drew me into the parish church, making quite sure first of all that the Reverend Pype was nowhere to be seen. The gaunt Norman nave was quite empty, though clusters of wedding flowers brightened the bare stone with colour and scented the air with lilies. I thought of all those high-born nuns who had once knelt here dreaming of anything but God. I walked on past the high altar. There in what Glyn had informed me was the retrochoir lay the stone coffin-lid of some early abbess, her carved hand emerging rather eerily from the tomb to grasp her wand of office. It looked more like a stout walking-stick, and I wondered how often she'd been compelled to wield it among her errant flock as they primped themselves in their extravagant clothes or scuttled giggling and dishevelled out of the Priory Tavern.

Suddenly I remembered Glyn talking about the carved corbels round the roof of the apse. Extremely rude, some of them, he'd explained: a good thing the Reverend Pype was as blind as a bat. I decided to go and see what he meant.

I walked round the back of the church and gazed up at the roofline. The sun was in my eyes, and at first all I could make out was a series of twisted shapes and grimacing creatures half-suspended from the overhanging stone. Then I manoeuvred myself so that the church tower blocked the sun, and peered again. The twisted shapes came dramatically to life. I wasn't sure if I was shocked, amused, or merely surprised; and I found myself instinctively glancing about me in case anyone was watching. I tried to tell myself that this was a church built for nuns, but this scarcely explained why intimate portions of their anatomy should be hallowed in this fashion. In any case nuns, as I understood it, were supposed to be brides of Christ, and this hardly seemed an appropriate way to announce the fact. Was Christ expected to appreciate yawning vaginas, thrusting breasts, couples athletically embracing, orgiastic tangles of stone limbs? I thought it was only Indian gods who went in for such antics. In fact it all made the bedhead presented to the admiral by the Ladies' Bridge Club of Bombay look positively demure.

Accustomed by now to gazing at rooflines, I found myself glancing up as I walked back under the arch of my gatehouse. I stopped dead, for there on the left- and right-hand side of the arch were two carvings I'd never noticed. They were considerably more battered than those protected by the roof of the church apse; none the less I could just make out that they were two figures.

The figure on the left seemed to be female. Maybe it was just centuries of weathering, or perhaps my imagination was by now attuned to these things, but she appeared to be naked, and covering her nakedness modestly with one hand.

The other figure was some kind of animal: at least it had four legs, so I assumed it was. And it was rearing up. Perhaps it was a dog; it was impossible to tell since the head was missing, and so were portions of its limbs and abdomen. Here was something I would need to ask the learned Dr Corrigan.

I glanced at my watch. It was half past five. There was just time for a quick shower and a change of clothes before setting off to collect Megan and Joan. I was viewing this evening with no pleasure at all. I had a vision of Caroline reclining dramatically on the sofa with one arm over her brow as though she was enjoying a fit of the vapours, and pleading total helplessness. And I knew what would happen next. I would get cross with her. She'd then complain that I was no friend of hers. And whatever came out of the meeting, I'd end up expected to do all the work.

But I had my own work to do now, and I was determined to make a go of it. St Cuthburga's herb farm was about to become a reality.

Drying myself on a huge bath-towel I gazed out of the window at my thirty-five acres. There had been no pilgrims today, or if there had been there was no sign of them now. The garden was empty. Except that it wasn't. I didn't quite believe it at first. But then I looked again. It couldn't be anything else. There, tethered in the middle of my hayfield was a large and extremely handsome goat. He was striped and shaggy, with a beard like Confucius, and he was contentedly munching at the summer grass, the size of his belly suggesting that he'd already consumed a fair quantity of it.

And then the phone went. It was Megan, and she was laughing.

'Sorry you weren't in when we called,' she bellowed. 'And when I say "we" I mean me and Jehoshaphat. D'you like him? Glyn wasn't sure you would. But my sister breeds them. I thought he might save you buying a mower. And you don't need to feed him. Just move the stake around a bit, and fill up the water-trough from time to time. He'll probably pee in it. Sounds like Niagara Falls when he does. Are you coming round? We'd better not be late for madam.'

Did I want this goat?

'I think he's lovely,' I said, trying to sound convincing. 'I always wanted a goat, but I failed first time round with David.'

Another snort of laughter came down the phone.

'I'll be just five minutes,' I added.

Half an hour later the expressionless Carmen was showing us into the vast drawing-room of Priory Hall. At first I didn't recognise Caroline. There was this elegant figure standing at the far end of the room. She was dressed in an eggshell-white linen suit and high heels; gold bracelets dangled on both wrists, and her hair was swept up into a French pleat to reveal what I was certain must be diamond earrings – would Caroline possess any others? She looked as though she was about to receive an ambassador, except that one hand displayed a long cigarette-holder which she casually raised to her lips as we approached.

She gazed at my jeans, Joan's leather boots and Megan's loud floral dress with an air of tolerant surprise, and then sauntered over to the drinks table.

'Mineral water for a business meeting, don't you think?' she exclaimed, her back turned to us.

She poured out glasses of Vitteloise and handed them round without a smile, then gestured to us to be seated while she gathered a sheaf of papers and pulled up a chair to join us. Joan and I exchanged mystified glances.

'Now, since I don't imagine any of you will have brought any practical ideas,' she went on, 'I shall tell you mine. Do please make any comments you wish.'

'Are you sure you need us to be here at all?' I said, feeling ruffled. I could see a smile begin to creep over Megan's and Joan's faces. Caroline gave me a stern look.

'Of course. I wouldn't have asked you otherwise, would I, Claudia?'

I was beginning to get irritated.

'You didn't ask us,' I said. '*I* did, if you remember.'

Caroline pretended not to hear.

'Right,' she went on, shuffling her papers. 'Now, the first suggestion. And this is where you come in, Megan. So please listen carefully.' Megan's eyes grew wide, and she took a gulp of her Vitteloise. 'I've decided to take down all these dreadful family portraits. None of our visitors are going to want to look at dead relatives, are they?' She gazed at us challengingly while her scowling ancestors gazed down. 'And in their place I'm going to hang all Megan's portraits of my father's mistresses.'

There was a moment or two of stunned silence as none of us chose to look at each other. We concentrated on our Vitteloise. I raised an eye cautiously at Megan, but her head was down. Joan gave an awkward cough. Caroline's long cigarette-holder was held in front of her like a dart waiting to be thrown. She blew thin coils of smoke into the air and began to tap her fingers on the arm of her chair. The only other sound was the rattle of her bracelets. Somebody had to say something, but what?

Caroline herself broke the silence.

'So you're all agreed, then,' she said. 'Good.' And she got up briskly and began to refill our glasses with mineral water. 'Well, that gave me another idea,' she went on. 'We could take commissions.' Megan's face gave a little jerk. 'I've been making enquiries at Longleat, Wilton and places like that, and the statistics are that almost half the men who visit great houses have three things in common: they're leisured, they're art-lovers, and they have mistresses. Well, there you go.' She looked enquiringly at Megan again. 'Portraits of the loved one – nude. I'll take forty per cent commission. And we'll make a fortune. OK?'

Megan said nothing.

'Now your turn, Joan,' Caroline continued. 'Bees. How many hives have you got?' Joan murmured that she had three. 'Right. Then make it thirty and we'll sell the honey, like Buckfast Abbey. After all, nobody had ever heard of Buckfast till they started keeping bees. And we'll undercut them. Again I'll take forty per cent. OK?'

I was dreading my turn.

'Claudia. Lots of ideas for you. Now, the medieval barn.

It's huge and it's empty, so we must fill it. The summer's no problem. We can have rock concerts, craft workshops, art exhibitions, flower shows. That sort of thing. You'll be good at organising all that with all your constituency experience. But winter – there's the problem. And here's the answer. We'll make it a conference centre. That's where the money is, I'm told. Financial conferences: Patrick can help there. Ecological conferences, land pollution, and so on; there's no end of things you can have conferences about. Then what about making it a literary study centre? All those poets who read their stuff in pubs; they'd much prefer a medieval barn, obviously. What's his name, that laureate fellow? Hughes. And John Betjeman, or is he dead? And we could invite a few Nobel Prize-winners. Christ, people would flock. And they'll all buy Joan's honey on the way out. Claudia, you could cook some St Cuthburga cakes. And Megan, you could stand at the door handing out brochures for "Nude Portraits of the Loved One". None of them will have brought their wives with them anyway. That's why people go to conferences, isn't it, to have an illicit fuck, all expenses paid?'

Caroline paused, looking pleased with herself, and lit another cigarette.

'Well, there you are. I told you you wouldn't have any ideas. Comments, any of you?'

I let a few seconds pass.

'Splendid, Caroline,' I ventured. 'And what exactly will *you* be doing?'

She looked surprised.

'Supervising, of course,' she said. 'Someone's got to see it all works smoothly. Have some more mineral water.'

I was already burping with Vitteloise, and said no. Megan and Joan were looking bemused. We glanced at each other, and the glance meant 'Let's get the hell out of here.'

Caroline showed us to the door. The audience was over.

I dropped Joan and Megan at their respective houses on the way home. Megan shook her head, and said nothing. Joan gave one of her flickering smiles and squeezed my arm. The gatehouse felt like a sudden haven of peace. I began to understand why women chose to become nuns.

It was eight o'clock, and I badly needed a proper drink. I'd just seated myself on the terrace with a reassuring glass of wine when the phone went. Oh, not my mother! Not David!

It was Caroline thanking me for all my wonderful ideas, and what a useful meeting it had been. Could she be drunk already, I wondered? I rather coolly thanked her for the mineral water.

No sooner had I returned to the terrace than the phone rang a second time. Had Caroline thought of something else I might usefully do? Run a private zoo perhaps? Organise a girl-guide jamboree? Build an inter-continental ballistic missile site? I said hello wearily. There was a brief pause; then a man's voice answered.

'Claudia Foscari?'

'It is,' I said.

'My name is Fergus Corrigan,' he explained. The voice was soft and unemphatic, with just a hint of Irish. She tried to picture a little white-haired leprechaun. 'Perhaps I could come and see you about the abbey. Would you be free some time next week? Whenever it suits you.'

Nothing could have suited me less. After Caroline's wild schemes and mineral water, now a dried-up medievalist was being thrust upon me. A day that had begun so brightly was ending in the deepest gloom. What was more, it was starting to rain.

I heard myself say, 'How about Thursday? And do please stay for lunch.'

Lunch! Oh Claudia, why the hell did you say that? And after I'd replaced the receiver I walked out into the evening rain just to make things even worse.

Four

By Thursday mid-morning my loot for St Cuthburga's herb garden was in some semblance of order. I was determined that the place shouldn't look a junkyard for my learned visitor, who was due to turn up at midday. Megan and Joan had stoically lent a hand laying out the innumerable trays of plants on the edge of the hayfield, while making sure that Jehoshaphat's tether prevented him from munching the whole lot during the night. With eyes like evil marbles he kept gazing purposefully in the direction of so much fresh salad; then, having tugged at his stake a few times, he shook his beard in disgust and wandered off to pee massively in his water-trough.

'I thought it was only Hindus who drank their own piss,' commented Megan, setting down the last tray of plants.

Joan and I were putting the finishing touches to my twenty-foot greenhouse, which now stood proudly in full sun by the boundary wall, at a discreet distance from the ruins of the old priory and the shrine of our patron saint. I didn't want to offend visiting pilgrims, whom in any case I was relying on to purchase large guantities of 'St Cuthburga's herbs' before the end of the summer.

The greenhouse had been a full-scale operation. The contractor had carried out the dismantling with great care, and had finally driven off with it in the direction of Norton Abbas while I drove to Exeter to return the key of the bankrupt garden centre to the bank. There I dutifully opened a business account with five pounds in the name of St Cuthburga Products. I also accepted the manager's insistent invitation to lunch, during which he enumerated all kinds of benefits the bank would be only too delighted to offer a young businessperson like myself if I'd perhaps care to discuss the matter further at his delightful weekend cottage on the edge of Dartmoor. He made the invitation more meaningful by dropping in the odd

phrase of Italian, smiling intimately as he did so. I smiled a
lot in return, felt glad I was wearing a bra, and left before the
coffee, though not before removing his hand from my thigh.
As I departed I awarded him a gentle Italian endearment in
return. '*Grazie, stronzo,*' I said as seductively as I could, trusting
he wouldn't understand that I'd just called him an arsehole.
The man simpered, then in an accent like a nail dragged across
a blackboard he replied, '*E grazie a lei, bella.*'

I told Joan this story, much to her delight. At the far end
of the greenhouse she continued to chuckle at the way I
referred to him as my 'bonk manager'. With every shelf she
put up the chuckles would rise in volume, and a comment
be thrown over her shoulder: they kept arriving like mortar
shells – first it was the likelihood of rising interest rates, then
it was soaring inflation, followed by credit squeezes. And so
it went on through the morning. I could see that bonk jokes
were destined to enjoy a long life.

Finally, still chuckling, she called over to Megan, and the
two of them departed, wishing me good luck with my *éminence
grise*. They hoped I had a Zimmer frame handy, they said.
By this time it was eleven o'clock. An hour to go. Apart
from Jehoshaphat, who was still directing his marble eyes
towards my boxes of plants, the garden was empty, and
almost orderly.

I felt nervous. It was hard to say what kind of nervous, but
it was mostly to do with the fear that I would be pronounced
totally unsuitable as a caretaker for so historic a site. At least
I hoped the lunch would make a favourable impression. I'd
decided on cold salmon with mayonnaise, which I'd made
early that morning, together with two different kinds of salad,
followed by an interesting variety of cheeses. All this seemed
appropriate for a hot summer's day, as well as being unlikely
to cause embarrassment should my elderly sage have trouble
with his teeth. I'd also pulled the stops out and baked a loaf
of rye bread, and in the fridge rested a bottle of Puligny
Montrachet which I couldn't afford. It would have to be
Bulgarian plonk until David's next monthly payment.

The next question was what on earth I should wear to
receive so distinguished a scholar. I thought about it hard

and ineffectually while fussing around my basil plants and pulling up the odd stray weed. The problem was, what kind of Claudia Foscari did I wish to be? The confident and capable businesswoman? The sophisticated foreign lady with the artistic heritage of Italy in her veins? Or the ever-so-willing *ingénue*?

Since I couldn't make up my mind, I decided in the end to be all three. For the confident businesswoman I remembered I had a pair of immaculate Katherine Hamnett jeans in stretch denim, chic and thigh-hugging at the same time: David had always found them far too sexy and therefore disapproved, even though I pointed out that at least they were the right political colour. Then, for the foreign sophisticate I thought of my lightweight linen jacket, cut into the waist and flared over the hips in the fashionable Edwardian style. It was also double-breasted, so that if the moment came for Claudia to become the *ingénue* I could unbutton it to reveal my soft cotton blouse in the sweetest rose-pink, with straps and little pleats and buttons down the front. A bit *Sound of Music*, but perhaps that was appropriate.

I wasn't sure what all this added up to in terms of *me*, but I was confident that it would look good; and in any case I didn't imagine distinguished medieval scholars spent much of their lives poring over fashion magazines, or indeed over women. No doubt Dr Corrigan had a wife who was comfortably encased in autumnal tweeds, her grizzled hair generously speared with pins. She probably had a fine display of lupins in her garden, and made elderflower wine.

I glanced again at my watch. It was now eleven-fifteen. I needed to get a move on; get off my knees, take a quick shower to remove the stench of compost and fertiliser, and assemble my carefully planned outfit. My hands were filthy and my shirt smeared with earth and patches of sweat. My hair felt as though Jehoshaphat had savaged it. Thank heavens I'd put no make-up on this morning, or it would now be running in dark rivulets down my face.

I straightened my back to get up, and as I did so the most sinister thing happened: as I moved, my shadow didn't. Or, rather, half of it moved. The other half became a second shadow. Instantly my stomach went into spasm. I was too paralysed to move. There'd been no sound, or none that I heard. For perhaps two seconds it was entirely clear that I was about to be robbed, raped and murdered, in that order. This was the end. There wasn't even time to scream.

Then, as the first flash of terror passed I decided I ought at least to know what my assailant looked like, and very slowly turned my head. My eyes started at ground level and gingerly worked their way upwards. The first sight they took in was a pair of very slim, sand-coloured jeans with two hands thrust casually into the pockets. Shock was by now giving way to bewilderment. I continued to raise my eyes: the jeans seemed to go on for ever, before finally giving way to a faded blue denim shirt unbuttoned at the neck to reveal a thicket of pale chest-hair. At this point the sun interfered; it was directly behind the man's head so that his face was in heavy shadow. All I could make out was that his hair was long and very fair, and glistened where the sun caught it; while out of the dark blur of his features a pair of intensely blue eyes were gazing down at me.

Whether it was relief or disbelief I had no idea, but I laughed. And the man smiled.

'Sorry if I frightened you,' he said calmly. 'Not at all what I intended. The name's Corrigan.'

He sounded so genuinely apologetic, his words uttered with that slight Irish sliding of the vowels. I got unsteadily to my feet. All kinds of sensations were bombarding me. To have expected a murderer, only to find some kind of Apollo, was hard enough to take. That this sun-god should also turn out to be the man I'd expected to be austere and stooped, was altogether too much. Could this really be the formidable Dr Fergus Corrigan, author of seven hundred learned pages on *The Dissolution of the English Monasteries*?

'And I'm Claudia Foscari,' I said shakily, brushing the soil off my hands; then, gathering up the remnants of my dignity, 'You're early,' I added with some indignation.

He apologised, while the intense blue eyes continued to gaze at me. A class at university had been cancelled, he explained in the same calm voice. And besides, it was a fine day, he added as though these were quite adequate reasons for scaring the living daylights out of me. He *had* tried the doorbell, but there had been no answer, so he'd decided to look around the priory estate until I arrived, in order to get some idea of what might need to be done. Then he'd caught sight of me in the garden.

His manner was disconcertingly intimate and relaxed, as though he already knew me well. As he bent down and pretended to admire my basil plants I had a chance to look at him properly. He was tall and sinewy, and moved with an easy catlike grace. He might have been forty, I thought, possibly less: it was hard to tell with such a lined and suntanned face, which managed to suggest that he'd just walked across the Spanish sierras with the sun bleaching his hair – which he was a little too vain to cut, I suspected. He prided himself on his Samson locks, I felt sure: they invited female fingers to run through them. No doubt his ego fed on a diet of adoring students.

'You seem hard at work,' he said in that same caressing Irish voice, raising his head to look at me.

I nodded, and swept the hair from my face with the back of my hand. He liked that, and already I was aware that we were conducting a discreet body-language which we would neither of us have been prepared to commit to words. The thought made me smile, and he liked that too.

'St Cuthburga's herb garden,' I said. 'D'you suppose she ever got quite as dirty as this?'

He didn't answer, but his eyes continued to gaze at me. I had a strong feeling that he would have liked to pay me a compliment, but had decided it was perhaps a little premature. Maybe he was also thinking, as I was, that thanks to the National Trust the two of us were likely to be seeing a good deal of one another, and that there would be plenty of time for such things, and indeed for anything else. Maybe, too, while I was busy readjusting my vision of a medieval historian, Corrigan was readjusting his view of the sort of woman who would choose to live alone in an ancient priory gatehouse. If so, the surprise was certainly mutual, though this too was unspoken. I knew what I could read in his eyes, as I was sure a great many women had done already, and had no doubt been very glad. But what, I wondered, was he reading in mine? I hoped it was 'Yes, you are clearly a dangerous animal, Dr Corrigan, as you know only too damn well. And I shall flirt with you with enormous pleasure, certainly think about you when I'm alone, maybe even dream about you fairly shamelessly; but I shall *not* join the queue of little admirers who I'm quite sure are even now waiting their turn to tumble into bed with you. I don't join queues, Dr Corrigan; I jump them, or stand aside. So, let's make this a delicious game, shall we? Your move.'

'Maybe the lady saint would like a clean-up,' he said in a voice now tinged with humour. 'So if it's OK with you I'll do what I promised and look around. It's quite some time since I've been here. . . . And by the way,' he added as he walked away, 'the name's Fergus.'

I waited until he was about ten yards from me, then I called out, 'Lunch whenever you like, Dr Corrigan. Nunnery fare of course.'

He paused, and I could see him smile as he made a gesture of thanks with his hand. Then, after he'd gone a few more yards I added, 'And by the way, the name of the lady saint is Claudia.'

He turned a second time and gave a little bow before continuing with slow, easy strides towards the ruins of the priory. I watched him for a moment, alarmed to realise that I was imagining him to be on the end of a long tether, rather like Jehoshaphat, and that it would be exciting to be able to pull him back whenever I wished. Unless of course *I* was the one on the end of the tether, which made me feel more uneasy. It's only a game, Claudia, I told myself firmly. Only a game. Then I went indoors.

I took a shower, and dried myself in the sunlight of the bedroom. From the window I could make out the tall figure of Corrigan strolling thoughtfully among the walls of the priory. Every now and then he would stop and bend down to examine something more closely; then he'd pull out a notepad from his pocket and jot down a few words before moving on, flicking his hair back from his face as he did so. The arrogant calm of the man, I thought, as if the world were watching and admiring him. Well, *I* was. I imagined possessing an invisible hand that could reach out and scrawl on his notepad, 'St Cuthburga fancies you.' There was a certain *frisson* about standing here at the window entirely naked gazing at him, knowing he was quite unaware of it. The rules of the game permitted such secret pleasures, I decided, though to have been observed would of course have broken those rules.

Just in case he chanced to look up I stepped back out of the sunlight and began to give some thought to what I should wear. Obviously the outfit I'd selected for the benefit of an elderly scholar was now entirely inappropriate. In any case I was *not* a capable businessperson. I was *not* steeped in the culture of Renaissance Italy, or indeed in any culture at all outside the walls of Raynes Park Comprehensive School. And I certainly had no intention of passing myself off as a sweet *ingénue*. So what was it to be?

For a moment I considered ringing Caroline, but that immediately seemed an extremely bad idea. For one thing I'd then have to let on about Fergus, which would make Caroline insist on meeting him. 'Bring him up to the house; I'm the one who's supposed to be dealing with the National Trust after all, darling. Would he like to stay the night? Oh go on, Claudia, ask him – be a good friend; it's about time something nice happened to me; you're quite sure he's not queer, are you?' Or else she'd assume that all I wanted was to take him to bed myself, in which case why the hell was I worrying about what to wear, for God's sake? 'Try wearing nothing,' she'd say. '*I* would.'

And indeed she would.

No, I must keep Caroline well out of this. It was my game, not hers. She could find her own Apollo to play with.

I decided that the best solution was to dress enigmatically. The Katherine Hamnett jeans in stretch denim, crotch- and thigh-hugging were all right, and they'd deliver one kind of message below the waist. But then I needed something entirely different for the top half. Nothing too severe: I didn't want him to imagine I really was St Cuthburga. But, well, sort of contradictory. Puzzling. So he wouldn't know quite what to make of it, and his imagination would have to work it out.

That was when I remembered David's shirt. I'd packed it by mistake, and had never got round to posting it back to him. David's shirts were from Turnbull & Asser – naturally; he never wore anything else, even on holiday. He was always the well-dressed Tory MP. Certainly never the undressed Tory MP. This one was in fine cotton, blue and white in conventional stripes; and of course it had long shirt-tails so I would never be embarrassed by a flash of his willy when he removed his Y-fronts. Yes, it would be perfect, just what I wanted. And of course it was hugely baggy, David being a large man, at least across the shoulders and chest.

I reached into the cupboard for it and shook it out. It certainly was huge; I would seem elfin inside it, though with nothing underneath it my blue-eyed visitor might have no trouble in noticing I wasn't exactly little in the right places. I slipped the shirt on in front of the mirror to see just how much of me was detectable through the fine white stripes. Just enough to make it look accidental when I moved, I decided. Now you see my nipples, now you don't. That should keep his mind off the Middle Ages.

Well, David, thank-you. And for once I felt grateful to him for his impeccable good taste. Had Turnbull & Asser ever been put to such good use?

Then a further thought came to me. It might occur to Dr Corrigan to wonder, as he gazed at me wearing a man's shirt, who was the man? And since we were engaged in this game of flirtation, that surely had to be worth quite a few points.

I laid out lunch on a small table by the open French windows. By now I was feeling a little ashamed of myself. What on earth was I doing weaving erotic fantasies round a man I'd met scarcely an hour ago, and with whom I'd exchanged barely a dozen words? I was thirty-two and behaving like a teenager. Was I just frustrated? Yes, I probably was: anyone married to David for ten years would be entitled to feel that. Yet I disliked the word 'frustrated'; it smacked of what the macho male always assumed a woman to be if she was bold enough to wear a low-cut blouse or raise a flirtatious eye. It meant 'available' or 'all she needs is a good fuck'. And even if I did, it wasn't that, I told myself. It was freedom. Something

I'd never experienced before. Freedom to fancy someone if I chose to without being made to feel guilty. My sole brief affair with one of David's fellow MPs had been so clandestine I'd felt like a thief in the night. I used to gaze in the mirror in the morning to see if my guilt showed. I'd longed and longed to be a blithe spirit, and now I was going to be.

I glanced out of the French windows and saw that Fergus was strolling back towards the gatehouse.

As he stepped into the house he looked hot, and I handed him a glass of chilled white wine. He looked surprised and pleased.

'I didn't expect all this,' he said, surveying the spread of lunch and then sinking into one of my wicker garden chairs. 'You promised nunnery fare. I'd imagined dandelion salad and holy spring water.'

His eyes continued to take in the spread of cold salmon and mayonnaise, salad, rye bread and cheese; then the bottle of Puligny Montrachet; and from time to time he took in me. I could see that my tight jeans intrigued him, though just a little less than the man's shirt and what he must quickly have observed to be nothing underneath. Those intense blue eyes told me a lot. I kept very cool, and served out the salmon and mayonnaise. He sipped his wine as I did so, and watched me.

It was another of those silences. I began to wonder what we would talk about? The old priory? Him? Me? It wasn't so much the ice which needed breaking as the heat. I decided I would leave it to him to break it.

'Tell me why you're here,' he asked quietly after a moment or two.

I looked at him cautiously.

'Because I left my husband,' I said.

He nodded as if to suggest this was a perfectly natural thing to do.

'David Hazlitt. Am I right?' There was a pause. 'Pillar of moral virtue. Bluer than blue.'

I laughed. I was also a bit thrown.

'Only politically blue.'

He gave a slight smile.

'And all you've kept of him is his shirt.'

I thought of saying, 'No, actually it's my lover's.' Instead I just shrugged, leaving a small area of doubt.

'So, you're alone,' he went on.

Again I didn't answer. I didn't need to: I suspected that nothing could have been more obvious than that I was alone. Fergus ran his fingers through his mane of fair hair and continued to gaze at me, not lecherously, but knowingly, with an air of cool assessment, mentally adding me, no doubt, to the list of future affairs he was contemplating when he wasn't so busy, when the right opportunity arose, when the evenings were long and dark, and a fire was blazing, and he had brought the champagne, and of course when the wife was visiting a sick relative.

'More wine with your cheese?' I suggested, carefully holding the neckline of David's shirt to me as I leant across the table.

Fergus understood the gesture, and smiled.

'Thank-you,' he said. 'And thank-you for everything.'

I knew that the 'everything' was me, and felt a little shock of pleasure.

Then, glass of wine in one hand, he turned to gaze out of the French windows.

'An interesting place, this,' he went on. He seemed to be reflecting on something rather than looking at it.

'Tell me,' I said. 'Why?'

There was another pause as his eyes continued to wander over the untended estate. Jehoshaphat was still munching away melancholically in the hayfield, and I noticed the honey buzzard had returned to his perch on the stone arch. I could see that Fergus had noticed it. Well, if he was going to be so bloody secretive, here at least I could get one up on him. I decided to await my chance to tell him what the bird was.

'Who keeps bees here, then?' he asked casually.

I told him it was a friend of mine called Joan. And he nodded.

'They nest here, honey buzzards, don't they? One of the few places in England. In Greece you see them feeding honeycomb to their young.'

I wanted to dislike him intensely for that, but he'd said it so naturally – just another scrap of knowledge a scholar couldn't help picking up in the course of a mentally active life.

'They must always have been here, I suppose,' he went on. 'Summer visitors flying in, always to the same place. A strange thought, isn't it? A thousand years. Your St Cuthburga would have watched them. She kept bees, I imagine. They all did.'

Clearly I'd lost that round. I decided to let him go on showing off.

'You were going to tell me what you found so interesting about this place,' I reminded him.

Fergus was still gazing thoughtfully towards the ruins of the priory. It was almost as though I was no longer there. Then he turned his head as if he'd suddenly remembered me.

'Oh, quite simply why it survived,' he said briskly.

'Survived what?'

He looked at me with an air of surprise.

'The dissolution. Why did Henry VIII spare Norton Abbey – or Priory as it had become by that time – in 1539? How did it manage to survive another hundred years until the Puritans finished it off? It's one of the unsolved puzzles of English history.' I was once more wishing I could dislike this man when he gave a sudden laugh. 'When you think that I've spent half my life studying the dissolution of the monasteries, and I've still not found out the secret of Norton Priory. Very galling. Well, perhaps I'll just have to make it up.'

'I thought scholars weren't supposed to do that sort of thing,' I said.

He gave a mischievous smile.

'I don't necessarily have to do it as a scholar.'

Until that moment I'd entirely forgotten about *Cardinal Error*, Corrigan's historical novel about Cardinal Wolsey written under the pseudonym of Carl Magnus. Even my mother in Bologna had read it, and I still hadn't. Now I felt cornered. At least I had the copy Glyh had pressed into my hands. I vowed that tomorrow I'd rush off to his shop and insist on paying for it.

'Do you enjoy being two people?' I asked.

I could see he was pleased that I knew he was Carl Magnus.

'It can be useful,' he said. 'If I used my real name I wouldn't be taken seriously as a scholar, would I? Besides' – and he gave another hint of a smile – 'a pseudonym is such a wonderful excuse for vanity. Throwing a cloak of mystery around yourself.'

Yes, I thought, you certainly are vain. But how is it that by admitting it you manage to make it such an attractive virtue?

'And you like mysteries, don't you?' I said rather boldly.

He laughed.

'Of course. Don't you?'

I wasn't sure what to say. He seemed to be playing this game rather better than I was. We were like a couple of fencers, and I was the one who was always backing away.

'Sometimes,' I answered.

The intense blue eyes were still boring into me. I wasn't sure if I was enjoying this or not.

'But the real fun is seeing if you can unravel them,' he went on. 'Wouldn't you agree?'

I'd never been flirted with quite like this before. As he said 'unravel' his eyes were unravelling me. It was exciting, and it was disturbing. I was losing this game so badly I decided to steer the conversation back to the mystery of the priory.

'About this place,' I said a little breathlessly. 'Do you really have no clue at all?'

The eyes shifted from me as if he understood that I wasn't going to be drawn any closer.

'Only one,' he said, putting down his empty wine-glass and picking at fragments of cheese on his plate. 'I did touch on it in *Cardinal Error*' – and suddenly he gave a broad smile – 'which you certainly haven't read: I'll give you a copy, and then you'll have to.' He laughed. 'No, the only clue is that Cardinal Wolsey's illegitimate daughter was packed off here as a nun. That might have protected the place, I suppose, though since Henry VIII had charged Wolsey with high treason years before that, why should he have bothered to spare the daughter? So I don't think it can be a very useful clue, do you? There must be a better one, wouldn't you agree?'

He kept asking these questions, as if I might have something useful to contribute. A strange feeling was coming over me. I wasn't able to account for it, but I couldn't help sensing that in some way I was being gently invited to collaborate with Fergus, to share his thoughts, even to join in some sort of investigation – of what, I didn't really know. But it was as if I were sitting here with two Dr Corrigans, both equally mysterious and equally persuasive; one of them persuading me to share his body, the other to share his mind.

Then a sudden remark made me think there might actually be three Dr Corrigans.

'You know,' he said, stretching out his long legs, 'you'd make a magnificent heroine for a novel, a runaway wife who becomes the beautiful guardian of the shrine of mysteries.'

And he looked at me as though he were already admiring his own creation.

'Don't heroines die?' I said firmly.

He gave another laugh.

'Not this one.'

'You promise? So, tell me then,' I asked, 'since you seem to know all about these things, what *do* heroines in ruined priories do with their lives?'

I poured the last of the wine into his glass, at the same time throwing him a glance that I hoped wasn't too provocative.

He raised the glass and looked at me quizzically over the rim of it.

'Well,' he said, 'maybe that's another mystery I should try and solve. What d'you think?'

Megan was painting a small canvas of wild-flowers when I called in for a cup of coffee the following morning to get away from a busload of pilgrims – thank God they hadn't turned up yesterday. Along the walls of her studio were stacked the portraits of the admiral's mistresses, which I'd never seen before. They were certainly very nude indeed, as well as an eloquent testimony to the admiral's far-flung travels in the service of Queen and Country. I tried to imagine them gracing the walls of Caroline's stately drawing-room as she conducted parties of eager Americans round Priory Hall.

'And how was your venerable scholar?' Megan enquired without turning her head from the canvas she was working on.

'If you really want to know,' I said, 'Apollo in tight jeans. Forty-ish. About six foot two. Blond. Gorgeous. Tricky. Sexy as hell. I liked him.'

Megan put down her brush, and looked astonished. Then she let out a guffaw, and her bosom shook.

'Well! So who's going to sleep with Apollo first, you or Caroline?'

I couldn't say I hadn't thought about it because of course I had, and Megan was someone you invariably told the truth to. It was one of her unnerving strengths.

'Who would you say was in greater need, Megan?' I asked cautiously.

She raised her eyes from the canvas and looked thoughtful.

'Well,' she said, 'let's see. You both have absent husbands, yours more absent than Caroline's, it's true. And from what you've told me, your sex life has been rather more of a desert than hers. In fact I wouldn't say hers has exactly been a desert at all: more like a jungle.' She gave another guffaw. 'So, on the face of it you win hands down, don't you? On the other hand' – I could see Megan was really getting into this – 'you're in the more vulnerable position. Caroline's never going to get hurt by any man: she's much more likely to cause him grievous bodily harm. But you could be. After all, you did tell me you wanted a year to find your feet, instead of which you might find yourself flat on your back – or is there another position more in favour these days? I wouldn't know. Glyn's an old-fashioned man, and anyway I'm too hefty for athletics. Joan would know, of course: she's an expert in these things, or used to be. She likes to do it in the bath. Christ, if I did it in the bath I'd get stuck or swamp the neighbourhood.'

It was another of Megan's cheerful monologues. The painting was quite forgotten by now; it struck me as rather comic that with all this fruity chatter she was in the middle of composing an innocent flowerpiece.

'On the other hand,' she went on, getting her second wind, 'he might not fancy Caroline at all. Not every man likes being told to unzip and get on with it and make sure you keep it up for half an hour. Christ, being her lover must be like *Come Dancing*.' There was yet another guffaw, then Megan gave me a serious look. 'Heavens, Claudia, the man would be mad not to fancy you more than her. Just look at you. You're young. You're beautiful. You're a touch exotic. Those eyes would beckon any man into bed. And you've got that unused look, if you'll pardon my saying so; I suppose it's what comes of being married to a man who could only manage it once every two months with his pyjamas on, I remember you telling me. How is he, anyway, your "ex"? Saw him on the box yesterday: looked very disgustingly clean.'

At this point Megan suddenly remembered her painting, and started to peer minutely at a spray of sweet-peas in a vase without waiting for an answer. I decided to leave without giving her one, and without having had the cup of coffee I came for.

'Oh, by the way,' she called out as I was halfway down the stairs, 'I'm under orders to deliver the admiral's nudes to Priory Hall. Patrick's coming down this weekend, Caroline says, so he'll be able to help her hang them. They're to be in order of residence apparently: Caroline's threatening to order little brass labels with the names, dates and country of origin inscribed on them, and I'm supposed to supply the information. Christ, one of them only lasted a week; I had to do most of the portrait from memory. How d'you imagine the label might read? "Felicidad, from Puerto Rico, in residence 14–21 May 1983."'

Heavy chuckles followed me into the street. With relief I noticed that the pilgrims' coach had gone.

For the next three days I was busy planting out herbs. Most of these I grouped in the little reclaimed rectangles of hayfield which I'd meticulously shaped, dug, composted, raked and frequently cursed. Others I arranged in dozens of earthenware pots which I labelled according to the various categories I'd thought of, 'Herbs for fish', 'Herbs for roasts', etc. Then there were the more exotic collections, 'Herbs from Italy', 'Herbs from Greece', 'Herbs from the Bible Lands'. I decided that 'Herbs of the Old Testament' could wait until I'd had a chance to consult Glyn; as church warden as well as master-chef he'd probably be able to save me having to sweat my way through 636 pages from 'In the beginning God created the heaven and the earth' to the Book of the Prophet Malachi.

'The St Cuthburga collection' I made up from all sorts of leftovers, some of which I couldn't even identify and may not have been herbs at all, though they smelled potent enough; and to signify that they had the saint's blessing I inserted in each pot a small label picturing the saint in roseate colours with arms crossed and eyes raised, which I'd acquired with ten per cent reduction for bulk from the local Catholic bookshop run by a lady of unctious piety who threatened me with a visit.

Then there were the hanging baskets, pots and urns of various shapes and sizes, all of which had to be packed with tomato plants, cucumbers, aubergines, sweet peppers, and anything else I'd managed to acquire in my ransacking of the bankrupt garden centre. It was already mid-season and I needed to hurry if the whole lot weren't to remain unripened and unsold with the first autumn frost. I squirted them with pyrethrum against greenfly, overdosed them with Liquinure and set them up in my new greenhouse in full sun, praying for the best.

St Cuthburga Products still only had five pounds in the bank, but when my bonk manager rang one morning to offer special terms for a business loan I felt able to refuse on the grounds that by mid-August profits would certainly have begun to pour in. He enquired solicitously if I were in good shape, making it clear that he would prefer to reassure himself personally on this matter – I was a lady customer he especially valued.

In the evenings I set about preparing suitable recipes which I intended to offer with a small extra charge to customers who purchased my plants. This proved relatively simple. I began with some of Anna-Maria's favourite dishes from Bologna, of the kind which had made her the shape she was (perhaps I should tell the bonk manager about her), adding to these a number of Italian recipes of my own invention which had once contributed to my reputation as a dazzling hostess among the Tory fraternity of Box Hill, even causing David to relent from his insistence on plain English cooking. Having exhausted these, I then did what all cookery writers do, which was to steal appealing recipes from other cookbooks, making small alterations in order to claim that such and such a dish was a special favourite among the olive-pickers of the Abruzzi.

Altogether I soon had an impressive sheaf of recipes which I planned to issue as *St Cuthburga's Cookbook: The Secrets of a Hungry Saint*. Megan had promised to provide a suitable illustration for the cover, with firm instructions from me that there must be *no* resemblance to any of the admiral's former mistresses. Glyn, who also offered several prime recipes of his own, also volunteered to help me with all the book-keeping and paperwork, as well as assuring me that he could easily arrange elegant and inexpensive printing through another of his golfing friends, who ran a stationery business in Exeter.

All in all, the days and evenings slipped by with hardly a spare moment.

If this feverish activity surprised me, the biggest surprise was that I never seemed to feel lonely. It was curious to think that I'd only stayed with David as long as did out of a deep dread of being on my own. This was entirely ridiculous since nothing could have been lonelier than spending evening after evening in our suburban house while David was trumpeting away in the House. That was when I started visiting Caroline, whom I'd met in a second-hand designer clothes-shop in Pimlico which she was running at the time. Caroline had been the first person to say to me, 'You're crazy. Leave him.' Then she'd added, 'He doesn't want a wife, he wants an adornment.' And, being Caroline, she'd decided to elaborate. 'Men who love power are incapable of loving anything else, least of all a woman. They love fucking, but that's not love, it's power too. And, Jesus Christ, David can't even do that!'

I should have known better – it always happened when my thoughts drifted to David. He rang. I'd just taken a break from *St Cuthburga's Cookbook* and was sitting on the terrace in the dusk gazing out over my not-very-medieval herb garden towards the evening light on the estuary. I shouldn't have been thinking about David, and I shouldn't have been congratulating myself on how peaceful life was, and how I was going to survive after all.

'Yes, David?' I said wearily.

'Are you all right?'

'Yes, David.'

'Are you sure?'

'Yes, David.'

'Look, I have an idea.'

'Yes, David.'

He then explained that it was about to be the summer recess – he made it sound like school breaking up. A colleague had offered him his farmhouse in the Dordogne for the second half of August, wouldn't this be the ideal chance to repair things? Just the two of us. No work. Lots of walks. Swimming in the river. Good food. Warm evenings. The sound of crickets. Any moment I expected him to say, 'Making love in the vineyards.' Instead it was 'And it would be so good to be able to tell the press we were together again.'

There simply wasn't any point in being angry.

'Thank-you, David, but I really don't think so,' I said. 'Besides, I'm working.'

'You are?' He sounded puzzled. 'What at exactly?'

I had no intention of letting him into my life.

'I'm running a business with friends.'

'May I ask what?'

I couldn't keep up this good behaviour any longer.

'We're running a brothel.'

'You're *what*?'

'Running a brothel.'

'Claudia . . . I don't think . . . I mean . . . You can't be serious.'

'Oh yes. A highly respectable clientele. Several MPs, probably colleagues of yours. A bishop or two. A high-court judge. A Nato general. Oh, and the head of the regional water board – quite insatiable he is. Why don't you tell the press about it? They'd be much more interested in that than in you and me. Got to go now, David; client waiting. Enjoy the Dordogne. Bye bye.'

I shouldn't have done it. But David was always hopeless at being teased, I could never resist it.

The phone went again ten seconds after I put the receiver down. I was glad because at least I'd have a chance to apologise and laugh it off. David didn't deserve to be so mocked, and

I needed to explain that I really was working, that I needed to earn a living, that I didn't actually think a holiday in the Dordogne was a good idea, that in any case I was afraid there wasn't any question of my coming back.

But the explosion of greeting was in Italian. It was Anna-Maria. And she was excited.

She was overjoyed that she'd got straight through to me, she said: she'd imagined having to talk to the Mother Superior since she knew it wasn't the hour when I was permitted to talk. The convent must have relaxed its rules, which meant I must be getting better. Was this so? It was such a relief; she'd been so worried about me. Now, she had something terribly important to say to me. She'd been talking to her friend the priest who had pointed out that since I'd married a Protestant it wasn't really a marriage at all; and if I was quite convinced it was all over with David I could obtain a legal divorce in England and then come home.

There had to be something deeply suspicious about Anna-Maria's sudden *volte face*. I made agreeable noises, and waited.

It would be so wonderful, she went on. A happy family again. So much to talk about. So much to do. Oh, so very wonderful. (Where was this joyful meander going to lead? I wondered.) So many people to meet. (Ah ha! Now we were getting closer.) I wouldn't believe how much people still talked about me; and of course they'd all seen photographs, and couldn't believe how beautiful I was; what a waste to be stuck in England where no one appreciated beauty except in racehorses. Why, only yesterday Signor Vespucci had enquired after me – I remembered him, didn't I? Signor Vespucci who owned the largest sausage factory in Bologna. Such a charming man, had known me ever since I was child. (Mamma, get on with it for God's sake.) A most handsome man too, though not quite as handsome as his son. Did I remember Luigi? Such a sad man: his wife died last year. Not that she was good enough for him, a man of his wealth and position. (OK, I get it, Mamma.) A beautiful house right on the Piazza Galileo, and of course the seaside house near Pesaro, less than an hour's drive in his Lamborghini. Such a lonely man now. And no *bambini*. Terrible to have no *bambini* for a man like that. Of course

David couldn't make *bambini*, could he? What do you expect in such a cold climate? A man needs warmth, and comfort, and a beautiful wife. Then the *bambini* come, wasn't that so? (And all that sausage to eat while I was pregnant.)

Well, at least it made a change from the pasta-makers.

'Mamma, I can't come to Bologna just yet.'

There was a stubborn silence.

'But soon you will?'

'When I'm ready, Mamma. I promise.'

I oughtn't to have said that. The voice immediately changed.

'Darling, of course. You need time. I understand that. Signor Vespucci will understand that. We all understand that.'

Christ, within twenty-four hours the whole of Bologna would joyfully understand that.

'Everyone will be so happy,' she added, her voice radiant. 'It is for the best, to come home. Such beautiful *bambini*.'

It was almost dark when I returned to the terrace. An owl screeched in the woods. A lone bat was stitching to and fro across the night. I loved it here. The thought of the Dordogne with David, or Bologna with the sausage heir, made me love it even more. I wondered when I would see Fergus again. And I wondered about the 'mystery' of this place. Perhaps Fergus was the mystery. I knew nothing about him whatsoever, except his physical presence. The long fair hair. The deep blue eyes. The private smile. The rangy walk. And the sudden switch of attention to his own private world; then inviting me to join it: 'You'd make a magnificent heroine for a novel.' What on earth was that supposed to mean? I didn't want to be re-invented; I just wanted to be discovered. That thought came as quite a shock. In ten years David had discovered nothing about me at all: it had been like living alone in a cell, sending the ghost of me out into the world to dress in powder-blue and be charming to the Tory ladies of Box Hill, or sometimes embarrass them by having one drink too many and blurting out something that made David wince.

Caroline was probably the only person who'd ever discovered who I was, which was perhaps why I loved her.

Again I should have known better. My thoughts always had

a telepathic effect. The phone rang, and it was Caroline. She was breathless and exuberant.

'Darling, I must see you. I'm just back from London, seeing lawyers. Well, one lawyer. I'm inviting him down: you'll see why when you meet him. But you're to lay off: he's mine. Or he soon will be. Can you come over tomorrow, in the morning? Lots of other things to tell you. Plans. The literary conference is going to be terrific. This autumn. Le Carré's coming. And Naipaul. Oh, and by the way, the pictures are here. Patrick and I are going to hang them at the weekend. I'm re-naming some of the rooms in the house for the benefit of the trippers, having notices painted above the door. The drawing-room's going to be "The Hall of the Mistresses". D'you like that? I've got other ideas for the bedrooms. And I've found lots of Daddy's memorabilia which I'm going to show in cabinets. Photos, letters and stuff. You wait. I'll tell you all about it. Christ, Longleat won't get a look-in when I've finished with this place. Fuck that Legover woman. Now I must get to bed. See you tomorrow. Good-night.'

Morning, for Caroline, would certainly mean late morning. I rose early, intending to spend at least a couple of hours on St Cuthburga Products. But the spirit rebelled: I felt like a day off. Overnight rain had freshened the pots and hanging baskets spread across the area of hayfield which I'd now cut with what resembled a giant electric hair-clipper. I'd managed to add this vicious-looking monster surreptitiously to the truck just before it was driven away from the garden centre, hoping its absence wouldn't be noticed; and it had savaged the grass almost as effectively as Jehoshaphat, who was now looking indignant that I should have introduced a rival. He gazed at me lugubriously from the end of his tether, his jaws making sideways chewing motions exactly like the blades of my giant hair-clipper. He was obviously trying to tell me something, and to underline the message he wandered off to piss even more vigorously than usual in his water-trough. Then he turned to stare at me with loathing while I tried to enjoy a peaceful breakfast on my terrace.

The rain had cleaned the air of midsummer dust, and already

at nine o'clock the sun was drawing the moisture out of the newly-mown grass in a veil of steam. The whole garden seemed to shimmer. The honey buzzard, perhaps disturbed by my hair-clipper, had forsaken his usual perch on the old arch and adopted a new look-out position on top of the abandoned topiary some distance further away. As I watched, his mate joined him on a neighbouring yew-tree, the tallest of them, the one which I recognised as the tree that had once been pruned into the shape of a giant phallus.

I'd quite forgotten about it until that moment. Suddenly I found myself wondering if Fergus had noticed it on his meanderings round the estate the other morning, and if so what he would have made of it. What part of the 'mystery' might it be? I was deeply curious, though it was scarcely the easiest subject to broach. I couldn't quite imagine myself asking next time he turned up, 'Did you know there was a huge penis in the garden?' But perhaps I could innocently enquire about topiary in general – might it have been the nuns who created it, and if so why might they have done so? Was there some significance in the shapes they chose? And then I'd wait and see what Fergus had to say. And if he didn't already know about it, I could always suggest he might care to take a look while I prepared a light lunch, and I'd look out for the expression on his face when he returned. 'Do tell me,' I'd say eagerly. 'I'm sure it's frightfully interesting.' After all, Fergus was the one who'd talked about the mystery of this place and now I'd found him another one, a huge botanical cock. Explain that one, Dr Corrigan. And I'd gaze at him with beautiful innocence and blink my eyes in horrified surprise.

I laughed. I wondered when I *would* see him again.

A coachload of pilgrims interrupted my musings. A tour guide led them along the path towards the ruins of the old priory, where they gathered round St Cuthburga's shrine in silence. It puzzled me what they got out of contemplating an empty sarcophagus. My recollection of holy shrines in Bologna was that they invariably contained bits of the dead saint – a finger or a toe-nail, even a whole skull if one was lucky – usually displayed on red velvet within a glass-fronted box behind the high altar. It had always struck me as a curiously pagan practice, yet these bits of bone were said to have potent spiritual properties, or so Anna-Maria maintained, and she had a season ticket to such places. Her ululations in the presence of holy mysteries were famous. But even Anna-Maria would never have clambered on to a long-distance coach in order to ululate over an empty grave: she needed something more for her money. Watching them, I felt sorry for my pilgrims – I'd begun to think of them as *my* pilgrims – and not for the first time wondered what I could possibly do to make their journey more rewarding. 'St Cuthburga's herbs' might very soon make a useful contribution to their pilgrimage, as well as to my pocket, but that still didn't seem quite enough. One evening after I'd cooked Glyn and Megan a guinea-fowl casserole I'd tried boiling one of the leg-bones overnight to see if the whitened relic, suitably encased, might pass as a fragment of St Cuthburga, but at dawn a smell of burning roused me from my dreams, and the idea was discarded along with the saucepan and charred guinea-fowl.

I continued to watch them clustered round the sarcophagus. Some were on their knees; others were crossing themselves. There were times when I wished I possessed such simple faith. I didn't even have a complicated faith. As a child I'd tried ever so hard, but nothing would ever stick. Eventually I decided that Anna-Maria had more than enough faith for two, and let her get on with it. Well, if I were wrong I'd presumably burn in hell, along with just about everyone I knew, except of course David, who'd be fluttering up there in some echelon of heaven specially reserved for the squeaky-clean.

The thought made me cross. How could a man go to heaven who couldn't even make love? After all, if the whole human race were like David, soon there wouldn't be anyone left to qualify for heaven, and what would the Almighty think about that? He might consider it to have been a waste of time creating the human race in the first place. In any case, if by some error of divine judgment both David and I did manage to get to heaven, I trusted it would be in separate compartments.

Out of the corner of my eye I caught sight of a familiar splash of red hair bobbing among the ancient quince trees; and then two other splashes of red hair. Joan had been doing something with her bees, and she'd dragged the twin flame-throwers along with her. The three of them were slowly making their way towards me, one of the twins bobbing his head to the rhythm of the Walkman clamped to his ears, the other swishing at the hayfield with a stick before wandering over to tempt Jehoshaphat with a tuft of grass, which he instantly rejected as superfluous, preferring a swathe of the boy's shirt.

'The things I do for Caroline,' Joan sighed, collapsing into a chair.

She threw her bee-hat and gauntlets on the terrace and said yes to coffee.

'Why *do* we do things for Caroline?' she went on, flicking her red hair back from her face and reaching for the coffee. The flame-throwers had by now slouched through the arch of the gatehouse and disappeared. 'What d'you imagine she'd do if we didn't?'

'She'd cope,' I said. 'We do things for her because we think she can't. She plays that one very well. Caroline was brought up to be served, and I was brought up to be a waitress. Perhaps that's why we get on.'

I laughed. But Joan only nodded gloomily.

'Well, I wasn't brought up to serve her.'

'But you do,' I said.

This time she just glared into her coffee-cup.

'Thirty bee-hives! Can you believe that? How does she expect me to conjure up thirty bee-hives?'

'Have you?'

Joan looked up at me fiercely.

'Well, I've managed to beg and borrow another dozen, and that's going to bloody well have to do. That's it. I tell you, I've been here since sparrow's fart: I don't suppose you even heard me drive in with them. Since then I've spent hours dividing up my hives, making nucleus after nucleus, making sure each frame I took out had a queen cell. Far too late in the year for that sort of thing, but there you are. Orders are orders. By next year they should all be breeding like hell.' Suddenly she laughed. 'And I tell you, Claudia, I shall personally direct the whole fucking lot to swarm in convoy in the direction of Priory Hall. Then we'll see how well her ladyship copes.'

Her mood restored, Joan picked up her bee-hat and gauntlets, and made her way towards the arch with a final wave.

After the pilgrims had departed – no doubt leaving yet
more prayers and pesetas in the little box by the entrance –
I decided to walk up to Caroline's via Glyn Davies' bookshop.
The window display was still the same, and the pile of Izaak
Walton's *The Compleat Angler* seemed not to have diminished.
As I was about to enter the shop the door opened and a slight
figure in a dark suit and dog-collar bustled out clutching a
small package. He didn't even glance at me, though I lowered
my head in case he did.

'Dropped by for his usual quota of feminist literature, did
he?' I called out to Glyn, who was at the back of the shop
replacing some of the books the Rev Pype presumably hadn't
bought.

Glyn looked round at me, and chuckled.

'Oh, don't joke about it, my dear. I once managed to convince
him that *The Female Eunuch* was the study of a rare species of
gudgeon. It was five years before I was re-admitted as church
warden after that. Now, what can I do for you?'

I told Glyn about my meeting with Dr Corrigan, who was
not – I said carefully – at all what I'd expected. Glyn's eyes
widened.

'Ah, what a lucky woman.' I stopped myself saying I rather
agreed. 'Such a fine mind,' he added. I nodded, thinking of
the skin-tight jeans and the blue eyes. 'No doubt he told you
a great deal about the priory.'

'A certain amount, yes. He seemed to think a great mystery
hangs over the place. How it managed to survive.'

Glyn sucked in his cheeks and looked pensive.

'Yes, indeed. One of those puzzles no one's been able to
solve.' Then his face brightened. 'Maybe now it belongs to the
nation, Dr Corrigan will unravel it. How fascinating, my dear.
So you could be seeing quite a lot of him, perhaps.'

I said I hoped so.

'Yes, such a fine mind,' he repeated. 'I envy you.'

'But I expect he's a very busy man,' I said, fishing cautiously. 'Academic work. Books. Articles. Television. Besides
his family life.'

That was the bait. As a fisherman Glyn would surely know about such things. Would he bite?

'Yes,' he said vaguely. And that was all.

I tried once more.

'Summer holidays, after all. Taking the wife and kids abroad, and that sort of thing.'

'Goodness, yes, I remember doing all that. Thank God they're grown up and can take themselves off. Now they just turn up with beards and fleas.'

Well, Glyn, you may be a great fisherman, I thought, but you're a bloody lousy fish. I gave up.

'I'd better go,' I said. 'Caroline calls.'

'My commiserations. Bear up well.' Suddenly, as he held open the door of the shop, his expression changed and his eyes crinkled with mischief. 'You know, my dear,' he said, 'I've just realised: you must be the only female occupant of the gatehouse whose portrait as nature intended won't be gracing the walls of Priory Hall. At least I trust it won't.'

Then he blinked and looked awkward, as if he'd uttered something he perhaps shouldn't, and made an elaborate performance of saying good-bye.

'Do call again, my dear. It's always a pleasure. A very special pleasure. And please offer my most sincere respects to Dr Corrigan when you next see him. Such a fine mind. Very fine.'

So I still knew absolutely nothing about Fergus. It irritated me that I was so intrigued by him. The more I didn't know, the more intriguing he became. I could always trying looking him up in Who's Who, I thought; except that Fergus was exactly the sort of vain bastard who would deliberately not be in Who's Who. All the same, I might try the local library. There'd be no point asking Caroline. She'd certainly have Debrett and Burke's Peerage, gathering dust on the shelves next to Patrick's racing almanacs. But I could already hear her voice: 'Darling, don't be ridiculous. What would I want with Who isn't Who?'

She was waiting for me in the cavernous drawing-room, made even more cavernous now that all the furniture had been pushed into the centre of the room. There was no sign of the ancestral portraits; instead Megan's portraits of her father's naked mistresses were propped all round the walls, giving the room the appearance of a harem. Caroline was standing by the large marble fireplace gazing from one mistress to another with a solemn expression on her face.

She looked across at me, and gave a laugh.

'It's just occurred to me, Claudia. What d'you suppose I should tell the children when they come back from holiday? I can hardly say "These are your aunts," can I?'

Then the solemn expression returned.

'Well, what d'you think? I've tried to put them in chronological order, with their names and dates underneath: I thought it would give the room a sense of historical continuity, especially as I found *this* in the attic.'

With that, she turned towards the marble fireplace where an exceedingly dark painting rested against one of the uprights. As far as I could make out it was a portrait of a young woman with a fuzz of curly hair. It wasn't possible to pick out anything else.

'I'd quite forgotten we had this,' Caroline went on. 'I must get it cleaned.' With that she pulled a handkerchief from the sleeve of her blouse, spat on it and gave the picture a vigorous rub. 'Now you see why Charles II was crazy about her. Look at those breasts.' With the aid of Caroline's spittle I could see that the young lady was naked to the waist. 'I told you about her, didn't I? The king built this house for her in sixteen-whenever-it-was; and of course he always got Sir Peter Lely to paint his mistresses. Not just Nell Gwyn, all of them.' She looked up thoughtfully. 'Think of receiving a knighthood just for painting mistresses. Perhaps Megan could become Dame Megan.' Caroline gave another laugh, and looked back at the picture. 'I suppose it could be quite valuable really. Anyway I thought I'd hang it there, just above the fireplace. The centrepiece of the room. My earliest ancestor. And it gives all Megan's portraits a kind of dignity, don't you think? A historical context, and that's important in an old family house. It's what trippers expect to see after all, isn't it?'

Feeling thoroughly bemused, I said I thought that was very likely so.

I continued to gaze round the enormous room in some astonishment. Megan's portraits were all of them life-size, and there must have been at least a dozen of them. Megan had explained to me that the admiral always had very clear ideas about how he wished each mistress to be painted, emphasising whatever part of her anatomy he particularly admired. As a result, one Indian lady was performing a kind of dance with finely-curved hands; a Spanish-looking creature was supporting her breasts, which must have required some strength if she'd posed for any length of time; an African woman had her buttocks towards the painter while she gazed at a mirror in the manner of *The Rokeby Venus*. And so on.

I found myself trying to imagine the expression on Pamela Leggatt's face when she made her next call of inspection on behalf of the National Trust.

Meanwhile Caroline was busy applying another coat of spittle to the mistress of Charles II.

'Now, I need your advice, Claudia,' she said, turning to me.

She leaned the Lely portrait back against the fireplace, strolled over to the centre of the room and picked up a folder from one of the tables. Then, reaching inside, she drew out a small sheet of yellowing paper, from one end of which dangled a golden ribbon that was fixed to the paper with a scarlet seal.

'We've got several of these letters,' she explained. 'We used to keep them in the bank, but I got them out specially so I can put them on show. As love-letters they're a bit disappointing really: not a man of many words, King Charles. Not much of "Thy breasts are like rosebuds", more like "Be on thy back at nine o'clock"; but here's one that actually refers to the picture. "To my mistress Lady Marchmount," it says. "Sir Peter hath rendered thy delicacies most prettilie." Now, here's the big question: Do I frame this and hang it next to the portrait, or should I keep it in the display cabinet along with all the other letters?'

I explained that I didn't have the faintest idea what she had in mind for the rest of the house, so I honestly didn't know.

'Well, all right then,' she said rather testily. 'I'll tell you all my plans over lunch. And now I suppose you'd like a drink.' Which meant that Caroline wanted one. She yelled to Carmen to bring in some champagne. 'But one thing I'm definitely going to do,' she went on. 'In the king's letter he spells "mistress" with a "y", so I've told the sign-painter to call this room "The Hall of the Mystresses". Makes it sound like Hall of the Mysteries, doesn't it? The trippers are bound to like that. Not that there's much mystery about it. Might just as well call it "The Hall of the Fucks".' She gave a giggle. 'But I don't suppose the National Trust would like that, would they? Ah, here's the champagne.'

She took the tray from Carmen and placed it on one of the tables in the centre of the room. Then she turned to the Spanish girl.

'Well, what d'you think, Carmen?'

I winced.

The girl's dark eyes passively surveyed the acres of flesh, and not a glimmer of expression formed on her face.

'Is very nice,' she murmured.

As she walked meekly out of the room I had visions of yet more lurid letters winging their way to the family in Salamanca.

'Come on,' announced Caroline. 'Bring your drink. Let's go and eat, and I'll tell you the rest.'

We'd scarcely sat down before she launched herself into her plans for opening Priory Hall to the public.

It was the first time I'd understood that Caroline, once set on a course, pursued it with a wild and ruthless logic. She might appear idle and helpless, but this was merely bluff. She was nothing of the kind. Once convinced of something, she was incapable of doubt, and equally incapable of compromise. All that well-bred languor fell away: she was like a general preparing for the decisive battle.

By the time we'd finished eating I was wondering if the National Trust might be grateful to return the house to Caroline's ownership.

She'd noticed, she said, that all the best stately homes open to the public had a theme. There was Blenheim Palace, for example, which had its military associations with the Duke of Marlborough. Longleat had its lions, Beaulieu its motor museum. She knew these places well – as a private guest, of course – and there were valuable lessons to be learnt from them. She'd given considerable thought to the matter, and it was entirely clear to her what the theme for Priory Hall should be. 'Mistresses.' After all, she went on, there hadn't been a single generation of her family since the seventeenth century which hadn't either kept, or been, a mistress. The family motto clearly acknowledged this: 'With Honour we Lie.' She admitted that the motto was supposed to carry quite another meaning, but this was only because the College of Heralds had insisted, 'the prudish buggers'.

Caroline paused while Carmen cleared away the dishes and brought in the fruit. Then she continued with her grand project. After the Hall of the Mystresses, she explained, visitors would be invited to enjoy the more private aspects of the family tradition. The small reading-room and library would be ideal for well-lit display cabinets containing not only the royal letters to Lady Marchmount – terse and to the point though they were – but the more romantic offerings in rhyming couplets by several nineteenth-century prime ministers, down to a positive gush of verbal erotica by Lloyd George, H. G. Wells, Augustus John and a host of other notable philanderers; and finally her own dear father's more stumbling literary efforts on Admiralty notepaper.

Caroline was by now looking exceedingly pleased with herself. She poured out the last of the champagne.

'Well, how am I doing?'

'Wonderfully,' I said.

What else could I say?

'And that leads us to the bedrooms,' she went on. 'Obviously one can't run the theme of mistresses without taking in the main field of action.' Her brow furrowed at this point. 'There's a bit of a problem here, Claudia, because the serious business of the house would naturally have been conducted in the principal bedroom, which happens to be mine, and I'm not bloody well letting American tourists gawp at my love-letters, or my underwear; and anyway I might be conducting some serious business myself, especially if my new lawyer comes to stay. So it'll have to be other bedrooms, and I'm going to label them. The King's Bedroom. Palmerston's Bedroom. The Archbishop's Bedroom. And so on.'

Caroline looked at me, and frowned.

'Now, the next problem is: What do I put in them? It's a bit of a cock-teaser to announce "Lloyd George's Bedroom" and then have nothing to show for it but an empty bed.' A thoughtful expression began to form on Caroline's face. 'I suppose I could always scatter a few photos of my mother around, couldn't I? Except that I'm not at all sure Lloyd George *was* her father. And I'm sure the National Trust would expect me to be historically accurate.'

She gave a sigh.

'Which reminds me, that Legover woman wants to call in again next week to talk about lavatories. I told her I thought we might find something more interesting to talk about, and that in any case Priory Hall wasn't a public convenience: Why couldn't they just pee in the bushes? But she seemed to think lavatories were important, the silly cow.'

Suddenly Caroline brightened.

'Oh, I knew I'd forgotten something. The family tree. Every stately home has one of those, and Americans certainly expect it. The duke told me that at Blenheim. So, anyway, I commissioned one when I was in London. On proper parchment, illuminated in gold and stuff. It'll be brilliant. None of your male line and all that rubbish. This'll be a tree of mistresses, going all the way back to Charles II and Lady Marchmount. We've got a complete record: my grandfather spent years researching it, tracing the family through the mistresses. We're all illegitimate, as I told you. All the proper sons and daughters were disinherited – by tradition. That's why we've been so successful: none of your aristocratic inbreeding. No chinless wonders in my family; we're the product of healthy lust. Anyway, I thought I'd hang the thing in the main hall so visitors can refer to it if they get confused.'

She stretched her arms above her head contentedly.

'So that's the plan so far,' she went on. 'Coming on well, don't you think? I'll tell the Legover woman about it when she's finished talking about lavatories.' Caroline was now gazing at me with a bright smile. 'You know, Claudia, I'm really rather looking forward to it after all. You will help, won't you; taking parties round and explaining things? I know you will. And Megan will be here of course, taking orders for "Nude Portraits of the Loved One". And Joan will be selling her honey. It'll be terrific. Now, let's have our coffee in the garden. I'm determined to tell you about my new lawyer.'

His name was Justin Whittaker, she said. Patrick had recommended the firm of which he was a junior partner: as solicitors they were decidedly grand, she explained, specialising in, among other things, disputes over family estates, and therefore all matters involving the interpretation of wills. Patrick was sceptical about the admiral's will, he'd told her. He now agreed with Caroline that there might be more to Pamela Leggatt's involvement with Priory Hall than merely being the representative of the National Trust. Had she actually been one of her father's mistresses? And if so might there be what were termed 'unacceptable motivations' behind his bequest? After all, the admiral had been old and infirm, perhaps somewhat gullible in return for certain favours. Caroline should seek legal advice, he'd suggested.

So she had. Young Whittaker was the man assigned to her. And indeed he was *young* Whittaker, seven or eight years younger than she was, perhaps ten, she explained. This was both a challenge and a stimulant: there'd be that much more she could teach him. After all, this was supposed to be the age of the older woman, wasn't it? Well, now was the moment to prove it.

He wasn't exactly pretty, she assured me. But swarthy. He must have powerful thighs and good balls, she felt sure. A sensual mouth. And thick black hair to run her fingers through, not like Patrick's ridiculous curls. And he wasn't married either, or living with someone – she'd found that out rapidly enough – so there'd be no hysterical phone-calls or tiresome outbursts of conscience.

'Might this possibly be a case of "unacceptable motivations"?' I suggested with a smile.

Caroline rose to that one rather well. She threw me a wicked look. As far as she was concerned, she said, if young Whittaker could manage to invalidate her father's will and bend to hers at the same time, she found nothing unacceptable about that whatsoever.

I left Caroline floating peacefully in the swimming-pool, her clothes strewn carelessly among the coffee-cups and the potted fuchsias.

'We'll talk about the literary conference another time,' she called out. 'I've asked Prince Charles to come: he's written a children's book, after all.'

There was a splash, and a naked bum appeared momentarily above the surface of the water.

I walked back down the long drive between the sentinel lime-trees feeling battered. Caroline's energy, once roused, was an assault upon the mind: one retreated from the blows. It was hard to retain any degree of detachment from even her wildest schemes. It was particularly hard to decide whether she was totally serious, as she pretended to be, or whether her outrageous projects were an elaborate mockery of the upper-class world to which she so unequivocally belonged. Caroline said the things no one else ever dared to say; she did the things other people only dreamed of doing; she raised her head where others would instinctively duck. Her affections and her loathings were as naked as the portraits that were soon to grace her drawing-room. Hers was a life entirely without masks.

Above all, she was a creature of extraordinary spirit. Here was a woman who within a matter of weeks had lost her father, her fortune, her house and her security. Her husband was away screwing his secretaries in London. Her own lovers, several of whom I'd met in London, invariably discovered urgent reasons to return to their wives after only the briefest taste of her demands. And yet here she was, brightly weaving a new tapestry of her life, drinking champagne, wallowing happily in her pool, and laying extravagant plans to captivate her new young lawyer.

Here, of course, was the fountain of her energy. Caroline always needed a burning project, and whatever plans she was laying for the future of Priory Hall, it was the golden prospect of a new affair which fuelled her spirit. She was a woman who could easily live without love, but never without the thrill of pursuing it.

By the time I reached the gatehouse it was uncomfortably hot. I rather wished I'd agreed to stay for a swim in Caroline's pool, but I knew it would provoke yet more questions about my love-life, or the absence of it, and what a waste my body was splashing around in the water instead of driving some man insane with lust.

That set me thinking about Fergus, and when he might perhaps float into my life again.

Once more my gift for serendipity proved infallible. On the garden table just outside the French windows I caught sight of a parcel. The wrapping was clumsy, and there was no note attached. I carefully pulled aside the strips of sellotape, eased the paper to one side, and stood gazing at a large bunch of yellow roses.

Still there was no note. My heart pounded less vigorously as it occurred to me they might have come from Glyn. But he would have said something, wouldn't he?

I carefully lifted the roses from the wrapping paper, and as I did so I saw there was a second, much smaller parcel which the flowers had hidden. Again there were clumsy strips of sellotape, which I tore away. Inside was an earthenware pot with a bushy plant, purplish in colour, with a hairy stem and tiny lilac flowers. It was no great beauty, though a strong aromatic smell rose from it as I lifted it on to the table.

Only then did I notice that a slip of paper had been wedged between the slats of the table. I pulled it out, and unfolded it. The paper had clearly been torn out of a notebook, presumably after the visitor had realised I was out. It was handwritten, and the writing was small and elegant, with the occasional flourish. My eyes went straight to the signature at the bottom of the page. And there was the name: Fergus, with a flourish on the 'g'.

'Claudia,' it began. 'Sorry to have missed you. I should have rung. The roses are to say thanks for the lunch. The plant is for St Cuthburga's collection. Summer Savoury – Latin name *Satureia horvensis*, appropriate for a nunnery whose gatehouse has a carved satyr above the arch. Had you noticed? This could just provide the clue I need. So far only a hunch. I shall need to delve into dusty manuscripts. Meanwhile, since you asked what heroines who live in ruined priories are supposed to do with their lives, may I offer one answer and take you out to dinner, preferably when you're not wearing your husband's shirt? I'll phone.'

I'd never believed people really did shiver at moments like this. But I did.

Five

One of the penalties of acquiring a hand-phone was that I now received calls I would otherwise innocently have missed. Having bought the thing, I became incapable of leaving it behind. It was like a pet dog that refused to be parted from its mistress. It accompanied me to the bathroom, the loo, the kitchen, and of course to the garden where its range just about extended to my favourite summer-evening retreat: this was an old tree-stump on the far side of the wood from where I could survey the expanse of marsh over which my honey buzzards would occasionally glide, and beyond this the tidal estuary speckled with white sails and combed into patterns by the sea wind.

I didn't always admit it to myself, but the single reason I refused to be parted from my new toy was in case Fergus rang. Instead, on consecutive evenings I got David, Anna-Maria, Caroline and finally a reporter from the *Daily Mail*.

David wanted to know if I'd reconsidered his invitation to a reconciliation holiday in the Dordogne. I said no, I hadn't. He made no mention of the brothel I'd told him I was helping to run, from which I assumed either he didn't believe me or he was worried that his phone might be tapped.

'I miss you,' he said plaintively.

I wondered what it was that he missed. Was it my company, my cooking, or my gifts as a Tory hostess? Or perhaps just the habit of having me around? It certainly wasn't my body.

'I really do. A lot,' he added.

I hated these conversations: they always had such heavy overtones of moral blackmail, as though I was being appallingly callous and unfeeling, betraying some precious gift he had offered me, and me alone.

'I love you. You know that,' he said.

Well, perhaps he did love me. But what exactly did that

mean? It had never seemed to me that what we had was love. The hours, weeks, years I'd spent agonising about it, going over it time and time again with Caroline, with other friends, even with David. At first I'd felt guilty, as though I'd somehow missed the point, and love was something I was simply incapable of recognising, like being colour-blind, or tone-deaf. I was defective. It was Caroline – bless her – who said, 'Balls!' That was when I began to think I might not be defective after all, that my instincts might be right. Even then the guilt didn't entirely vanish. Wasn't I perhaps laying too much emphasis on this sex thing, just because I wasn't getting it? After all, when we were old it wouldn't matter, and we'd still be able to love one another, wouldn't we? 'No' was Caroline's response. 'Not if you've *never* had it. Listen, darling. If you've never at some time wanted to fuck each other every minute of the day, then you haven't got a marriage; you've got an arrangement – a friendship if you're extremely lucky. You might just as well be brother and sister, without even the forbidden pleasures of incest.'

Caroline's own sex life might be a total mess, but she would never have made the mistake of believing you could get along without it. 'Once a month through a gap in the pyjamas is *not* a marriage, my darling. Get out of it.'

It had still been hard not to feel guilty. After all, it wasn't just that David had married me. I'd also married *him*.

'I always have loved you,' he was saying. 'Nothing has changed.'

I wanted to shout, 'Oh Christ, that's just the point, David. Nothing has changed. Nothing could change, because you are what you are.' I had to keep remembering that.

And, remembering it, I said nothing. To my relief neither did he. And at least this time he didn't spoil it by dragging in his bloody career. That was his true love. I was the support mechanism, and now I'd removed the support.

He merely said a sad good-bye.

I sat for nearly an hour after that, until it was almost dark, gazing at the estuary and the movement of the tide until the sight of it began to soothe my nerves like soft hands.

The following evening it was Anna-Maria who phoned.

In a state of excitement she explained that Signor Vespucci would love to pay for my flight to Bologna. Whenever I liked. His son Luigi remembered me well. Remembered how beautiful I was. She was sure he'd be happy to show me round the sausage factory, only a short drive away in the Lamborghini. And of course the whole family would soon be at their seaside house near Pesaro. She was certain they'd welcome a visit from me, with a chaperone, of course. Cousin Bianca would be ideal. I'd love Luigi's mother; I'd so enjoy shopping with her and helping with the cooking. She'd be able to tell me all about Luigi. Then of course the sea-bathing would be excellent, and with my figure and a nice bikini . . .

'Sorry, Mamma, I can't come this summer. The nuns need me here.'

That put an end to it. The good nuns could always be relied upon to take precedence, at least for a while.

The next evening it was Caroline.

'Where are you?'

'In the garden, enjoying the sunset.'

'Why?'

'Because it's beautiful.'

'Jesus, how romantic you are.'

'Yes.'

'Now listen. I have to tell you. That Legover woman's been here talking about lavatories. And do you know she promptly rushed off to use one the moment I ushered her into the Hall of the Mystresses.' Caroline gave a snort of pleasure. 'After the stupid woman returned, looking pale, I pointed out Charles II's letter and explained about the family tradition and the theme I'd chosen for the house. And to reassure her I showed her the splendid genealogical tree I've just had made, illuminated with the names of all the famous lovers in our family, prime ministers, archbishops, generals, poets, and so on. But she still didn't seem at all happy, Claudia: she kept saying she'd have to consult her superiors. I told her that sounded a bit feeble to me, and in any case wasn't the National Trust supposed to have an eye for beauty? Well, here it was all around her, I said. Acres of it in all the shapes and colours anyone could desire.'

Caroline gave one of her rippling laughs. I could tell she

must have thoroughly enjoyed the encounter. She was getting her own back.

'Oh, by the way,' she went on, 'the Trust are giving us a gardener. Something about the medieval garden and the topiary. Anyway, that'll be your department, Claudia; I'm far too busy with my literary conference. The Legover woman seemed to like that idea rather better than the paintings, especially with Prince Charles coming. Listen, darling, I must go. My young lawyer's coming for the weekend, so you're *not* to come to dinner, or even a drink. Promise? This is the age of the older woman, and you're by no means older enough.'

'I promise,' I said, smiling.

The evening after that it was the *Daily Mail*.

'Claudia?' the reporter enquired chirpily. How had he found out where I was? And what the hell was he doing calling me by my Christian name? 'We'd like to know if you're intending to go back to Mr Hazlitt.'

'Oh, would you?' I answered archly.

'Well, are you?'

What annoyed me was that now I was the one having to think about David's bloody career. I might not care much about it, but I didn't want to make things worse for him than they already were.

'I'm thinking of going into a nunnery,' I said firmly.

There was a momentary silence. I'd been rather clever, I thought. David would know it wasn't true, and as far as the press were concerned any government minister whose wife runs off to become a nun had clearly married a screwball.

The reporter sounded astonished.

'You mean you're going to become a nun?'

'Very likely,' I said.

'Could you tell us why?'

'I'm afraid that's a matter for myself and the Good Lord,' I replied.

He tried again.

'Is there another woman in Mr Hazlitt's life?'

'Yes,' I said brightly. 'The Mother of Parliaments. But then she screws everyone, doesn't she?'

Before the reporter had a chance to say anything more

I switched off the phone, hoping Fergus wasn't about to contact me.

I went on sitting there until it was almost dark, watching the bats weaving in and out of the trees. The silence was broken by the screech of an owl. Glancing round I caught sight of it, hunting purposefully over the meadow before disappearing like a pale ghost into the darkness over the marsh.

Fergus never did ring during these romantic sojourns in the dusk. He rang when I was in the bath.

'Claudia.'

The voice was low and velvety. There was something incredibly sexy about lying here in the warm water and being addressed by a man I fancied with the phone resting just above my naked breast.

'Oh hello,' I answered, trying to sound surprised and casual. I wondered if I should make the water ripple so that he'd know where I was. 'I have to thank-you for the flowers.'

'I'm sorry I missed you,' he said. 'I've tried to phone once or twice, but you're a busy lady. I hoped I'd see you before I went away.'

Ah ha! All right, I know. You're taking the wife and kids on holiday. Probably the Dordogne. Just think of it: if I'd accepted David's invitation we could have arranged a nice little family get-together. A friendly dinner *à quatre*. I bet she's pretty. And I bet she needs to be.

'It's cropped up rather suddenly. Channel 4 want me to do something in Burgundy. Not wine, alas. Romanesque churches. Cluny. I did my doctorate on it. I've got to stroll round the place being wise apparently.' (Rubbish! With your tight jeans and blue eyes, who's going to look at you and give a fuck about Cluny?) 'Only ten days. Then what about that dinner – if the nuns will let you out, that is?'

I hoped my sigh of relief wasn't audible.

'Oh, I really don't know, Dr Corrigan,' I said. 'I'll have to ask permission from the Mother Superior.'

'Of course. I fully understand. Maybe you'd feel happier if she came too.'

'Yes, that would be really nice. Thank-you.'

This seemed the right moment. I gently splashed some

water over my left breast. There was silence for a few seconds.

'Where exactly are you?' he said.

'Oh, just in the bath.' I tried to picture his face. 'And since you ask, dinner would be lovely. I might even be dressed by the time you come back.'

Was I being entirely shameless? Yes, of course I was. The things one could get away with, playing games.

'Only if it's not too much trouble,' he said.

It was my turn to laugh. Then I made another gentle splash.

'Enjoy France in the meantime, won't you. And make sure you look wise.'

'I promise. And don't let the water get cold.'

He named a date towards the end of August. He'd phone as soon as he returned, he said. He was looking forward to it.

'And me,' I echoed. 'And thank-you for the other plant, by the way. What am I supposed to do with it?'

'I'll tell you more about that when I see you,' he said. 'And about the satyr. I've dug up some rather interesting stuff. Very strange. But take a close look at it, and see what you think.'

After I'd rung off I lay there wondering. It was so totally unfamiliar to me, flirting with a man on the telephone with his voice sounding softly over my naked body while he pictured me lying here. A man I'd only met once, and rather briefly. Was it a dangerous game? And should I be playing it? As Megan had said, I was the one likely to get hurt. I knew nothing about Fergus whatsoever; yet he knew everything he needed to know about me. I thought about that for a moment, and realised I found it very, very sexy: the excitement of not knowing, while he did. It was like having a phantom lover. Was I just being romantic again? Or was it the effect of ten years living with David, who was certainly no phantom and even less of a lover? I wasn't sure. All I knew was that I was free: I could risk whatever I liked, whatever I dared. It was something I'd never known.

Joan was insistent that I should hold a launch party for St Cuthburga Products. The flame-throwers could do the pouring and the handing-round, everyone could be relied upon to purchase something even if they didn't need it, and we'd get started with a bang, wouldn't we? The local paper would certainly send some pimply photographer along. I might even invite my bonk manager, Joan suggested, then he and I could swap 'special offers' behind the medieval barn.

'Thank-you, Joan. No,' I said.

In the end I vetoed the whole idea on the grounds that a party would be certain to mop up all the profits I made on the plants and besides, I might have nothing left to sell to my next coachload of pilgrims.

This turned out to be a wise decision since the very next morning I received a breathless phone call from a Catholic organisation in Exeter. The lady was delighted to announce the arrival in two days' time of five coaches containing one hundred and fifty pilgrims who were at present offering their devotions to Our Lady of Walsingham, in Norfolk, after which the climax of their spiritual journey was to be a visit to the shrine of St Cuthburga in Norton Abbas. Naturally I was aware, wasn't I, that this month was the one-thousand-two-hundredth anniversary of the blessed saint's canonisation?

'Of course,' I said.

This, I realised, had to be my 'launch'. There were barely two days to get ready. I needed to get moving.

I rang Megan.

I rang Joan.

I didn't ring Caroline.

Glyn – I could have kissed him – volunteered to drive to Exeter and pick up five hundred copies of *St Cuthburga's Cookbook: The Secrets of a Hungry Saint*, and to have the printer's bill made out to Glyn Davies Books. I could repay it at my leisure, he assured me, whenever I'd sold enough copies.

Joan, who'd by now completely forgotten the launch party, answered the call to arms by arriving at midday with six trestle-tables roped precariously to the top of her car, and later returned a second time with two dozen pots of honey.

Megan placed herself in charge of the greenhouse, systematically removing the dozens of hanging baskets, urns and pots, and arranging them welcomingly on two of Joan's trestle-tables. The cucumbers, peppers and aubergines had been spectacularly boosted by my overdoses of Liquinure; and by the time I'd embellished each basket with a label picturing the saint in roseate colours it was self-evident that only the hand of God could have been responsible for such wondrous fecundity.

On the other four trestle-tables I laid out the smaller earthenware pots, carefully grouped as 'Herbs for fish', 'Herbs for roasts', 'Herbs from Italy', 'Herbs of the Old Testament', and so on, ending with my somewhat dubious 'St Cuthburga collection', which seemed to contain a number of herbs which suspiciously resembled stinging-nettles and ground elder. But rather than remove them and leave bare patches on the soil, I decided it was best to conceal these intruders behind pictures of our saint with arms crossed and eyes raised. Joan's comforting view was that if Jesus could change water into wine, then St Cuthburga could surely manage to turn nettles into sweet basil.

Finally, so long as it didn't rain, I proposed to carry out a small table from the living-room and pile it high with copies of *St Cuthburga's Cookbook*. Megan's original illustration for the jacket had looked more like Jonah being swallowed by the whale, and I'd tactfully rejected it. She'd then come up with a design of such sickening piety that I felt sure we were on to a winner.

I was less sure about the opening page, which was also Megan's idea, and which she'd craftily slipped in without showing me. With the Christian market in mind she'd headed the first recipe 'Give us this day our daily bread' in an elegant gothic script. Beneath this she'd drawn a bearded figure seated on a cloud whom I assumed to be God the Father. His right hand was raised in blessing, while his left hand pointed earthwards towards the divine instruction, 'Take one pound of stone-ground flour.' If this weren't bad enough, she'd spelt 'when the dough has Risen' with a capital 'R', accompanying it with a small drawing of the Resurrection.

'I'm afraid Glyn will get sacked from being church warden a second time if the Rev Pype catches sight of this,' Megan said wistfully after I'd remonstrated with her. 'But never mind,' she added with a smile. 'A little blasphemy is always good for the soul.'

Megan's contribution apart, I was actually rather proud of my book. Quite a number of the recipes were original, and at the modest price of £4.50 it might conceivably pay the rent on the gatehouse all by itself, should 'Herbs of the Old Testament' fail on stony ground. Glyn, of course, had agreed to stock the book, and to risk the rage of the vicar by displaying it prominently in the window next to his cherished volumes on fly-fishing. After all, Glyn pointed out, St Cuthburga had included several excellent recipes for fish.

On the morning of the great pilgrimage I received a further phone-call from the Catholic organisation informing me that the caravan of coaches was due to arrive around eleven o'clock. There'd been overnight rain, which had pleasantly freshened the plants, but now the sky was clear and there was every promise of a hot August day.

Megan had put on her favourite dress splashed with crimson-and-white dahlias, each bloom crowning a bulge in the flesh beneath.

Joan wore her standard outfit of tailored jeans and leather boots, though her froth of red hair was now partially imprisoned by a headband.

The flame-throwers had been hauled along to man the stalls in case any of us was required to escort pilgrims round St Cuthburga's estate.

Meanwhile I waited nervously by the gatehouse arch.

Punctually at eleven the convoy came in sight, moving slowly up the High Street accompanied by a cacophony of horns from cars which had presumably been held up for miles. Fixed to the windscreen of the first coach were the words 'Saintly Tours'.

They drew up one behind the other opposite the parish church. And as the coaches disgorged their pilgrims I caught sight of a stooped figure in black standing in the middle of the path below the west window, his legs planted astride, arms folded and chin thrust forward beneath a mouth that was stitched tight and eyes that were hungry with fury. Then the lips parted, and I could make out two inaudible words,

'Catholics' and 'Women'. Like Horatius guarding the bridge, Jonathan Pype was defending his faith.

There was no problem picking out the tour leader. A small, youngish woman dressed in pastel shades came bounding towards me.

'Mrs Hazlitt?' she asked breathlessly.

I nodded, and we shook hands.

'And I'm Judith Burroughs,' she explained. 'I'm the secretary of Saintly Tours. This is such a wonderful experience for us. Truly wonderful. It rained for Our Lady of Walsingham, but St Cuthburga has blessed us with sunshine.'

I said they were all entirely welcome, and she thanked me vigorously. She had a smile that had been stapled to her face, and she kept swivelling her head to make sure her flock were following. Many of them were still being disgorged from their coaches, step by careful step. Glancing anxiously at a few of them, I began to wonder if Lourdes might not have been a more appropriate venue. I wasn't at all sure about St Cuthburga's healing powers, and began to wish I'd labelled some of my pots 'Herbs for the halt and the lame', 'Herbs for senile dementia', perhaps even 'Herbs for the afterlife' since I had severe doubts whether a number of my pilgrims now hobbling towards the gatehouse would ever make it through the morning.

'I think it's wonderful that so sacred a place should now belong to the nation,' Judith Burroughs was proclaiming to her flock as they began to gather round her. 'The previous owner must have been a man of true spirituality.' She turned to me. 'A naval gentleman, so I understand, Mrs Hazlitt. And much-travelled. He must have acquired an awful lot of wisdom in all those foreign places.'

I restrained myself from replying, 'Well, certainly an awful lot of women.'

'Oh, absolutely,' I said.

'Then, God bless our Royal Navy,' she added emphatically. 'So, here we all are then.'

To my relief Judith Burroughs seemed to know exactly how to tend to her flock. She'd been to Norton Abbas several times before – 'of course' – she assured me as she gently eased her followers through the arch of the gatehouse and along the path

towards the ruins of the old priory. 'One keeps being drawn
back to places like this. It has a uplifting quality, wouldn't you
agree, Mrs Hazlitt?'

'Oh, most definitely,' I said.

With some relief I left her to her troupe of pilgrims, some
of whom were making heavy weather of the gravel path. Then
suddenly she turned.

'There's just one thing I forgot to ask, Mrs Hazlitt,' she said,
hurrying over to me as I was exchanging bemused glances
with Megan and Joan. 'I remember on an earlier visit coming
across some remarkable trees of great antiquity that the blessed
nuns must at some time have shaped most lovingly into holy
symbols. You are acquainted with these, I'm sure.'

I tried not to look troubled, and said yes I was aware of such
trees, though I couldn't altogether recall the holy symbols.
What I couldn't say was that unless I'd missed something the
only symbol clearly recognisable in the ancient topiary garden
was the gigantic phallus, which I'd not yet summoned up the
courage to mention to Fergus, or indeed to anybody.

'Then perhaps you'd be so good as to guide us there once
we've made our small offerings to St Cuthburga,' she went on.
'My memory of the place is a little unclear, and I know that
our friends here would be deeply moved to see such unusual
evidence of devotion surviving after so many centuries. Such
ingenuity. Such a labour of love.'

I looked at the ecstatic face of Judith Burroughs and wondered if we could really be thinking of the same labour of love,
and if so what on earth did she believe it to be?

'Of course,' I said hesitantly, 'if you're quite sure your friends
won't be too exhausted to walk that far,' I added, grasping at a
straw. 'Some of them are not too youthful, and it *is* a rather
hot day.'

Ms Burroughs gave a girlish flutter of her eyelashes and a
bright laugh.

'When the flesh is weak, Mrs Hazlitt, the spirit rises to our
aid.' Then, as she turned to hurry after her flock, she paused a
second time as she caught sight of the trestle-tables laden with
herbs, and the bold painted sign announcing St Cuthburga
Products, which Joan was in the process of erecting above the

tables laden with her honey and my cookbook. 'Oh, look. How wonderful,' she exclaimed, 'to be able to take a living memento home with us. What an uplifting idea. We shall certainly avail ourselves of this.'

I smiled gratefully. This had to be the best news of the morning. If we could somehow survive St Cuthburga's phallus, perhaps we could really be in business.

I watched them from a distance as they shuffled intently round the walls of the old priory, then gradually congregated by the open sarcophagus, which they took turns at peering into as if hoping that a fragment of the saint might still remain there. Many of them had brought small bunches of flowers, which they proceeded to lay in the grave. Others wandered over to pick posies of wild-flowers from the verges of the hayfield left untouched by my electric mower and Jehoshaphat. Those who could kneel knelt. Heads were bent in prayer. There was a flutter of handkerchiefs, mopping tears, drying eyes, blowing noses. And suddenly I was reminded of Juliet's grave in Verona, which Anna-Maria had dragged me to in a romantic moment when I was a child; and I remembered the love-letters, the poems, the little heart-broken offerings which had littered the bare stone and which presumably the yawning attendant had raked out every evening in readiness for the next invasion of tears. Young love. Old love. The yearning to transcend mortality and loneliness was the same.

I always left St Cuthburga's flowers where they'd been laid until they withered. I wondered what the attendant at Juliet's tomb did with the love-letters.

After a while I saw Ms Burroughs gathering her flock around her. She was saying something, and I imagined this was my cue to join the congregation. Feeling distinctly uneasy I made my way towards them. The stapled smile welcomed me from afar.

'Ah, here is Mrs Hazlitt,' I heard her announce. 'She has most generously offered to conduct us to another holy site which I feel sure you will find rewarding. As many of you will be aware, the Benedictines were great gardeners. They made important contributions to horticulture, no doubt because they were forbidden to eat meat.' I could see she was relishing this display of knowledge. 'In addition to vegetables and medicinal plants, for which they were famous,' she went on, 'the Benedictines were among the first Christians to perfect the art of topiary, which we know from Pliny the Younger was first practised by the Romans. Well, I'm pleased to tell you that a unique survivor of this art is to be found here at Norton Priory, though alas time has all but obscured the spiritual purpose to which the nuns dedicated it. However' – and once again the stapled smile was directed at me – 'Mrs Hazlitt will be able to direct us to one remarkable example which I feel sure all of you will instantly recognise. This is a yew-tree which has been cut into one of the most universal symbols of mankind's hopes and aspirations. I feel sure you will all of you recognise it. Mrs Hazlitt, do please lead us to it.'

I was aware of one hundred and fifty pairs of eyes gazing at me. Instinctively – helplessly – I closed my own. I hoped they would think it was in prayer. Oh, St Cuthburga, come to my aid; remember that I was brought up a good Catholic, and perform a small miracle. Forget about turning stinging-nettles into sweet basil; just transform that yew-tree into anything you choose so long as it's not a giant prick.

The walk from the priory ruins to the overgrown topiary garden was perhaps four hundred yards. Looking back I could see how, every ten yards or so, our progress was flagged like marker-buoys by pilgrims who had fallen by the wayside. They were leaning against trees, slumped on the grass verge, or just standing in the August sun mopping their brows. I glanced anxiously at Judith Burroughs.

'Perhaps I should have labelled this path the Via Dolorosa,' I suggested.

For the first time the staples fell from her smile, and she gazed at me with disapproval for a moment. Then the smile re-formed and she began to coax her weary flock joyfully onwards. And onwards, slowly, they came, until finally we were all of us clustered round the huge shaggy yew-tree in the centre of the abandoned garden. The silence was broken only by the sound of wheezing breath, and the occasional moan.

She gazed up at the giant tree and began to part its lower branches. I looked elsewhere.

'There,' she announced, raising both arms triumphantly. 'Pilgrims, cast your eyes upon this. The firm shape. The upward thrust. The broadening and narrowing of the tip. Here is proof of our sisters' devotion long ago. As foretold by the prophet Isaiah: "And there shall come forth a rod, and the spirit of the Lord shall rest upon him." Pilgrims, perceive before you the Tree of Jesse!'

I'd been in the gatehouse scarcely two months and already my old life had drifted far away over the horizon.

Only occasional and discordant echoes reached me from those farther shores. The *Daily Mail* duly reported that 'The estranged wife of the MP for Box Hill, David Hazlitt, has gone into retreat, announcing her intention to take the veil.' The reporter found it appropriate to add that in the eyes of Mr Hazlitt's colleagues in the Commons the dance of the seven veils would have been a more popular vocation for me to choose, and that my charms would be sorely missed. The paper managed to unearth a rather audacious photograph to prove its point. David's reaction was to issue an outraged denial from his holiday retreat in the Dordogne, then to phone me suggesting I might benefit from psychiatric treatment. I reminded him that it wasn't only the wives of government ministers who told lies to the press, and that he was bloody lucky I didn't tell them I was running a brothel. At this point the local French switchboard conveniently cut him off.

An hour later Fergus rang, also from France, to tell me he'd come across a copy of the paper, and would I please delay my final vows until after our date for dinner? I said I'd think about it. I was longing to tell him about my pilgrims and the Tree of Jesse, but thought better of it. The silence on the telephone was just long enough for me to sense that there were other things he would have liked to say, and to be intrigued as to what they might be. I said I was looking forward to seeing him, and he said the same. There was another silence. It was like a knowing touch of fingers.

But for most of the time there was scarcely a moment to think about Fergus, or indeed about anything much. Clearly it wasn't only Saintly Tours who were aware it was the centenary of St Cuthburga. The coaches now came in waves. The gravel path to the open sarcophagus became worn with the sandals of pilgrims, young and old, though mercifully no one repeated the request to be shown the topiary garden. More mercifully still, we were now doing a roaring trade in herbs, urns, hanging baskets and Joan's honey. As for *The Secrets of a Hungry Saint*, by the end of that week I was urgently on the telephone to the printer in Exeter ordering a reprint of one thousand copies. Megan's recipe entitled 'Give us this day our daily bread' was a conspicuous triumph, one excited group of pilgrims even suggesting we award it the shorter title 'Manna from Heaven'. Before the end of the week I was able to hurry over to Glyn's bookshop and proudly present him with the first cheque to be drawn on the account of St Cuthburga Products.

We were in profit. I could pay the rent. With any luck, by the end of the summer I might have earned enough to pay the rent for the entire winter. I might even become financially independent of David. Then I really would feel free.

After the last coach had departed early that evening Joan, Megan and I celebrated in the garden with a bottle of champagne. And then another.

'Oh God, I can't walk,' announced Joan, stumbling against the table as she rose to leave. 'What will the flame-throwers think of their mum? Fuck it, I don't care. Whoops!'

Her legs did a little shimmy in the direction of the gatehouse arch.

'I think I'll let you navigate and then try and follow,' said Megan with a hiccup. 'Sail before steam. Here we go.' And she rose uncertainly, legs well apart in an attempt to keep balance. 'Got to stabilise the cargo, Glyn always says. Ballast amidships. Well, I've got plenty of that.' She gave out a burp. 'Oh dear. All your bloody fault, Claudia. We were clean-living people in this town till you arrived.'

'Balls!' Joan called out over her shoulder, at the same time reaching out for the stone arch as if it were trying to run away from her. 'Come on, Megan. This way. Take it at a run.'

Megan set off. She tacked heavily towards the gatehouse, arms flailing, and muttering nautical instructions to herself. 'Lee-o. Lean to starboard.'

Perhaps I'd drunk less than they had, or just felt responsible for their safety: I wasn't sure which. But I followed them out on to the cobbled entrance, grateful that neither of them had more then a hundred yards or so to stagger home, and equally grateful that the Rev Pype hadn't chosen this moment to observe his flock, particularly since one of them was the wife of his church warden.

Suddenly I noticed that Joan was gazing up at the arch. Leaning back unsteadily, she raised one hand to shield her eyes. Then she gave a laugh.

'Well,' she said loudly, pointing upwards with the other hand. 'After all these years. The things you notice when you're pissed. Look.'

What she was pointing at were the two battered carvings which decorated the outer arch on either side. At first I assumed she was indicating the female figure modestly covering her nakedness.

But Joan shook her head vigorously.

'Not her. *Him*. The other one. The animal. Can't you see?'

It was the figure I'd always imagined to be a dog rearing up on its back legs, though so much of its anatomy had been hacked away it was quite impossible to be sure.

'See what?' asked Megan, who was having trouble seeing anything.

'What he's got missing, for Christ's sake.'

Something clicked in my head: it was that evening when Fergus had left me a note accompanying the roses and the strange herb. I'd been too busy with St Cuthburga Products to give it any further thought. Now I remembered he'd said something about the gatehouse having a carved satyr above the arch. And on the phone he'd urged me to take a look at it. But, having no idea what a satyr was, I'd never bothered.

This must have been what he'd meant. I gazed up at it again. Someone had certainly done his best to render the creature unrecognisable: I could even follow the long marks of the chisel where parts of it had been removed.

'Go on, Joan,' Megan was saying, sounding disgruntled. 'Tell me. What *is* missing?'

Joan spread her arms wide and let out a bellow of a laugh.

'It's his prick of course. A huge erect prick.'

I blinked. After the phallic topiary, now this. Without thinking I blurted out, 'Well, well. That makes two of them.'

Joan gave me a very strange look.

I lay in bed puzzled by why it was that my new life seemed to be surrounded by cocks. I baulked at the idea of telling Caroline: she would only laugh and point out that if one of them were actually a tree and the other one had been removed, then neither was much use and wasn't it about time I found myself a real one? But since the only real one was hundreds of miles away in France until next week, there wasn't a great deal I could do about it.

On a less personal note, I was curious to know what a nunnery was doing being so blatant about that aspect of male anatomy which its immates were most particularly forbidden to enjoy. I could hardly imagine it to have been prescribed in the Rule of St Benedict, yet already I'd come across a phallic yew-tree and an excited satyr, not to mention all those extremely frank corbels carved round the roofline of the parish church, which had once been the nuns' chapel, I reminded myself. Fergus had suggested in his note that the carved satyr on the gatehouse arch might offer a clue to the mystery of the place. He'd also told me on the phone that he'd made a few interesting discoveries about Norton Priory, which he was keen to tell me about. I was equally keen to hear about them: on the other hand, if these discoveries were related to erotic topiary and mutilated satyrs, I did wonder how relaxed our dinner conversation was likely to be. It was hardly a conventional avenue of budding romance to be conversing about phallic symbols in a medieval nunnery.

I kept picturing David's lay-preacher's face should he ever hear about all this. Then one night I dreamt that in ten years I'd got David entirely wrong, and at that very moment in the Dordogne he was tearing the clothes off some reseacher in the summer moonlight, *not* wearing his Y-fronts or his pyjamas, and sporting an erection that my satyr would have been proud of.

The vision didn't survive the dawn, but it did spur me to

visit the town library – early before the next coachload of pilgrims was due to arrive – in order to look up what a satyr actually was.

Hall's *Dictionary of Subjects and Symbols in Art* caught my eye. I turned to 'Satyr'. It immediately followed 'Satan', which I thought might be significant. 'In ancient Greece,' Mr Hall explained, a satyr was 'one of the spirits of the woods and mountains' – attendants of the god Bacchus and with goat-like features. 'They were lazy and lecherous and spent their time drinking and chasing nymphs.' In medieval allegory they personified Lust, and with the female followers of Bacchus they participated in orgiastic rites known as the Bacchanalia. The author concluded with the more tender observation that, as fertility symbols, they sometimes gathered fruit from the trees in the company of nymphs.

Walking back to the gatehouse I tried to reconcile this description of a satyr with the life of the holy nuns. There surely had to be some straightforward explanation of why there should be such a carving over the entrance to a priory.

Perhaps, I decided, the pagan myth of satyrs being spirits of the woods gathering fruit from the trees in the company of nymphs had simply been Christianised – in other words, sanitised – like so many other pagan myths; and my satyr was simply the divine spirit who presided over the autumnal gathering of quinces. 'Nymphs' had become 'nuns'. This seemed entirely likely. There remained the problem of the satyr's erect penis. But then I only had Joan's drunken word for it that it *was* a penis. Most likely it was a leg, or a tail, which Cromwell's soldiers had hacked off quite indiscriminately in their state of Puritan rage. And in that case perhaps my phallic yew-tree was indeed the Tree of Jesse, just as the lady from Saintly Tours had excitedly maintained. As for the church corbels along the roofline, wasn't it true – I remembered David explaining this most solemnly during some bleak weekend in Herefordshire – that stonemasons were encouraged to portray the works of the Devil on the outside of churches, signifying that they had been cast out from the inside?

These explanations satisfied me for all of the three minutes it took me to walk back to the gatehouse. Then I paused, gazed up, and my explanations collapsed. There really couldn't be any doubt about it. What Cromwell's soldiers had removed with their angry chisels was – quite clearly – a cock.

The hooting of a car horn made me turn round, and there drawing up on the pavement beside me was Caroline's dark-blue Mercedes. To my surprise she had all her three children in the car with her. Less surprising was that their faces were a group study in rebellion. They were huddled in the back seat like the three furies. Caroline, on the other hand, was radiant.

'They're all going to stay with my sister until term begins,' she explained thankfully.

'Whom we loathe and detest,' came mutterings from the back seat. Caroline took no notice.

'I'm just taking them to the station. I hope there *are* trains to Inverness today.'

The elder daughter, maybe fifteen and disgracefully pretty under the scowl, made her face as ugly as possible.

'Inver-fucking-ness! In August! What a place to chill out.'

This, too, washed harmlessly over Caroline. She leaned cheerfully out of the car window.

'I'll be back this afternoon. Come over to dinner. Carmen wants to cook a paella. And I haven't seen you for ages – been tied up with that stupid Legover woman. *More* lavatories. Enough to give anyone the hot flushes. I'll tell you all about it. And about my lawyer. Oh, and I've got a brilliant idea for my literary conference. Seven-ish?'

And without waiting for an answer she drove off down the bus lane and through the red lights.

For the rest of that day I was occupied with pilgrims, three coachloads in the morning, and two more in the late afternoon, one of them from France. In the midst of all the genuflection a party of serious twitchers arrived laden with cameras and binoculars to peer at the honey buzzards. Jehoshaphat took exception to them standing in his field, and several camera-cases found their way into his stomach. To add to the confusion several of the French pilgrims obviously didn't know about English birdwatchers; they got it into their heads that all these raised binoculars were being employed to track some divine mystery, and hurried over excitedly to enquire what species of miracle was being performed in those distant trees. Unfortunately none of the twitchers appeared to understand a word of French; and from my vantage-point by the herb stall I was able to watch the blundering attempt at an *entente cordiale* as the English contingent tried vainly to share their passion for a buzzard, while the French eagerly scanned the woods through borrowed binoculars in search of the Holy Dove.

But since neither party showed the slightest interest in my pots of herbs, or in *The Secrets of a Hungry Saint*, I soon lost interest in both of them.

As the last coachload of pilgrims pulled away from the gate-house, and the twitchers gathered up such gear as Jehoshaphat had spared them, I set about my usual evening task of collecting up the cash, packing away the books and finally turning the hose on my herb pots, urns and hanging baskets, which to my great satisfaction were already reduced by almost half. And next week – Eureka! – I would have more than enough money to pay my first rent.

Finally, before taking a bath and dressing to go and see Caroline, I treated myself to a glass of wine in the evening sun. I'd long ago learnt that any meeting with Caroline needed to be fortified by a little alcohol. Here was another of the small pleasures I'd discovered since leaving David. In ten years of marriage I'd scarcely touched a drop, mainly because David didn't – except of course ceremonially when hosting some gathering of the party faithful. In the early days I used to scheme to get him drunk, out of pure curiosity to know what he'd be like if he were. Might he be outrageous? Wonderfully witty? Even randy? I never managed it. The self-control never slipped. It wasn't until I met Caroline that I learnt to accept a drink without a twinge of guilt. 'Fuck it,' she exclaimed. 'If you're married to a man like that, you bloody well need it.'

Even then I used to stick to vodka so David wouldn't smell it on my breath when I went home.

'There have never been drinkers in our family,' he'd announce smugly, sipping his permitted glass of Christmas sherry. His other favourite line was 'There's never been a divorce in our family.'

Well, here were two temples of virtue I was about to defile. Would he survive the shame?

The thought came to me that if I'd never been married to David I would probably have liked him, as of course I once did. And now that in a sense I was no longer married to him, I almost found it easy to like him again, even admire him. He was a *good* man. He was a much better person than I was. I'd never known him be unkind or mean. There was no malice in him. He'd never lied to me.

Suddenly I switched off this train of thought. Jesus, Claudia, what the hell are you talking about? Guilt has got to you again. Marriage isn't about *liking* someone. And life isn't about being good. It's about being real. And David isn't real. All that goodness is a shield behind which he protects himself from the world.

I helped myself to a second glass of wine after that.

I would have liked to stay here on the terrace until the sun went down and the bats started to flit between the trees. It was so richly peaceful gazing out over my borrowed acres. With every evening spent like this I could feel my year of freedom blossoming inside me. Surprisingly it was like the freedom I'd felt when (so fearfully) I'd taken myself to England at sixteen, not knowing what lay ahead, but knowing I would make something happen, that I would push life my way. After ten years of being the passive wife, it was bewildering and wonderful to feel like this again. And what would I reap from it, I wondered?

Finally there was only time to change hastily before driving up to Caroline's. She'd either have draped herself in designer clothes, I decided, or be stark naked by the pool, so there was little point trying to compete. I threw on jeans and a cotton blouse.

But I was wrong. She hadn't changed at all. I found her bent over a table in the garden, her face invisible behind a curtain of blonde hair as she pored over a sheet of paper laid out in front of her, weighted against the evening breeze by what I imagined to be the customary vodka-and-tonic.

She had a biro in one hand, and didn't bother to look up.

'I've been drawing up a shortlist,' she announced severely, as if I'd been there all the time. 'How many speakers d'you think we need, Claudia?'

'Speakers for what?' I asked.

Caroline clicked her tongue impatiently, then glanced up at me with a frown.

'The conference, of course.' Suddenly the frown evaporated. 'But I haven't told you, have I? Of course not.' She swept her hair back from her eyes and gave a mischievous laugh. 'I just thought of it this morning: the theme – what it's going to be. I haven't told anyone yet.'

I waited expectantly. It was clear she was about to test it on me. I was to be the guinea-pig, not a role I coveted.

'Well, there's no point in holding just another literary conference, is there?' she began. 'Authors wanking about their art. Who cares? There's got to be a subject, an idea.' She paused for approval, and I nodded cautiously. 'Right,' she went on, 'so why not tie it in with the theme of the house? Family mistresses going right back to Charles II. We'll make it a literary parallel, and call it "Mistresses in Literature". What d'you think? Brilliant, isn't it?'

I must have looked puzzled, because the frown returned.

'They've been terribly important when you come to think of it,' she said emphatically. 'Where would literature be without mistresses, after all? Much more important than wives. Anyway,' she continued, ignoring whatever expression was on my face, 'I've been jotting down who we should invite to speak. We want plenty of variety, don't we? So I thought we might kick off with Antonia Fraser: she knows all about that sort of thing, and she's written a book about Anne Boleyn who was Henry VIII's mistress before she became queen. That'll be a good start – give the conference some historical weight. And Antonia'll bring in the heavies: Pinter and people like that.'

Caroline took a thoughtful sip of her vodka-and-tonic and lit a cigarette.

'Well, after that we need something more contemporary. A bit racier, to catch the public eye. Who knows all about mistresses? I thought of Alan Clark: he's had plenty. But he doesn't really write about them, does he? Except in the margin, so to speak. So what about that American woman who wrote about Nancy Reagan having it off with Frank Sinatra in the White House? Kitty Kelley, that's her name; and now she's about to blow the gaff on Prince Philip. Does that count as literature? Anyway, she'd be good news. And she'd come over to publicise her book, wouldn't cost us a penny. Terrific.'

Caroline was looking extremely pleased with herself. I was getting increasingly lost. Was the National Trust really likely to buy all this?

'And surely there must be someone writing about that Camilla Parker Horse woman. Andrew Morton maybe. Shall we ask him? What d'you think?'

I muttered something incoherent.

'And Lloyd George, of course. There must be a biographer of him around somewhere. And since he's supposed to have been my grandfather, that would link it nicely to Priory Hall and the family. Yes, that's a great idea.'

A longer sip of vodka-and-tonic. Caroline began to look thoughtful again.

'But I do want it to sound serious,' she went on. 'Not just gossip.' She took several long draws on her cigarette. Then her eyes brightened. 'I know, religion. That's what we need. This *is* an ancient priory, after all. Religion. What mistresses are there in the Bible, Claudia? The trouble is, I've never read it. Have you?' I said nothing. Caroline stubbed out her cigarette violently. 'Got it. Marina Warner. She's written a book about the Virgin Mary, hasn't she? Perfect. God's mistress – he never married her, did he? Am I right? Well, *am* I?' I said I believed she was. 'Good. That's it then. I'll get in touch with them all tomorrow. And I'll also try and rustle up the odd Nobel Prize-winner: there are plenty of them knocking about, after all. Then I'll block-book the King's Arms and the Royal Devon for the first weekend in December. Cut-price out of season; they'll be only too delighted.'

She swept her fingers through her hair and gave out a long sigh of contentment.

'Now. The barn. That should seat two hundred, I've cal-culated. I know a firm in Exeter who'll supply the chairs. A caterer'll arrange buffet lunches. Oddbins the wine. I'll get posters out. A few ads in the serious press. Fifty pounds a head for the weekend: pay your own expenses. D'you think that's about right? That's ten thousand quid all told. And if fees and stuff eat up half of it that's still five grand clear profit in a single weekend. Christ, four conferences like this a year and all the costs of Priory Hall are met automatically. Wow, Claudia! And that Legover woman can get stuffed.'

Then she saw my face. I couldn't hide a sense of utter disbelief. This was a totally mad scheme, and I couldn't see any way it was going to work.

'You don't like it, do you?' she said fiercely.

By now I was feeling thoroughly uncomfortable, and longed to get out of saying anything at all.

'It's not that I don't *like* it. It's just that . . .'

Caroline spared me having to finish. She gave a contemptu-ous snort, and drained her vodka-and-tonic.

'You're hopeless. Bloody Italian peasant. No imagination. Where did you say you went to school?'

'Raynes Park Comprehensive.'

Caroline's expression said, 'No wonder.'

At this point she at last decided to fetch me a drink. I should have known it would be the worst bottle she could find in her cellar: it still had the number stuck on it where someone had won it in a raffle. Caroline herself had refreshed her vodka-and-tonic, and proceeded to gaze at me over the top of it with poisonous eyes while I sipped the stuff. This wasn't going to be the best of evenings, and I wished I was still sitting on my terrace waiting for the bats to flit between the trees.

But perhaps I was wrong to be sceptical. You could never tell with Caroline's wild ideas. All that ferocious energy and total fearlessness. She might well be capable of bullying the entire literary mafia into traipsing halfway across the globe to Norton Abbas because they didn't dare say no. And maybe the old barn would be packed out with people falling over themselves to pay their fifty quid. And Caroline would indeed clean up.

'I'm really sorry, Caroline,' I said.

She ignored my apology, and tossed her head.

'And how are your little efforts with the salad going?' she asked. Now she was getting her own back. A sharp smile appeared on her face, and immediately went again. 'I must remember to come and buy a lettuce from you one evening when the shops are closed.'

I thought it was best to say nothing.

We sat in silence for a while. I took small sips of my disgusting wine while Caroline savoured her vodka-and-tonic. Every so often she glared over the top of it.

And then suddenly she let out one of her rippling laughs.

'Claudia, your face!' she exclaimed, still laughing. 'You'd make a hopeless actress.'

With a joyful smile she got up, seized the wine bottle and tipped its contents into the flower-bed.

'Yuk. Serve you bloody well right, being so snooty about my plans for survival. Now let me get you a proper drink.'

And with that hip-swinging gait of hers she strode into the house, emerging a few moments later with a bottle of champagne in one hand and two glasses in the other. She placed these on the table, removed the champagne cork and poured out the glasses. Then she handed one of them to me.

'Cheers, darling. And fuck the National Trust. They may think they've got my father's house, but they're not bloody well having his cellar.' She sat back contentedly in the late-evening sun, and closed her eyes. 'D'you know, Claudia,' she went on dreamily, 'every time he acquired a new mistress he'd order six cases of champagne from the Wine Society. But no mistress ever lasted longer than three cases. So I've got something to be grateful to him for, the old bugger.'

A smile of pleasure spread across Caroline's face. Then she opened one eye and peered at me.

'Are you really all right, Claudia? With the rent and things, I mean?'

I nodded and said yes I was. I explained about the herb stall, 'St Cuthburga's collection' and the rest of them. And the urns and hanging baskets. And about *The Secrets of a Hungry Saint*, and Megan's blasphemous illustration for

making bread. I'd made enough money for several months'
rent already, I said.

Caroline opened the other eye, and looked astonished.

'Christ, you're clever.' She leant over and poured out two
more glasses of champagne. 'You know, I love having you
here.'

Carmen brought the paella out into the garden. Caroline had
drunk enough champagne to thank her very sweetly, which
surprised the girl.

'Think of being a Spanish virgin in Norton Abbas,' she said
reflectively as Carmen disappeared back into the house. 'Can
you remember being a virgin, Claudia?'

'Of course I can,' I said, laughing.

'I can't,' she insisted.

She swore that amnesia had blotted out everything in her
life before that event because it had been such a dreadful
experience.

'Mind you, it hasn't always been a lot better since,' she went
on cheerfully, her mouth full of paella. 'And if you ever go to
bed with Patrick you'll know exactly what I mean. When he
told me he was heir to the smallest county in England he never
explained that he had a cock to match. I've often thought of
divorcing him under the conditions of the Trades Descriptions
Act. D'you think I could?'

We were back on familiar Caroline territory. Poor Patrick.
I didn't add that his secretaries never seemed to find cause
for complaint. It also occurred to me that even the smallest
county in England must surely provide enough to cover
Patrick's losses at Lloyd's, and that perhaps I shouldn't be
taking Caroline's financial disasters too seriously.

But of course it wasn't really about money. The loss of
her house was something much more personal. For Caroline
money was merely a nuisance when you didn't have it,
whereas the house was her past, her life, where she belonged.
To be losing it was far worse than losing money. I was grateful
not to feel any such ties, even though I sometimes felt a touch
of envy. I'd never owned anything much that was my own.
As for houses, Anna-Maria's flat in Bologna had been more

a family menagerie than a place you could belong to. The house in Leatherhead had been David's, with the local Tory matrons given the freedom of the place, and me the suspect hostess and resident kitchen-maid. And now the gatehouse, which if it belonged to anyone was in the joint ownership of the nation and the ghosts of Admiral Romsey's mistresses. In every place I'd lived in I was the squatter.

'Tell me about your new lawyer,' I said, changing the subject. 'Did he come up with anything at the weekend?'

Caroline gave a throaty laugh.

'Did he come up with anything? He didn't have a chance to come up at all because the bloody children were here, weren't they? They kept poking their heads round the door, the little bastards.' She dug deeper into her paella. 'But I'm working on it, darling, I assure you. The wiles of the older woman.'

I smiled.

'Caroline, I actually meant had he come up with some way of contesting the will?'

She shrugged.

'Not very successful on that score either. He says that even if the Legover woman *was* having it off with my father – and Patrick's bloody sure she was – it would be damned near impossible to prove "unacceptable motivations" without proof of dirty tricks. And since my father's life was one long dirty trick, what would be the point of that?' She laughed, and poured us both some more wine. 'No, Justin has far more interesting uses than that. I've invited him down again. He's terribly sweet.' She looked quite dreamy for a moment. Then she gave another throaty laugh. 'And God, I bet he's huge and hairy.'

Then, just as I imagined we were settling in for one of Caroline's erotic flights of fancy, her mood changed.

'Meanwhile, there are other things on my mind, Claudia,' she said, rising to her feet. 'Let me show you. I tell you, the battle lines are drawn.'

She disappeared into the house and returned a couple of minutes later with a large brown envelope. In the other hand she was holding a lantern which she placed in the centre of the table. She lit it, and replaced the glass cylinder.

'Now,' she said meaningfully. 'In the dusk of Priory Hall I shall show you what the powers of darkness think they've got in store for me, may they roast in hell.' With that she ripped open the envelope testily and laid out the contents on the table, pushing aside the remains of the paella and adjusting the lantern so that it shone evenly on whatever it was she was anxious to show me.

'This pretty thing arrived by the second post today. Look.'

I peered down at a closely typed letter of several pages under the ornate heading of a firm of London architects. Accompanying the letter were several sheets of what were obviously ground-plans – three of them apparently of Priory Hall, one plan for each floor, and a further plan which was devoted to the garden area around the house.

Caroline stood back with her hands on her hips. She thrust out her breasts as if preparing to take on the enemy.

'Well, look. *This* is what they propose to do to *my* house, the arseholes.' Her forefinger stabbed at one of the drawings. 'They want to rip out half my kitchen to make loos. *Four* of them, plus a low-level one for little boys to widdle in. Can you believe it? And I suppose they'll want those little pictorial signs for "His" and "Hers", won't they?' Caroline gave a snort, followed by an angry chuckle. 'On second thought perhaps I should tell them they may put them up on the condition that I'm allowed to put up a prick-and-balls sign pointing to the Hall of the Mystresses, you know, like the Romans used to do for their brothels.'

The thought seemed to temper Caroline's anger for a moment. But not for long.

'Then ramps. Look. Ramps everywhere. It's like a bloody geriatric ward.' There was another snort, and the forefinger stabbed down a second time. 'And what about this? "*Baby-feeding area*", it says here. And a room for changing nappies.'

Hurricane Caroline was by now in full fury.

'And they want an office too.' She pulled out another of the drawings. 'And d'you know where they want to put it? In my nursery. My old nursery when I was a girl. Can you imagine it? Claudia, I love that room. I'm not having some spotty clerk sitting there with his halitosis and dirty finger-nails, surrounded by National Trust posters of Roman drains. It's *my* nursery.' It was such a plea from the heart. And suddenly her face had become quite soft, as if she were still that little girl. 'Nanny used to read *Winnie the Pooh* to me in that room. And she'd stick all my drawings round the walls.'

I thought Caroline might burst into tears. But she merely gulped, then turned her attention briskly to the plan of the garden and outhouses. And that refuelled her anger.

'Now look at this. *That* is my rose-garden. And they want to make it a fucking car-park.' She looked up at me in amazement. 'A car-park! What's wrong with parking in the town? Or walking?' She peered down at the plan again. 'And what's this say? "A roofed-in area for powered buggies." What the fuck are powered buggies? Oh, perhaps it's a misprint for "buggers".' That made her laugh, and she poured herself another glass of wine. Then her eyes fell on something else, and the hurricane was whipped up again.

'What's this? "The shop."' She slammed her hand down on the table, and some of the wine spilt over the plan. '"The shop!" Christ, those are my stables. They can't do that. That's where I used to keep my pony. Oh, I loved that pony. It's a shrine, that place, Claudia. Much more important a shrine than bloody St Cuthburga's grave.' She paused mournfully for a moment, then leant forward over the drawing again. 'Something's been scrawled here next to it. What does it say? "Shop for selling booklets, postcards, perhaps small reproductions of the more important paintings in the house."'

Caroline gave a loud guffaw.

'The more important paintings in the house. Oh Claudia, that's a real hoot. Now I *do* like that. Can't you just see it? Repros of all Megan's nude paintings of my father's mistresses. Oh yes!'

She paused. Then she gave a long sigh.

'No, no, no, no, no!' she said menacingly. 'No. No.'

At that moment I began to feel a few spots of rain. Caroline knocked back her glass of wine, grasped the bottle and turned towards the house. The lights of the great drawing-room picked out Megan's life-size pictures of her father's mistresses. The room seemed alive with flesh. Out here the spots of rain were becoming heavier, fizzing into the lantern. I picked it up.

Caroline looked back at the garden table.

'I'll leave all this rubbish to rot in the rain,' she said, glancing down at the architect's letter and the spread of drawings. 'May God piss all over them.'

In the light of the lantern Caroline's face looked strangely vulnerable.

'I'm determined to keep this place, Claudia,' she said quietly. 'You know that, don't you?' Drops of rain were falling from her blonde hair and down her face, like tears. 'It's mine, and it's going to stay that way. I don't know how, but I'm going to do it.'

Wine-bottle in one hand, she laid her free arm on my shoulder as we walked back towards the open French windows.

'I'm going to get thoroughly pissed this evening, Claudia,' she added. 'Because from tomorrow, my darling, it's war.'

Six

To hell with the pilgrims. I decided to award myself the weekend off. Catholics, after all, were forever enjoying their Saints' Days: Why shouldn't St Cuthburga have one too? So I made out a notice with my marker-pen and attached it to the railings outside the gatehouse. 'Old Priory Closed Sat. 6 p.m. – Mon. 9.30 a.m.' In smaller letters underneath I'd added, 'Enquiries to Glyn Davies Books, 47 High Street.' Glyn, who glowed with pride at my commercial efforts, had replenished his stock of *The Secrets of a Hungry Saint* – his 'international best-seller', he called it, adding with a wry smile, 'well, quite a few visitors to Norton Abbas are foreigners, aren't they?'

The late-summer heatwave had returned after the thunderstorms, and I savoured the prospect of having my thirty-five acres entirely to myself, with just Jehoshaphat and the honey buzzards for company, and perhaps Megan or Joan to split a bottle of wine with me in the evening as the sun went down.

Yes, that would be great. I thought of David moping in the Dordogne, sweating and unsuitably dressed, and Anna-Maria in Bologna lamenting that I'd stood up her favourite sausage-maker; and I felt even better. I was good at being alone, I'd come to realise. Why did people always assume that a woman on her own must be pining for a man, but that a man on his own must be having a terrific time? It was true that I could do with a lover; but just a lover, nothing more, none of the day-to-day tedium. Ten years with David had killed that for me.

And yet Caroline called me a romantic. Perhaps wanting to be alone was part of being a romantic, floating through each day on unattainable daydreams. Was that really me?

The church clock struck six. I was off duty. There was nothing I need worry about. I felt a delicious sense of aimlessness, brushing aside any thoughts of 'I should do this', 'perhaps I should do that'. I kicked off my shoes and wandered barefoot through the meadow. The grass was cool after days of rain, and tiny brown crickets exploded from under my feet. The air gave out a warm rank smell of summer.

I lay down and closed my eyes, pulling my skirt up to my thighs to feel the breeze blowing in off the estuary. It felt sensual, bare legs stretched out in the grass, midriff naked below the half-unbuttoned blouse, the breeze stroking my skin, wisps of hair playing with my face.

My head became filled with imaginings. They had no focus, only sensations, appetites, needs; they stirred around my brain and within my body. Maybe the spirit of this place was getting to me; the effect of being surrounded by so many cocks – the tree, the satyr, the whole damned *Kama Sutra* above my bed. Or maybe I'd simply been celibate too long. After all, at thirty-two wasn't I supposed to be just entering my prime? 'Damn you!' as Caroline always said in an aggrieved tone. So what was I doing lying here wasting it on dreams?

I ran one hand under my blouse on to my breast, and felt the nipple harden: it was as though sparks of electricity were shooting through my body. Involuntarily my buttocks and legs moved against the grass, and my breast seemed to burn under my hand.

And then . . . another hand closed over it.

Thank God not all reactions are quite instantaneous: there must have been a fraction of a second before terror had a chance to grip me. And in that split-second came a voice, very softly: 'Claudia.'

I didn't even open my eyes. I reached up with my other hand and ran my fingers through Fergus's hair, pulling his head down towards me. I could feel the roughness of an unshaven face. A tongue explored my lips, my mouth, my throat. His body pressed down on to mine, and I curled my legs round his thighs. I only sensed him removing his clothes, then felt his hands remove mine, peeling me very gently, until I lay naked on the grass. His lips hovered over my body, touching here and there, my eyes, ears, neck, breasts, down over my belly, between my thighs: his tongue sought out my clitoris, stroking it until I heard myself gasp as I came. Then as my head fell back he drew my hand to his prick and I ran my fingers along it, guiding it deep into me, my muscles closing around it. I could hear my own voice: 'Fuck me. Just fuck me.' My fingers clawed his back. I bit his tongue. I cried: such unruly and wonderful tears, as if all the pain that had ever been in my life was being washed away.

When I did open my eyes he was gazing down at me, leaning with one elbow on the grass while his fingers began to trace every contour of my body as if they were modelling it. I could feel little convulsions as they brushed my vagina, my nipples, my neck, my lips. I never wanted him to stop. And he went on gazing at me, those intense blue eyes fixed on mine.

And still we said nothing, either of us.

It was something I'd never experienced, to be gazing up at a man I scarcely knew at all – knew almost nothing about – and yet I knew his body as intimately as my own: I could love it, be wanted by it, roused by it. And he by mine. I was lying here, naked, for him. There was nothing to be said: it was all in the eyes, and in the touch. I didn't need to know any more.

The church clock broke the silence, striking seven. Fergus sat up, folding his arms round my knees. I noticed how deeply suntanned he was, his hair longer and more bleached. He was, I thought, quite disgracefully beautiful.

'Well,' he said, leaning forward and laying his hands over my breasts. 'Perhaps I should tell you that I actually came to bring you flowers.' And he smiled. 'I left them on your table. Flowers from France. I got back this afternoon.'

I reached up and ran my fingers through his hair.

'And is this how you always bring flowers, Dr Corrigan?' I said, laughing.

His fingers circled my nipples, and I gave a shudder. He bent forward and kissed them. Then he looked up at me.

'Of course. How else? Especially if the woman has a body like Venus and is lying almost naked in the grass.'

I pulled him down on to me, pressing the light stubble on his face against my cheek.

'I'm glad you didn't only bring the flowers,' I whispered.

Fergus raised his head again.

'I came with another good intention as well, to ask you to dinner.'

I pressed him closer to me.

'You mean, that was just the *hors-d'oeuvre?*'

I heard him chuckle, his face against mine.

'If you like.'

I rolled away from him, and sat up. I gazed down at his body for a moment, then threaded my fingers through his chest-hairs and down his stomach. I closed my fingers round his prick.

'I think I'd love to have dinner with you,' I said.

I'd never behaved like this in my life. Was this what it meant to be a liberated woman? I thought of all those years of wearing powder-blue, and having to go through a quick inspection parade for David before we drove off to some Tory function.

So, now that I had a completely free choice, what should I wear this evening?

'Are we going somewhere smart, Fergus?' I called out.

He was lounging on the sofa with the glass of white wine I'd just poured him. How could a man manage to look quite so glamorous in faded jeans and a white shirt open to the waist?

'Well, are we?' I asked a second time.

I was leaning over the stairs wrapped in a bath-towel, my wet hair bound under a second towel. He glanced up.

'Unless you count my company as smart, no.'

'That doesn't exactly help,' I said, dabbing bathwater from my face. 'What about the other people?'

He looked at me quizzically.

'There won't be any other people?'

'I see. You've booked the entire restaurant, is that it? Just us in the middle of a large room?'

He laughed.

'Not so very large. It's where I live. I'm cooking dinner for you.'

I was puzzled. So what was this? My mystery lover. No wife and kids? Or perhaps they were all on holiday, and the mouse was free to play with me. I had no intention of asking; I didn't even want to know. I felt a wickedly warm glow: it meant I'd be spending the night with him. Then a late breakfast with coffee to wake me up, in a borrowed dressing-gown. Thank

God I'd taken the weekend off, and I wouldn't have to worry about Saintly Tours.

I gazed at him as I went on drying my hair.

'Do you cook as well as you make love, Dr Corrigan?'

Fergus smiled, and sipped his wine. I could see his eyes do a circuit of the towel wrapped round me, unwrapping it.

'You'd better be the judge of that, Mrs Hazlitt.'

'I shall look forward to it. I'm sure you've had plenty of practice.'

Life seemed to me entirely delicious at this moment. I finished drying my hair. Then I opened my wardrobe. There wasn't a great deal of choice: David had never exactly lashed out on designer clothes for me. He'd liked me to look sensible, though sometimes I'd managed to break the rules.

My eyes lit on an outfit I'd worn only once with David. I'd bought it in my free-and-easy days as a waitress, just after I'd lost my virginity, and perhaps in celebration of that, or in compensation for the experience having been so awful. It was a sort of pyjama job, Indian, in shiny white silk caught at the ankles. A loose white cotton top went with it, cut square at the neck rather deep – a great deal too deep for David's liking. The only time he'd seen me wear it was to a Tory garden party with no bra underneath. Considering the company of middle-aged MPs this was unwise. Christ, it had been like Richmond Park in the rutting season. So many notes were slipped down my cleavage I'd felt like Juliet's tomb in Verona. Somehow they managed to fall right down to my ankles, and when I undressed that night they all tumbled out over the bedroom floor like voting papers. David didn't speak to me for nearly a week. And the Indian pyjama job was banished. It was back to powder-blue.

I put the outfit on and gazed at myself critically in the mirror. I realised my body must have filled out a curve or two since the days of the Tory garden party; 'matured' perhaps would be a more complimentary way of putting it. At any rate a note posted into my cleavage now would certainly stay where it was. I had a feeling Fergus's hands might like that. His eyes had hardly been off my breasts from the first moment he saw me.

Now it was just the final touches. I remembered that the

outfit went with a pair of gold sandals. I slipped these on, and above one of them I tied a gold anklet with a tiny bell, so he would hear me coming in the night (as if he hadn't heard me coming enough already – God, you're a vulgar woman, Claudia, I thought). Finally I added a heavy Indian necklace in chased silver which did an inviting swoop between my breasts, just in case the cotton top mightn't prove to be invitation enough.

I let my hair very loose, still glistening from the shower, and in the mirror my eyes looked especially large and dark beneath it. The *houri* look, I decided. I felt like one.

'Will this do?'

Fergus just gazed at me as I came down the stairs. His eyes travelled very slowly upwards from my anklet to my necklace, rested there for a moment, then met my own eyes. He gave a slight smile.

'Not bad for a nun.'

And then the phone went. I grabbed it.

'Claudia, I'm back,' came David's voice.

'Ah . . . well . . . really,' I said, glancing nervously at Fergus. 'How was the Dordogne?'

How on earth was I to get rid of him?

'I've had lots of new thoughts,' he went on. 'I'd like to come and see you, before the Commons are in session. Might we arrange that?'

I threw a look of horror and raised my eyes to the ceiling. Fergus rose from the sofa, put down his empty wineglass and came and stood very quietly behind me, resting his hands on my hips.

'David, I'm sorry, but I'm just about to go out to dinner,' I said uncomfortably.

Suddenly I could feel Fergus's hands reach round under my blouse and cup my breasts. He lifted my hair and began to nibble at my neck. I almost dropped the phone.

'You're going out?' David was saying. 'Good. I'm so glad you've got friends,' he went on in that familiar patronising voice.

My nipples were being gently massaged between forefinger and thumb until they stood out like acorns.

'Yes,' I said. 'I'm . . . in . . . very . . . good . . . hands.'

One of those hands was already sliding down between my thighs. I could feel myself getting wet as involuntarily my hips began to twist and press against Fergus. I was aware of choked sounds coming from my lips.

'Are you quite sure you're all right, Claudia?' David was saying. 'You sound very breathless.'

'Yes . . . absolutely . . . all right,' I gasped.

'Oh, good.' And he went on talking. I was always so good with people, he assured me; everyone always said that in the constituency; they all missed me so much, and so did he. All the time Fergus's hands were stroking and exploring me until I could feel an orgasm about to explode inside me, and I just had time to blurt out, 'David, I really . . . do have . . . to go,' before I came, crashing the phone down as wave after wave of pleasure sent me collapsing on the sofa.

'God, you're a pig, Fergus,' I said, regaining my breath. 'That was my husband.'

'I know.' He tried to look contrite. Then he smiled, and took my hand. 'Shall we go?'

The church clock was striking eight as we sauntered towards the gatehouse arch. Fergus had eased my blouse off one shoulder and was resting his hand on the bare skin. This, I thought, was just the moment for the Reverend Pype to make his invitation to Harvest Thanksgiving, and as I heard the gate click ahead of me I hurriedly brushed the hand away.

But it was Joan.

We stopped. She stopped. She gazed from one to the other, then back again at Fergus. Her eyes widened, and her mouth dropped.

'This is Dr Corrigan,' I said rather foolishly. 'Fergus, this is Joan. She keeps bees here,' I added for some reason. And then, 'We're just going out to dinner.'

Joan was still looking at Fergus in his open shirt and and tight jeans. I could see her trying to will away some of those forty-two years, smoothing her blouse to make the most of her small breasts, and giving her red hair a casual toss. Then she looked at me again, her eyes taking in the gold anklet with the little bell, the cotton top pulled off one shoulder, the heavy necklace resting between my breasts, dark nipples undoubtedly showing through.

'So I see,' Joan said heavily. Then with a giggle, '*Bon appétit!*'

I smiled awkwardly, and we walked away.

'Is it really that obvious?' I said the moment we were out of earshot.

Fergus just smiled.

'Sex is always obvious, isn't it?' And he leant over and lightly bit my bare shoulder. 'What's your perfume? Giorgio?'

I looked at him sharply.

'I wonder how you know.'

'Just a guess.'

'Oh yes?'

I preferred not to think about it.

We stopped by a red two-seater parked near the wall of the old priory. He *would* have an open Alfa-Romeo, I thought. I noticed the GB plate, and wondered if he'd driven back from France in it just this afternoon, and who might have been in the other seat.

'I thought these were reserved for blondes,' I said, climbing in beside him.

Fergus glanced at me as we pulled on to the road. I'd come to recognise that amused half-smile, and wondered if he'd copied it from Harrison Ford.

'I make exceptions sometimes,' he said.

We turned eastwards out of the town towards Totnes. He drove fast. At traffic-lights other drivers gave us predatory looks – just as often women as men, to my annoyance, particularly since the women were invariably young and willowy, while the men were puffy and middle-aged. I'd never realised I was quite so competitive: it certainly wasn't a quality David had ever brought out.

'I've no idea where you're taking me,' I said contentedly, settling back into my seat and enjoying the wind in my hair.

Fergus gave me another glance.

'Do you want to know?'

'No.'

It was true. I wanted to know as little as possible. Each

time I found myself bursting with curiosity I tried to shut off my mind. This was my year of freedom. My vagrant year. What I longed for were all the experiences I'd never had in ten years of being married to David. I longed to make up for the drought. And I was determined to feel none of the ties and obligations that had suffocated me all those years. I didn't want domestic commitments or social bonds. I certainly didn't want marriage. I wanted to feel life in my veins, take what it had to offer without asking questions, give myself to whatever I wished. This evening on the summer grass had been entirely perfect. It had all happened as if by some divine accident, my phantom lover taking me in my dreams. It had cut through everything, all the niceties, politenesses, anxieties, self-questionings, all the social foreplay, all the cautionary tales spun out by well-wishers about how he'd certainly be married, a total shit, dump me tomorrow, probably be into whips and rubber masks, most likely a closet homosexual.

I didn't want to hear any of it. This was a high-voltage dream, and I was loving every moment of it. My whole body vibrated as if it had never been alive before. Perhaps it hadn't.

I put my hand inside his shirt as he drove.

'I like your body,' I said.

There was that private smile again.

'Good. Yours isn't so bad either.'

In retaliation I tweaked his chest-hairs. He responded by sliding his left hand inside my Indian pyjamas and running his forefinger under my pants and down to my clitoris. I bit my lip and closed my eyes

'Fergus, we'll crash.'

'What a way to go.'

I remembered I'd once counted the orgasms David had ever given me, and had never got beyond the fingers of one hand, and even those had been self-induced, 'after the event', as they say. Christ, I'd beaten that number already today – and the night hadn't even begun.

'Why are we turning on to a cart-track, Fergus? Is it something I did?'

'You'll see.'

The car bumped along a precipitous track overhung with

wild rhododendrons which from time to time brushed against the windscreen of the car, making me duck. Glancing down to my left, all I could make out were sheer rocks and the occasional glimmer of a stream far beneath us. I was glad Fergus had abandoned my clitoris for the steering-wheel. With his deep suntan and his blond hair blown back from his face, he looked absurdly handsome. I wanted to touch him again, then had visions of the car's wheels spinning upside-down on those rocks, and folded my hands carefully on my lap.

A thought crossed my mind. What on earth was so gorgeous a man doing being the author of a seven-hundred-page tome on the dissolution of the English monasteries? That was an enigma I couldn't fathom. But I rather enjoyed not knowing the answer: it meant that I knew even less about him, and that was the way I wanted it.

We rounded a headland, and suddenly there was the sea, mother-of-pearl and calm, shimmering in the late sun. And ahead of us where the track ended I could see a house, huddled against the rock. At first it seemed no more than a tiny cottage, in rough stone painted white, and with a slate roof. Then as we approached I saw that it spread out lengthways on the farther side: a long picture-window spanned what appeared to be an extension in reddish wood. And beyond that I could make out an open space, a terrace perhaps, with strange trees and cactus-like plants here and there, and a piece of sculpture of some kind just visible, mounted on a plinth overlooking the sea.

'This is it,' Fergus was saying, drawing the car up in front of a narrow door. 'Casa Corrigan. Used to be a coastguard's cottage. Now it guards me. Or I it. You'll like it.'

'I already do,' I said.

I had no idea what to expect. Since I hardly knew Fergus, how could I know what the place he lived in would be like? Or was it just one of the places he lived in, and somewhere else – in Exeter maybe – a large bustling house was filled with squabbling children, predatory students, and university wives gathering in Mrs Corrigan's businesslike kitchen to drink coffee from sensible brown mugs? But in that case why wasn't he there, the dutiful husband home from France, instead of sweeping up a new mistress into his love-nest overlooking the sea?

I was determined *not* to ask him.

'Why don't you explore?' Fergus said casually, as if there were no secrets. 'I'll get some food together. D'you like wild mushrooms? I bought them in France yesterday, in the market.' And he tipped a heap of shiny black mushrooms on to the wooden kitchen table. 'They look deadly, don't they? They're called Horns of Plenty. Seems appropriate, doesn't it?' And he turned towards me with that half-smile and ran his hands over my breasts and hips. 'I'll come and find you with a glass of wine. Then we can eat in the garden, if you could call it that.'

And he laughed.

The kitchen was small, part of the original cottage I imagined, with a single small window low down – little more than a porthole – from which all that was visible was the sea far below. But one of the inner walls had been broken through, and sliding glass doors led directly into the new extension which was flooded with light and filled with sofas and brightly coloured cushions, and a long pine table that was piled with papers and files. A computer and a CD player occupied a smaller table by the wall. Except for a massive stone fireplace in the centre, the wall itself seemed to be built entirely of books. As I skimmed the shelves I began to feel daunted: I counted four different languages in addition to English. The Italian ones I could manage easily enough. There were editions of Dante and Ariosto, biographies of people I'd never heard of, ancient-looking photographs of illegible documents. But the majority of the books – whether in Italian, German, French, Spanish or English – consisted of volumes of early history. Why did historians write at such inordinate length? I pulled out one particularly massive tome on the history of the Normans in Sicily. The author appeared to hold about a dozen professorships, all listed in italic print after his name. Then I noticed a dedication in a tiny neat hand: to 'Dottore Fergus Corrigan', followed by effusive Italian compliments suggesting that only with the help and guidance of his distinguished colleague could this work have been undertaken.

I realised that I'd never quite imagined this new man in my life to be a scholarly heavyweight, and felt a little anxious that such intellectual firepower as Raynes Park Comprehensive had equipped me with might prove painfully inadequate. If Fergus believed the mind to be an erogenous zone, I feared his interest in me might rapidly fade. What substitutes might there be for an intellect? I would need to work hard on that. Caroline, who had no intellect at all, might know the answer.

Turning my back on the books, I opened the sliding glass doors and wandered out into the garden. This was walled in on two sides by rock and seemed to consist largely of rock, across which swathes of brilliant coloured flowers draped themselves like fishing-nets. Benches were arranged round a wooden table in the centre, and on the third side ran a low stone wall, beyond which I could see that the garden must drop straight into the sea.

It occurred to me that this would be an ideal setting for a discreet murder: perhaps I should do Caroline a favour and invite the Legover woman here.

'You see what I mean,' Fergus was saying, his eyes following my gaze. 'It's not a garden; it's just a place to be, particularly just before the sun hits the sea. You wait.'

I began to explore the house, a little fearful that I might learn too much, and yet deeply intrigued. I made my way up the narrow staircase. The door facing me was open. It was the bathroom, very small, with a towel thrown over the rail, and a sponge-bag still unpacked. No clues there. I went back into the passage. The next door led into what I took to be the spare bedroom: just a single bed, with a wash-basin next to it, no towels, all rather bare except for a few severe photographs of old churches on the walls. I wondered if he'd taken them himself.

That left just one more door, which had to be Fergus's bedroom. It felt extremely odd to be entering my new lover's bedroom, particularly since I'd yet to share a bed with him. I hesitated for a moment, then opened the door cautiously. The room was a lot larger than I expected. There were bookshelves everywhere. Persian rugs on the floor. A large double bed neatly made-up, with several unpacked suitcases strewn across it. And, facing the bed, a mirror from floor to ceiling. Vanity, vanity, Dr Corrigan. I rather liked that: after all, he had a great deal to be vain about.

Next to the mirror stood a large wardrobe. Again I hesitated. Here was the moment of truth. I told myself firmly that it didn't matter to me in the very least if there were women's clothes hanging in that wardrobe.

I opened it. And there weren't any.

I tried the chest of drawers that stood beside the wardrobe. But there were no lacy panties, no bras, tights, trinkets. Just very male underpants and a pile of shirts and T-shirts.

It puzzled me. There was no getting away from it: here was a man who apparently lived alone. At least he lived alone *here* – or, if not alone, then he made sure the little admirers came and went without leaving a trace. After all, I would be doing the same, wouldn't I? A lover for the night, and then gone.

I couldn't resist feeling the bed. It was soft and firm, and I wondered which side I would sleep in. Then I gazed out of the window: I wanted to know what I would see in the morning light.

Fantasies, Claudia. Fantasies. I closed the door and made my way out into the garden. After the cool stone house the summer evening felt close and warm. The garden was small, like a cradle in the rock-face, and around me the brilliant flowers were catching the last of the sun. It was as though someone had taken a paintbrush and smeared the rocks red, pink and purple.

I gazed about me, but there was no sign of Fergus. I removed my Indian sandals and sat on the low wall overlooking the sea, my arms hugged round my knees. The only sound was a muffled thud of waves on the rocks far beneath me. The sun was low and huge above the horizon, and its reflection zigzagged across the water towards me like a sea-serpent, growing longer and paler as I looked. I'd never felt so far away from my old life. Everything around me seemed to exist purely for my senses. It was as though they'd never been alive before; as though my body had never been alive before.

On a sudden impulse I took off everything I wore except my gold anklet, and stood in the last of the sun. And as I gazed out at the sea I heard myself say – maybe I said it aloud – 'Well, David, here is your wife. Well, Fergus, here is your mistress.'

It was one of the most perfectly sensual moments of my life, waiting to be made love to as the sun went down.

Nothing told me he was even there until I felt his fingers run very softly down my bare back. And when I turned round, he was naked. I closed my eyes as the fingers continued to trace my body like braille: then he lifted me in his arms, and gently carried me to the carpet of scarlet flowers draped across the smooth rock. Our bodies crushed the flowers.

It was dark when he finally set out the wine and the wild mushroom risotto on the garden table, with a lantern which flickered over his nakedness. It was a still summer night under the stars, and his body was lithe and beautiful. I ate ravenously, and gazed at him across the table, wondering how many more times we'd make love before the night was over. How often could men do it? Virtually my only experience was of a man who could scarcely do it at all. Perhaps wine and food recharged the energies.

Both the risotto and the wine were finished when Fergus suddenly said with that half-smile, 'I haven't done you very well, have I? There's nothing to follow; all your fault – too many distractions.'

I smiled, and reached across the table to touch him; and suddenly the idea came to me, God knows from where.

'Why don't I do it? All I need is some honey, cinnamon and a few nuts.'

Fergus looked surprised, and got up. He went back into the kitchen, and in a few moments returned with the things I'd asked for.

'Great,' I said, taking them from him. 'Now, why don't you just lie down over there on the flowers? Whatever colour you like.' I laughed. He was looking even more surprised, but did as I asked without a word. I gazed down at him for a moment, then lowered myself astride him and very carefully began to spread honey along his prick with my fingers. As I felt it harden I added a pinch of cinnamon to the tip, and finally garnished my creation with flaked almonds. It looked wonderful rising into the lantern-light, and I smiled. 'You told me you were exhausted, Fergus,' I whispered; and I leant over and began to curl my tongue round it and lick off the honey and the nuts. 'Perhaps we should call this Resurrection Pudding. I may even add it to my holy cookbook.'

For a long while Fergus lay there groaning with admirable self-restraint, until suddenly he grasped my hips fiercely and tugged me towards him. And it was like riding a wild thing.

I'd never made love on top of a man, I realised some moments later as I lay there with my heart beating violently and my forearms resting on either side of him among the cool flowers. I could feel him limp inside me, and I raised my head and kissed him with a taste of honey.

I had no idea what time it was when he lifted me and carried me towards the house. But I was conscious of the stars, and the sound of the sea. And in the cool bed I fell asleep in his arms.

'Places do things to people, don't they?' Fergus said. He was gazing down at me and playing with my hair on the pillow. 'And I don't need to ask you what this place does to you.'

How long it had been daylight I had no idea. Fergus was stretched out next to me, propped up on one elbow. I reached out and ran a hand down his thigh.

'Must have been the wild mushrooms,' I murmured. 'Or the wine. Or, just possibly, you.'

He gave a chuckle.

'D'you want to sleep?'

I shook my head.

'I want to look at you.'

He smiled very gently, and stroked my breasts.

'And what do you see?'

'A lover,' I said, 'who makes me want to think of nothing else but making love. Shameless, isn't it?'

'Totally. And what's wrong with that?'

'Nothing. It's just that I've never felt it before.'

'Never?'

I shook my head.

'I probably shouldn't say that to you, should I? It'll make you even vainer than you are. But it's true.'

The intense blue eyes gazed at me searchingly.

'I wouldn't have believed it. But I'm glad.'

'Why wouldn't you?'

I looked up at him with curiosity. His eyes wandered over my body, and he rested one hand between my legs.

'Because of yesterday evening. You were amazing.' He leant over and kissed me. 'And if that's what ten years married to a capon does to you, I'm grateful I was around.'

'So am I,' I said quietly. 'Very.' I placed my hand over his hand, and closed my eyes. 'It's called hunger.'

We lay there for a while. Eventually Fergus murmured something about coffee, and I felt him get up off the bed. I heard him open the bedroom door and go downstairs.

Half-awake, I thought back to last night, bewildered that it could really have been me. What made me smile was remembering the hot glances David's colleagues in the House used to throw me, and all those whispered propositions at cocktail parties: it wasn't until now that I realised they'd all assumed I was a little raver in bed, and that David must have something unexpected under that sanitised exterior. Instead of which, apart from one brief affair I'd spent ten years as a cold fish on a slab, touched by nothing more unexpected than a half-cock of a thing every few months or so whenever David had made a successful speech in the House. And that, I'd always imagined, was me, the cold fish on a slab; and that, I'd imagined, was life. And oh God, was I wrong.

Was it possible that being sexually passive induced passivity in general, I wondered? And if so, might this account for my having done so little with my life during all those years with David? In which case the opposite might be equally true, which would explain the new energy and forcefulness I felt within me. The thought filled me with wonder and delight.

'Tell me, was I so very shocking?' I asked as Fergus wandered back into the bedroom bearing two cups of coffee.

He put down the coffee and gave me his private smile.

'You must have noticed how shocked I was.'

I reached up and curled my arms round him.

'Is that why you were so huge? I dread to think what would have happened if I'd added yeast.'

He laughed, and kissed my eyelids.

'Dangerous eyes you've got.'

'With you it's not just eyes, Dr Corrigan,' I said. 'Isn't that what they all say?'

He didn't answer. And I was glad: even as I said it I knew I didn't want an answer. It didn't matter to me what his life was. What Fergus gave me was something I'd never known. I no longer felt like a deprived woman. Depraved perhaps, but certainly not deprived. I now knew that my body was not a dead thing.

'It's extraordinary, isn't it,' Fergus was saying, 'that lust should be one of the seven deadly sins. Where would we be without it?'

'Married to my husband maybe,' I suggested.

Fergus gave me another wry look.

We had breakfast in the garden around lunchtime. The scarlet flowers draped across the rocks had a somewhat beaten-up appearance after our endeavours of last night, and my Indian outfit and golden sandals still lay strewn where I'd discarded them. Fergus had lent me his dressing-gown, which smelt deliciously male. Fergus himself was barefoot, with a white bath-robe wound loosely round him. Unshaven and rumpled, he had a fallen look about him. I didn't dare think what I looked like. I'd carefully avoided the mirror. How long did love-bites take to heal?

'What are you thinking about?' Fergus asked.

I hadn't realised I'd been thinking about anything. But now that he'd asked I was conscious of a curious thought that had been buzzing in my head ever since I woke up. I didn't know quite how to put it to him – it sounded too ridiculous: none the less it was there, and wouldn't go away. It was triggered off by the remark Fergus had made while I was still half-awake. 'Places do things to people, don't they?' he'd said. Well, maybe it was true. I knew what this place did to me, as the detritus around me demonstrated only too well. But it was also the gatehouse and the old priory. Might there not be something about the spirit of that place which had induced me to enjoy erotic daydreams in the meadow, and then make violent love with a man I scarcely knew? *Genius loci*, wasn't that the phrase?

If it were true that such a thing existed, then there could only be one presiding genius at Norton Abbas, and that was a phallus.

'I was thinking about a tree,' I said.

Fergus gazed at me quizzically.

'A tree. I see. A Christmas tree? A family tree? The Tree of Life?'

He was enjoying humouring me.

'One that's like your prick, only quite a lot bigger, I'm sorry to say.'

He smiled.

'Probably just as well. But what d'you mean?'

I told him about the phallic yew-tree in the priory garden, adding that the secretary of Saintly Tours had claimed it was a Tree of Jesse, but after close inspection of the real thing I was now totally convinced it was a prick.

I imagined Fergus would mock me, suggesting that any woman who'd been married to a eunuch for ten years would be bound to see pricks wherever she looked. But he didn't. He looked intrigued and very serious.

'Describe it to me.'

Never having been asked to describe a phallus before, I decided that the best thing was to demonstrate. I reached over and pulled his dressing-gown aside, and held his penis between my fingers. Fergus looked surprised, but didn't stir, though the penis began to.

'Well,' I said, 'it's got a trunk which rises up . . . like this.'

'Jesus, Claudia.'

I was trying not to laugh.

'Then it goes all smooth and broadens out into a kind of rim all the way round . . .'

'Claudia.'

'. . . before tapering in at the very top . . . Fergus . . . Fergus, I'm sore!'

It hurt, but I suppose I deserved it. I could have done with some honey. It was also uncomfortable among the breakfast things.

'You're a devil, aren't you?' Fergus said, struggling to regain his breath.

I removed one arm from among the coffee-cups.

'And you're also terrific,' he added, laughing.

'I was only trying to answer your question,' I said, getting up painfully from the table. 'You did ask.'

Fergus began rather shakily to clear away the chaos of breakfast.

'I'll make some more coffee. I think we could do with it.'

When he returned a few minutes later he had a mischievous expression on his face. He put down the tray and seated himself on the wooden bench opposite me. I noticed that next to the pot of fresh coffee and the cups lay a thick folder of papers.

'After all that love-making I think it's time I told you a story,' he said. 'D'you mind?'

I shook my head. Whatever it was, I felt sure it was nothing compared to the story I would have to tell Caroline about this weekend, if I ever dared.

'Don't ask me whether it's a true story, because I don't know. It could be,' he went on, looking at me very intently. 'It's about the secret of Norton Abbas, and why your tree fits in perfectly. You have to show it to me, by the way. The real thing this time, not the demonstration model.'

Fergus gave a laugh and sipped his coffee.

'This is detective work. And I love it,' he said. 'There's not a historian in England who'd believe what I've come up with; but then most historians have the minds of librarians. No imagination. For me the only true history is fiction: we know so little of what really went on that we need to fill the gaps, which is why I wrote *Cardinal Error*, and thank God I did; it bought me this place.'

This sudden change of mood in someone who'd been screwing me on the breakfast table ten minutes earlier was thoroughly confusing, but I was listening.

He looked at me mischievously.

'So, the story will probably end up as another novel,' he went on, 'and people can believe it or not as they like.'

Again I felt I was being invited to be a fellow conspirator. Or I was already being woven into his fiction – the mistress-heroine of his imagination – and perhaps I didn't really exist for him outside it? It was curious feeling, and yet I realised it suited me. It kept Fergus the way I wanted him, my phantom lover.

'Here it is then. The outline, OK?' And he swept his hands through his hair before placing them in front of him on the table like book-ends. 'There's a letter in the British Museum,' he began, 'written by one of the advisers to Henry VIII's chief minister, Thomas Cromwell. It's dated 1537, exactly the moment when Cromwell was in charge of smashing the English monasteries. The letter's mostly about the need for drawing up an inventory of monastic possessions; but in the course of this it acknowledges – almost in passing – that of course Cromwell appreciates that the nunnery at Norton has a certain power over the king, as if this were common knowledge at the royal court, and the king's chief minister needed to be careful. There's no mention of what that power was, and no one has ever been able to find out.'

Fergus was beginning to look extremely pleased with himself. Then he reached for the folder on the table in front of him and pulled out a sheet of paper.

'This is where my detective work comes in,' he continued, holding up the sheet of paper. 'I copied this out in the Bodleian Library in Oxford, just before I went to France. It's a mish-mash of a manuscript called "Ashmole 61", but I seemed to remember that it contained transcriptions of various documents relating to Norton Priory, mostly the equivalent of laundry bills. But then I came across this.' And Fergus handed me the sheet of paper. 'It's a recipe for quince honey. Evidently the nuns used to make it at Norton. For some reason the recipe is a twelfth-century translation from the Greek. Presumably it must have been brought over from the Eastern Mediterranean at some earlier date, and then someone at the priory translated it. So it was obviously considered to be valuable. But why?'

I tried to read it, but by and large it seemed to make almost complete nonsense. I handed it back to Fergus, who smiled rather patronisingly and read it out aloud.

Take quynces ripe and pare and heue hem smal,
And al for smal, but kest away the core.
In honey thene upboile hem, lese and more
De pepur with yt boyling, smalest grounds,
This is the first mannere, the seconds
Is to boil with honey till well thicke,
Thene largelich for meruelles the satur rote.

He looked up at me. I made a face.

'What the hell does all that mean? What language is it supposed to be?'

Fergus continued.

'It's called Middle English. The sort of language Chaucer used.'

'For Christ's sake, I'm Italian. How am I supposed to know things like that? Now you've shown off, Dr Corrigan, how about giving me a translation?'

He gave a chuckle, and replaced the sheet of paper in the folder.

'Well, most of it's just a straightforward recipe, interesting only because it tells us they grew quinces. They're still there after all, or their successors are. And that they kept bees: your friend Joan still does, when she's not calculating how many times we'd already made love that afternoon.'

I wished he wouldn't look so darned pleased with himself. I was the one who had to face Joan after all, not him. And she'd be merciless, insist on knowing everything. I put on a grumpy face. But Fergus wasn't looking.

'The really interesting bit is the last line,' he went on. 'There's the real clue. "Largelich" is a survival from Anglo-Saxon, meaning "generously". "Meruelles" – the "u" is a "v" – means "marvels" or "miracles". So, in order to produce miracles from this dish, you need to add generous amounts of . . . of what? Well, the magic ingredient is something called "satur rote". "Rote" means "root". Of a plant obviously. And "satur" is "satyr".'

Fergus looked at me enquiringly across the table.

'Now, how many bells does that ring, Claudia?'

My irritation had evaporated. Maybe this was only the seeds

of a novel, but I could feel myself drawn into it. After all, there was the carved satyr above my gatehouse, with its chopped-off penis, as Joan had pointed out. There was all that copulatory stuff round the church roof. And there was the phallic yew-tree in the topiary garden, which I needed to show Fergus. And now this.

'Seriously, are you telling me that the nuns at Norton Priory used to make aphrodisiacs?' I asked. 'Is that it?'

Fergus raised his eyebrows and gazed questioningly at me.

'It would seem like it, wouldn't it? That's my theory anyway. And now let me run with it and see what you think. First of all, what do we know? Well, there's this mysterious letter to Thomas Cromwell reminding him that the priory has a special power over the king. And it's 1537, just as the monasteries are in the process of being dissolved, with the king pocketing the loot. But wait a minute, 1537 is also the year Henry's son was born. His long-awaited son. The future Edward VI. So, maybe there's a connection there, between Edward's birth and this supposed power the priory is said to have over the king. After all, we have this curious recipe from the priory for something that's said to produce "miracles". Mightn't the "miracle" be the royal son and heir? In other words Henry had been gorging himself on this aphrodisiac which the nuns provided for him. Makes sense. It was popular folklore at that time that male children were supposed to be the result of increased sexual ardour. And it worked for the king, didn't it?'

I had just about enough knowledge of English history to grasp some of this. But in any case I was riveted: Fergus was like a man on fire. His book seemed to be bursting out of him already. He drained his coffee and went on.

'So that was the power Norton had over the king. It had given him his son and heir. But hang on a minute. Edward was a sickly child, and not likely to live very long. In fact he died at sixteen. So wouldn't Henry have wanted another son to make quite sure? *We* know he had syphilis, the poor bugger, but *he* didn't. And the only way to ensure another son, as he saw it, was to use the magic powers of Norton Priory. All the other monasteries could be looted and destroyed, but not this one. It was special.'

Fergus paused, looking extremely contented.

'Well, there you are,' he went on. 'And *that's* why the nunnery survived, at least until the Puritans a century later, who weren't exactly into aphrodisiacs. That's my theory anyway. How does it grab you?'

I laughed.

'I just love the idea of the National Trust owning an aphrodisiac factory. Will you tell them?'

'God, no. And you'd better not tell your husband either, particularly if he's likely to be the environment minister. I can just see him getting up in the House and spluttering about love-potions. Mind you, from what you say he could clearly do with one.'

It was mid-afternoon. The sun was pouring on to the little cradle of a garden, burning off the rocks. Fergus went indoors to fetch suntan lotion. When he came back the mischievous expression had returned.

'You know about plants, Claudia, don't you?' he said, gently smoothing Ambre Solaire on my face and arms, then peeling my dressing-gown aside and doing the same to my breasts. I closed my eyes. 'Do you happen to know about aphrodisiacs?'

I shivered as his fingers began to circle my nipples.

'Yes, I do,' I said breathlessly. 'And they're wonderfully effective right now.'

Fergus completed the massage and sat back back to admire his handiwork. I looked down at my body and it shone like a *Playboy* centrefold. Not bad for thirty-two, I thought. Living with David I'd begun to feel forty-two, and rising sharply. I tried to remember if in all those ten years he'd ever touched my breasts, and I could recall only once, when he was thrilled at being appointed a PPS. Fergus's eyes were more of a turn-on than David's hands had ever been.

'"Satur rote",' he said, still gazing at me. 'The root of the satyr plant. You've got no idea at all what that might be?'

I shook my head, and he looked thoughtful.

'Then we need to find out, don't we?' he said. 'Some historical research.'

'For your book?'

'Perhaps.'

'And what d'you think you'll call it?' I asked.

Fergus gazed at me with those intense blue eyes without saying anything for a moment. It was as though he were trying to wring the title out of looking at me, drawing me into his fiction. There was something possessive about that gaze. It frightened me a little; and I loved it.

'Perhaps it shouldn't be set in the past at all,' he said reflectively, 'but take place now. The search for the secret, and what happens.' He laughed. 'I think I'll call it *The Devil's Work*.'

I felt entirely foolish walking towards the gatehouse in my Indian outfit and golden sandals just as the congregation were emerging from evensong. The Revernd Pype was among them, thin hands clasped against his chest, a pallid smile on his lips. He saw me, and the smile withered. Then I caught sight of Glyn, who waved cheerfully.

I closed the gate behind me gratefully . . . and there was Joan. She was striding towards me across the meadow with that bouncy walk of hers, clutching her bee-keeping gear and wearing her usual leather boots and pale-blue jeans. Her hair was frothy and tousled. She stopped abruptly when she saw me. Her head did a sudden jerk, and a look of wonder crept over her face as she gazed at my outfit. Then she cocked her head on one side and let out a throaty laugh.

'A bit slow bringing the bill then, were they?' she said loudly, and laughed again. 'But then I'm afraid the service is terrible round here, isn't it?'

And to make matters worse she just walked off, still laughing.

Oh well, what did I expect? I asked myself as I wandered into the house. I plucked up courage to look in the mirror, and promptly closed my eyes. God Almighty! A very high neckline for you over the next week or so, dear girl, I muttered to myself. I ran a bath and lay there soaking, raising first one leg out of the water and then the other, trying not to count the bruises.

I found myself wondering what Fergus was thinking now as he drove back to his hide-out on the cliff. Was he congratulating himself on his new catch, one more notch on the bedhead?

Was he making comparisons, awarding Brownie points? Legs.
Breasts. Eyes. Hair. Appetite. Nine out of ten perhaps, all in all.
One point deducted for my not having fallen helplessly in love
with him. Though maybe he preferred it that way, not having
a soggy doormat to walk all over. And certainly there'd be a
bonus point for initiative; I couldn't imagine any of his other
ladies had ever served him Resurrection Pudding.

I winced as I thought of it. What on earth had got into me?
Well, *he* did, I suppose. That made me laugh. I ran some more
hot water, and felt better.

So, where did I go from here? Possibly nowhere. But even as
I considered that, I found myself doubting it. I wasn't certain
what it was, but there was something about Fergus which
suggested more than the charming reprobate. One had only
to look at him to know how much he liked women, how much
he enjoyed being fancied by them, toying with them, making
love to them. And I was sure that his women were by and
large interchangeable, merely the sum of various desirable
parts which came in a pleasing variety of sizes and shapes,
each reacting a little differently to his attentions in subtle
ways, thereby preventing monotony. They were a slightly
changing menu, and perhaps changed every day as in any
good restaurant.

And yet there was something more. Maybe it was just my
own vanity, matching his vanity. But it was as though he
were casting a net around me, wanting me as a mistress –
most of all that, without any doubt; but also as a rather
special possession, to be valued for rather special reasons.
What those reasons were I found it hard to fathom, except
that they seemed to be to do with this place and what his
imagination was making of it. It was as if he were asking
me to be his invention, his necessary heroine. I was his
dark swan.

The thought made me laugh: it was like being fucked
between the covers of a book. But it also surprised and
excited me. After all, if I was to be part of his floating world,
wasn't this my floating year? I'd cast away all my anchors.
I'd wanted the drift of chance to carry me on its currents, to
feed on experiences as they came my way. Never to withdraw

from them, but to indulge, if necessary over-indulge; and then maybe one day to wake up knowing who I really was.

Was this merely romantic slush, I wondered? Perhaps it would all just drift away on the tide, leaving me with foolish and wonderful memories.

Before I had a chance to decide, the phone rang. I reached out of the bath and picked up the hand-phone.

'Jesus Christ!' came a bellow in my ear.

The sound was deafening. I hadn't even spoken a word. Caroline sounded furious.

'Where the fuck have you been? Come over. I've got a million things I need to tell you. What the hell have you been doing all weekend?'

I curled my big toe round the chain of the bath-plug, and pulled it.

'Making love,' I said.

Seven

One day the honey buzzards had gone, and I knew it was autumn. 'To Africa,' Glyn said in his knowing way. 'They'll be back in the spring provided they don't get shot to bits all over Europe.'

The pilgrims had mostly gone too, back to wherever pilgrims go, taking with them a great many of my herbs and reassuring quantities of *St Cuthburga's Cookbook*. Glyn was excited about the idea of a second edition. 'Make it fatter,' he urged me. And he pressed half a dozen of his own recipes on me. 'Most saintly, I assure you,' he said with a twinkle. '*Coq au vin* with communion wine, things like that. Megan'll do the illustrations for you.'

I also had a few new recipes of my own. The question was, dare I include Resurrection Pudding? I loved the blasphemous vulgarity of the idea, but since the book brought in a fair slice of my modest income I couldn't afford to have it seized under the Obscene Publications Act. I confided the problem to Joan, whose eyes grew as round as saucers when I described what the dish consisted of, and how I'd come to invent it.

'Jesus,' she said in a startled voice. 'Well, that has to be a first for Norton Abbas. *And* a novel use for my honey. Yes, of course you must include it in the book. You may have to tart it up a bit, as it were. And Megan will love making the drawing.' Joan looked reflective for a moment. 'I wonder who she'll use as a model. I don't imagine it's Glyn's sort of thing, do you?' She chuckled. 'We could give the Reverend Pype a signed copy for Christmas. He could do with some resurrecting.'

We were standing on my terrace drinking wine. If we hadn't already got through the best part of a bottle I doubt if I'd have told her about my weekend with Fergus. She'd been pressing me about it for weeks, irritated that I'd already told Caroline, and doubly irritated that all Caroline would volunteer was 'Well, they didn't play tiddlywinks, darling. What d'you expect?'

'I'm just bloody envious,' Joan said moodily, sipping her wine. 'D'you realise I haven't had an affair since before the flame-throwers were born? Sixteen years. Jesus!' She laughed. 'And then I went and married him. Mind you, I had to.' She looked at me crossly. 'I tell you, Claudia, it's a real curse being the faithful type.'

I kept my lip buttoned. According to Caroline, Joan spent much of her time trying to get Patrick into bed. Who was telling the truth, I wondered? Caroline's own reaction to my weekend was entirely in character. She stopped swimming, hauled herself out of the pool stark naked, and glared at me.

'Right,' she said, dripping water over the table where her champagne glass stood empty. 'Just remember you're my tenant, Claudia. So the next time you make Resurrection Pudding I insist on a tasting in lieu of rent, OK?'

She then went on to tell me about the county planning officer whom she'd invited over, hoping to put a stop on the National Trust's plans for converting Priory Hall.

'I'm afraid I may have blown it,' she said. Then she gave one of her ringing laughs. 'Not like you with Resurrection Pudding, darling, I assure you, though I'm sure he'd have liked that. Dreadful little man with a beer belly. Can you believe it, he imagined the real reason I'd got him over was to get a good fuck. He actually took out his willy and said did I know what it was. I said, "Well, Mr Tinsley, looks like a penis to me, only smaller." He zipped up and hurried away after that, looking furious.'

Caroline gave a sigh, and waved to Carmen to bring out the champagne bottle.

'I was feeling quite shaken,' she went on. 'I mean, I'm happy to enjoy a man's willy as much as the next woman, but please! Not on a county planning officer with a beer belly. I'd almost rather have Patrick.'

I tried not to smile as I watched Caroline standing there, still dripping from the pool, a towel slung vaguely over her naked torso as she held out a glass to Carmen who appeared to find this behaviour entirely normal.

'Caroline,' I said, feeling doubtful about this story, 'I can't believe county planning officers normally flash their cocks at ladies in the execution of their duties. What did you actually say to the man?'

Caroline gave me a haughty look.

'Say? I merely said I'd be grateful to anyone who could help me. Maybe I said I'd do *anything* for such a person. But that was all.' The haughty look wilted a little. 'It is true that the top button of my blouse came undone as I bent over to show him the National Trust's plans. But even so, one does expect a certain finesse from these chaps.'

'You mean your boobs fell out,' I said.

'How crude you are, darling. I couldn't help it, could I?' She gave a proud sniff. 'Anyway, thank God I looked at the man's card after he'd gone, and discovered he was only the assistant county planning officer. So I got straight on the phone to his boss and insisted he come and see me himself. "And if you're going to flash your cock at me," I said, "I trust it's more adequate than your assistant's." There was a heavy silence on the other end, and then he promised to fit me in on Friday. Well, that made me roar with laughter, and he spluttered a bit. So I may have blown it after all. Ah well,' Caroline added with a shrug, 'if all else fails I'll just have to go straight to the ministry, won't I?' Suddenly an expression of horror came over her face. 'Oh Christ, that's your husband, isn't it?'

'Not yet,' I said. 'But you'd better hurry. He rang to tell me it's "promised" at the next government shake-up.'

I got up to leave soon after that.

'You're always rushing off these days,' Caroline called out after me. 'Ever since you found yourself a lover, damn you!'

It was true I was spending less time with Caroline. And it *was* related to Fergus. I never knew when he might appear. Sometimes he'd phone, but more often he just turned up. The university term was imminent, and he was working hard in Exeter, he said casually. I never asked him anything more. .I never even knew what kind of domestic set-up he had in Exeter, and I chose not to know.

Sometimes he only stayed an hour or two, and I'd throw

some supper together for us; or he'd turn up with a lobster or smoked salmon, and calmly take over the kitchen. Sometimes he stayed the night, and we'd make love in my huge bed beneath the carved *Kama Sutra*, which Fergus would examine with keen interest, hoping – I suggested – he might learn a few new tricks.

At first we'd lie there naked all night. Now, as the nights grew cooler, I'd throw a duvet over us before we slept. And I'd snuggle under it next to him and wrap my arms round his chest.

I was happy. It seemed absurd to realise that it had taken me until the age of thirty-two to learn what love-making could be like. I'd always imagined it was only men who couldn't do without it (David excepted, that is), and that women fell into it, so to speak, in order to please them. That had certainly been Anna-Maria's philosophy of life, if not her experience; and nothing in my own life had ever put it to the test. But now, if three or four days passed without Fergus appearing, my appetite would be entirely shameless; it was straight upstairs. And as I scattered my clothing across the bedroom floor I'd find myself wondering how I could possibly have lived with my husband for ten long years, those desert years marked out by striped pyjamas and midnight snoring. Christ, they might have gone on for ever.

Occasionally Fergus would sweep me off to the coastguard's cottage on the cliffs. The scarlet flowers were dead by now, and it was too cold to make love in the garden. Fergus would light a fire, and we'd lie in front of it propped against the sofa. We'd talk idly, and then the firelight playing on naked skin would suddenly stop us talking.

'D'you always buy your condoms from the same chemist?' I asked one evening. 'Doesn't he give you a peculiar look?'

Fergus looked surprised, and then laughed.

'You make it sound as though we're abnormal,' he said.

Perhaps because it was such a strange new world for me, I'd rather assumed we were. But maybe it was just abnormal for me. I'd never met anyone who liked to make love all the time. Caroline talked as if she did, but I'd noticed there was a distinct absence of lovers in her life, except of course in the past, and maybe they were mostly talk too, like the Italian racing driver with three balls. Caroline's life was like a theatre of love which rarely seemed to get beyond the rehearsal stage. She had an erotic mind, but I was beginning to think she found the real thing rather messy; hence her dismissive treatment of Patrick, who all too evidently did have a sex life. Jesus, each time he came down for the weekend his eyes would strip me naked.

Fergus's eyes did just the same, though in his case it worked. It was as if our clothes were simply items of provocation, attractive wrappings inviting instant removal. We lived as two bodies which enjoyed one another, and I wondered how long it would last, and what might there be left once the fires had died down? Two people who had nothing whatever to say to one another? I knew I didn't believe that. I was playing the old truck of raising a fear in order to enjoy the comfort of dismissing it. I had a shrewd feeling that, given a chance, Fergus and I would have things to share for the rest of our lives. And that prompted a greater fear – that we would never have such a chance. It would be suicidal for me to even hope for it.

Other thoughts played in my head during those early autumn days. I kept remembering Fergus's remark after we'd spent our first night together. 'Places do things to people, don't they?' he'd said suddenly. That was before he'd told me his theory about the old priory, and why it had been protected by Henry VIII when all the others were being pulled down. And he'd produced that weird recipe for quince honey which he claimed was an aphrodisiac. If only he could discover what the magic ingredient was, he kept insisting. I remembered the name: 'satur rote', the root of the satyr plant. Fergus was going to consult the botany department at the university, he said, to see if they could throw any light on the mystery.

Was it all true, or was it an elaborate fantasy he was constructing in order to write a book about it? *The Devil's Work*, he wanted to call it, with me as heroine, he'd suggested. So I wasn't only his mistress, I was also his fiction. I was beginning to feel like Alice in Wonderland, no longer certain what was real around me. Supposing I was only behaving as I did because of this place: all those pricks everywhere, the tree, the satyr above the arch, the *Kama Sutra* above my bed. And Fergus's prick was one more. Perhaps I'd been bewitched, by Fergus and by this place, and the Devil really had got into me. This was undoubtedly what David would think. Anna-Maria might well agree, and suggest I needed a good Bolognese sausage-maker to sort me out. Well at least, I decided, that would be a better fate than being burnt as a witch, as I certainly would have been a few hundred years ago, and as no doubt the Reverend Pype would like me to be right now.

What kept me anchored to reality was the thought that, bewitched or not, I was damned if I was going to return to David, and somehow I needed to survive and pay the rent. So, with the danger of night-frosts becoming imminent I began to move all my remaining herbs, pots and hanging-baskets into the long greenhouse.

Thankfully Megan appeared in time to lend me a hand. She was in an unusually serious mood: there was none of the customary monologue which invariably reminded me of dominoes, a chain of haphazard conjunctions which only ended when there were no more pieces to play. It wasn't until the plants had all been safely stored away that she finally revealed what was on her mind. She picked up her shoulder-bag from the terrace where she'd left it, delved inside it, and pulled out a small folder.

'You've set me an artistic problem,' she announced portentously, clasping the folder to her ample tweeds. 'It's your bloody Resurrection Pudding – how to illustrate it. Glyn says I need to remember that the book is designed for the eyes of the pious, and therefore I should disguise the anatomy of the beast; which is all very well, but as *what*? How can you disguise a penis, for God's sake? I don't know why the hell you couldn't have smeared honey and cinnamon over some other part of your lover's body.'

Megan was looking quite aggrieved, and began to mutter as she fumbled inside the folder.

'Well, here's one idea,' she said grumpily, handing me a sheet of paper.

I gazed at it, and burst out laughing.

'Oh Megan,' I gasped. 'Well, at least a French loaf fits the title. Bread does rise, after all. But what's that funny bit at the end?'

Megan clicked her tongue and snatched the sheet of paper from my hand.

'It's an uncircumcised loaf, can't you see?'

I was doubled up. Megan just stood there with her hands on her hips, glaring at me, her face flushed with irritation.

'Well, it's obvious you've got absolutely no idea what it's like being an artist,' she growled. 'All right, you don't like it. What about this, then?'

And she pulled out another sheet from the folder. Then, just as she was about to hand it to me, I saw her mouth quiver, and her eyes begin to water. And as she continued to gaze at the sheet of paper her entire body started to tremble. She shook her head, and small spluttering noises issued from her mouth. In alarm I thought for a moment she might be having a fit; but then the spluttering noises turned to gulps of laughter, and a huge grin spread across her face.

'I can't . . . I can't believe I've done this,' she said between gulps. 'I always thought it was stupid idea, but Glyn was so insistent. So I persisted. And look what I persisted with.'

She thrust the sheet of paper at me, and there, rampant and bright yellow except for its coating of nuts, was an enormous banana.

'And that's not all,' she went on, waving another sheet in front of me. 'How's this for a meringue?'

A long white object rose up the page.

'It looks exactly like the Leaning Tower of Pisa,' I suggested, 'with the tourists as nuts.' And suddenly I felt awful. I threw my arms round Megan. 'God, I'm sorry,' I said. 'I'm being really unkind. I should never have asked you. And you were trying to be so helpful.'

Megan stepped back and gazed at the three sketches, one after the other. Then she swept her hair back from her eyes, and looked at me.

'No, you're perfectly right. Imagination's not my forte. I should stick to flowers and mistresses.' She gave another glance at the three sketches. 'So, what shall we do with these ridiculous things?' She looked at me questioningly; then her face brightened. 'Oh, I know.'

With that she turned on her heel and clumped purposefully down the path and across the open meadow, waving her three sheets of paper in the air as she did so.

'Jehoshaphat,' I heard her call out. 'Jehoshaphat, dinnertime.'

And as I watched Megan's brave art-works disappearing into my melancholy goat, I knew that St Cuthburga would not after all be exhorting next year's Saintly Tours to practice fellatio on their loved ones. And I swear that a small tremor of piety overcame me at the thought.

Anna-Maria would have been proud of me.

The small private study where Caroline did almost anything except study now sported a notice painted on the door, 'The War Room'. The table which filled at least half the room was awash with papers and correspondence, some of it arranged in folders marked vividly in red biro 'Literary Conference', 'County Planners', 'Solicitors', 'Historic Buildings Commission', 'Legover Bumf' and – to my surprise – 'Husband', to which she'd added in brackets 'Patrick' as if at first she'd forgotten his name.

It was clear that Caroline was waging her war on many fronts. She even dressed for the part, having taken to wearing a voluminous beige garment which reminded me of wartime photos of Churchill's siren-suit, except that where it should have been buttoned it frequently wasn't, leaving any visiting member of her war cabinet in no doubt that Caroline liked to wear nothing whatsoever underneath. I was reminded less of Winston Churchill than of an early James Bond film.

'The first thing we have to do is to hold off the enemy,' she announced, tossing her blonde hair back over her shoulders in a defiant gesture. 'I've been reading a lot about siege warfare, and the trick if you're besieged is to make sure you've got plenty of food and drink to last you till winter sets in, by which time the buggers attacking you will have to piss off or have their balls frozen off.' She laughed. 'Well, thanks to Marks & Spencer's we've got the food, and thanks to my father we've got the drink.'

And she reached over to a cupboard marked 'Battlefield Rations' and pulled out a half-empty bottle of vodka.

'What this means, Claudia,' she went on, plunging one hand into the ice-bucket and dropping a heap of cubes into two glasses, 'is that if I can keep the builders at bay for another couple of months it'll be winter and they won't be able even to think about tearing the place apart until the spring. And I'm pretty sure I've managed that OK.' She sloshed vodka plentifully over the ice, filled up the glasses with tonic, and threw me a lime to cut up. 'I insisted the National Trust let me approve the builders. Well, that's been easy so far: I simply don't approve any of them. "This is a historic building," I explain. "I can't have just any old bunch of yahoos whistling and farting around the place." The Trust are getting extremely cross with me, but why should I give a fuck? Cheers.'

I refused the second mega-vodka, but Caroline was clearly fuelled by hers. I remembered reading that Churchill was plastered throughout the war, and still won it. So perhaps this was a good omen.

Caroline reached for the folder marked 'Historic Buildings Commission', which I noticed had a fair number of wine-stains splashed across it.

'I'm also galvanising this lot,' she said, pulling out a sheaf of letters and flicking through them with her fingers. 'They may be just another useless quango, but they're finding out for me if there's some law prohibiting a "change of use" for a Grade I listed building. Priory Hall isn't actually Grade I, though it soon will be: Patrick's father decides on the listing. Which reminds me, I must tell him to pull his finger out or I'll withdraw marital rights from his son, which would be no great matter, I can tell you.'

There was another of her rippling laughs, washed down with a slug of vodka.

'Then there's that bloody Legover woman.' Caroline reached for yet another folder. 'A total pain in the arse, she is. D'you know, Claudia' – and she thrust a letter in my direction – 'she's actually threatening to have me evicted if I don't take down the portraits of my father's mistresses? *Evicted* from my own house. The cheeky bitch. So, shall I tell you what I'm doing? I'm opening the Hall of the Mystresses to the public the weekend after next: I've put an ad in all the local papers and the *Telegraph* have agreed to send a reporter. The BBC are covering it too: Marmaduke promised me. A pound a head: that's pretty reasonable for all that flesh, don't you think? And I'm getting some T-shirts printed with Megan's portraits on them: "tit-shirts" I suppose I ought to call them. Would you be prepared to stand at the door modelling one, Claudia? Oh, please do. You'd look terrific. And I'd pick the one who looks most like you, that busty little tart from Puerto Rico. Sorry, that sounds rude, doesn't it? I didn't mean to be. Have another drink.'

Caroline's schemes continued to pour out as liberally as her vodka. Scarcely a day now passed without her summoning her war cabinet. Besides herself it consisted of me, Megan, Joan, Patrick if he happened to be down for the weekend, and some-times an outside 'adviser' whom Caroline had dragged in.

The first of these was her new solicitor, Justin Whittaker. Caroline had evidently abandoned her efforts to get the young man into bed, having transferred her gaze to the county planning officer – the real one this time – who she claimed looked exactly like Paddy Ashdown.

'I decided Justin had guilt where other men have balls,' she explained languidly while we were in the kitchen mak-ing coffee.

As usual Caroline treated men she'd ceased to fancy with abrasive contempt. If the poor man did have any balls, I thought, they would certainly have run for cover by now.

'Well, Justin,' she announced, sweeping back into the War Room with the tray of coffee, 'what other ways of challeng-ing the will have you managed to come up with after all this time?'

The young man looked her courageously in the eye.

'It's not easy to challenge a legitimate will, Mrs Uppingham,' he replied, 'unless—'

Caroline interrupted him.

'Legitimate!' She gave one her special laughs. 'My dear man, nothing in my family has ever been legitimate, including me. You know that.'

'I was about to say,' the solicitor continued with just a touch of irritation, '*unless* one can prove that there were "unacceptable motivations", for which I'm afraid there's no evidence in this case, or unless it can be shown that Admiral Romsey was not of sound mind at the time he made it.'

Caroline gave another hoot of laughter.

'Of sound mind? My father? You must be joking. He was as nutty as a fruitcake, the old bastard.'

The solicitor lowered his eyes and coughed into his hand.

'Then there would need to be independent witnesses prepared to testify about his mental state, Mrs Uppingham. Doctors perhaps. The family lawyer. The vicar.'

There was a snort from Caroline. Then she yawned. I could see that her mind was already elsewhere. She wasn't going to win this one, and she knew it.

'Ah, Justin,' she said in a tired voice, 'the gods are not on my side, are they? The only witnesses I could possibly call would testify to the one and only thing that was ever sound about my father, his prick!'

I knew that this would be the last time any of us would see young Justin Whittaker.

'Did you think my father was "of sound mind", Megan?' Caroline enquired as the solicitor's car disappeared down the avenue of lime-trees. I could have sworn it looked relieved.

'I'm afraid so, Caroline,' Megan replied.

'Joan?'

A nod came from Joan.

Caroline gave a long sigh. Then she picked up the folder labelled 'Solicitors' and flung it on the floor. She glared at it for a moment, then she swept out into the corridor. Facing the open door was a photograph of the admiral in full dress uniform which she'd hung as a kind of *entrée* to the Hall of the Mystresses. He was like a sultan standing majestically at the entrance to his harem.

Caroline stood gazing at it for a while. Then I saw that she was shaking. She raised one hand above her head as though she was about to slash the photograph with her nails. Instead she reached forward and very gently brushed a speck of dust from his cheek.

'Oh, Father,' I heard her whisper.
And she placed her hands over her face.

If I thought Caroline was about to crack up. I soon learnt that I should never underestimate her. Having drawn a blank with her young solicitor – professionally and sexually – she'd now decided to beam her attentions on both fronts towards her new-found friend the county planning officer.

'Jesus, he's a hunk,' she exclaimed. 'I could eat him. That wonderfully battered look, battered from having had just about every woman in the county, I bet. Anyway I've invited him to dinner. And Claudia, you must tell me what to wear.'

For once Caroline had paid *me* a visit at the gatehouse. It was late in the afternoon, and a low mist was settling over the meadow, with Jehoshaphat's head just poking up above it. I'd been clearing up the last of the mess left by St Cuthburga's herbs, and sweeping up the first of the autumn leaves. The new gardener provided by the National Trust had, I noticed, already been hijacked by Caroline exclusively for her own garden at the big house. He was deaf-and-dumb – 'Called Hal,' she explained, 'though the way he says it makes it sound like Howl, so I'm calling him Howl. At least being deaf he won't hear the noises I make.'

I wasn't sure what noises she had in mind, but I had a strong suspicion they might be related to the county planning officer.

Caroline gazed about her, almost as if she'd never been here before.

'What's that?' she exclaimed suddenly, pointing across the open meadow.

'Jehoshaphat,' I said.

'What is he?'

'A goat.'

She nodded approvingly.

'We could all do with one of those.' She laughed as she turned to me, then her face became intense. 'Claudia,' she said, 'I'm determined to have at least one more lover before I'm forty. I'm going to hit middle age with a bang.'

And she laughed again.

In fact Caroline was looking radiantly pretty and young, as she invariably did when she was hatching a romance. The prospect of an affair seemed to do something for her skin, ironing out the scowl; whereas when an affair went sour, she would go sour too, and age ten years. At the moment, though, she would pass for thirty.

'Caroline, I can't go on calling him your county planning officer,' I said. 'Does he have a name?'

She looked quite surprised.

'I suppose he must have. I can't remember. I've always called him "you".' Her face brightened. 'Oh, I know. He's a Gerald – I think. Yes, it is Gerald. He signs his letters that. Gerald Penrose. He will insist on writing to me as "The Hon", and I hate that. There's nothing honourable about me at all, as you know. In any case I'm only an "Hon" because I happen to be married to Patrick's four inches. God, I bet Gerald's got a lot more than that. What's Fergus like?'

I had no intention of sharing details of my lover's anatomy with Caroline, and steered the conversation back to the county planning officer.

'I have to tell you, Claudia, I didn't behave very well,' she said. I tried to look surprised, trying to remember when Caroline had ever behaved well. 'I took him out to lunch, you see, and turned on the "damsel in distress" quite shamelessly. I'd practised all morning. The helpless look. Tears in the eyes. Hands shaking just a little. Then I realised it was all perfectly true, so it came out horribly naturally. The daughter who'd nursed her dying father only to find herself disinherited. The wife whose feckless husband screws every bimbo he can lay his hands on. The beloved home gone for ever. Investments sinking with every oil tanker. Oh Claudia, I collapsed sobbing into the lemon sorbet.' Caroline looked at me with a wicked smile. 'That rather set me going, I'm afraid.' she went on. 'The truth began to get stretched a bit. Children about to be plucked out of school because we can't pay the fees. Family heirlooms sold. Jewellery gone. Can't even afford the MOT on my car. And now the house is about to be torn apart by some ruthless old harridan who was certainly my father's mistress. And what's more I was alone, alone, alone. Every day I said to myself if it weren't for the children I'd kill myself.'

'And how did your Mr Penrose take all that?' I asked.

Caroline had the look of a naughty child, and gave a giggle.

'Deeply moved he was, darling. Took my hand. And do you know, Claudia, I kissed it. Disgraceful, wasn't it? Then I gave a heart-rending sigh – I'd been rehearsing it in the mirror – and looked at him pleadingly with my mouth half-open like they used to do in films. Well, it always worked when Marilyn Monroe did it, so it was worth a try.'

'And did it work?'

Caroline leant back against the garden table with her eyes closed and let out a long sigh exactly as I imagined she'd rehearsed for Mr Penrose. Then she opened one eye and gave another giggle.

'Oh yes,' she said skittishly.

A damp autumn mist was gathering round us, and we went inside. I lit a fire while Caroline chatted away. The literary conference on 'Mistresses in Literature' was creating quite a buzz, she assured me. Lots of promised celebs. Bookings pouring in. I still harboured the suspicion that it was one of her wilder fantasies; on the other hand you could never be quite sure with Caroline, and I made a mental resolution to be well out of the way that weekend rather than endure a literary jamboree right on my doorstep. The last thing Caroline would enjoy was the sight of a real live mistress receiving her celebs as they drifted in past the gatehouse.

After a while she returned to her dealings with the county planning officer. An absolute pussycat, she assured me: the marine commando appearance was just a veneer. 'Gorgeous man,' she went on. (I suspected she mightn't have found the pussycat quite so gorgeous if he hadn't purred on command.) The important thing was that his sympathies lay entirely with her; he was outraged that she should have been deprived of her birthright simply because of a senile father's whim, particularly a house that had been in the family for over three hundred years. Gerald Penrose was a good West Country man of principle, Caroline insisted. Salt of the earth. Obviously he couldn't commit himself to anything in writing, he'd told her; none the less there were a hundred and one ways a county planning officer could obstruct applications for the renovation of historic buildings. He would do his best.

'God, he can do his best in any way he wishes as far as I'm concerned,' Caroline added with another faked sigh. 'A candlelit dinner should do it.' A dreamy look came into her eyes. 'Gerald's just the sort of man I should have married, you know, Claudia.'

I laughed. Caroline didn't think I should have done.

'I'm perfectly serious,' she added, looking ruffled. 'Marrying Halfwayuppingham was a huge mistake: well, a little mistake, speaking anatomically.'

That restored her good humour.

'For Christ's sake, why haven't you offered me a drink yet?'

I smiled, and did my duty with a vodka-and-tonic.

'Oh, I do like you,' she announced, lounging back on the sofa, clinking her glass. 'For one thing, you listen to me. No one else ever does. Am I a frightful bore, Claudia? Be honest.'

'No,' I said truthfully.

Caroline looked pleased.

'You know, I'm going to win this battle, don't you?' she went on after a moment or two. 'Even if I end up in jail.'

'I'm sure they'll find you a very open prison, Caroline,' I suggested, seating myself opposite her by the fire.

She laughed.

'As open as my marriage, d'you think? Now, give me the update on yours.'

'Dead. Stone dead. You know that,' I answered.

She gave a reassuring nod. I thought of all those evenings with Caroline I'd spent a year ago agonising over whether or not to end it, and whether I had the courage just to walk out. There'd been so many things I was frightened of then, confronting David, being alone, ending up alone, being poor, being lost, seeing the boat I'd missed drawing further and further away, or perhaps making yet another mistake and having to go through it all a second time. 'Rubbish,' Caroline had always replied. 'Ridiculous. Women like you don't end up alone and lost: you're alone and lost *now* because you're with the wrong man.'

I used to wonder how Caroline could manage to be so sensible about other people's lives when she was so unsensible about her own.

'Does David agree that it's dead?' she asked.

I said it was hard to tell: that David was a stubborn man, and marriage for him was like a legal brief he was determined not to lose – his image of himself was of a man who didn't fail. It was nothing to do with love; he didn't really know what that was; having a wife was a necessary part of the orderly life, and if you didn't have one you were deprived, something was missing. He would even have liked children – he'd often said so – and he'd have been an excellent father, I felt sure, doing all the right things; except what he never seemed to grasp was that in order to have children you also needed to do the right thing in bed. I think he felt that somehow children ought just to happen so long as you slept in the same bed.

Caroline smiled into her vodka-and-tonic when I told her that.

'Well, in my case they did just happen, one after the other.' She gazed up at the ceiling thoughtfully. 'You know, I've never understood it. You can have the best fuck of your life with no protection at all, and nothing happens: then one day it's wham-bam-thank-you-ma'am at the safest time of the month, and bingo! You're pregnant. Mind you,' she went on with a chuckle, 'at least Patrick always knew how to do the right thing in bed, even if he did it badly. Now he's doing it badly with all his secretaries, but they're interchangeable, unlike me. That's the difference. Can I have another drink, please?'

She thrust her empty glass towards me, and at the same time swept both legs elegantly over the arm of the sofa, tilting her head back over the other arm so that her blonde hair cascaded to the floor. Her blouse outlined her breasts like clingfilm.

'God, I feel randy,' she announced loudly.

From her upside-down position she may not have realised that she had an audience. I was busy pouring out her vodka, and saw nothing; none the less I was aware of an unnatural silence, and turned round. Fergus was standing by the open

French windows, his long hair glistening with mist and curling palely over the collar of his trench-coat. In one hand he grasped a bottle of wine, while from the other dangled an unplucked cock-pheasant. I could see his eyes crinkle as he looked down at Caroline with that amused half-smile of his.

She seemed frozen for a moment. Then she did an awkward half-swivel, twisting her head round and sweeping her hair back from her face, her bottom in the air, one hand resting on the floor.

'Oh my God,' she said, followed by a gulp, and a hoist of her legs so that she was now squatting on all fours on the sofa gazing up at him. 'You must be . . . obviously.' Caroline turned her head to look at me with a slightly shocked expression. She glanced back at Fergus, then at the pheasant, finally again at me. I could see her gathering her self-composure round her. She laughed.

'Well. All that and a cock too, Claudia.'

'What did you think of her?' I asked when Caroline had finally gone.

'Difficult lady,' Fergus said.

He was plucking the pheasant in the kitchen, a glass of wine by his side. I came up behind him and slid my arms round his waist.

'Sure you wouldn't rather have brought the cock for her?'

Fergus tilted his head back so he could kiss my hair.

'Not unless I wanted it bitten off, and I can think of better things to do than that.'

'When?'

He gave a soft laugh.

'As soon as it's plucked. First things first.'

'I rather think that's what Caroline had in mind. She fancied you rotten. But then every woman does, I suppose. It must get rather boring.'

'Very.'

I gave a tug at his chest-hairs. He said 'Ouch' and went on plucking the pheasant.

'So, where have you been? I haven't seen you for almost a week.'

I immediately wished I'd never said that: it broke my rule about never enquiring into Fergus's life. I would like to have taken it back; I much preferred the idea of Fergus walking in unannounced out of the misty night and taking over the kitchen, and later taking over me. As it was, Caroline had lingered until I imagined I'd have to kick her out. I'd watched her flirting many times before: she had her own special way of doing it, lowering her voice to a soft bedroom purr and making sinuous movements of her body as she walked round the room, accompanied by remarks that weren't exactly provocative but were designed to make a man wonder what the hell the words really meant. I knew perfectly well what they meant; they were the sounds of Caroline on the hunt.

'Where have I been?' he answered casually. 'In London. I had to see my publisher. I also found out a few interesting things in the British Museum. And I wanted to go to Kew, about aphrodisiacs. Interested?'

He'd finished the pheasant. I took the knife from him, grasped his wrists and drew him to the sink, where I turned on the tap and washed the blood from his hands. Then without bothering to dry them I steered his fingers on to the buttons of my blouse, coaxed them undone, and laid his wet hands on my breasts.

'Do you really need an answer?' I asked.

Cold water was trickling down my stomach, and I shivered.

'I'd much rather have been here with you,' he said, and took one of my nipples in his mouth.

I shivered again. Then I realised it was the first time Fergus had ever said anything that suggested he sometimes missed me. I was excited and a little frightened. Would this mean that from now on I'd always be waiting for the next time, and if it didn't happen would I start to wonder if he cared at all? And did I even want him to care?

I wanted him to make love to me.

I dropped my clothes one by one on the staircase between long French kisses. His own clothes lay strewn around the bedroom floor, and I reached out and drew him down on to me. It was as if we hadn't made love for a year, and I closed my eyes as the bedroom ceiling began to spin. And as we lay there panting I found myself smiling at the thought of all those noises which Caroline was glad the deaf-and-dumb gardener couldn't hear. Did women all make the same noises? I was damned if I was going to ask Fergus.

We ate the pheasant extremely late. It wasn't quite burnt, but I enjoyed satisfying the lesser hunger after the first had been fed.

Fergus gazed at me over his wineglass. As always his gaze was mysterious, not frightening but as if he were calculating something, fitting me into some pattern of thought that lay invisibly buried behind those intense blue eyes. I never knew if it was really me he was gazing at, or some fictional heroine he was busy inventing, creating, modelling as a sculptor models a clay figure, just as his hands had modelled my body while we made love. Perhaps Fergus really was the Devil who had taken possession of me, and I was the Devil's Work. The thought made me feel uncomfortable.

'Tell me what you found out in London,' I asked.

His forehead became furrowed for a moment, and he sat back. Behind him, outside the narrow kitchen window, the street-lights were blurred with mist, and a midnight silence had fallen on the town.

'Your saint,' he said. 'St Cuthburga. I discovered a few things about her. She was a royal lady, as you know. Sister of the king of Wessex. Well, it seems she became a missionary, mainly in Germany.'

The switch in Fergus from romantic lover to medieval scholar always threw me. Here was yet another mystery of the man which I could never quite grasp. He even seemed to look different when he talked in this way. Almost ascetic. The face elongated. The eyes deeper set.

'But she travelled a good deal further afield than Germany,' he went on, 'which was brave for any lady at that time, particularly a royal lady, though no doubt she'd have had a faithful entourage, and stacks of jewels to give to all the princes and abbots she visited. It would have been quite a royal procession, I imagine.' Fergus paused, and looked at me with a slightly ironic smile. 'As an Italian, you'll be interested to know she spent a lot of time there, mostly in Rome where she was no doubt much fêted. And then she came back here, to Norton Abbas.'

I waited. What was I supposed to make of all this? Why did scholars take so long to get to the point? It wasn't as though Fergus was exactly slow in other directions: an hour or so ago his underpants had looked as if they were draped around a flagpole.

'Well, here's my guess,' he said, draining the last of his wine. 'Our lady would have been showered with gifts in Rome, without any doubt. So, what kind of gifts might she have been offered? What would be good enough for a royal visitor from England who was also a leading figure in the Church? Something pretty special, one imagines, designed to enhance the fame and prestige of the priory she'd recently founded. A helping hand from one holy sister to another. Obviously not gold: she had plenty of that already. Rich clothing? Not for a nun surely. So, what else? How about a rare manuscript: after all, monasteries were the centres of learning in a barbaric age, and learning needed to be spread.'

'Fergus, please. Just tell me,' I said.

This time he laughed.

'OK. My view is that what our royal lady Cuthburga brought back with her was the original of the recipe which I came across in the Bodleian Library. It would have been written in Greek because that's where it came from in the first place: what I copied out was the translation made at Norton Priory. But not only did she bring back the recipe; I suspect she also brought with her the actual magic ingredient, otherwise nobody would have been able to make the stuff, would they?'

Fergus looked pleased with himself. He paused for a few seconds, letting all this sink in. The magic ingredient, I thought; and I remembered the words 'satur rote', the root of the satyr plant.

'OK, I'm with you so far,' I said. 'Go on.'

'Well, that's more or less it. The rest follows. Whatever it was, the recipe worked. Hence her fame. And hence her canonisation after her death. D'you buy that?'

I made a face.

'Do I buy it, Fergus? Honestly, how can I? You're not seriously telling me that a royal nun got canonised for manufacturing aphrodisiacs?'

Fergus was grinning.

'Why not? There are far more unlikely saints than that: the Catholic Church is full of them. It makes perfect sense. A potion that produces more children for God. What better reason for sainthood? And what's more' – Fergus leant forward across the table with a triumphant smile on his face – 'we know that whatever the magic ingredient was, it was still around at the time of Henry VIII eight hundred years later. So it must have been something that grew here. And if it survived for eight hundred years the strong likelihood is that it survives here today. That it grows somewhere in your garden.'

By now I'd convinced myself I didn't believe a word of all this. I also had a strong suspicion Fergus didn't either, and that his imagination was merely playing an elaborate game in order to build an intriguing plot for his book. In other words Carl Magnus, author of best-selling *Cardinal Error*, had taken over from Dr Fergus Corrigan, medieval historian and famous fucker. And right now I wished he'd stick to the latter.

'But aphrodisiacs are a load of rubbish, Fergus, surely.'

He raised his eyebrows.

'Perhaps. Who knows? If they were used for eight hundred years, maybe they aren't rubbish.'

'Huh!' I said. 'So, what do you think the magic ingredient might be, then?'

Fergus shrugged his shoulders.

'I don't know any more than you do. But there are a few candidates. The people at Kew Gardens said they hadn't been asked such a sexy question in years. They got quite excited about it. The most obvious root-aphrodisiac, they explained, was mandrake, *mandragora*. A member of the nightshade family. It comes from the Mediterranean, has a forked root vaguely human in shape, and it's apparently mentioned in the Book of Genesis – Leah employs it in order to lie with Jacob. How's that for learning? Then there are the roots of the sea-holly, called "eringoes", which Falstaff enthuses about in *The Merry Wives of Windsor*, or so the Kew people inform me.

Well, Norton Abbas is pretty close to the sea, so it could be that, couldn't it? Or it could be that herb I brought you once. Remember? Summer Savoury. It's got the right sort of Latin name, *Satureia*; but at Kew they say it's only ever been used as a feeble alternative to sage in soups.'

Fergus paused, and his brow became furrowed again.

'Somehow I don't believe it was likely to have been any of those.' He laughed. 'I just don't see a woman getting canonised for cooking sea-holly, making soup or doing funny things with nightshade. Besides, *mandragora* being a Latin word, presumably the Romans would have brought it here long before, and as for sea-holly and Summer Savoury, they're both native plants: they were already growing on her doorstep, so to speak.'

It was almost one o'clock in the morning, and my eyes were leaden with tiredness. Fergus stetched out his hand and ran his fingers through my hair, then down over my shoulder and breasts.

'I'm boring you to tears. And I must go. I'm lecturing in the morning.'

He got up and put his arms round me.

'I bet your students don't need eringoes or mandrake roots,' I said. 'They've got you.' And I kissed him. 'Do they send you love-letters?'

Fergus gave me his private smile, then nibbled at my ear.

'All the time.'

'Then you offer them private tutorials, I suppose.'

'Of course.'

'Which they leap at?'

'Yes.'

'And offer themselves to you.'

'Usually.'

'And you accept.'

'It would be impolite not to.'

'Oh, what a hard life you lead, Fergus.'

'I know.'

'What would you say if I went back to my husband?'

'That you were a bloody idiot.'

I nodded. I knew I should have found something sharp to say.

He looked dishevelled and unshaven in the half-dark as I walked with him to the French windows. The mist had lifted, and the priory garden stretched away into a pattern of faint silhouettes against the night. I could hear an owl. Everything else was silent. I kissed Fergus good-night; then I waited until the metallic whine of his Alfa-Romeo became a fading echo through the town, and finally a distant acceleration until the hills and the woods muffled it. My Devil was driving home.

Home. What was that? I wondered. The coastguards' cottage alone, or the house in Exeter bursting with children? And then I made myself stop wondering.

Everything was silent again. Even the owl. I lingered for a moment in the blackness of the garden. It had been an evening of love, and of mysteries. But then Fergus was a mystery too, and so was what I felt for him.

The last question I asked myself was: can one learn quite so much about love-making without learning a little about love? I wished I knew the answer.

Eight

Now the woods were stripped of leaves I could gaze from the gatehouse right out over the estuary. All summer it had been more of a boating lake, with coloured dinghies fluttering over it like butterflies, and water-skiers cutting zigzag patterns across the tide. Now it was empty and grey, and the only movement was the ripple of the wind, with the occasional fishing-boat rearing and dipping towards the open sea.

I preferred it this way. Throughout the summer it had seemed to lie beyond the boundary of my retreat: now it felt included within it. The distant sea reminded me of being in Fergus's cottage, waking in the chill morning and peering out of the window wrapped in his dressing-gown. I'd never lived near the sea before. In Bologna it had merely been something blue on a travel poster which Anna-Maria would drag me to every August and sit bulging on the beach while I'd glance disapprovingly at the foreign tourists who dared to bathe topless. And I used to think that if Anna-Maria were ever to enter the sea topless it would be like letting a school of porpoises loose.

I'd spent the morning clearing up huge quantities of leaves, raking them into wooden compost bins which I'd laboriously moved from outside the medieval barn. If Caroline was going to hold smart conferences in the place I didn't imagine visiting Nobel Prize-winners would welcome their pearls of wisdom being coated with the smell of rotting vegetation. Now my back ached, and my hands were blistered. What the hell was I doing this for? A year ago I'd been the unpaid social secretary for the Box Hill Conservative Party. Now I was an unpaid gardener for the National Trust.

But at least I didn't have to wear powder-blue, or smile.

Not that I felt much like smiling at present. David was finally insisting on coming down to visit me. He wasn't sure when he could get away from the House, he said, but he desperately needed to talk to me. Christmas was coming up, and wasn't that a perfect time for a reconciliation? We could go away together, just like old times. I shuddered at the thought: old times had been bad times. And Fergus had already hinted at a surprise he had in store for me at Christmas.

'I want a divorce, David,' I said. 'I really do.'

There was a silence. Then the patient lawyer's voice came down the phone.

'Why don't we just talk about it?'

David always believed he could talk his way into anything, anything, that is, except bed.

'If you really want to,' I said wearily.

But perhaps that *was* the right thing to do. Perhaps I should just get it over with. Stop running away from him. Stop playing games.

There was something unexpectedly final about that conversation. The thought of being free of David made me feel intensely relieved, and at the same time a little frightened. I started thinking about money. I'd had so many unexpected windfalls that I'd come to live in a state of euphoria about my finances. Money had fallen on me like manna from heaven, and I'd begun to believe it always would. But now a more sober review showed me that although I could probably just about survive until spring, it was likely to be a bleak winter deprived of all pleasures of the flesh except (I trusted) Fergus's prick.

There was only one answer, I decided: I must exercise my one and only professional skill. Within an hour of David phoning I took myself off for a discreet look at various restaurants in Norton Abbas in order to decide if there was one I could tolerate working in, and which might also be prepared to tolerate me. I ruled out the Taste of Bangladesh and Op's Chinese Cuisine, and finally plucked up courage to walk into the Ristorante Mamma Gina ('Tuscan Specialities') and offer my services on a part-time basis. The one stipulation I made was that I wasn't free to work on Saturday evenings: I was prepared to lay tables any other days of the week, but Saturdays were for Fergus to lay *me* (though I put it rather more delicately than that).

Maybe it was because I was Italian. Maybe it was because Mamma Gina embraced me like a long-lost cousin. Maybe it was because her husband could hardly prise his hands off my buttocks. But to my surprise the deal was on: three nights a week, Thursday, Friday and Sunday. I'd start on November 18th, in exactly one week's time. I was 'Signorina Foscari', which rapidly became 'La Bella Claudia' as soon as Mamma Gina departed and Il Padrone's hand found its way to my left buttock.

Experience with Anna-Maria's favourite priest had long ago taught me how to deal with the likes of Il Padrone.

All that had been yesterday, not exactly a red-letter day, but none the less a day of reckoning; a small corner turned. And now this morning it was back to basics, gathering up autumn leaves. Life was not feeling particularly glamorous.

I was strolling back towards the gatehouse carrying my rake and gardening gloves when I caught sight of Megan and Joan coming towards me through the arch. They had the look of an official delegation. Or might it be a conspiracy? I would soon find out. Relations with both women had become, if not exactly strained, then somewhat guarded since my affair with Fergus. They seemed uncertain how to respond, and treated my relationship with a certain prurient envy. None the less I had something they knew they couldn't have, and never *would* have. So neither of them knew whether to be thrilled for me as a friend, or to wait for it all to end in tears as I deserved.

I greeted them from across the meadow. They were looking unusually serious.

'Claudia, we're both of us worried,' Joan announced as I approached. And then she laughed. 'It's all right. Not about you. No cause for worry there, I can see from your face. It's Caroline.'

'Her stupid bloody conference,' Megan chipped in. 'Mistresses in Literature, for God's sake. It's simply not going to work, is it? And she thinks it is. But it's a fantasy. It'll be a complete disaster. You know that. She's invited half the literary world, and because she's Caroline they've all said yes to get her off the phone. But they're never going to turn up, are they? She'll be lucky if she gets some nondescript poet who'll read his unpublished "Elegy for the Minke Whale", and that'll be it, and everyone's going to demand their money back.'

I'd had very much the same thoughts, but hadn't dared say so to Caroline. In my experience interfering with Caroline's plans was always doomed to failure; she only hated you for it, and you simply had to let her get on with it. And she usually managed somehow to pull it off.

'So what are we supposed to do about it?' I asked cautiously.

They had a solution. We went indoors and they explained. The conference was due to start on Saturday morning, December 3rd, and continue through until Sunday afternoon. Two whole days.

'So we need two fail-safes,' Joan insisted. 'First an alternative conference that we can actually guarantee will happen. And secondly a slap-up dinner in a restaurant which we'll bill as a celebration, but in fact it'll be a comforter, so that Caroline can dilute her tears in buckets and buckets of wine, and we can all tell her we love her even if we'd sometimes like to wring her bloody neck.'

I made a mental note that under no circumstances was that dinner going to be held at the Ristorante Mamma Gina. I was not going to lose my job as a result of Caroline throwing bread and tantrums all over the restaurant.

'What do you mean, an alternative conference?' I asked.

'Well, we thought we could rustle up a few local people,' Megan said rather unconvincingly. She noticed the expression on my face and wriggled her flesh in an attempt to look more confident. 'Glyn, for example.'

I looked at her, puzzled.

'And what does he know about mistresses?' I asked a little unkindly.

Megan threw me a sharp look, and then laughed.

'He could always pick *your* brains.'

It was my turn to laugh.

'*Touché*,' I said.

'Well, Glyn happens to know everything there is to know about Anne Boleyn,' Megan went on. 'She may not be literature, but we can't have everything. This is an emergency.'

I nodded, feeling deeply unconvinced by all this.

'OK, Glyn on Anne Boleyn. Then who?'

Megan glanced at Joan, who looked uncomfortable.

'Well, there's this local historian I know, and he's passionate about minor Elizabethan love-poets.'

I blinked.

'Minor Elizabethan love-poets? Terrific. The hungry hordes will go a bundle on them. They'll be queuing down the street.'

Joan looked at me disapprovingly.

'You're not being very helpful, Claudia. Could you get your mind out of bed?'

'All right, I'm sorry,' I said, and felt mean. 'I wish I could come up with something.'

Megan threw another glance at Joan.

'Perhaps we could do that for you. D'you think you could ask . . . ?'

I didn't let Megan finish.

'Oh no, absolutely not. That's *out*.'

Joan leant forwards and put her hand on my arm.

'Oh, come on, Claudia. For the good of the cause. I'm sure he'd do it if you asked him. And he's famous. He looks gorgeous. And he's not only written about mistresses, he'll have one in the audience.'

I didn't know whether to be angry and just smile graciously. I felt dreadful. I was being pilloried.

Joan's hand gave my arm a reassuring squeeze.

'Just think about it. Please.'

That made it worse. I didn't want to think about it.

'All right,' I said weakly.

This was *not* going to happen, I vowed to myself . . .

'And we had one other idea,' Joan went on.

I stood up and looked suspiciously at her. Then I caught her eye and laughed.

'All right, I know. My husband. You want him to come and talk about the mistresses he's never had, and the wife he hardly ever had either. Is that it?'

Joan gave a broad grin.

'No. Try again. Someone even more sanctimonious than your husband.'

My mind was a blank. Could there really be such a person?
'I give up.'
'Think of a lecture on "Sin and Redemption" to round off
the conference. Give it a proper moral perspective. A rousing
finale. Doesn't anyone you know come to mind?'
It dawned on me most horribly.
'Not the Rev Pype?'
Megan and Joan both nodded.
'But he hates women,' I said, looking at them in amazement.
Joan's eyes lit up.
'Precisely. That's the whole point. Caroline will get so furious
that she'll answer him back, and after a good slanging match
she'll feel the whole conference was a triumph after all. You
know how she loves a punch-up.'
By now I was more than ever convinced that it was all
a total nightmare, and determined somehow to keep to my
first resolution and be as far away from it as possible. Then,
as if she were reading my thoughts, Megan killed that idea
stone dead.
'We thought we'd have a shift system looking after Caroline,'
she said in her most matronly voice. 'The first shock's going to
be terrible for her, and the last thing we want is her hanging
around waiting for her celebs to arrive, and all she gets is Glyn
and a local historian. Claudia, you'd be the ideal person to do
that: keep her away for the first hour of two. Then once it's
under way Joan and I'll take over, and you can do another
stint in the afternoon. After that it'll be the evening and we
can all prop her up in the restaurant. Sunday she'll have a
hangover, and that'll fire up her temper beautifully for the
final scrap with Jonathan Pype.'
I could see this was a *fait accompli*, and there seemed very
little I could do about it short of saying bluntly no. Life with
David was beginning to feel almost bearable by comparison.
Or perhaps I should reconsider Anna-Maria's sausage-maker
after all.
'And *do* work on Fergus, won't you?' was Joan's parting
shot. 'I'm sure you could reward him with all sorts of special
privileges afterwards.'

Again there was that sharp edge of envy in her voice.

I sat by the fire after they'd gone, realising that I'd never encountered female jealousy before. I'd felt it myself once or twice when I was having my brief, guilt-ridden affair, and I knew the man was only smothering himself with aftershave so his wife wouldn't know where he'd been. Afterwards I'd lie in bed next to David snoring in his striped pyjamas and picture my lover all brisk and *macho* after plundering me and wondering if he had the energy to do his wife a favour that night. I hated it. It dirtied the mind. What I loved about my relationship with Fergus was that there was none of that. I wasn't jealous because I didn't know, and I didn't know because I wanted it to be only what it was, two people drawn to each other's bodies. A feast of wanting.

But Joan and Megan invariably made me feel I was cheating, stealing sweets without paying for them. Well, perhaps I was. It was a wonderful feeling. And if it should end in tears, then let it; that was the risk I was prepared to take. Their envy was because I was prepared to take it.

Something else was constantly on my mind, the knowledge that everything in my life here was temporary. Somehow this made it richer; it compelled me to seize each moment in case it might be the last. This place itself was temporary. I could be evicted. Caroline could be evicted. It was the same with Fergus. Whenever he appeared, or phoned, I never knew for certain that he would do so again, or if from tomorrow he might suddenly cease to exist in my life. When he kissed me it could be for the last time. When he withdrew from me it might be forever. Yet I felt strong enough to survive that. I now knew I would do something with my life, even if I were alone.

Perhaps my self-preoccupation made me pay less attention to Caroline's plight than as a friend I should have done. She was fighting for survival and all I was doing was going off and getting laid. I'd invariably come back from a weekend with Fergus feeling guilty.

And then, invariably, the unexpected would happen.

A few days after the rescue meeting with Megan and Joan, the phone went.

'D'you want to hear about it, Uppingham versus Legover?'

came Caroline's voice unannounced. She sounded cock-a-hoop. 'Come over and celebrate.'

It was a Sunday evening, and I'd just walked in through the door after a weekend with Fergus in the coastguard's cottage. I was looking forward to an early night, but Caroline was insistent.

'I don't want to hear what you've been doing, or how tired you are. Just come over. Now.'

Reluctantly I clambered back into the little Fiat and drove up to the big house. The drive was sodden with fallen leaves from the lime-trees, and the grass verges looked as though the tank corps had been conducting exercises. My headlights caught a large sign wedged into the lawn near the front door, 'Hall of the Mystresses', with an accompanying arrow on to which someone had slipped a condom. I'd completely forgotten about Caroline's open weekend. It had evidently been a success.

I rang the bell and her younger daughter, Samantha, opened the door. When she saw me she giggled, then clapped one hand to her mouth bashfully. I recognised her T-shirt: printed across it was a reproduction of one of Megan's portraits, with two large breasts exactly where Samantha had none.

'Chloe's got one too,' she said. 'Mummy's a bit cross.'

Chloe was Caroline's eldest, aged fifteen. Samantha was almost eleven. They were home so rarely for weekends I'd almost forgotten their existence.

'Why is she cross, Samantha?' I asked cautiously, closing the front door behind me. Being cross was such a normal state for their mother that I wondered what special indignity could possibly have been inflicted on her.

Samantha giggled again, and didn't answer. She skipped away and ran upstairs.

I found Caroline reclining dramatically on a sofa in the drawing-room with her back to me. She was wearing a wine-coloured house-coat and smoking a cigarette. She only half-turned her head as I came in.

'Claudia,' she said languidly. 'Help yourself.' One hand waved vaguely in the direction of the drinks tray. She gave a contented sigh and blew a plume of smoke towards the ceiling. 'A triumph! You missed a triumph, darling,' she went on, sounding anything but cross. 'Five thousand people in two days. Five *thousand*! That's five grand in cash, plus the sale of T-shirts. Legover's furious.'

'Why? Samantha seemed to think *you* were.'

Caroline swung her legs round and sat up.

'Oh, that.' She gave a snort. 'I'll come to that. But let me tell you the rest first.'

It was the papers that did it, she explained. The tabloids picked it up from her ads in the local press. The *Sun* really went to town; rang her up on Friday to ask who all the mistresses were, and sent a photographer down to take pictures, got Megan to pose in front of her portraits. Then the reporter phoned the National Trust who said they knew nothing about it and that it was all quite outrageous; they intended to take legal action.

'And that was what brought the Legover woman hurrying down.' There was a gleam in Caroline's eyes as she related this. 'Well, I told her it was my house, and I could do what I bloody well liked with it,' she explained haughtily. 'The creature spluttered and said it wasn't my bloody house, and she'd have me thrown out. I just laughed.'

Caroline was thoroughly enjoying herself.

'Oh Claudia, everywhere she looked she nearly had a heart attack. It was wonderful. And I'm afraid I *was* a bit naughty. As soon as I heard she was coming I rushed off to the chemist and bought one of those surgical appliances. Then I hung it on a recruiting poster and altered just one letter so that it read "Support the National Truss". She just ripped it down; but as she did so she caught sight of Michelangelo's figure of God the Father which I'd carefully cut out so that it pointed towards the garden. She composed herself sufficiently to ask, "And what is *that* for?" So I told her it was for the loo.'

Caroline paused as if knowing perfectly well what I was going to ask. And I did.

'In the garden, Caroline? But I didn't think you had a loo in the garden.'

She clapped her hands with pleasure.

'Exactly. That what's the Legover woman asked me. And I just smiled and said that all over Europe people just peed in the bushes, or wherever they chose; so why not here? Besides, I told her, pee is wonderfully good for rhubarb.'

'Judging by the sign in your front garden, that wasn't the only thing people did in the bushes, Caroline,' I suggested.

She just shrugged.

'Oh well, if you invite people to visit a Hall of the Mystresses you can't be too surprised if they bring their own, can you?' she said lazily. 'I must ask Carmen to remove the thing.'

I could see another wide-eyed letter winging its way to Salamanca.

The Legover woman then stormed off, Caroline explained, though not before assuring her that she'd be hearing from the Trust's lawyers within a week.

'And not before being accosted by my charming daughters,' she added. Samantha had reappeared quietly at the door, and Caroline tried to look disapproving. Then she burst out laughing. '*This* one,' she exclaimed, pointing at the girl, 'offered to sell her a T-shirt, saying she'd look great in it particularly since she'd been one of her grandfather's mistresses, hadn't she, and why wasn't there a portrait of her in the drawing-room like all the others?'

Samantha looked at her mother indignantly.

'I was only repeating what Daddy told me,' she announced with an air of injured innocence.

'Yes, darling, very loyal of you,' Caroline said wearily. 'I'm sure the Legover woman appreciated the thought, just as I'm sure she appreciated the fact that you were wearing two grapefruits under the T-shirt. Now why don't you go and change for supper?'

Samantha put on a sulky face.

'I was just trying to look like Chloe.'

'It's true that Chloe doesn't need any grapefruits, darling,' Caroline said in that resigned voice mothers use for their precocious children. 'And nor will you very soon. But please try and keep whatever Daddy says to yourself in future. Now go and change, Samantha.'

The girl went off in a huff. Caroline turned to me with a wicked smile.

'Of course I was tickled pink, really. I don't believe I've ever loved my children more. Jesus, Claudia, you should have seen the woman's face. And she doesn't even know what's coming to her. Wait till I tell you what my lovely county planning officer has come up with. Will you stay to supper? Please do. I haven't had a real gossip with you for ages. I feel terrific. *And* five thousand pounds richer. So let's open a really good bottle of wine – God bless my dreadful father.'

The letters from the county planning office were master-pieces of official obstruction, and anyone on the receiving end would be excused for blowing his brains out. Each was addressed to the National Trust, attn. Mrs Pamela Leggatt, copy to The Hon Mrs Caroline Uppingham, Priory Hall, Norton Abbas, Devon.

What Mrs Leggatt would not have had the chance to see were the short handwritten notes, addressed to Caroline personally, which accompanied the copy of each official letter. In this way Mr Gerald Penrose, or 'Gerald' as he signed himself on these notes, must carefully have by-passed his own secretary as well as County Hall records and all computer systems, presumably trusting to Caroline's tact (how very unwise) in being prepared to burn them, swallow them, or secrete them about her person should any official enquiry ever be mounted.

The letters had been sent every few days or so, one after the other, perhaps deliberately to produce a staccato effect on the unfortunate Mrs Leggatt, who must have felt morning sickness coming upon her each time she opened one.

'I've always hated officialdom,' Caroline declared, spreading Mr Penrose's sheaf of letters across the large mahogany table in the drawing-room. 'But, my God, I love it now. So let's start from the beginning. This one's about the special ramps for wheelchairs.'

She handed me a three-page letter, closely typed, and headed 'Priory Hall – Facilities for the Infirm'. I'd never met Mr Gerald Penrose, yet I could tell from the wonderful obfuscation of language that he was enormously enjoying himself making the simple matter of a ramp sound like an operation worthy of the builders of the pyramids. Towards the end of Page Two the fog of words finally parted as he explained that he'd taken careful measurements, and was of the opinion that the only suitable access for wheelchairs was through a side door facing the stables which, since the Trust wished to convert these into a shop, would cause dangerous obstruction to visitors wishing to purchase items from the aforementioned premises. On the other hand . . . The letter then continued in its serpentine fashion to offer various ludicrous alternatives each of which would involve the cooperation of structural engineers, sanitation experts and quite possibly archaeologists, over whom his department had no direct authority. Special applications would need to be made to these separate bodies, and such investigations would, of course, take time, there being much pressure of work during this post-recession period.

'Brilliant, don't you think?' Caroline was hugging herself with joy. 'Now take a look at the note Gerald sent with it.'

And she handed me a small slip of paper with no letter-head. The handwriting was bold and florid. 'Dear Mrs Uppingham,' it read, 'I trust this will keep the halt and the lame from your door – for a while at least. The lunch was most enjoyable. I look forward to the return match. My deepest respects, Gerald.'

'Now here's the one about the four extra loos. Have another drink to help digest it.'

Caroline's idea of a brandy would have immobilised a St Bernard. I sipped it gingerly, and flicked my eyes down several pages of Letter Number Two. Mr Penrose had taken a cautious line over the extra lavatories, acknowledging that these were indeed necessary, but expressing concern that the sudden influx of several hundred visitors on a hot and thirsty day might impose an undue strain on sewage pipes intended for modest domestic use. A survey would of course be necessary, requiring excavation to the extent of some five hundred yards, this being the distance between Priory Hall and the public thoroughfare. So a thorough survey was essential due to the likelihood that the roots of ancient lime-trees lining the drive would already have fractured the ancient pipes, the replacement of which, on a scale adequate for such large usage, might endanger the life of the aforesaid trees which, as he understood, were the subject of a preservation order.

'Oh, what a lovely man,' Caroline chortled, inhaling deeply from her brandy-glass. 'Now here's his accompanying note.'

Again it was the same unheaded notepaper. 'Dear Mrs Uppingham, I think the enclosed may prove more effective than your suggestion that visitors squat in the bushes. The return match was as delightful as the first. I am away for the next few days, after which I should be delighted to accept an invitation to dinner at Priory Hall. I look forward to it. My warmest regards to Mr Uppingham. Yours affectionately, Gerald.'

I raised my eyebrows and looked at Caroline. She pretended not to notice, and without a word handed me Letter Number Three. This was headed rather curiously 'Nappies and Car Park'. I got the feeling Mr Penrose was growing weary of official language, and the letter which followed was altogether more crisp in tone. He pointed out – and I could almost see the smile on his face as he wrote it – that although the ordure of babies was likely to be of smaller volume than in the case of adults, its disposal would none the less be by the same channels; and since these were under review ('see my letter of Nov. 12th') no decision could as yet be reached in this area. As to the car-park which the Trust planned to create in what was at present Mrs Uppingham's rose-garden, the letter continued, it was the policy of the council to view with disfavour projects likely to disfigure areas of natural beauty, as he was sure the Trust would be the first to support. Furthermore he understood that Mrs Uppingham's rose-garden was held in high esteem in horticultural circles, and had even been the subject of a television programme.

Caroline was looking mischievous.

'Well, it's quite true,' she said. 'A programme on pest control did once feature my rose-garden to demonstrate what can happen if greenfly and black spot go entirely untreated. And the expert made a point of saying what a very beautiful rose-garden it must once have been.'

I laughed.

'And now the note, Caroline.'

She handed it to me without a word. The handwriting was becoming quite familiar by now. 'Dear Mrs Uppingham, I trust the nappies are well disposed of. Yes, Friday evening will suit me admirably. I look forward to it. My regards to Mr Uppingham, and I only regret that he may be unable to be present that evening owing to pressure of work in London. Yours affectionately, Gerald.'

'Caroline,' I said, 'you're even more unscrupulous than I thought.'

She put on a wistful expression and eyed her brandy studiously.

'Ah well, darling, a girl's got to do what a girl's got to do,' she said with a sigh. 'Sometimes there are sacrifices you just have to make in the interests of a good cause.'

Another sigh, and a longer sip of brandy.

'Oh, of course,' I said. 'Very noble of you, Caroline. Now let me see the next letter. I'm anxious to see how the good cause is going.'

She passed it to me, then began to peer intently at her fingernails. The letter was headed 'Stables – Proposed Commercial Premises'. To my surprise Mr Penrose adopted a friendly and cooperative tone. The council would have no objection to the former stables being used for trading purposes, he assured Mrs Leggatt: indeed it appeared admirably suited to such a function, provided of course, he added, that no structural alterations of any kind were made to the building. The Trust would naturally be the first to appreciate that stabling dating from the seventeenth century was of rare, if not unique, historical importance, particularly since all the original fittings appeared to be in place and in excellent condition. The Trust would be required to respect the stalls, manger, stone water-trough, stone flooring with central drainage, not to mention iron rings in the walls, original stable doors and all other existing features, any damage to which might incur a withdrawal of trading licence and possible legal prosecution. Mr Penrose ended by wishing the Trust well in this enterprising venture.

'That would seem to cook Pamela Leggatt's goose pretty thoroughly,' I suggested with a laugh.

Caroline was already handing me the accompanying note. It was even briefer than the other three.

'Darling Caroline,' it said, 'I kiss your breasts. Gerald.'

*   *   *

Fergus promised not to turn up at Mamma Gina's to sample my skills as a waitress. But he'd be there in spirit, he assured me, eyeing the appalling mauve outfit I was required to wear, which had clearly been designed for some anorexic teenager and not a woman with a full-bodied Italian figure like mine. The mini-skirt just about hid my pubes, and the mini-blouse did an even less successful job of covering my bosom.

On my first evening Mamma Gina's husband Carlo appreciated my outfit with both hands. It also inspired a party of local rugger-buggers to get vigorously drunk as they ordered bottle after bottle in order that I should lean over and pour wine into their glasses. If there were such a thing as verbal rape, then I was gang-banged that evening. The entire lexicon of football-speak was directed at me. They kicked up and under, they scored, they put it in straight, they got it clean between the uprights, they awarded penalties for a forward pass, they made it into touch, they shoved over for a try.

I began to understand how easy it would be to hate men.

'Know about rugby, sweetheart, do you?' said one of them who had a slobbery grin and was marginally less pissed than the others. 'Know it's about handling balls? Yeah, I bet you do.'

He turned and brayed at the others. There were guffaws all round. I was trying to concentrate on making out the bill.

'She can handle my balls any day,' came a voice from further down the table.

'She'd drop them, Kev. Too heavy.'

'Drop her knickers, more likely, Des. That'd have you beating about the bush.'

This convulsed them. Then the one with the slobbery grin shouted above the laughter.

'Nah, you got it quite wrong. It'd be a knock-on, wouldn't it? With a pair of knockers like that it'd have to be.'

I placed the bill in front of him without a word. He was far too busy braying to see me pick up his lighted cigarette from the ashtray and drop it neatly down the front of his tracksuit trousers.

'Enjoy beating about the bush,' I said.

The man leered uncomprehendingly, then suddenly shrieked and began to beat at his genitals while his mates hooted and jeered.

I stood back, assuming I'd get the sack for branding the balls of a customer. But fortunately Mamma Gina had been listening in on the exchanges, and was suddenly there behind me with a face like Medusa.

'Dirty, feelthy boys,' she spluttered. 'You go now, and you not come back, or I get the police.'

There was a strong smell of burning pubic hair, and the man with the slobbery grin was by now holding his beloved crutch tenderly.

But the nightmare had a sequal. No sooner had the rugger-buggers departed than the door opened and a downcast woman in autumnal tweeds entered the restaurant, her bulk masking the male companion following her.

Mamma Gina fussed around them and ushered them to a table by the window while I went to fetch two menus and the wine list. Still feeling rather distracted after my encounter with the rugger-buggers, I placed the menus on the table without even looking at the two customers. But as I did so it was as though the temperature of the room suddenly plummeted ten or twenty degrees, and I became aware of a thin male hand trembling on the red tablecloth. Blue veins stood out like the delta of a river, and small tufts of black hair sprouted along the fingers.

I raised my eyes and found myself gazing down at the bald pate of the Rev Jonathan Pype. His eyes didn't meet mine. They were directed like pale-grey gimlets at a point just above the edge of the table where my thighs at last met the hem of my mini-skirt.

There was a sharp intake of breath, followed by a slushing sound from the vicar's mouth. He gave a gulp, glared across at his companion, whom I took to be his wife, and muttered several words in an outraged undertone of which only one word was distinguishable.

'Babylon!'

He then glanced about him as if hoping for some handy fire and brimstone, and staggered to his feet.

'Disgusting,' he spat in my general direction. 'You should be ashamed.'

In truth I *was* rather. It hadn't been my choice of outfit.

Carlo noticed that the vicar was about to depart, and hurried over with an engaging smile.

'Something is not right, sir?' he said, still smiling.

Jonathan Pype threw him a furious glare.

'I don't expect my wife to be subjected to this kind of nudity.'

Carlo's face became sad.

'The lady does not enjoy the mini-skirt?'

It may have been a delayed reaction to the rugger-buggers. Or perhaps it was the vision of the gargantuan Mrs Pype in a mini-skirt. Or just the absurdity of this entire evening. But I burst out laughing.

From somewhere blood managed to rise into the vicar's face. His eyes watered, and with a final glare at my offending thighs he brushed past Carlo. Then, hustling Mrs Pype before him like some docile sow, he seized their two coats from the peg and wrenched open the door. The words 'Catholic whore' drifted in out of the night.

I looked around me, bewildered. I had lost another bunch of customers. Clearly I was being employed to empty the restaurant.

Carlo was raising his eyes heavenwards.

'Protestants,' he hissed. 'No love of beauty.' Slowly his eyes descended, undressing me as they did so. 'Such beautiful legs.' Carlo's hands began to mime other portions of my anatomy he appreciated. He re-created my body in air, then clapped his hands ecstatically. 'Oh *Bella Claudia*, we should be in *Eetaly*, not Devonsheer.'

By now I was growing rather sick of all this.

'*Bella Claudia* or not,' I said sharply, 'if you want me to go on working here, Carlo, I think I'd better wear something decent.'

Mamma Gina was gazing on tolerantly all this time, with a knowing smile on her lips. I imagined she must have witnessed this performance many times before. And I wondered if she had once been the shape Carlo had drawn in air, and why she seemed to care so little about her husband's lecherous fantasies.

The restaurant began to fill up again. Finally, around midnight when the last customers had left, she drew me aside.

'He a good man, Carlo,' she assured me in a low voice. 'But he no good cook.' Mystified by why she should be telling me this, I nodded politely; whereupon she plunged a large shiny hand into a drawer beneath the till and brought out a photograph of an exquisitely handsome young man. '*He* very good cook,' she said.

'Your son?' I asked.

Mamma Gina looked at me askance, then burst out laughing.

'Son?' She went on laughing. 'No, no, he my lover. Very good cook. How you say? He fucking good. Carlo no fucking good. No good cook.'

The truth dawned.

'You mean *cock*.'

She smiled radiantly.

'Yes! That what I say, very good cook. Big. Strong. Carlo no good cook. Is all' – and she imitated her husband's mime with her hands – 'is all in the sky. Sky no good. Cook is good. So we happy. Carlo happy with the sky. I happy with the cook.'

At that moment the kitchen door opened, and there wiping his hands on a cloth was the same exquisitely beautiful young man. He was dressed all in white, and he smiled at Mamma Gina. I turned away to hide my own smile, because the beautiful young man *was* the cook.

Joan always picked the quinces in the old orchard as late in the year as possible, never before November when they were properly ripe, she assured me. There were vast quantities of them, enough to feed the entire West Country on quince jelly if she ever felt like getting round to it. What she really liked was the smell of them, rich and heady, almost intoxicating. This was why she picked them as late as she dared before the first sharp frost, and then carefully stored them on long slatted racks in the tumbledown shed which she also used for some of her bee equipment.

'I don't know why I bother,' she said one misty evening as she passed the gatehouse on her way back from the orchard. 'Two-thirds of them always get thrown on the compost heap in the spring. It's a stupid ritual I have. I pick them, store them, and chuck them away.'

I laughed.

'I know perfectly well why you're bothering this year,' I said.

Joan looked put out, and gave her red hair a toss.

'I don't know *what* you mean,' she exclaimed.

'But he hasn't been helping you today, has he?'

She gave a shrug, and didn't reply.

It was obvious to everyone that Joan's extra energy in gathering the quince crop was directly related to the man who'd volunteered to help her. What she didn't know was the reason why Fergus had suddenly decided that picking quinces was far more urgent than lecturing at the university or writing books. I suspected Joan secretly believed it was entirely due to her, and that Fergus harboured a ravening lust for her trim little body. Certainly she now dressed in order to make the best possible display of it. Megan claimed that she'd caught her selecting a new Wonderbra at Marks & Spencer's.

Suddenly I was seeing a great deal of Fergus. For the moment whatever else was in his life was entirely secondary to picking quinces with Joan, after which he'd come and spend the night with me. I was beginning to feel I was his lover by proxy.

'Fancy her, Fergus, do you?' I asked, propping myself up on one elbow and gazing at him. 'I know. The appeal of the older woman. Redhead. Never had an affair before. Or so she says. Irresistible, isn't it?'

Fergus gave me one of his half-smiles, and reached out to run his hands over my breasts.

'Jealous?'

I placed my hands over his.

'It's sexy being jealous.'

'Good.'

'Beast.'

'I know.'

It was Sunday morning. Now that all the leaves had gone it

felt as though we made love in full view of half the county. By raising my head a mere inch or two I could take in a whole stretch of coastline from the estuary westwards towards Cornwall. Closer, the chimneys of Priory Hall rose above the avenue of lime-trees, which I was quite sure did *not* have a preservation order on them as Caroline's planning officer claimed. Closer still, the tangled shapes of Joan's quince-trees stood out against the tidal marsh, and next to them was the crumbling brick shed where Fergus and she had been storing fruit for the past few days.

Fergus had a plan. He smiled self-mockingly as he told me. However absurd the idea of a medieval aphrodisiac might appear, he was determined to pursue it, he said, at least as a piece of detective fiction. It would make a good story. *The Devil's Work* was progressing, he assured me, and I was emerging as a delightfully dangerous heroine. When I asked what was to become of me in the end, he said he couldn't possibly know until he'd discovered the magic ingredient and tried out the nuns' recipe. So, next year he intended to make an inventory of everything that grew in the priory garden, and get each plant identified by a botanist friend at the university. Whatever the 'satur rote' might be, he would find it.

At this point I laughed and suggested he was obviously losing his marbles, and why didn't he just make up the entire story instead of pretending it was real? Fergus merely gave me another of his private smiles and said if that was the case, since I was his heroine, perhaps I'd prefer our love-making not to be real either?

That was unanswerable, and to prove it I pulled him down on top of me.

After he'd left around mid-morning I lay there convinced more than ever that the love-bubble we lived in would survive just so long as Fergus was writing his book; then at the final full stop the bubble would burst and it would be as though we'd never met. And my free-floating year would be over.

I tried not to think about that. I tried to believe I didn't care; that it was all a delightful game, and games come to an end when the whistle blows.

Something a great deal more imminent than love-games

was also occupying my mind, Caroline's Literary Conference. By now Megan, Joan and I had taken all possible rescue precautions: Plan B was ready to be put into operation. Glyn was hard at work preparing his lecture on Anne Boleyn, and Megan's local historian had agreed to enlighten the audience about minor Elizabethan love-poets. The Rev Pype had leapt at the opportunity to deliver a valedictory oration on 'Sin and Retribution', convinced – according to Glyn – that this was to be a contribution only marginally less valuable to the Christian community than the Sermon on the Mount. I'd long since abandoned pointing out that nothing could be further from 'Mistresses in Literature' than the vicar's puritan fundamentalism; but both Megan and Joan insisted that the conference needed some sound and fury to round it off, and that Caroline would certainly expect it, and indeed rise to it.

One merciful relief was that Fergus had already been booked to chair a medievalists' seminar in Cambridge that weekend. None the less he'd agreed to persuade a university colleague to speak about the role of mistresses in French Romantic poetry, which at least would add scholarly weight to the proceedings.

It all sounded entirely grim to me, and I dreaded to think how many people would be rushing to demand their money back. Then there would be unpaid hotel bills which Caroline would be compelled to meet, not to mention the cost of specially installed heating, microphones, acres of little chairs, and the no doubt hopelessly inadequate sanitary arrangements which Caroline had only considered at the very last minute, having finally been persuaded that five hundred paying guests might not be entirely happy to be asked to squat in the bushes on a chill December morning.

Patrick, down for a long weekend as a respite from his bimbos, was even more dismayed by the coming débâcle. As if the disasters at Lloyd's weren't enough, he moaned. In any case, he pointed out, the customary practice was for conferences to be organised by a team of experts who would attend to everything, and merely take their cut of the takings. But Caroline was adamant. She dismissed such suggestions as so much unnecessary bureaucracy; all that was needed, for Christ's sake, were a few phone calls and a great deal of common-sense. The conference was her idea, and therefore her responsibility. The trouble with us was that none of us had an ounce of guts or imagination. Besides, she rounded on Patrick, she had no intention of sharing the profits with anyone; and what the hell was he doing daring to offer her advice on finance when his own stupidity had already brought about the loss of the entire family fortune?

Patrick looked bleakly around for support, only to see defeat on our faces.

He cut the weekend short.

Altogether it was a nightmare which made my first evening at Mamma Gina's seem like a children's tea-party.

On the Saturday of the conference I awoke before dawn, convinced that the tumbrils were already rolling and the guillotine was a mere two hours away. As daylight began to spread across the winter meadow I gazed over towards the medieval barn, now decorated with a large banner saying 'Literary Conference'. The path leading to it had been smartly re-laid with gravel, and painted signposts were planted here and there indicating 'Toilets', 'Cloakroom', 'Buffet' and 'Bar'. A profusion of Portacabins filled the open space between the barn and the ancient priory wall, each with a bright-red pennant fluttering cheerfully. I had to admit that so far Caroline's organisation looked remarkably impressive, and I experienced a desperate hope that the conference might actually work out after all.

Then I caught sight of Jehoshaphat, standing motionless as far away as his tether would permit; and his expression of fateful gloom seemed to be telling me what I knew in my heart to be true.

Mine was the morning shift. Somehow I needed to keep Caroline away from the danger area for as long as possible. Joan and I had worked out an elaborate system of coded messages to shield Caroline from the full impact of the disaster. She was to stand guard by the gatehouse telephone in order to keep me in touch as people started to arrive around nine-thirty. Megan had undertaken to sell tickets, installed in a little pill-box by the entrance. One of the flame-throwers would be on duty at the barn to show visitors to their seats. His twin brother was to act as roving messenger and scout, directing cars into the meadow (from which Jehoshaphat was to be temporarily banished), and with instructions to ring me on the hand-phone should anyone unexpected or undesirable arrive.

It was the best we could do. I felt it might have been just about adequate for a village fête.

As I drove out of the gatehouse arch I caught sight of Megan trudging towards me, wrapped up miserably like some straggler in the retreat from Moscow.

'I had a dream last night,' she called out, 'that we'd put up road-signs re-directing everyone to Torquay, and then gone off in the opposite direction and got blind drunk. D'you think it's too late to do that?'

We exchanged brave smiles, and I drove on. It was beginning to rain. Oh God.

Caroline's Mercedes looked more than ever like a hearse in the morning gloom. I parked my little Fiat behind it, and pressed the front doorbell. Nothing happened for a long while, and I began to fantasise that Caroline had done a bolt and was even now sipping her first glass of champagne Club Class heading for the Bahamas.

Eventually she opened the door herself. I scarcely recognised her. She was dressed to kill. A black wrap-around skirt ended at her ankles, revealing polished black boots. A matching Edwardian jacket flared out over her hips, and beneath it a white silk shirt rose up to a tie-neck. Her long blonde hair was swept high into a coiled plait.

'The right image for a literary hostess, don't you think?' she said confidently, ushering me indoors. 'I intend to make an entrance.'

She glanced disapprovingly at my jeans.

'Absolutely,' I muttered, feeling more uneasy by the minute.

'Now, how about a drink before we go down? What have we got, half an hour?'

She glanced at the time. I found myself wondering if they were real diamonds in her Cartier watch.

Champagne at nine o'clock in the morning was probably

the best thing for both of us. It cushioned my despair, and it provided an invaluable delay before Caroline insisted on making her grand entrance. I was already planning other delays, my last resort being a car crash, preferably involving the police who would waste hours taking statements and demanding to see my licence and insurance, which I would conveniently have mislaid. Caroline would then be abusive, and with any luck get hauled off to the police station for serious interrogation.

She kept looking at her watch.

'I'm a bit surprised I haven't heard from any of them,' she exclaimed, tapping her champagne glass impatiently with her finger-nails. 'But I suppose literary people are like that, aren't they? Don't bother with the little niceties any more than I do. Perhaps that's why I like them.'

I was bemused by the idea of Caroline, who only ever read the *News of the World*, being the social hub of the international literary world.

'Who exactly have you asked?' I ventured cautiously.

She gave me a vexed look, as though I'd asked something tiresomely trivial.

'Oh, I can never remember their names,' she said airily. 'Well, a few of them I can. Antonia Fraser. Harold Pinter. Alan Clark. Marina Warner. Oh, and Andrew Morton of course.' She paused, and carefully plucked a few specks of dust from her jacket. 'I could probably recall the others if I had time. I just rang Melvyn Bragg and asked him who the top writers were. He was very sweet; gave me their phone numbers and told me how to spell their names.'

'You mean you . . . just . . . made phone-calls?'

The vexed look returned.

'Of course. What else did you expect me to do? I phoned all over the world. Took me days tracking them down. Then I phoned their publishers and told them to pay the air fares and the hotel bills.'

I blinked.

'And what did you actually say to these writers whoever they are, Caroline?'

'Well, naturally I told them what it was all about. The

"Mistresses in Literature" idea. I said it seemed obvious to me that great authors never wrote about their wives, but only about women they were having affairs with. Then I said I assumed they all had mistresses themselves, unless of course they were gay, and that people would love to hear how they wrote about them. So altogether it was terribly important that they turn up.'

'And they agreed?'

'A few of them put the phone down. But mostly they laughed and said it was a brilliant idea.'

'But did they actually agree to come?'

Caroline clicked her tongue irritably.

'Well, they didn't give me a signed affidavit, if that's what you mean, for Christ's sake.' She gave me a dismissive glare. 'Look, Claudia,' she went on, and I could see her making a special effort to be tolerant, 'there's always a trick with something like this. You put all your efforts into landing your big fish, and once you've done that, then everyone else falls into line. They're terrified of being left out, particularly since the South Bank Show is doing a "special". Did I tell you that, by the way? Perhaps I forgot. Authors love to be on television: it makes them feel they're actually communicating with someone, especially since their books so rarely do.'

I wondered how Caroline knew, since she never read any.

'So, who *is* your big fish,' I asked.

I waited for her say it was Jeffrey Archer, or perhaps Barbara Cartland, or maybe someone nobody had ever heard of who happened to be married to a distant cousin of Caroline's. Who the hell, after all, was likely to give a second of their time to attend some tinpot conference in Norton Abbas? I prepared my face for the great let-down.

Caroline was gazing nonchalantly out of the window.

'I'm lucky, I suppose,' she said wistfully, 'because he happened to be in Stockholm this week receiving his Nobel Prize.' She turned to me with a patronising smile. 'I expect even you may have heard of Juan Diego Morelleja.'

I felt suitably crushed. And astonished. To have described Morelleja as a 'big fish' would have been insulting to say the least. The words 'literary giant' seemed more appropriate:

even I – as Caroline had unkindly put it – was aware of the man acclaimed everywhere as South America's literary genius. Even David, who rather pooh-poohed fiction as a rule, had been known to drop his name with some respect. Fergus had once said he'd give his right arm to be able to write like Morelleja.

The notion that this man was actually prepared to trek here to this medieval seat of Catholicism seemed . . . well, beyond imagining.

'How did you persuade him to come?' I enquired extremely cautiously.

Caroline was once again gazing reflectively out of the window. She gave a little shrug.

'Oh, I just left a message for him in Stockholm. It's not that far away, after all; and anyway, he'll enjoy a few days' peace and quiet in the English countryside after all those dreadful jungle trips he keeps making.'

'And you've told everyone else he'll be here?'

Caroline turned her head with a frown.

'Yes, of course. That's why they're all coming.'

I closed my eyes. I tried to bend my mind round the fact that all of literary Britain was apparently at this very moment hastening to Norton Abbas because Caroline had left a message with some hotel receptionist in Sweden suggesting that the most successful writer in the world might enjoy a couple of windswept winter days in the English back-of-beyond in the company of someone he'd never met or even heard of. This was madness. Caroline, I decided, could sort out this débâcle on her own.

Suddenly the phone went. I grabbed it. A croaky voice crackled on the other end. It was one of the flame-throwers.

'Is that you, Miss Foscari?' came the voice.

'Yes,' I said nervously.

'There's someone here asking for Mrs Uppingham. Says he's One.'

'One what?' I demanded, in no mood for games.

There was a pause. I could just make out a murmur of voices in the background. Then the croaky voice came back.

'One Diego More-something-or-other. What shall I do with him?'

My mouth felt dry. I just handed the phone to Caroline.

'Here he is,' I managed to say.

Caroline beamed as she took the phone.

'Juan, how wonderful. Tremendous. And is Van with you? . . . Oh, great. Right, I'm on my way down. Five minutes. Sorry about the weather.'

She put the phone down, turned to the mirror admiringly for a moment, and then strolled casually towards the door. I could feel myself blinking rather hard.

'And who, as a matter of interest, is Van?' I said, following her.

Caroline turned as she reached the door.

'Van? That's Juan's wife. Lady Vanessa Stanhope. Used to be married to that ghastly prat Henry Tarrant. She and I were at school together. That's how I got him. The old girls' network, if you like.'

She laughed and grabbed my hand.

'Come on, Claudia. This is going to be fun.'

She was still humming as we made our way to my car.

'Oh, by the way,' she said, clambering in beside me, 'I meant to tell you, I've invited all the press. You *will* look after them, won't you? There'll be some Italians there because of Umberto. And Germans too of course, with Günter Grass. Maybe a few Russians. And ITN naturally. But I'm sure you'll manage.'

I tried to laugh.

Nine

The bewildering triumph of the conference had a high-octane effect on Caroline, revitalising her assault on the National Trust and her determination to gain the support of the local authorities by any means at her disposal.

'The great thing about going to bed with a planning officer is that he knows exactly where to put it,' Caroline announced in ringing tones a few days after the literary razzmatazz was finally over, and the celebrities and the press had departed.

It was one of those remarks she was apt to come out with whenever she felt the conversation was flagging. I could see from her face that the idea was already inspiring further extravagant thoughts.

'And since Gerald's so good at knowing where to put things,' she went on, 'I wonder if he might think of somewhere to put the children.' She sighed. 'Oh God. Three weeks' holiday in an English winter. Chloe will be in love and sob all the time. Joel will be locked in the bathroom counting his pubic hairs. And Samantha will have her usual Christmas tantrums. I *hate* Christmas. I suppose you'll be going away with your lover, Claudia.'

I said I was.

'Shit,' she muttered. 'What a time to leave a friend in need. Ingratitude. Where are you going?'

I said I didn't know.

'Oh Jesus. Little romantic surprises, eh? Aren't you bored with Fergus yet? How's his wife?'

Caroline must have asked me that question a dozen times.

'I don't believe he's got one,' I answered guardedly. 'Or if he has, then she's buried away in his past somewhere.'

'Ah. You wait,' she said with a laugh. 'She'll crawl out of the woodwork one of these days like a death-watch beetle. They always do.'

I said nothing. There were so many things Caroline could never grasp about my affair with Fergus. First of all, she had no understanding whatsoever of the word 'contentment'. Having set eyes on him – admittedly upside-down – she perfectly realised why I should have wanted to leap into bed with Fergus: that 'Greek god' look, the long fair hair, the penetrating blue eyes, the air of mystery and rather frightening intelligence. I'd have been a complete idiot not to fancy him, she said; she only wished she'd got there first. But four months later, and I *still* wanted him. This was quite beyond her, and she never stopped expressing her disbelief. Of course the first few times with a lover were always exciting, she acknowledged: it was someone new and different. New shapes. New smells. New sounds on the pillow. But after that it wasn't new and different any longer, was it? So you'd have an orgasm or two, and that was nice, but then he'd still be straining and banging away, and by now you'd be thinking about who was going to win Wimbledon or that phone call to the builders you'd forgotten to make. Four months of that. Jesus.

And Caroline would gaze at me incredulously.

Then there was my not knowing whether Fergus was married, or indeed anything about him at all. This was even more beyond her. Caroline always found out everything about a new lover between the first and second fuck, she assured me; if not earlier. It was just natural curiosity, especially about the wife. It was vital to know about her straight away. Why had he married her? When had he begun to get bored? Did she have affairs too, and if not, why not? And then she'd start telling him about Patrick, and how when you'd done your best with four inches for a few years you desperately needed something more substantial – and now would he kindly get on with it?

I'd learnt a great deal about Caroline's sex-life in the two and a half years I'd known her. Invariably it seemed to follow the same course, the pursuit of distraction. The guiding thread of her life was boredom, and she was as easily bored *with* men as she was without them. She once moaned to me that God had shown woefully little imagination in providing only one primary sexual organ per person; and, what was more, they were all much the same – one went outwards and the other went in. Since He had managed to populate the Garden of Eden with sixty-seven varieties of bumble-bee – or so Joan had informed her – why had He been so uninspired as to create only one pair of prototypes for the human race? God had deliberately condemned us all to monotony, she complained, and then expected us to worship Him. Bloody cheek. No wonder they crucified His son.

These perorations were usually delivered – along with much alcohol – as a curtain-raiser to a meeting of the war cabinet; and in the run-up to Christmas these meetings (and perorations) were becoming increasingly frequent. Joan, Megan and I would be assembled like disciples round the drawing-room table, where the press cuttings on the conference were carefully displayed like battle-honours among the glasses and bottles of champagne. And then Caroline would launch into some mighty opinion. There seemed to be no shortage of these: her recent conquest of the world of books had armed her with an unshakeable confidence that other conquests would soon be hers. There was something about doing battle with the National Trust which stimulated the crusader in Caroline, or so she liked to think.

'Crusader, my arse,' exclaimed Megan one afternoon after Caroline had hurried off to the loo, leaving us standing there in the drawing-room like courtiers. 'She just adores making trouble. Look at the trouble she's put me to these last couple of weeks. I've been slogging away morning, noon and night.'

We'd all been mysteriously summoned to what Caroline described as an 'unveiling ceremony'. Megan had been sworn to secrecy: all Joan and I knew was that this was to be Caroline's response to a court order requiring Mrs Uppingham to remove the offending portraits from the great drawing-room on pain of eviction. Pamela Leggatt had followed up the court order by announcing her intention to inspect the 'cleansed' premises personally the following week.

'Right, Megan,' Caroline called out as she swept back into the room. 'Demonstration, please.' She turned to Joan and me. 'Now I warn you, this may not be entirely flawless: we've only had one rehearsal.'

Megan grasped a lightweight step-ladder which had been

resting by the French windows, and set it up carefully in front of one of the large nude portraits of the admiral's mistresses. It was the painting of the Puerto Rican barmaid who Caroline claimed looked exactly like me, though any resemblance was now confused by the Christmas decorations which Carmen had been instructed to drape over and around the portraits until they resembled multi-coloured wigs.

The ladder creaked alarmingly as Megan began to climb it, and Joan stifled a giggle. Megan's brawny arms were now spread out above her as if she were a bill-poster; and suddenly I noticed that what I'd taken to be one of Carmen's Christmas decorations was in fact a roll of canvas neatly fastened beneath the picture-frame. Megan carefully eased something free with both hands, then gradually lowered the roll down the face of the painting until it exactly covered the entire surface.

At first all I could make out on either side of Megan were large areas of painted sky with fluffy clouds. Then, as she descended the step-ladder, a cluster of little pink cherubs, each with tiny wings, began to emerge, frolicking angelically on yet more clouds.

Megan pulled the step-ladder away and stood back.

'I copied Tiepolo,' she explained proudly.

I had no idea who Tiepolo was, and kept an appreciative silence. So did Joan. But Caroline strode up to the painting, peered closely at one of the naked cherubs, and let out one of her rippling laughs.

'Judging by his winkie I assumed you'd copied Patrick,' she exclaimed. Then she put on a straight face. 'Except that Patrick's circumcised, if you look closely.'

Caroline was enjoying herself.

The show took almost half an hour. Megan must have lost several pounds – and a great deal of perspiration – clambering up and down the step-ladder in front of picture after picture. Joan and I watched in bemused admiration as one by one the admiral's mistresses disappeared beneath pots of geraniums, bowls of fruit, a dead chicken, several more cherubs, a sailing-dinghy, the Norton Abbas parish church, and finally a lifelike study of Jehoshaphat.

We applauded. And when Megan demonstrated how, by

applying Cow Gum along the inside edges, each canvas could be made to fit its frame without even a wrinkle, we applauded even more.

'Such versatility, Megan,' Joan said, strolling admiringly from one canvas to another. 'And what a work-rate. All this in two weeks!'

Megan sat slumped in a chair after her labours.

'The things one does for Caroline,' she muttered as I came over to offer my congratulations.

But everyone always did things for Caroline. And if there'd been moments when the three of us vowed never to lift a finger for her again, Caroline's *coup de théâtre* with the 'Mistresses in Literature' conference had entirely dispelled such resentments.

We all had our special memories of that event. For me it was the sight of Caroline on the platform with her arms round two Nobel Prize-winners. For Joan it was the moment when I informed the rather intrusive reporter from the *Sun* that Tolstoy had unfortunately left to catch an early train. For Glyn, still overwhelmed with relief at not being required to give his talk on Anne Boleyn, the golden occasion was when a dozen internationally famous writers voluntarily gathered in his bookshop in order to sign copies of their work. Megan preferred the incident when a heavily painted lady in the audience rose to announce that she'd been the mistress of quite a number of celebrated authors, none of whom had ever written a single word about her; and in order to prove that this conference was not merely so much hot air, please would one of writers assembled here be prepared to correct this oversight in return for the customary favours?

Caroline herself opted for the bizarre climax of the whole weekend. 'There's only one possible candidate for immortality,' she exclaimed, shaking her head at the rest of us. 'The Rev Pype. He got the biggest cheer of all.'

It was true that Jonathan Pype, entirely undeterred by the company, had strode to the platform just as Caroline was winding up her valedictory address, and had proceeded to deliver his passionate sermon on 'Sin and Retribution'.

So perhaps, on second thoughts, my favourite moment was

Caroline's expression of perfect joy as she watched the faces of the assembled *notorati*, all of them imagining that here was a venerable master of English prose whom none of them dared admit they'd never heard of.

Mamma Gina had decided to adopt me. Her round face would brighten into a smile as I entered the restaurant to begin my evening duties.

'Eh, bella Claudia,' she'd exclaim loudly, enfolding me within damp arms.

I loved the way she pronounced my name. For so many years I'd been *Claw*dia, which I hated: it made me sound like a lobster. To be *Clow*dia again was a return to childhood. I could feel the Italian sun in her voice.

After the restaurant closed around midnight she'd taken to beckoning me to a table near the kitchen and pouring out two glasses of grappa. It was a special bottle which came from her native Lucca, tall and slender as if made specially to accommodate the sprig of tarragon that rose within it.

She'd slide one of the glasses across the table towards me while Carlo grumpily busied himself in the restaurant doing the clearing-up which should have been my job.

'No, no, let 'im do eet,' she insisted. 'Ee touch the ladies, so ee clear up their bloody mess. Lazy bugger.' Mamma Gina enjoyed throwing out English terms, the meaning of which I suspected she didn't always know. Meanwhile her lover would eye me cagily from the kitchen. He was Sicilian, I learnt (so much for 'Tuscan Specialities'), and Mamma Gina made it clear that she paid him well for his services as a 'good cook'. 'Ee fock beautiful,' she assured me, leaning her enormous breasts heavily on the table. 'Carlo, ee no fock beautiful. All is dreams, and looking down the blouses.'

Our midnight grappa soon became an invitation to mutual confidences. I realised that for all the sixteen years I'd been in England there'd never been anyone from my own country I could share thoughts with; no one who understood what it was like to have been brought up in Italy, with all those warm and suffocating bonds, and then to have broken away. There were so many things I scarcely needed to explain to Mamma

Gina. The sense of no longer belonging anywhere, of having cast oneself out, of having a wandering heart forever pining for what one had voluntarily shed, of feeling homesick for a home one didn't want.

'But you so *bee*-u-tiful,' she'd say, shaking her head. 'Why you'ave no home? No man? *Bambini?*'

There were moments when she sounded just like Anna-Maria.

One evening I told her my mother believed I was in a convent being cared for by the good nuns; and her eyes widened.

'O, *Spirito Santo*. You a virgin?'

I laughed.

I explained that I'd been married for more than ten years, and now I'd walked out.

'Why? He terrible man?'

I felt like saying 'he no good cook', but restrained myself.

'We just grew apart,' I said cautiously.

Mamma Gina looked puzzled. I realised that she assumed all married people grew apart – as she and Carlo had – but this didn't mean you broke up the marriage. You just made accommodation. You found 'a good cook', and if necessary you paid him well for it.

And accommodation, I realised, was exactly what David would choose. Separate beds. Then separate rooms. Separate lives. Except that there would be no accommodation for 'a good cook'. The Box Hill constituents would never put up with that.

The following evening the last customers left early, so the grappa ceremony began soon after eleven. Mamma Gina always turned on the television the moment the restaurant was empty. Not that she ever did more than glance at it, but it flickered away behind me in the corner of the room, occasionally evoking a response from Mamma Gina when something caught her eye.

'She fuck about. You tell.'

'He bad breath in bed.'

'He lousy cook.'

'Shame no tits.'

I learnt to ignore these interpolations, and rarely turned

round to register what had inspired them on the screen. But on this particular evening her eyes began to wander to the TV set more frequently than usual, until our conversation about the corruption of Italian politicians – usually an inexhaustible topic with Mamma Gina – stuttered almost to a halt, and all I could hear was a volley of ribald comments relating to whoever it was occupying the screen behind my back.

'Oh, ee *bee*-u-tiful man!'

'Ee real good cook. You tell.'

'Oi, oi! She fancy 'im big way.'

'She gonna take 'im off fuck straight after show.'

Eventually Mamma Gina could bear my inattention no longer, and shook my arm.

'Eh Claudia, you look. You want man like that fuck you?'

This time I did look. It was Fergus.

Perhaps it was the grappa; all the same I should have kept quiet.

'He *does* fuck me,' I said.

There was total silence. The woman interviewer was winding up the show. The camera did a final close-up on Fergus, who had put on his private smile, then pulled back to reveal the studio audience as the credits rolled. Mamma Gina was gazing at me, her eyes watering. She blinked for a moment or two; then, as if reaching for support, she grasped the bottle and poured out two more glasses of grappa.

'Santa Maria,' was all she managed to say.

From that evening onwards Italian politicians never got a look-in on our conversations over grappa. Mamma Gina was obsessed by my relationship with Fergus. At first what intrigued and confused her was the idea that someone who served as a waitress in her restaurant should be having an affair with a man who appeared on television. She assumed that people she saw on the screen inhabited an Olympian world rather like Megan's cherubs fluttering among the clouds; and if they ever did come down to earth it was only to get married and divorced, or occasionally to run into trouble with the law.

But having finally accepted that one of these Olympians actually climbed into my bed, she immediately decided I needed a manager, and that she was the very person.

'He gonna do decent thing marry you?' she asked furiously a few evenings later.

I reminded her that I was married already, and she looked at me sharply.

'Then you divorce lickety-split?' I had no idea where she'd got such a phrase from. 'And you gonna marry Mr Fergoose have big party here with Mamma Gina.' She looked thoughtful for a moment. 'I think ee very good cook, Mr Fergoose. I tell. I think your 'usband no very good cook.'

How right she was. And I burst out laughing. She looked at me disapprovingly.

'You listen Mamma Gina,' she said firmly. 'She know few things. Bad cook is bad life. You no want mistake two times.'

Again how right she was.

It was nearly one in the morning before I got back to the gate-house. A little woozy from grappa, I fell into bed conscious that my life seemed to be turning into an Italian soap opera. Then it struck me that most of my youth had been an Italian soap opera too, with Anna-Maria singing the arias. The only difference was that Anna-Maria had been hell-bent on marrying me off first to a pasta-maker, then to a sausage-maker, whereas with Mamma Gina the target was 'Mr Fergoose'.

I fell asleep wondering how Fergus would enjoy his new name, and whether Mamma Gina was right about the TV interviewer 'taking 'im off fuck straight after show'.

In the night I dreamt of him with another woman, and awoke angry with myself for being miserable. It was still dark, and I made a determined effort to dive back into my dream so that I could announce, 'I don't care.'

But I couldn't, and I did care. Suddenly my year of freedom seemed very chill.

The next morning was Saturday, the Saturday before Christmas. For the first time almost since I could remember I felt a longing for Italy. Here everyone had their own lives except me. Even Caroline, on the edge of losing everything, in the end had her husband and her children; whereas I had an ex-husband and no children. It even seemed significant that I lived in a gatehouse, a place you passed through on the way to somewhere else.

I sat there feeling too depressed to stir myself. Where had all the excitement of summer gone?

I was still drowning my self-pity in coffee when the phone went.

'Claudia, I'm in London,' came Fergus's quiet voice. 'I need to ask you something.'

I miraculously no longer wished to be in Italy.

'Ask away,' I said as calmly as I could.

'About Christmas. Are you prepared to be surprised?'

I laughed.

'When do you *not* surprise me, Fergus?'

'Then one more won't disturb you, will it?'

'I like your surprises,' I said.

'Good. In that case I'll call for you on Thursday. About lunchtime, OK? And I'll whisk you off in the afternoon.'

'In your sleigh?'

'Not exactly.'

I laughed.

'You can whisk me wherever you want – I'm yours for Christmas. I might even let you unwrap me.' (Perhaps I shouldn't have said that, I thought.) Suddenly I felt fragile and insecure. 'I *do* want to see you, Fergus,' I added rather urgently.

Oh God, I shouldn't have said that either. I was breaking my own rules: I'd vowed to keep this affair sexy and light. No dependence. No confessions of need. No jealousies. No cravings of the heart. No wounded hopes. No pining for phone calls that never came. This was supposed to be my year of freedom, not slavery. Fergus was the last man in the world ever to fall in love with. How could I have allowed myself to forget that?

I was so thrown by a sense of imminent disaster that it was a second or two before I could take in the two little words that floated down the phone into my ear.

'Me too,' he said.

Caroline with her three children around her was a caged lioness. She paced the house snarling while they followed her about, entirely unmoved by her outbursts of irritation.

'Oh, for Christ's sake get it yourself.'

'How many times have I told you not to use my bathroom?'

'Turn that bloody music down. It's driving me mad.'

'Why do you have to use that frightful aftershave when you don't even need to shave yet?'

'I don't care if you do wear the same size bra as me: you're not to nick mine.'

'That bottle of gin was half-full yesterday, and I don't drink the bloody stuff; so what are you trying to tell me?'

'I don't give a damn what Joanna's mother lets her do: I want him out of the house by midnight.'

'No, you certainly *won't* ask Carmen if bull-fighters are good in bed.'

'What d'you mean, "Daddy's girl-friend"? How dare you?'

In a rare moment of peace Caroline sank into a chair and gazed at me fiercely.

'Obsessed by sex, the lot of them. I don't know.'

'I wonder where they get that from, Caroline?' I said.

I laughed. Caroline didn't.

'Bloody Christmas,' she muttered. There was silence for a moment; then she gave a deep sigh. 'And tomorrow Patrick'll come down laden with presents and good cheer, and they'll be all over him. "Daddy, Daddy, let me show you this. Daddy, Daddy, I got this prize at school! Daddy, Daddy, let me ruffle your hair." Yuk! You could vomit. And I'll be in the kitchen cursing that the bloody turkey won't fit in the oven, and the Christmas pudding I made last year is seething with maggots.'

There was another sigh.

'*And* the Historic Buildings Commission are refusing to list the house Grade I, the bastards. What's the use of having a father-in-law who's the head of it if he refuses to do me a favour in my hour of need? He even had the nerve to say to me, "You don't live in Blenheim Palace, you know." Well, that's the end of favours for Patrick; and if one of his bimbos phones I'll tell her she can have him, all four inches of him.'

Then she brightened.

'But I have to tell you about the Legover woman this

morning.' Caroline gave a girlish chuckle and stretched out a hand towards the table, and I saw her fingers fumble for the glass of vodka-and-tonic which wasn't there. She turned her head, surprised, and glanced at me fiercely as though I might have stolen it; then her expression became conciliatory and she leaned back comfortably in her deep armchair.

'Oh, be a sweetheart and pour me a drink, Claudia. My usual. Not the cooking sherry; I bought that specially for the Legover bitch.' She let out a giggle. 'What I didn't realise was that I gave it to her in one of those joke glasses that tip the whole lot down your cleavage when you sip it. Joel must have sneaked it in among the others, the little beast. So that wasn't a very good start. But anyway, when I'd cleaned her up a bit I invited her to inspect the paintings. I didn't tell her they were by Megan, of course: I just let it casually slip that my great-grandfather had collected Renoirs and that I'd decided to replace the nude portraits with a few of the less valuable ones. The fat cow clearly knows fuck-all about art, though she did stare hard at the picture of the parish church and said she never knew Renoir had visited Norton Abbas. "Oh yes," I said gaily, "often. Very close friend of the family was Renoir. So was Picasso, of course. We've got lots of his too, but I decided not to hang them since your members seem so frightfully stuffy about naked flesh. Perhaps they never see any; and judging by the look of some of them, it's just as well."'

Caroline sipped happily at the vodka-and-tonic I'd poured her.

'Well, I've no idea whether the silly bitch believed a word of it,' she went on. 'But I could see she didn't dare risk making a fool of herself. She just puffed up her bosom and said nothing.' Caroline stretched out languidly, admiring her legs for a moment before giving her blonde hair a casual toss. 'You see, Claudia,' she added with a thoughtful air, 'the great thing about having been brought up as disgustingly privileged as I was, is that people half-believe you might have done just about anything. So, if I say that my grandmother was the mistress of the Archbishop of Canterbury, people believe it.' She looked at me impishly and gave a laugh. 'As it happens, of course, it's perfectly true.'

Then as if to demonstrate one of the benefits of privilege, Caroline held out her empty glass for me to refill.

'Anyway, that's the good news,' she continued. 'One crisis averted. No eviction. I'm still in there fighting. The bad news is that Gerald's efforts at blocking the National Trust's building application look like coming unstuck.' Caroline made a grimace. 'Apparently the chairman of the county council has suddenly been appointed to the board, the crafty buggers. So Gerald's being leant upon heavily by his boss. He says building work may have to begin in the spring after all.' She looked at me sharply and gave a theatrical sigh. 'So I'll just have to find something else, or someone else, won't I? Such a shame. I shall miss Gerald. But it's no good a man coming up if he can't come up with the goods, is it?' Another sigh. 'And he's been such a good lover. How's yours?'

As usual the circuit of Caroline's talk had returned to my sex-life.

I avoided the question by wandering over to the French windows and announcing that it was snowing.

'Really?' Caroline leapt up and stood next to me as we gazed out into the night and watched the huge flakes drifting down, white against the far trees, then suddenly black against the light from the house.

She put an arm round my shoulder, and I realised that she was crying.

'When I was a child there always seemed to be white Christmases here,' she managed to say after a while. 'We'd all go sledging at night down the long field above the marsh.' The voice managed to waver into a laugh. 'I'd shove snow down my sister's jumper, and my brother would pee his name in the snow. And Daddy would creep into our rooms as Santa Claus, but he'd be drunk and trip over, and I'd hear him say "Fuck!"' There was a pause, and I could feel Caroline's hand grip my shoulder more tightly. 'Now it's going to be a white Christmas again, and it'll be the last one.'

'But you can stay here, Caroline,' I said. 'They're not going to kick you out.'

She shook her head violently.

'No. How can I stay here once they're turned the place into a funfair? I couldn't possibly. We'll go. We'll just go.'

I glanced at her. Caroline's face was flushed and moist with tears, and she was staring fixedly out into the falling snow.

Suddenly she took a deep breath and wrenched her arm away from my shoulder. I saw her raise the other hand holding the vodka glass. She gazed at it for a moment as though it was a holy chalice; then in a swift movement she spun round and hurled the glass the entire length of the room, where it smashed against the wall, just managing to miss Megan's painting of cherubs and her portrait of Jehoshaphat.

'FUCK THEM!' she screamed. 'THEY SHALL NOT HAVE THIS PLACE!'

There was an eerie silence in the house, broken a few seconds later by the pattering sound of footsteps. One after the other Caroline's three children thrust their heads round the door, and grinned. The heads disappeared. Caroline took no notice.

Still breathing heavily, she turned back to me, and I could see her struggling to compose herself.

'Claudia, I mean it,' she said. 'I really do. I'm quite determined. I'll put a bomb under it first. Perhaps the IRA would oblige if I asked them? I mean it.'

I could believe it.

We walked away from the French windows and Caroline sank back into her armchair. She was quite calm by now: the vodka glass had cleared the air. She lit a cigarette and blew the smoke thoughtfully up towards the ceiling.

'I've been thinking, Claudia,' she said. 'Several thoughts, which is unusual for me.' And she laughed. 'You never knew my father, which was lucky for you – he'd certainly have groped you. He was terrible in all sorts of ways, but then so am I, *and* I need another drink.' Caroline sprang out of the armchair and bounded over to the drinks cupboard. 'But like me,' she went on, glancing at me over the tilted bottle of vodka she was pouring, 'he was foul to his family and loved us all fiercely. And he loved this place. He really did. I *know*, I just know, that he would never, never, never have given it away just like that. There has to be a trick somewhere, something we don't know. I've thought about it for six months now, and the longer I think about it the more certain I am of that. I know about the will. I know what the fucking lawyers say. But I still know I'm right. And I'm going to hang on until I find out. Christ knows how, but I shall.'

Caroline walked back across the room, handed me a drink, and, having slumped back into her armchair, took a long swig of her own.

'So, what's the next move?' I asked. 'If Gerald's come to the end of his usefulness, what now? Who's next in line?'

A cunning look came over Caroline's face, and she stretched out her long legs, twisting her feet to and fro like windscreen wipers as she did so.

'Well,' she said, and paused to admire her legs a little longer. 'After the county planning officer I thought I might try the Church.'

She clearly wasn't into explaining, and I decided not to press her. If her grandmother had been the mistress of the Archbishop of Canterbury, there seemed no reason why Caroline shouldn't ensnare at least some suffragan bishop, if not the Papal Legate, should this further her cause, whatever that might be. I assumed she wasn't setting her sights on the Rev Jonathan Pype.

'Meanwhile, my darling, I've got to survive,' she went on. 'Twenty thousand a year expenses for this place. I'm banned from opening the Hall of the Mystresses, thanks to that Legover cow. But the literary conference made quite a bit, so I've been thinking of some more events I could organise. Now tell me, what d'you think about a medical conference? Paediatricians perhaps. Children's health's all the rage at the moment, isn't it, the little buggers?' I nodded uneasily. 'And then what about a rural crafts show? This place is stiff with potters and weavers: you can't move in Devon for people doing things by hand – everything except masturbate.' Caroline gave one of her rippling laughs. 'Then we could have a rock festival, couldn't we?'

'Oh no, Caroline, I wouldn't,' I said. 'It'd turn out to be a drugs festival.'

Caroline made a face.

'Well then, a Summer Fête. How about that? All sorts of

stalls, and we take twenty per cent. Antiques. Megan can paint people's portraits, clothed unless they insist. Second-hand books – Glyn can fix that. Second-hand clothes – I've got all that designer stuff I never wear. And Joan can sell that quince honey you're always on about. And then all your amazing herbs, belladonna or whatever they are.'

'That all sounds a much better idea, Caroline,' I said.

I looked at my watch. It was nearly nine o'clock. I'd been here more than two hours, and tomorrow I had to get ready for Fergus's 'surprise'. But how on earth did one get ready for a surprise? I tried to imagine what I might want it to be, and it discomfited me to realise that I didn't mind so long as Fergus would be there.

'And now I suppose you've got to go,' Caroline was saying rather fiercely. 'Another candlelit supper while I'm stuck here with the brats. And, oh shit, I haven't even fed the little buggers. Don't ever breed, Claudia. Your boobs droop. Your belly droops. And your man goes off with a bimbo, leaving you with the nappies.' She gave me another glare. 'And when are *you* off? Tomorrow? Christ, I hate you.' She laughed as she said it, then came over and threw her arms round me. 'And have a super time, won't you. I'll miss you. I really love you, you know.'

Once again I realised why one always forgave Caroline everything. And as I drove away from the lights of the house, the sounds of her yelling at the children gradually faded into the darkening snow.

It was mid-morning and I'd just finished packing for my 'surprise' Christmas when I caught sight of Joan peering through the French windows. Her bee equipment lay dumped on the terrace, along with a capacious anorak. It was clear that she'd removed this in order to reveal an unusually tight blue sweater. And it was equally clear that she was wearing this because she hoped Fergus might be here.

He wasn't, and as she stepped inside Joan looked disappointed.

'So you're being whisked away for Christmas,' she said with a slightly disapproving edge to her voice. 'The farthest

I ever get whisked at Christmas is the kitchen all bloody morning.'

Joan kept glancing about her just in case Fergus was lurking somewhere after all. She fancied him: she always had from the very beginning when she'd caught us sneaking out to his car, me in a rather dishevelled state, and Fergus with his hand sliding my dress off my bare shoulder. It had turned her on, and each time they'd met since then he had turned her on even more. Fergus, who saw that Joan's bees and quinces were essential to his medieval alchemy, behaved disgracefully. After helping her pick the quinces, he'd continued to spin his charms round her by showing her the medieval recipe he'd discovered and persuading her to follow it, explaining that the last line referred to a mysterious plant – the 'satur rote' – which he hadn't yet identified, but which would turn this harmless confection into a powerful aphrodisiac.

Joan's whole body had gone into spasm as he explained this. 'You're shameless, Fergus,' I said after she'd left. 'Has any man ever made a woman wet her knickers over a medieval manuscript? If I hadn't been there she'd have whipped them off.' Fergus had awarded me a sideways glance, and that slightly mocking smile of his. 'All in the interests of research,' he'd announced solemnly.

Ever since then Joan invariably found it necessary to tend to her bees whenever she knew Fergus might be here. Never can bees have been so well loved. It wasn't that I was particularly jealous. I trusted him, perhaps unwisely but none the less I did. Besides, I felt sure that he was only the latest in a long line of men whose erotic phantoms quickened Joan's rather mundane love-making with her husband. Joan was an expert in vicarious adultery.

As for Fergus, I was convinced that he didn't really believe a word of all this aphrodisiac nonsense, and all that stuff about Henry VIII desperately wanting another son: he was just keeping an elaborate game going so that he could weave the plot of his book around it. He was pretending to live out his fiction, casting a spell on those around him so that they should believe it wasn't fiction at all. It wasn't for nothing that he was calling the book *The Devil's Work*.

By now Joan had stopped glancing around her. Fergus clearly wasn't here.

'So, when he's supposed to be picking you up, then?' she enquired as casually as she could.

'Around twelve-thirty, though he's driving down from London and I dare say the snow may delay him,' I said, hoping this might discourage her from staying; and for the same reason I resolved not to offer her any coffee, and immediately felt mean.

Joan glanced at her watch. It was a quarter to twelve. I could see her weighing up in her mind whether or not she could justifiably hang around for another forty-five minutes.

And then the doorbell went.

Fergus normally just walked round the back and came in through the French windows. But perhaps the 'surprise' was something heavy which he could only lug as far as the front door. I caught sight of Joan giving her lips a lick and her bosom a little thrust as I made my way to the door.

'Coming,' I called out cheerfully. Well, to hell with Joan being here. I'd simply say she happened to be passing, then rather ostentatiously start laying the lunch table for two.

I could feel my smile broaden as my hand lifted the latch. My body tingled. I'd put on a low-cut blouse which always sent Fergus's eyes plunging, and I could feel my nipples harden at the thought.

I opened the door. Standing in the melting snow, carrying flowers, was David.

Shock creates a time-warp. Probably it was two or three seconds at most, but in that ocean of time I swear I relived the entire ten years of my marriage, all the frustrations and despair, the delusions and the helplessness, the weariness and the capitulations, the guilts, envies, loneliness, emptiness, futility, anger, the enormous sense of waste. And now here he was, bearing flowers. It was yet another peace mission: we should try again, we have too much to lose, we mustn't run away, you are the woman I love, you are the woman I want to grow old with.

My God, how I grew old with you, David.

'May I come in?' he said gently.

'Of course.'

I felt numb. I heard myself say, 'This is Joan.' And then, for some reason, 'She keeps bees.'

This was appalling. The silence was like a time-bomb. If only something would happen. Anything. A flash of lightning. A huge fart. Anything at all.

'Pleased to meet you,' David muttered.

I realised that Joan had absolutely no idea who this man was.

'Er . . . my husband,' I explained belatedly. 'David Hazlitt.'

We just stood there, the three of us, in the middle of the room. David was still holding the flowers. My eyes begged Joan not to leave. Hers flicked to and fro, from David to me and back again, a look of bewildered fascination on her face.

'Perhaps I could put these in a vase for you,' she announced breathlessly, relieved no doubt to have an excuse to leave the room and then no doubt to slip quietly away by the side door.

Oh no you don't, I thought, grasping the flowers myself and laying them on the table. My brain was scrambling desperately to form a plan of action. It was almost twelve o'clock. Fergus could be here at any moment. My suitcase lay packed only just out of sight by the kitchen door. We were leaving – where the hell *were* we leaving for? – straight after lunch, Fergus had said. It was Christmas Eve: What on earth was David doing here? A terrible thought struck me: This couldn't be the 'surprise' Fergus had promised, could it? Arranging a showdown with my husband? A duel perhaps? A punch-up? That certainly *would* be the Devil's work. No, not even he would do that.

But how in God's name was I supposed to get rid of him?

'Would you mind leaving us to talk?' David said suddenly to Joan.

I was almost relieved. At least we'd soon know what this was all about. Joan threw me a sympathetic glance, and without bothering to say good-bye to David let herself quietly out of the front door.

Then I surprised myself.

'How dare you?' I said, spinning round to face him.

'You didn't ring. You didn't write. Who the fuck d'you think you are?'

David always hated bad language, and for years I'd never used it in order to avoid the pained expression on his face.

This time there was no expression on his face at all. I noticed it looked thinner. His hair looked thinner too. His suit was dull. He wore a nondescript tie. He was horribly clean-shaven. I was gazing at a man who was no part of my life at all.

'You're my wife,' he said quietly. 'That's why I came.'

Perhaps he meant the remark to sound humble. It didn't sound in the least humble to me, and at that moment everything that was Italian in me suddenly took over, everything that for so many years had been buried away under powder-blue.

'I AM NOT *YOUR* ANYTHING, DAVID,' I shouted.

He looked startled, then began to make placatory gestures. Oh God, he was going to be reasonable again: I could feel it coming.

'All right,' he went on in that same soothing tone of voice. 'I know I shouldn't have just turned up like this. And I'm sorry. Really sorry, Claudia. It was an impulse. But I woke up this morning and it was Christmas Eve; and it came over me that Christmas was a time to repair things, a time for a family to be together.'

I was beginning to feel quite sick, and my heart sounded as if it had an amplifier attached to it.

'Family. What the hell does that mean? We *aren't* a family, for Christ's sake, David. We never have been. My family's in Bologna, and yours is the House of Commons. What we've had together is more of a public convenience.'

That was a bit crude, but never mind. It was what I felt.

David was shaking his head.

'I'm sorry you feel like that. It's not how I see it. You've been something precious to me. You still are.'

I had to stop this. I could feel it all about to begin again. The gentle pleading. The baring of the tender soul. The inner, loving David if only I would understand. Everything was there for me if only I could reach out for it. No one would ever be as close to him as I was. Jesus, five minutes of that and I'd be the one made to feel inadequate, prepared to smash this lovely, precious, growing thing we'd created between us.

'I don't want to be *precious*, David.' I could hear a cold fury in my voice as I said it. 'I'm not a jewel. I'm not a work of art. I'm not something to be gazed at and admired, kept in a glass case. I want passion. I want joy. I want laughter. I want sex. All the things you don't understand. All the things you're actually terrified of.'

This was cruel. And it was also true.

Then, having let go of all that, a strange thing happened. I felt sorry for him. I found myself thinking – almost with tenderness – 'You're a good man, David. And that makes it so much harder. Why can't you be a total shit?'

He was just standing there. I could feel him searching for something to say. For a dreadful moment I thought he might break down, and then what would I have done?

'Don't you think—' he started to say.

I jumped in.

'No, David. I know what I think; I don't need you to do it for me. This is *it*. I want a divorce. I want an end.' And then I added, 'I want to stop hating you.'

He looked surprised. I tried to hide my own surprise at what I'd just said. Then very slowly he nodded, and I knew that for the first time in his life he'd lost.

'All right,' he said softly.

It wasn't relief that swept through me; it was a sudden wave of terrible sadness, and I wasn't even sure what it was sadness for. Perhaps it was a kind of farewell to an enemy I'd needed: that during all these months of being a fugitive I'd secretly been relying on David always being there on the edge of my life. Loathing him had been a prop. And now I really was alone. I felt frightened.

I walked with him to the door, saying nothing. I was aware how dignified he was. If he'd been my brother I'd have liked him so much. I'd have teased him, and he'd have exasperated me, but I'd have liked him and felt close to him. My bachelor brother, that's what he would have been, and that's what he should have been. Big brother David.

'I'll ring,' I said, meaning it.

He merely nodded, and walked towards his car.

As he did so I froze. A few yards away, gazing up at the gatehouse arch, was Fergus. Next to him was Joan. She caught my eye, and winked. She was pointing up at the mutilated carving of the satyr, and laughing.

'Poor bastard, having an erection chopped off like that,' I heard her say loudly. 'I wonder if it reminds Claudia of anybody?'

I was glad David was out of earshot. His car was already pulling away down the street.

'I thought I'd better keep Fergus here while you were busy,' Joan called out, looking pleased with herself. 'I did explain.'

Fergus gave me a quizzical look.

'Not one for subtlety, your friend, is she?' he said.

Then, ignoring Joan, he put his arms round me, and held me. His face was rough and unshaven, and I buried myself in it. Suddenly Fergus released me, turned his back to the gatehouse and steered me towards his car. I watched him open the door of the red Alfa-Romeo, reach inside and pull out an enormous fur coat.

'D'you think you could fit this into your luggage?' he said.

I took it from him. The weight of it almost pulled me over. God know how many wolves had lost their lives for it. Fergus noticed the astonishment on my face, and laughed.

'It's not a gift, I'm afraid. I rented it. But you're going to need it where we're going.'

I stopped myself asking where, and just looked at his face. And in that silent meeting of eyes I knew there was no point pretending: there was no way I was going to stop myself loving this man.

Ten

All around us and far away the lake was fringed by a wilderness of white forest, with patches of intense violet trapped here and there in the shadows. The sleigh held us like a shell, and everywhere the ice we sped across was a deep blue, deeper even than the sky. I grew puzzled about this since the lake was entirely snow-covered, and snow – I'd always understood – was white. Fergus explained with great confidence that it was all to do with ultra-violet rays and because the sun at this latitude was so low on the horizon. When I challenged him that he'd just made this up on the spur of the moment, he laughingly agreed; then he threw me a questioning glance as if to say, 'Well, how about all this? Are you enjoying it? Say something.'

Perhaps it was sheer happiness, but I felt too dazed.

'What *can* I say? What can I possibly say?' was the best I could offer.

I raised my voice into the wind and shook my head, as far as was possible in a fur hat from which only my nose protruded. Fergus looked at me, laughing.

'Well, try,' came a muffled sound from somewhere within his own all-enveloping fur hat.

'OK, it's the most magical place I've ever seen. I don't believe I'm here. It's unreal. It's a wonderland. I love it. And for Christ's sake how is one supposed to steer a reindeer across a frozen lake?'

'You don't. It knows.'

'Knows what?'

'Where we're going.'

'And where *are* we going?'

'I don't know. Across the Arctic Circle, the guide in front said.'

'How are we supposed to know when we've crossed it?'

'Stop asking ridiculous questions.'

'It's a perfectly sensible question. There aren't exactly signposts. Do *you* know?'

'Of course not.'

'You told me you knew everything.'

'I was lying.'

'Beast. And what happens if the ice breaks?'

'We die. But it won't. It's probably ten feet thick.'

'How d'you know?'

'Because this is Lapland. It's not the Round Pond.'

'It's just occurred to me, Caroline's probably serving Christmas pudding right now.'

'We must send her a postcard. You can buy special Santa Claus Arctic Circle stamps.'

'My saliva would freeze sticking the bloody things on.'

'Hey, hold the reins looser. You're half-throttling the poor beast.'

'You take over, then, and I can admire the scenery.'

'D'you really like it?'

'It's magic.'

'And did you like the Concorde?'

'Of course . . . And Fergus,' I shouted into the wind, 'I love you. Can you hear me? I said I LOVE YOU!'

It was as if being catapulted here at twice the speed of sound had left all the fears and anxieties of my life trailing far behind me out of sight. I was lost in a white dreamland, and at this moment I wanted to go on dreaming for ever. It was barely two hours since the Concorde had glided down over the frozen forests which seemed to have no end, and I'd watched the snow being spun into wild flurries as the engines finally deafened us to a halt on what I took on trust was a runway. Only a few hours earlier it had been breakfast before dawn at Heathrow. And before that we'd danced away the night at some secret place Fergus knew, where there'd been champagne and dinner in a private alcove and the candlelight had felt like the touch of soft fingers on my skin.

And now here. Christmas Day in a wilderness of ice and sky, with reindeer and the promise of log fires in the forest, and at the end of the day the hugest bed in Lapland in a suite of rooms overlooking a frozen river.

'Where am I? What am I doing here?' I kept saying to myself. And how did Fergus discover there was a travel firm which arranged Christmas flights to Lapland by Concorde?

A white fox sped across the ice in front of our sleigh.

The cry of an eagle resounded across the lake as the giant bird tilted against the sky and plunged among the fir-trees.

Through the wind came the distant howling of what I assumed must be wolves.

I pulled my fur hat further down over my face against the cold, and wriggled my body deeper into the coat Fergus had brought for me.

'Please tell me,' I shouted. 'Why are you doing all this for me?'

Fergus either didn't hear, or pretended not to hear.

We fell into silence: there was only the sound of the sleigh and the buffeting of the wind.

All the time we'd been crossing the lake the huge sun had barely cleared the distant fir-trees, as if it were rolling along the tops of them. Now very gradually it began to dip behind the trees, and suddenly the wind dropped, as though it had been extinguished by the setting sun. Everything became silver and still. And as I gazed around me I realised that the white wall of trees was growing nearer, until unexpectedly they parted, and one after the other the sleighs ahead of us vanished between them. A moment later a hidden creek opened up before us, and the trees closed above our heads. After the vastness of the lake, suddenly we were drawn into a tunnel of grey dusk, and all around us the laden branches were a fretwork of ice and snow which made a sound like soft breathing as we passed.

I felt bewitched by the wonder and strangeness of it all. Neither of us spoke.

Then, 'Look,' I said quietly.

And there in the half-darkness I could see points of light, clusters of them, darting along the edge of the ice like winter fireflies. Ahead of us the sleighs were stopping, and people were stepping out on to the snow.

As we drew closer I could make out a village of wooden

houses, each roof so deeply hung with snow that it all but sank into the winter landscape. In a clearing among the houses a huge log fire was sending a cascade of sparks into the night. And by the light of the flames I caught sight of a long table set with rows of wooden goblets and tall wooden jugs.

'Where are we?' I whispered.

Fergus glanced at me, and in the almost-dark I could just detect a smile.

'D'you want me to make it up, or tell you the truth?'

As we stepped out of the sleigh villagers gathered round us on the ice, each holding a lantern. They were dressed from head to toe in fur, with boots that looked like elephants' feet and long ear-pieces dangling from their hats. They grinned at us, murmured some sort of greeting, shook our hands, and swinging their lanterns began to guide us towards the village and the long table where a dozen or so people from the sleighs ahead were already gathered, warming themselves by the log fire.

Then one of the villagers grasped a wooden jug and began to pour a whitish liquid into the goblets. Steam rose from each goblet as he passed them round.

I took mine, and glanced at Fergus. He was looking solemn. Then I sipped it. It was sweetish and powerful, and I didn't dare ask myself if I liked it.

Our guide turned towards us all and raised his goblet.

'Welcome,' he said. 'Welcome to a Lapland Christmas night.'

He raised a toast. We responded. Then we stood there in the Arctic night, all of us, gazing about us without speaking, the snow between the wooden houses reddened by the light of the lanterns and the fire; and beyond, the frozen silence of the forest.

I thought of childhood stories of people lifted away into their dreams and returned years later only to find the hands of the bedroom clock had scarcely moved. And I wondered if this was happening to me, and what the spell was that had brought me here. And in what time and place would I waken?

Someone was refilling my goblet, and I felt dizzy.

And still there was no sound except the crackling of the flames and the faint whispering of the trees.

The spell seemed to lift as we began to move away towards the sleighs. A pair of lanterns was fixed to the front of each, then the sleighs were turned towards the darkness of the creek where we had come. Fergus clambered in after me and took the reins, and we began to move. The lanterns in the procession ahead of us momentarily lit up the silver fretwork of branches like ghosts as they slid overhead, until suddenly the roof of the forest parted and there was nothing above but a million stars. Our sleigh gathered speed across the frozen lake, and as I gazed around me I was aware only of a vast curtain of darkness on which were studded tiny points of light from the moving sleighs, which flickered and wove in and out of one another like a silent dance of fire. And above me an eternity of stars.

If this is dream-happiness, then let me dream, I thought.

'What are you thinking?'

I gave a start as Fergus pressed his lips to the nape of my neck, then reached on either side of me to hold my breasts in his hands. He began to squeeze the nipples very lightly between his fingers until they tingled and grew hard. I shivered and lay my head back against his shoulder.

'How do you expect me to tell you anything if you do that? Disgraceful. I'm a married woman, remember?' I laughed, and turned my head to kiss him. 'But if you really want to know, I was thinking how strange it is to have made love on the Arctic Circle . . . Have you ever done it before?'

Fergus gave my ear a gentle bite.

'God, no.' His lips were placing the lightest of kisses down my neck and along my shoulder. 'I'm a man of the sun: you know that. Olive-trees and thyme-scented hills. Hot afternoons. Siestas. Warm flesh.'

And to prove it he bit mine.

'You're dreadful,' I said, laughing. 'So, why did you bring me here?'

He took his hands from my breasts and began to run his fingers through my hair, combing it methodically across my shoulders and down my back, then parting it by running his tongue down my spine. I shivered again.

'Because it's Christmas, and I wanted to give you a surprise,' he said.

We'd pulled the bed over to the window, and I was sitting upright with my arms around my knees gazing out at the lights of the small town as they shimmered on the frozen river. It must have been some time during the night, though that meant nothing since it was almost always night in this place except for an hour or so. And in the summer, I thought, it would almost always be day. Tomorrow, the guide said, we'd seize the daylight to take snowmobiles through the forest. There'd be another Lapp village, he assured us, and another welcome with hot reindeer milk mixed with honey and local spirit, just as we'd been given after our sleigh-ride across the lake.

Fergus had enquired what the 'local spirit' might be, and was none the wiser for the answer. I suggested it might have included the magic ingredient he was so keen to discover, judging by its effect on his love-making within two minutes of returning to our hotel room. 'Christ, you're enormous,' I said, then I laughed. 'But perhaps you're absolutely minute on the Equator: let's not go there.' We then gorged ourselves so hungrily we almost missed the official 'Christmas Banquet' which the guide had promised would introduce us to yet more Lapp hospitality. This turned out to be Lapp ice-maidens in unlikely local costumes who served us with everything we might wish and, in Fergus's case, a great deal more than *I* wished. One of the ice-maidens took being Lapp rather too literally by seating herself on his, displaying most of her Arctic Circles as she did so and wriggling her bum against his crutch until, in a flash of Italian temperament, I reached over and shoved her sprawling to the floor.

Fergus treated the whole event with infuriating calm, merely suggesting as we left the room that he could see no harm in enjoying a bit of Christmas spirit. I vowed to withhold all extra-marital favours thereafter, and promptly broke my vow within minutes of returning to our hotel room.

'Now you know why I brought you here,' Fergus said, still breathing heavily.

Then we slept.

And now we were gazing out into the frozen night, which might, for all I knew or cared, already be morning.

It was all so absurdly unlikely, a naked man and a naked woman staring into the Arctic night; and maybe this sense of unreality was why we found ourselves suddenly talking of things we'd always deliberately curtained off from our lives. Or perhaps, having told Fergus openly that I loved him, I felt too close and too vulnerable to keep those curtains drawn any longer.

It began almost accidentally. Fergus was half-lying next to me. I could feel his eyes taking in my body, and I could sense that if he hadn't already exhausted himself on me quite so greedily he would have liked to make love again. His penis lay across his thigh, extended just enough to suggest keen interest but clearly incapable of lift-off, and I tried not to smile. I gave the poor beached thing a gentle stroke with my thumb and forefinger, and it made a feeble effort to rise before slumping back again across his thigh. My reservoir of body fluids being drained rather dry, I felt privately relieved, and withdrew my hand just in case it should suddenly remind him of Resurrection Pudding.

'You know, there are little things I notice about you when you sit like that,' he said thoughtfully, breaking the silence. 'They're very sexy and I love them.'

'Go on,' I said. 'Tell me.'

And I prepared to wallow in self-indulgence.

'All right. In no particular order. The little moles on your shoulder, four of them: you can't even see them, can you? So I feel they're mine.' And he touched them lightly with his fingers, one after the other. 'Then, the way your hair falls over your body, like a dark waterfall: I want to bathe in it, scoop it up in my hands, run it over my face.' This was getting better and better. 'And your breasts, how they make a hidden valley underneath them when you lean forward, and when you lie back it disappears.' Fergus's hand explored first one valley, then the other. I caught my breath. Jesus, how could he do this? 'And the outline of your spine; I love running my fingers down it, then across to your hips, holding them when I make love to you.' Suddenly he gave a chuckle. 'Then of course your toes, specially the little ones; they make me smile and I want to nibble them like little potato chips, and put my tongue between them to make them wiggle about.'

I loved the way he could turn eroticism into laughter, and back again. I smiled, and felt happy. I was always happy with Fergus. Whatever the mood, there was joy in everything we did.

A crowd of thoughts jostled in my head. It was such luxury to have my body admired, and desired, after all those years with David when it might as well not have existed. I'd never known life could be like this, to feel constantly on fire, to want and be wanted, to have no reserve, no shame, no inner hunger shrivelling away unsatisfied.

'What if you stop noticing those things?' I asked.

It seemed an impoortant question. But Fergus looked startled.

'Why on earth should I?'

'People do. Men do. And women grow old.'

I'd never put a question like that to him before, and I realised I wanted him to say something wonderfully noble and romantic, like 'You'll never grow old to me; I shall always desire you.'

He didn't. He just seemed puzzled.

'It never occurs to me,' he said after a second or two. 'Never. What we have is *now*. I love it, and I love you.' His face suddenly looked defensive. 'How can I tell what will happen? I don't even want to think about it. Why should we need to? We're happy; isn't that enough?'

Perhaps that was the moment when I knew for the first time where our relationship lay, and where its boundaries lay. And a strange mixture of feelings overcame me. It was the first time Fergus had ever said openly that he loved me, and this filled me with joy. At the same time I was suddenly aware of a gulf, not between us but between how we saw ourselves. It struck me that it might be the difference between a man's and a woman's need for love, and how those differing needs coloured the fabric of our lives. Ever since I'd known Fergus I'd chosen – just as he had – to live our life together entirely spontaneously, without a thought for what might have existed before, or might possibly exist tomorrow. It was a life lived off the cuff; and it had made every day, every meeting, all our love-making, something as fresh as spring. And for all those months I'd sincerely believed that this was right for me, that it was what I needed and what I wanted.

And now I knew I was wrong. I needed more. I wanted the promise of tomorrow. And Fergus couldn't give it. I knew then that what we had between us would one day come to an end, even while I longed for there never to be an end.

How absurd it all seemed. For years I'd lived with a man who had promised everything, and given nothing. Now I had a lover who was all-giving, and could promise nothing.

It struck me that I ought to be deeply unhappy. And yet I wasn't. There was almost a sense of relief. Now that I knew precisely where I stood I was free to make the most of it. Claudia, I told myself, you are having a wonderful romantic affair: embrace it, love it, but don't call it anything else.

And I closed the curtains to shut out tomorrow.

It made me smile to realise that it took a flight to the Arctic Circle to teach me about the man I'd been sleeping with all these months. Lapland should carry a mental health warning, I decided; or maybe the 'local spirit' the Lapps put in their reindeer milk was actually a truth drug.

Or else there was something about this fairytale landscape which drew unexpected confessions out of Fergus.

Or just that I was behaving rather recklessly.

'For Christ's sake, Claudia,' he called out urgently in my ear. 'A reindeer may know where it's going, but a snowmobile doesn't. You need to *steer*.'

We were in this contraption rather like a fairground bumper-car, and I had just hit a tree. Snow and ice showered down all over us.

'D'you think I'll lose my licence?' I said, laughing.

I got the hang of it after that, and we skimmed through the silver forest through shafts of pale sunlight. I felt exhilarated, and began to sing Italian love-songs at the top of my voice.

Fergus glanced at me.

'I've never heard you sing before.'

'You've never told me you loved me before.'

After a while we reached the frozen lake we'd crossed yesterday, and I could see the tracks of the snowmobiles in front leading along the edge of it in the direction of the town. We must keep within sight of each other, the guide had insisted, but since we could make out the distant roofs of the town, and the tracks leading to it, this seemed a good moment to play truant. I switched off the motor and our snow-carriage glided to a halt. And in the sudden silence the expanse of blue ice seemed even more vast, with its unending fringe of fir-trees far beyond, and an enormous orange sun suspended above it.

We gazed and gazed. I remembered Fergus saying how places did things to people. And he was right. I knew exactly what ten years in the Box Hill constituency had done to me – and shuddered. I knew what Fergus's coastguard cottage did to me – and gave quite a different shudder. But what about this winter fairyland?

'Any minute now you're going to ask me what I'm thinking, aren't you?' I said eventually.

'How d'you know?'

'Because you always do when I'm not saying anything.'

Fergus laughed.

'So, what *are* you thinking?'

'Lots of things.'

'Like what?'

'Like the fact that I know almost nothing about you at all except what you are when you're with me.'

'That's because you've never asked.'

'I know. I never wanted to. But now I do.'

He looked at me with that teasing smile.

'I'll tell you anything you want.'

That threw me for a second. He said it so casually, almost as if I was asking him the time.

'I suppose I never asked in case I didn't like the answers,' I went on. 'For one thing I always imagined you were married. Are you?'

Fergus shook his head.

'Were you?'

'Yes.'

'And what happened?'

He looked puzzled for a moment, as if he weren't entirely sure of the answer.

'The usual thing. We split up.'

'Tell me, would you?'

'OK. It was a long time ago. We were very young. Students. In Belfast. No money. My father worked in a shipyard. I was a scholarship boy. She was training to be a teacher, and I was studying medieval history of all useless things.' He laughed. 'I think I loved it partly because it was useless. I like living in other worlds; that's why I write, I suppose. It's not the best recipe for living in this world, and it certainly wasn't the best recipe for marriage.'

'So, what went wrong?'

He looked thoughtful, and then told me very simply, as though he'd have told me right at the beginning had he considered it important. Or it may have been that sitting here in an Arctic wilderness with the temperature minus God-knows-what, we both knew we had about ten minutes left before frostbite set in, so he'd better get on with it. How many marital confessions, I thought, would benefit from being delivered in a deep-freeze.

'Oh, it was a divorce made in heaven,' he said lightly. 'She was itching to get stuck into the day-to-day world, and I was itching to get out of it.'

He did manage to spell it out a little further than this. The two of them moved into a tiny flat in Liverpool. She longed to settle down with a family, have him around in a safe job, watch TV together, take the kids out on Sundays – all that sort of thing. Fergus's vision hadn't been quite like that. He'd also just managed to get his first university post, but it was in Leeds. So he weekended, and they spent most of each weekend squabbling about it. She didn't want to live in Leeds. Finally she agreed to, whereupon he promptly got a better job in Manchester. So, more squabbles. And still no children. The weekends grew rather less frequent. He became more and more involved with his work. She pointed out indignantly that she'd had to give hers up when they moved.

'It's the old story, isn't it? And if there were someone to blame, I suppose it had to be me,' he went on. 'If I were determined to be a free spirit I should never have married. Obviously.'

'Did you love her?' I asked.

There was a pause, as if he didn't quite know the answer.

'I told myself I did, at first; though looking back it seems more like an act of fate, as if I were obeying orders – or mostly disobeying them. It's what comes of being an Irish Protestant: you get the worst of both worlds, Catholic hypocrisy and Puritan guilt.'

'And how did it end?'

'The best way possible for both of us. She found somebody else.'

'Didn't you mind?'

'Of course. But mostly my vanity. The rest of me felt hugely relieved. I was free.'

'And you've stayed free.'

'Fergus just nodded. I'd liked to have asked him what that meant, but the Arctic cold was beginning to seep into my bones, and I suddenly had visions of two human icicles being found in the morning. I pressed the starter button and headed our little snow-machine in the direction of the distant town. The sun was already grazing the tops of the distant fir-trees, and the lake had turned a dead, deep grey.

I only said one thing more. And it took all my courage.

'Does your freedom have any room for me, Fergus?'

He turned to me in the half-light with a look of utter astonishment.

'But my darling, whatever would freedom mean without you? Nothing. Nothing at all.'

It was a lovely thing to hear, yet the longer the words echoed in my head the more I understood what they meant. They meant no ties, no promises, no commitments, only the present stretching wherever chance might lead it.

'So, when he goin' marry you, Mr Fergoose?' demanded Mamma Gina for the third or fourth time that week. 'You goin' divorce no good cook 'usband lickety-split.' Then she added a thoughtful embellishment. 'You listen Mamma Gina: I tell you good cook make *bambini*, plenty *bambini*. That why I no *bambini*: Carlo bad cook. Now I 'ave good fuck too late. You young, you no fuck too late.' Her expression became suddenly quite fierce. 'But you careful you no fuck in Lappaland no more: Mr Fergoose cook he drop off, he no stiff fucking, he stiff icicle.'

And she made a vigorous chopping motion with her hand in order to assure me.

Mamma Gina's vision of my Christmas spent in the frozen north had grown increasingly fanciful over the weeks since my return. She was quite unable to grasp that there might be such things as hotels, cars, beds, restaurants in 'Lappaland': she was convinced that Fergus and I had celebrated Christmas in an igloo accompanied by polar bears and a few grunting Eskimos, boring holes in the ice to spear fish which we then ate raw. This scenario I eventually traced to a television documentary she'd once seen about life in Labrador, though when I pointed out that Labrador was in Canada, not Europe, she dismissed the information as entirely irrelevant.

'Is the same. No difference. You no fuck in Lappaland no more, Claudia. You listen Mamma Gina. You fuck in nice warm bed, no iggaloo. Mr Fergoose cook he fall off.'

I gave up after that and promised to be more sensible next time.

Not that I felt like being in the least sensible at the moment. Day by day I was overcome by the kind of hysterical happiness which comes of knowing that it can't possibly last. Fergus's impassioned plea for freedom had left me feeling that I'd been swept up into a whirlwind of love which would inevitably one day hurl us apart. It was all too obvious an omen that my own 'year of freedom' should have won me a lover for whom freedom from all worldly ties was nothing less than a philosophy of life. I'd come to understand this, if not a great deal else, about Fergus; and it seemed to explain not only the way he behaved towards me, but also his fondness for the obscure byways of history and his urge constantly to spin webs of fantasy around them – the novel he was composing about the old priory, his elaborate theory relating to King Henry

VIII's sex-life, and of course his determination to discover the secret ingredient of some supposed aphrodisiac. Then there was his lonely house wedged into the cliffs from where he could project all his dreams on to the distant ocean. There was even the manner in which he first made love to me, appearing out of the sun like the god Apollo to embrace my own dreams as I lay there in the grass.

Why on earth should I be in love with such a man, I kept asking myself? No good could possibly come of it, I was quite convinced: in my heart I didn't want to be the focus of a man's dreams and fantasies, the subject of his fiction, his accomplice in shaping an unreal world.

So, why didn't I just dismiss him from my life?

However, when I posed myself this question an entirely different Fergus would suddenly appear before my eyes. I saw in front of me an irresistibly beautiful man whose very presence set fire to me, who made me laugh with joy, whose mind was an enticing labyrinth in which I could wander and never tire, and who opened miraculous vistas of love before me with every glance of his eyes and every touch of his fingers. This was not a man who lived in 'other worlds', as he claimed, but someone who brought the most brilliant sunlight into the grey world I lived in, so much so that it had become hard to imagine that world without him.

At this point I'd pull the plug on trying to solve all these contradictions, and remind myself that he made me very, very happy. Each fragment of my day seemed blessed. I walked on air. One morning Megan appeared at the door and stood in astonishment as she caught me singing while I did the housework. She clicked her tongue. 'The men in white coats will be round here if you go on like this,' she announced sternly, readjusting several of the bulges in her anatomy. Joan, spotting me carrying my shopping cheerfully through the February rain a few days later, was rather more forthright. 'Damn you,' she called out, looking bedraggled, 'Why can't you go back to your husband and be bad-tempered like everyone else?' Then she laughed, and I made her a cup of coffee and told her what Mamma Gina had said about Fergus's prick getting deep-frozen, and she laughed even more.

She was still laughing when Anna-Maria phoned from Bologna.

'I hope I've managed to catch you between prayers,' she said in a nauseating tone of piety. Then, hearing Joan chortling in the background, she added, 'Ah, the cheerfulness of nuns. How God's light must shine on you all.'

The pious note didn't last. Within seconds she was reminding me of Luigi Vespucci, the sausage-maker's son, whose Lamborghini she'd caught sight of only this morning – he must have been on his way to visit his father who was so terribly ill in hospital, and unlikely to see another spring. Luigi, of course, would then inherit the business, and what a tragedy it was that he had no wife to share his joys and responsibilities, and with all that money coming to him too.

As I put down the phone I had a vision of myself as Anna-Maria saw me, gift-wrapped in God's light and awaiting only the embrace of the sausage-maker's son to open my eyes to true happiness and eternal pregnancy. *Bambini* like Luigi's sausages, round and fat and factory-made.

'Oh Joan,' I said, feeling suddenly tired, 'will I ever be able to explain to my mother who I really am?'

Joan put her head on one side, and looked at me quizzically.

'You could always get Caroline to do it for you.' She let out a giggle, 'It'd be like a Berlitz course in human relations.' Then, abruptly changing the subject, she added, 'And where the hell is Caroline anyway? I haven't set eyes on her for weeks.'

It was true. Nobody had seen her. I'd phoned three or four times. Mostly I got Carmen, who merely volunteered, 'I no know,' and when I pressed her said it again in the same flat voice: 'I no know.' Once I got Patrick, who said he didn't know either: he'd come down for the weekend as usual only to find the house totally empty except for Carmen, who was glumly watching television. The children were all back at school, and as he couldn't remember which schools they were at, he explained, he couldn't ring up and enquire about their mother. Did I know?

I said, 'Of course not: you're supposed to be their father, Patrick.' He sighed as though this wasn't really his fault, and please would I come up to the house and keep him company?

'It's so cold here,' he went on pathetically. 'We could just go to bed. Would you?'

'No, Patrick.'

'Oh, why not? You're so sexy.'

'That doesn't mean I want to go to bed with you. Besides,' I added, 'Caroline says you've only got four inches.'

Patrick gave a squawk of indignation.

'Lies. God, what lies. I have to tell you I'm remarkably well-endowed. Caroline's just short-sighted.'

I could hear him chuckling down the phone.

'All right then,' he went on with an exaggerated sigh, 'neglect me if you must. You don't know what you're missing. One day you'll regret it.'

'I can probably live with that, Patrick. And now I must go.'

There was another sigh.

'Then I'll just have to get drunk.'

'What's new?'

I put the phone down, aware that in other circumstances I might well have chosen to have an affair with Patrick. Just brief and casual, with an empty house and no one to find out. There was something infuriatingly attractive about his narcissism: he was like a middle-aged naughty little boy, whom you'd scold, only to find yourself ending up in bed with him. Clearly an awful lot of women did. Self-deprecating vanity brought him easy conquests because no one need take Patrick seriously, thereby removing any danger of guilt. A one-night stand with him would be like nicking a bar of chocolate when no one in the shop was looking.

I imagined him getting self-pityingly drunk all alone that evening. But immediately I knew this wouldn't be true: it was the sort of thing he said in order to trap you into doing what he wanted. Under the veneer of helplessness Patrick was just about the most self-sufficient man I'd ever met; and this, I suspected, was the secret of any successful relationship a man might have with Caroline.

And this thought set me wondering once again what on earth might have happened to her.

Three days later I was in Glyn's bookshop. Fergus had just left for the university. Glyn had seen me waving him off in the little red Alfa-Romeo, and had beckoned me with a bright smile to come over to the shop.

As usual there were no customers, and Glyn assured me that the vicar had gone fishing.

'Oh, my dear,' he added confidentially, his eyes bright with mischief, 'the fat's really in the fire. Jonathan's been given a new curate – and it's a woman. Can you imagine it? The bishop's got a wicked sense of humour. I've advised her to get a sex change quickly if she wants to survive.'

He chuckled to himself, his thin hands fussing over a pile of new books on the central table. Among them I noticed several copies of *Cardinal Error* which Fergus had graciously signed for him, the signature 'Carl Magnus' scrawled across the title page in a florid sweep of the pen, very different from the elegant precision of 'Fergus Corrigan' with which he'd signed two copies of his *Dissolution of the English Monasteries*.

I wondered which of the two was the man who shared my bed, or perhaps it would be best just to congratulate myself on having two lovers in one.

I was still gazing at the two signatures when there came the sound of screeching brakes in the road outside, followed by an ominous crunch and a tinkling of glass. There was silence for a moment, then raised voices. One of the voices was immediately familiar. I closed the books and hurried out of the shop.

Caroline was standing in the road, hands on hips, berating a speechless truck-driver in shirtsleeves whose arms were tattooed with two naked women trapped in a jungle of the man's hair. He kept opening his mouth, but no words came. Caroline was in full flow.

At first I couldn't work out what the commotion had to do with her, or what she was doing there anyway. The truck, with a load of scaffolding, had halted with one front wheel on the pavement just outside Glyn's bookshop. Clearly it had taken the sharp bend opposite the gatehouse and been forced to pull over hastily to try to avoid an oncoming rental van which – equally clearly – had been cutting the corner. Its front wing was now folded comfortably round one of the truck's wheels.

Caroline was gazing alternately at the intrusive wheel and at the truck-driver. Her torrent of abuse was unabating, and no traffic could pass either way. There was much hooting of horns, then the wailing of a police siren.

This was hardly the moment to enquire what Caroline was doing driving a rental van, least of all on the wrong side of the road. Suddenly she caught sight of me and with a look of outrage pointed furiously at the truck's wheel.

'What the fuck does this oaf think he's doing driving that thing through the middle of a peaceful country town?' She swung round to face the truck-driver again. 'Haven't you heard of by-passes?'

I just had time to reflect that Norton Abbas had no by-pass when a police car threaded its way along the pavement and three uniformed officers leapt out, one of them shouting rapid instructions into his mobile phone, another brandishing a notebook, the third hastening towards the two combatants. I could see the truck-driver's clenched fist raised menacingly, and the naked lady on his forearm preparing at any second to leap at Caroline.

One of the policemen hurriedly parted them and began trying to take a statement. Witnesses were gathering round. The two other officers firmly pressed them all back, and I could no longer hear the flood of abuse which, from the expression on her face, Caroline continued to hurl at the truck-driver.

Glyn and I stood and watched, bemused. From this distance it was all a brilliant piece of mime: their gestures told me precisely what was being said. First there were the two statements, which clearly bore no resemblance to one another. The truck-driver then produced his licence. The policeman examined it, gave it back to him, and turned to Caroline. From her face one might have imagined she'd been asked to strip in public. With a look of outrage she threw her hands in the air, and gave a dismissive toss of the head. The second policeman put his hands rather menacingly on his hips, whereupon Caroline turned her back on him and strode towards the van, wrenching open the driver's door.

But with one foot on the step she suddenly caught sight of the third policeman making his way round to the back of the van with the clear intention of opening it. Caroline immediately brushed past the other two officers and slammed her hand on to the policeman's wrist, shaking her head violently as she did so. There followed a heated conversation, with Caroline barring the way to the van's rear door, a 'they shall not pass' expression etched on her face.

A moment later and she was explaining something to all three officers extremely carefully, making supplicatory gestures while her face became gentle and appealing and her hands began to work overtime. They stroked a policeman's arm; they were clasped together in front of her bosom; she buried her face in them; she wiped away a tear. Then suddenly she looked up, darted to the side of the road and grabbed a small child who'd been standing agog with its thumb in its mouth. Its mother was too dumbfounded to move as Caroline dragged the child in front of the three officers who gazed down solemnly at it while she went through another repertoire of dramatic gestures, finally slapping her open palm to her forehead and shaking her head vigorously.

The performance over, she paused as though for applause. By now the policemen were looking pensive; then one after the other they nodded their heads and turned gravely away. A notebook was closed, a pencil put away, a mobile phone clipped back on to a coat pocket. They got back into their car. The child ran anxiously back its mother, who cradled it with an expression of horror on her face.

Caroline stood there for a few seconds, looking entirely composed and serene. She turned to the crowd and smiled. She even smiled at the truck-driver. And at this moment I stepped forward. She saw me and without the slightest change of expression motioned me to get in the van.

She climbed in next to me and started up the engine. There was a grinding sound as she reversed away from the truck and we were off. I caught a glimpse of the truck-driver, still standing wide-eyed: then as we pulled away I saw him mouth an obscenity and helplessly wave a clenched fist, and as he did so the naked lady tattooed on his forearm seemed to perform a dance amid the jungle of hair.

'Well,' I said as we rounded the corner on the right side of the road, 'are you going to tell me what that was all about?'

Caroline turned the van through the palatial gates and

into the long avenue of lime-trees. She was humming to herself.

'Oh, just a little quick thinking.'

'And the child?'

'I told them I'd swerved because it ran across the road.'

'Did it?'

'No, of course not. I just saw it in the crowd and thought I'd better act quickly.'

I shook my head.

'And this van, how did you manage to stop them looking inside it?'

She gave a laugh.

'I told them it was full of bee-hives.'

'And is it?'

'Claudia, don't be ridiculous. What would I be doing with bees?'

'So, what the hell *is* in it?'

Caroline didn't answer for a moment as she concentrated on parking the van carefully in front of the house next to the dark-blue Mercedes.

'Well, I'll show you,' she said, opening the driver's door and jumping on to the gravel. 'God, it's nice to be home.'

I made my way to the back of the van and watched her reach up to turn the handle of the rear door. Her expression told me nothing at all. She was still humming as she swung the door wide open.

'How d'you like that?' she announced cheerfully.

Inside, reclining next to each other separated by thin strips of sacking, were three skeletons.

One thing I'd learnt about Caroline was that she dared to do what others only dreamt of doing, just as she dared to say what others only wished they had the nerve to say. There was never a restraining hand of doubt. Decorum was a concept unknown to her, and embarrassment an absurd human frailty experienced only by those too spineless to stand up for themselves.

'Just help me carry the bloody things: they won't bite you,' she said testily, clambering up into the back of the van. 'We'll put them in the stable for now. Howl can deal with them later.'

Howl, I remembered, was the deaf-and-dumb gardener the National Trust had provided for her, and whose real name was Hal. Caroline somehow managed to imitate the way he spoke without appearing cruel, rolling her lips around her face and uttering zoo-like noises.

Caroline offered no explanation of her macabre acquisitions until the three skeletons were safely laid out on the floor of the old stable, and the door bolted. My own squeamishness had been a little relieved once I noticed that the bones were not about to fall apart in my arms, but were securely wired together so that it was possible to lift each skeleton in one piece, though I swore that their teeth chattered in my ear as I carried them.

'I think we both deserve a drink after that,' she said firmly.

We peeled off our coats, washed the dust of death from our hands, and sank gratefully on to the sofa.

'You look a bit pale,' Caroline exclaimed accusingly.

I managed a laugh.

'It's not every day I act as a grave-robber's accomplice, Caroline,' I said. 'Perhaps you'll now tell me what the hell this is all about.'

She curled one leg elegantly over the arm of the sofa, sipped her vodka-and-tonic and began to look extremely pleased with herself.

'Well, this is the plan,' she began. 'And you've got to help me.'

I listened.

This was Phase Three of the battle plan, she explained. The first two had only been delaying tactics, first refusing to agree with the Trust's choice of builder, then using her charms to persuade County Hall to withhold planning permission.

'A real shame,' she said, gazing wistfully out of the window. 'Gerald was such an eager lover. I do like uncircumcised men – that funny wiggly bit at the end, rather like the nozzle of a balloon. Hey,' – and she turned towards me with a bright face – 'I wonder if that's where "blow job" comes from? Christ, I never thought of that before, did you, Claudia? Do *you* prefer uncircumcised men?' She paused, mercifully not expecting an answer, and stared down at her vodka-and-tonic. 'Oh, I shall miss Gerald,' she sighed, shaking her head.

I was beginning to wonder if Caroline's thoughts would ever return from the bedroom. But after another sigh or two, she carried on.

'So, as I told you, the next target had to be the Church. And that's what I've been doing for the last week or so.'

I had visions of Caroline, having bundled her children back to boarding-school, promptly setting out to seduce half the General Synod, and I was eagerly waiting to hear how this managed to result in her returning with three skeletons in the back of a rental van.

'It came to me quite suddenly just before Christmas,' she explained. 'The old priory. This was all once Church land. Nuns lived here for God knows how many hundreds and hundreds of years. Right?' I nodded. 'OK. Nuns die like everybody else. Their souls may go to heaven, or wherever, but what about their bodies? They got buried, didn't they? But where? Do you know? And your beloved saint, St Hamburger or whatever she's called, where's she buried? I know there's some kind of stone water-trough in the garden that fruitcakes come and throw flowers into, but there aren't any bones in it, are there? Empty. Not exactly *habeas corpus*.' The thought made Caroline smile. 'So where is she, then? There aren't any nuns' graves in the parish cemetery, because I've had a good look. They're all fishmongers and master-masons, people like that.'

Suddenly it was all beginning to dawn on me. I felt I knew what was coming, and that it was vintage Caroline.

'Well, we can soon fix that, I thought,' she went on, swinging her other leg over the arm of the sofa and admiring the effect in the long mirror on the far wall. 'D'you know, Gerald used to say I had the best legs of any woman he'd ever seen? And then he'd part them.' She let out one of her rippling laughs. 'God, he had a pair of balls on him: I tried weighing them on the kitchen scales once, but then Carmen walked in . . . Now, where was I, Claudia?'

'Weighing Gerald's balls.'

Caroline clicked her tongue in irritation.

'No, I know. Bones. The nuns' cemetery. Since it has to be

somewhere, why not in my garden? All we need is a bit of evidence, and that's what I've been busy collecting. I'm going to get Howl to bury them around the house as soon as the ground's a bit less frozen. Then I shall announce to the National Trust that it's consecrated ground. And they can bloody well stuff their building plans.'

I was lost for words. If it had been anyone other than Caroline I should probably have buried my head in my hands and let out a despairing moan. But with the triumphant literary conference still fresh in my memory I thought it was just conceivable that Caroline could actually pull it off. It should at least gain her another stay of execution while laboratory tests were carried out on the bones. But whose bones were they? In the rambling unlikelihood of Caroline's tale I'd never got round to asking the most obvious question. I got up from my chair and looked at her.

'The skeletons, Caroline, tell me, where the hell did you get them from?'

She glanced up at me and gave a chuckle.

'Lateral thinking, darling: that's the secret. You know Joan's husband, Geoff, is my doctor, don't you? Well, I had to go and see him about a new coil, and while he was fitting it we got talking about this and that, as one does while having a coil fitted. I asked him about the problems of studying anatomy since he was studying mine, and he told me it was all quite different at medical school these days: it's all done with computers apparently, like everything else. Christ, computers will start fucking one another soon, won't they, then we'll be redundant.'

I feared we might be about to whizz off on yet another of Caroline's flights of sexual fantasy. But she checked the impulse, and carried on.

'Well, that gave me the most brilliant idea. If they study anatomy through computers nowadays, then what about all those skeletons medical schools used to be full of? They must be redundant as well. Not too many people have need of a few old skeletons, but by God I did. So "Geoff," I said once he'd finished fitting my coil, "can you please let me have the names of all the medical schools in Great Britain? The whole lot." And he did. He didn't ask why, he just did it. So I rang them the next morning, one after the other. Of course most of them thought I was off my trolley, and hung up. But three of them didn't. I offered them a good price, and they took it. And there you are. I hired a van and off I went round the country gathering my cargo of old bones. And now let me get you another drink. You're a white wine person, aren't you?' She gave me a wry smile. '*Bone* dry, would you say?'

And she swung her legs off the sofa with a laugh.

'And by the way,' she went on, handing me my glass, 'another thing came out of having my coil fitted. Geoff's going to help me with my paediatricians' conference in the spring. I'm getting down to it next week. I've got plenty of time now I haven't got a lover. How's yours?'

I just smiled, which made her cross.

'Don't you realise how much I need gossip?' she said. 'Sometimes I think I'd fall apart if no one was prepared to make me laugh.'

So I told her about Mamma Gina and her warning that Fergus's prick would drop off if we carried on making love in 'Lappaland'.

'Oh, I love it, I love it,' she exclaimed. 'Go on.'

I left her a little while later, warmed by a second vodka-and-tonic and by exotic tales of Mamma Gina. Then I wandered back to the gatehouse through the February drizzle. Splinters of glass still lay by the roadside as testimony to Caroline's brief encounter with the truck and her spectacular hoodwinking of three Devonshire police officers.

No one else could have put on a show like that, I thought. No one else could be quite so ruthlessly brazen. Caroline always played everything by the rule-book, without ever acknowledging that she'd set the rules. So, why did everyone manage to love her in the end, even while doing their best to loathe her? Was it because she personified the hidden anarchist in us all? Yes, perhaps it was that, or partly so. Yet there was something else. When I thought about Caroline's unceasing battles, it was as though she were taking on the entire nation single-handed in order to preserve what she felt to be hers by divine right. They were ludicrous battles very often, but they were always heroic battles, against the odds. What few people were aware of was just how much pain lay only a centimetre or two beneath the armour-plating of Caroline's self-assurance, or how much raw courage she constantly needed to summon up. Hers was the kind of bravery that was all too easy to dismiss, or to mock; and in knowing that I would never dream of doing such a thing I'd come to realise how very close, and how deeply valuable, our friendship was to me. I loved her.

Eleven

It tickled me that I should be busy planting herbs while Caroline was busy planting human bones. The long frost had held up both enterprises until well into the second half of March, and now I was hurrying to make up for lost time in anticipation of the rush of spring pilgrims which the secretary of Saintly Tours had eagerly promised me.

Caroline phoned in high spirits to announce that Howl should have finished burying the skeletons by this evening, and if there were any bones left over would I like them? I could sell them as holy relics perhaps: it might help pay the rent.

I saw her point, but said no. In that case, she insisted, at least I must come over for a drink to celebrate. But I'd been feeling less than well for the past day or so, and again said no. I could hear the irritated click of her tongue.

The fact that the ground had remained frozen for almost six weeks was a setback for me, but a near-disaster for Caroline. The stable had seemed an entirely safe place to keep the skeletons – after all, Caroline reminded me with a laugh, they could hardly make a bolt for it, could they? But she'd forgotten one thing. The stable was where Pamela Leggatt was keen to have the National Trust shop; and now that planning permission had at last been granted she was equally keen to bring her marketing people round to assess its possibilities. Caroline was at her wits' end. 'They're coming this morning!' she screamed down the phone. 'What the fuck shall I do?'

'Say you've lost the key,' I suggested.

'What if they've got a spare? They probably have.'

'Then tell them you've got a dog with rabies and you're awaiting the extermination squad.'

She liked that idea, and phoned half an hour later to say it had worked beautifully. There was a pause before she added, 'But darling, we don't have rabies in this country, do we?' Then she gave another laugh. 'Ah well, there's always a first time.'

Now that the bones were all safely buried among the rose-bushes around the house, it was just a matter of waiting until the drainage people arrived with their excavator; then the nuns' cemetery would be duly discovered. An ex-lover of Caroline's, now a suffragan bishop, had been prevailed upon to pronounce it 'consecrated ground'.

She felt thoroughly gleeful about the whole business.

'I wonder how long laboratories take to date human bones?' she said. 'I'd better plan my next move in case it's only a matter of days. There is one idea I'm working on, but I shall need your advice, Claudia. You're not going back to Lapland or anything, are you?'

I said I thought not.

'Taking Mamma Gina's advice, eh, in case Fergus's prick drops off? Mind you, if it were Patrick's you wouldn't notice.' The ripple of laughter spilt out of the hand-phone across the garden. 'And by the way, the paediatricians' conference is ON. The first weekend in May. I'm on the blower morning till night. We shall make medical history: you wait.'

This time, I determined, I was *not* going to be here to witness history being made. Caroline would have to pull off another miracle without me.

There were just two weeks to go before Easter. Megan and Joan had been helping me all morning, potting and planting out the herbs I'd been carefully nursing in my greenhouse. Easter would be big business, Joan assured me: hadn't Chaucer said that this was the time when everyone longed to go on pilgrimages? ('How the hell do you expect a girl from Bologna and the Raynes Park Comprehensive to know anything about Chaucer?' I retorted.) But she'd get the flame-throwers along to help. She'd make sure they didn't bring their Walkmans, and wore something other than slashed jeans and their 'The Pope's a wanker' T-shirts.

'Anything to boost sales,' I said. 'I need to keep my bonk manager happy: he's threatening me with another "feed-me-and-feel-me-up" lunch.'

She laughed.

Now I was on my own. It was thrilling to see this place for the first time in the spring. I was made to feel like a country girl at heart. Wild daffodils were beginning to appear in the meadow leading down to the tidal marsh and the estuary, and wood anemones were opening like stars in the sun around the beech-trees. Soon, Glyn promised, there would be cowslips, so long as I could keep Jehoshaphat from devouring them; and bluebells, great splashes of them. And the migrant birds would start arriving. I'd need to learn their songs, he assured me, because they were such shy and invisible creatures: willow warblers, whitethroats, blackcaps. Nightingales, too, if I were lucky.

I was still Italian enough to be amazed at the English love of insignificant little brown birds. In Italy everyone assumed they were all the same, the only point of interest being whether or not you could eat them.

Then of course there'd be my honey buzzards, which perhaps even the Italians might find too indigestible to eat, though Glyn assured me a terrible number of them got shot on migration, Italian manhood always needing to prove itself at the point of a gun. One day the birds would simply cease to appear, and that would be the end of an era, he added sadly: after all they'd been coming here ever since the Middle Ages, even earlier, feeding on the bees the nuns kept.

That had put me in mind of Joan's quince honey, and I wondered if Fergus would manage to discover the magic ingredient he was searching for, the 'satur rote'. How on earth did he imagine he'd be able to identify it? I'd asked him a few days ago and he'd gazed at me with that private smile of his, which usually meant he knew something he wasn't prepared to divulge. 'Something'll turn up,' he said. 'I know it. I'll just keep my eyes open.'

Right now I could scarcely keep my own eyes open. Whatever the bug was that I'd caught, I felt very odd. And my breasts itched: they felt uncomfortable against my blouse.

After a snack lunch I lay down and slept for the best part of an hour, and woke feeling refreshed. Fergus was due to turn up during the afternoon: we'd decided that the long-neglected topiary garden could do with some care and attention before the waves of visitors started to arrive. We'd already made a start on restoring the urns, castles, pyramids and heraldic beasts. Now the big question was: What to do about the phallic yew-tree? At present its rampant form was visible only to the keenest of eyes, the passing centuries having disguised it sufficiently to invite any number of imaginative interpretations. But a little hard work with the pruning shears and there was no way the secretary of Saintly Tours would be able to exclaim to her pious flock, 'Behold the Tree of Jesse.'

By late afternoon Fergus and I were standing beneath its ancient branches, having completed the job of tidying up the shrubs around it.

'Well, now comes the moment of truth,' I said. 'Do we go for it, or not?'

Fergus looked at me questioningly.

'You're the one who has to deal with Saintly Tours.'

'And you're the one who has to deal with the National Trust.'

He nodded thoughtfully.

'True.' Then his eyes crinkled and the shadow of a smile formed on his lips. 'And since I'm their historical adviser I think I owe it to them to be historically correct. Wouldn't you agree?'

And with that he seized the step-ladder, eased it through the jungle of outer branches and began to clamber up it, a saw grasped in one hand, pruning-shears in the other.

'If this doesn't give me a castration complex, nothing will,' he called out from somewhere amid the upper branches.

Fragments of yew-tree began to fall about me. I stood back and watched.

'I wish I had a camera,' I called out as the outline of the giant phallus began to emerge from the tangled foliage. 'The Trust might enjoy publishing it in their magazine. I wonder how they'd caption it? How about "One of our long-standing members revealed"?'

I could hear Fergus chuckling among the branches.

By dusk the job was completed. I was fairly horrified gazing at the thing, a huge erection standing up against the skyline. I wondered if I should perhaps throw a tarpaulin over it on pilgrim days, claiming that the tree was being treated for a rare fungus.

Fergus suggested a more reverential approach, that a tasteful plaque be set up beside it: 'In respectful memory of Admiral Romsey, this tribute from his many female admirers.'

I looked at him and laughed. If I'd imagined that Caroline stood for the anarchist in us all, I was beginning to think that Fergus in his quieter way was the more disruptive of the two. Something I'd come to realise about Fergus was that he trod his own path with a kind of ruthless logic. Because he was beholden to no one it never seemed to occur to him that certain truths might sometimes be best hidden. He was a man who could see no virtue in making concessions to propriety or censorship: if a former nunnery were found to possess a fine example of phallic topiary, then let it be revealed, let the truth be known, whatever offence it might cause to those cherishing the belief that monasteries had always been havens of virtue. As a historian he knew perfectly well it wasn't so; then why on earth pretend otherwise? Society was not going to fall apart as a result; and if certain people became apoplectic, they had it coming to them for being so naive.

And that was all there was to be said about it. Let the tree-phallus stand for all to see.

After Fergus left that evening for a late seminar at the university I stood outside in the dusk wondering, just as I had over Christmas, what lasting partnership could possibly exist with such a lone and free spirit. I knew precisely where we stood: we loved one another along separate paths, which ran parallel and within sight of each other, but which could never meet. It wasn't the life I would have chosen, but it was how it was.

I woke up the next morning feeling ragged, as though sleep had merely induced more tiredness in me. Rain was lashing at the windows, and threatening clouds were racing low above the trees. I could see no earthly reason why I should get up: it felt like a day that was best buried.

And then the phone went. The hand-phone by my bed was missing: God knows where I'd left it. I threw a dressing-gown round my shoulders and hurried downstairs.

It was Anna-Maria. She sounded surprised to get me; then I remembered she still believed I was in a convent, probably mumbling Ave Marias on my knees somewhere.

'Darling, I'm coming,' she announced excitedly in Italian. 'For Easter. Coming to visit my Claudia. My baby.'

Oh, Jesus wept. What on earth could I say?

'Mamma,' I began, and got no further.

'No need to worry,' she went on. 'I arrange everything. Flight. Train. Hotel. I phone you when I arrive – Good Friday. You tell the good nuns to let you out. I have to go now. I so happy, my baby.'

I stood stunned by the telephone. It was too early for a drink. Besides, I hadn't felt like a drink for several days: I must *really* be ill, I kept telling myself. Even coffee, just the smell of it, made me feel sick. I needed a pick-me-up, I decided. I'd ask my doctor, Joan's husband, Geoff. I scarcely knew him, but Joan had asked me to dinner in a couple of days' time: I'd have a word with him then.

But Anna-Maria. God Almighty. I poured myself some apple juice and gazed mournfully out of the window at the lashing rain. What a prospect! My mother expecting me to be in the care of the good nuns, and coachloads of Easter pilgrims being confronted by the largest penis in the western world. At the same time. What made it worse was that both disasters were of my own making.

Fergus had left this morning for some conference in Paris, and was getting paid for it, the jammy bastard. Caroline was away collecting her offspring from their various boarding-schools, assuming she could remember where they were. Joan had gone shopping in Plymouth for the day, and Megan was visiting her grown-up daughter in Cardiff.

I phoned Mamma Gina.

'Help!' I said. 'Can I come round?'

I was due to work in the restaurant this evening, but this was urgent.

'You trouble with Mr Fergoose?' she bellowed down the phone.

'No. With my mother.'

'Then you come see Mamma Gina.'

I pulled on a coat, grabbed an umbrella and hurried across the road and down the High Street. The large welcoming figure of Mamma Gina was waiting for me by the door. She thrust an espresso and a brandy towards me as I slumped opposite her at the familiar little table. I could only gaze at them, and the smell of coffee made me feel slightly sick.

'You unwell,' she said, shaking her head. She felt my forehead. 'You fever.'

It didn't feel like a fever. I drank some mineral water and began to tell her as calmly as I could about Anna-Maria. It was comforting just to talk, and Mamma Gina didn't even laugh when I told her my mother believed I was living in a convent.

'Oh, my dear, no problem. Anna-Maria just like *all* Italian mothers, would like daughter locked safe in convent until married off. She quite normal, your mother.'

And she placed a large red arm round my shoulder.

'You bring 'er ere. Mamma Gina deal with your mother lickety-split. I tell 'er. No problem. She sound just like me.'

It shook me to think that Anna-Maria could possibly be like anybody else, least of all like Mamma Gina. But maybe she was right. I began to feel a lot better.

'Now you need champagne,' she announced, opening the large fridge behind her and grasping a bottle which she opened with a deft twist of the hand.

She poured out a glass and placed it in front of me. Even the sight of those bubbles turned my stomach, but I closed my eyes and took a sip, praying I wouldn't vomit. To my astonishment it tasted like nectar. Well, I thought, I can't be all that ill.

'And where Mr Fergoose?' she asked.

I explained that he was in Paris, and she looked disapproving.

'Huh. And when your divorce?'

I said it was in the hands of the lawyers, but that these things rumbled along very slowly. David was being very nice, I added, and in return I'd agreed to keep quiet about it until after the government reshuffle when he fully expected to become environment secretary, which could be any day now.

Mamma Gina looked mystified.

'Why ee want to be secretary? That girl's job.'

I explained it wasn't quite like that, and a secretary of state wasn't exactly a secretary.

She looked even more mystified.

'Huh,' she said. 'He no good cook and now he want girl's job. Maybe he homo-what-you-call-it, your 'usband.'

I didn't say that it had sometimes occurred to me.

'Now I got go cook,' she announced, rising heavily from the table.

After a quick double-take I decided she probably meant helping to prepare lunch. The Sicilian lover could be seen stirring large pots of sauce in the kitchen, and Carlo was hurrying around the restaurant laying tables.

I walked back to the gatehouse feeling altogether more cheerful. The rain had stopped, and there was even a hint of milky sunshine. I put on my gumboots and moved Jehoshaphat's stake further away from where he might nibble the spring flowers. He followed me with eyes like evil marbles and tried to munch the seat of my jeans. I stroked him, and he peed massively. Why, I wondered, was I so fond of this dreadful creature?

By the evening of my dinner with Joan I'd managed to prepare what I hoped were enough baskets and pots of herbs to satisfy my Easter pilgrims. I'd also taken delivery of a fresh edition of *St Cuthburga's Cookbook*, already paid for by last year's sales. I was glad I'd been sensible enough not to include Resurrection Pudding, even without Megan's appalling illustrations. One seasonal indiscretion, in the shape of my phallic yew-tree, seemed quite enough without inviting the wrath of the faithful even further.

The last thing I wanted was to go out to dinner. I felt permanently tired and would have loved just to watch television and retire to bed early. But I pulled myself together, put on my tight-fitting Katherine Hamnett jeans and a turtle-necked cashmere sweater: the casually sexy look should bring out the envious streak in Joan, I thought; perhaps it might even spark a glint in Geoff's eye. Then I took myself down the High Street to the door whose brass plate was so rigorously polished that the doctor's name was half smoothed away. It made me realise how much older than Joan he must be.

'Jesus, look at you,' she said, holding the front door open for me. A pair of oven gloves was slung over one shoulder, and her red hair had been drawn tightly back with a band. She looked sharp and harassed. 'I don't know,' she went on, giving the door a brisk shove as I stepped past her. 'When I wear a floppy sweater like that I look even smaller; you just look more voluptuous than ever. It's grossly unfair.'

I didn't tell her I was only wearing it because my breasts felt sore.

'It's just you tonight, I'm afraid,' she went on, steering me through into the kitchen which was filled with a rich smell of casserole. 'No man to drool over you, except Geoff. Sorry Fergus couldn't make it.' She handed me a glass of wine. 'You don't mind talking to me while I cook, do you? Geoff's got a patient. He'll be free in a while.' She opened the oven door and waved clouds of steam away from her face. 'So, Fergus is in Paris, is he?'

I thought this was probably her way of saying, 'You'd be mad to trust him, or why hasn't he taken you with him?'

'He is,' I said.

I didn't want to talk about Fergus. Joan invariably did. So did Caroline, of course, but that was different. Caroline was really only interested to know what he was like in bed, whereas Joan was more prying. It was as if she were always hunting for something which would undermine my relationship with Fergus, or make it appear vulnerable. It wasn't exactly malice. Maybe it was envy. Or maybe she simply wasn't at ease with other people's happiness. And yet she was kind, though I suspected her kindness could only be fully extended to those who were suffering a little. I was always on my guard with Joan.

'D'you think you'll marry him?' she went on, vigorously mashing potatoes before spattering generous dobs of butter on a bowl of carrots.

'I'm not even divorced yet,' I said defensively.

She glanced at me as though she knew this was a feeble answer. Then she noticed I wasn't drinking my wine.

'That's not like you at all. Anything wrong?'

I shook my head.

'I just don't feel like it.'

Joan gave me another sharp glance. Then she laughed.

'You mean you're going to watch me getting pissed all evening while you and Geoff sit there looking disapproving. He never drinks a thing, as you know.'

'Actually what I would love is something bubbly,' I said, suddenly remembering the glass of champagne Mamma Gina had handed me. 'Is that terribly rude of me?'

She gave another laugh.

'Oh God no. Thank heaven for that. A perfect excuse.' And she hurried over to a cupboard and hauled out a large crate. 'A grateful patient of Geoff's sent us this for Christmas, and I've never liked to open it on my own. The real stuff too. Oh, great. I'll shove a couple of bottles in the freezer for ten minutes if you can wait that long.'

And she eased the two bottles among the packets of frozen vegetables, and closed the freezer door.

'Are you really all right, Claudia?' she asked suddenly. 'You don't seem yourself.'

I said it was true I wasn't feeling myself, and that I'd wanted to ask Geoff for some sort of pick-me-up. And at that moment he appeared. He gave me a formal hand-shake and a rather tired smile. I'd never made any kind of contact with Geoff: he was a man who seemed to extend the same kind of detachment towards the rest of the world as he employed towards his patients. There was never any small-talk in his company, and often no talk at all. I often wondered what he and Joan shared, and whether perhaps her sharp bubbliness had the opposite effect on him, of making him flat.

'Claudia needs something to pick her up,' she announced without any preliminaries. 'She's feeling low.'

Geoff's face brightened just a little now that medical matters had been raised.

'Tell me then,' he said quietly. 'Come next door for a moment and we'll see what we can do.'

I followed him into his surgery and he sat in his large leather chair, fingertips together, while I seated myself opposite him on the other side of his desk.

'So, tell me then,' he said again. 'What's the trouble?'

I felt deeply uncomfortable. I hadn't wanted a formal consultation: none the less here I was. I related the vague symptoms I'd been aware of for the past week, even the little things like not liking the smell of coffee or the taste of wine.

Geoff said nothing, just let me burble away. I loathed it, and wished I'd just taken myself off to the chemist and asked for a tonic.

Then he looked at me questioningly.

'Everything else all right? Your periods regular, are they?'

I've never understood the terrible power of instinct. It was as if I'd been shot, and was waiting to feel the pain. I heard my own voice say something about being a few weeks late, adding rather pathetically that this wasn't particularly unusual, but . . . my voice trailed off, and there was an awful silence. Then Geoff gave a polite little cough.

'I think I'd like to give you a pregnancy test.'

Morning after morning I kept telling myself, 'There are women all over the world who would give anything for a moment like this: they cross continents to visit fertility clinics, they take their temperature before making love and stand on their heads after it, they pray to St Margaret of Antioch, they spend their life's savings on quacks and potions. And here I was, for ten years pronounced infertile by the most eminent gynaecologists (yet always – just in case – protected by either diaphragms or condoms, and sometimes both), PREGNANT!

I wished black humour could be funny.

I wished I wasn't me.

For days my thoughts had been rushing around trying desperately to sort themselves out amid tidal waves of panic, alternating with bouts of helpless inertia and sheer disbelief. I kept crying. Much of the time I didn't know what I was doing. The phone rang and rang, and went unanswered. Mail piled up on the kitchen table unopened. Megan called and I hid in the loo. I couldn't deal with seeing anybody. Everything inside and outside my head was unrecognisable. Day after day all I was conscious of was this alien thing growing inside me. And I didn't even know whether I wanted to love it or hate it.

It was Saturday. The end of the worst week of my life, I kept telling myself. But there was something that made it even worse. Fergus's conference in Paris was due to finish yesterday. He'd be flying back this morning. He'd have left his car at Heathrow, and be driving down this afternoon. Then of course he'd phone, wouldn't he? Maybe he'd already phoned from Paris, several times perhaps: he almost certainly had – all those calls I never answered.

I felt even more panicked. At first I didn't quite understand why. Should this not have been a joyful moment? I thought of all those millions of women who, with their hearts thumping and tears in their eyes, must have waited for this very moment when they could ring up their loved ones and announce breathlessly, 'Darling, oh darling, I'm pregnant. Isn't it wonderful?'

My mind cleared. It *wasn't* wonderful. It was the end. Fergus and I didn't have a relationship like other people. Fergus had never wanted children: he'd told me so clearly enough. He was a free spirit. His love for me was something completely without bonds, and it could never possibly survive if those bonds were imposed. Our love was a floating world, without anchors: that was its glory, and it was what I'd come to accept.

If I told him I was pregnant Fergus would do one of two things. Either he would disappear, a rejection which I would find agonising; or else he would offer to marry me out of a sense of duty, which would destroy everything we'd ever had together.

I knew one thing more. If I had an abortion it would kill that love anyway, because it would kill something within me, not only my child, but whatever made me what I was.

I could scarcely believe where my thoughts were taking me. But there could be only one answer: I wouldn't tell him, and I wouldn't see him. That was *it*.

He wouldn't know. He might never know.

I would keep the child, and in that child would be the living memory of Fergus. That was all of him I would ever have.

It sounded horrific. It sounded like the most absurd self-punishment. I felt as though some massive fist had struck me, and I held on to the chair, watching my hands go white with tension. I couldn't quite believe it. Was I asleep and would soon wake up, and the birds would be singing?

But I wasn't, and it didn't go away. I was right: I knew I was. It had to be this way; there was no other. I would have the child; I would find a way of supporting us both; and then . . . there was a single minute ray of light far away in the distance, and my eyes were full of tears as I gazed at it. Once we were together, the child and I – once we were all right, once we no longer needed Fergus, were no longer vulnerable – then, if by some chance he were still around, I could go to him and say, 'I'm Claudia. Remember me? Here I am. I still love you.'

I never knew the mind could generate such pain.

I kept the phone off the hook all afternoon, and did robotic and meaningless things to pass the time: I didn't even remember what I'd done. But I was aware of the clock. Four o'clock. Five o'clock. There was no point trying to ring him before six. I made myself walk across the meadow, letting Jehoshaphat nibble my hand surprisingly softly. (Could the little bugger be feeling sorry for me?) I made myself look at the spring flowers, and at the evening sunlight on the estuary where the sailing-boats glided so peacefully. I walked through the beech-wood and looked at the quince blossom in the orchard, then stood and watched Joan's bees crashlanding on the entrance to their hives, their boots (as they looked like) stuffed with golden pollen.

On the way back to the gatehouse I avoided the phallic yew-tree: phalluses had done quite enough damage already, I decided. And I avoided St Cuthburga's tomb: virgin martyrs seemed even less appropriate to my condition. But there suddenly, on its favourite perch above the ruined arch, was one of my honey buzzards. It was like seeing an old friend, and I felt quite sentimental. It had come safely through a long journey. Would I?

I glanced at my watch. It was five minutes to six. My stomach felt taut, and my head swam. Now was the time I had to do it. I went indoors.

Suddenly it was as though I was someone else. I watched myself pick up the phone, tap out the number, and listen as it rang, five, six, seven times. What would I do if he was out, or on his way here? Then I heard a click, and it was Fergus's voice saying 'Yes?' I swallowed. I heard myself telling him I had something terribly important to say, and he must believe me: please, he really must. I couldn't go on seeing him, I said, so coolly, so firmly. (Could that voice be mine?) I couldn't see him at all. He must believe me, I repeated several times.

I didn't give him a chance to reply. 'I *will* explain,' I heard myself say. 'I *will*, one day soon. I promise. I absolutely promise. But not now. Please. Just let me be. It's got to be this way. I can't say any more; I really can't.'

Perhaps I should have put the phone down straight away. But I hesitated. I thought he might have leapt into his car and driven straight here; and that would have been infinitely worse. I had to hear his voice.

'I see,' he said very quietly. There was a pause, then, 'Well, what can I say? Nothing. There isn't anything to say, is there? You've just told me to go away. An ultimatum.' His voice was flat: I hardly recognised it. I heard him give a little cough. 'It's all pretty obvious, I suppose,' he went on. 'David's been pressuring you, hasn't he? And you're going back to him.' I shook my head, but no words came. 'Of course. It makes sense,' Fergus said. 'I should have known it was bound to happen.' There was even a dry laugh in his voice as he said it. 'You've had your year of freedom, and now it's over. So. It was good while it lasted. Good luck.'

He didn't even sound unkind, or angry.

I almost choked on a 'Thank-you.'

'But if you should think again . . .'

He left the sentence unfinished. Fergus was too proud a man to plead, but there was a note of terrible hollowness in his voice, which cut through me like a dagger.

I had to end this immediately, or I would never be able to end it. I murmured something incoherent, and said good-bye. Then I put the phone down. Why couldn't I have explained that it was nothing whatever to do with David? Maybe knowing that he believed that left me feeling free-er.

There was a terrible silence in the room. I gazed about me, seeing nothing. How could I have done that? I'd just told the only man I'd ever loved to get out of my life. I wanted to scream.

I took the phone off the hook and just sat there, appalled, God knows for how long. I was aware of the light gradually fading, and still I couldn't move. I stared and stared into the darkness, and it was as though the darkness was my own life. Every so often I heard the church clock strike.

Some time later – heaven knows how long – I managed to take myself to the bedroom, and lay down without undressing.

I cried most of that night.

It surprised me that the morning came. The sun had the nerve to be shining. I was exhausted. I felt middle-aged. My mind was a desert. All I knew was that I'd done what I had to do. Now it was just a question of living through it, minute after minute after minute.

I was setting out on the long journey to becoming a single mother.

I kept surprising myself. I'd always imagined that if the sun were to disappear from my life, all would be night. But eyes grow accustomed to the dark.

There are also things one has to do, not only eating, dressing, making the bed, paying bills, but external things which intrude and make demands.

The first of these was Anna-Maria. I realised I must stop refusing to answer the phone, since my mother would then turn up unannounced. At least with a warning of her imminent arrival I'd have a chance to prepare what I was going to tell her.

What on earth *was* I going to tell her?

I'd forgotten what a hybrid of pragmatism and fantasy Anna-Maria was. She rang breezily from one of the local hotels late on Good Friday to announce that the flight and the train had been most satisfactory; ditto the hotel booking; that she'd just enjoyed an excellent English dinner, even if the vegetables were not as fresh as they should be; and that she hoped I would call for her at a decent hour after breakfast, say about nine-thirty. She'd already enquired about the priory, she assured me, and was pleased to be told that the entrance was easily within walking distance. She had brought her stout shoes.

I could only admire her. Here was a woman who hadn't visited England since before I was born, and whose English, so I'd always imagined, had only been up to murmuring 'Yes' when my father had fancied his pretty au pair girl and clambered into her bed. Clearly I was mistaken. Somehow she'd managed to make herself understood perfectly well, even in Norton Abbas.

She was waiting for me in the hotel lounge, dressed as though for Sunday Mass – gloves, hat, little veil pulled back. I realised with a thud of dismay that of course she believed she was about to visit a convent, and would be required to genuflect and mumble before stony altars. Yet another little lie to be disentangled.

We embraced fondly. She smelled of overripe melon. She cried a little, and made mother-hen noises. What a long, long time it had been, she said. Oh, how she'd missed me. Suddenly her sharp eye began to search me. At first I wondered if she'd somehow spotted that I was pregnant. Then I realised she must be wondering what kind of convent permitted make-up and jeans. I should have thought of that. I still had no idea how I was going to explain away where I lived. Not a convent cell, but my comfortable gatehouse. But at least I would not – absolutely *not*, I vowed – show her my bedroom. The *Kama Sutra* bedhead, even if I placed a Bible beside it, might not convince her that the good nuns were quite as good as I'd always led her to believe.

All along the street Anna-Maria gazed keenly about her, every so often uttering approving murmurs at the tourist shops which offered saccharine Madonnas in bright porcelain and models of the parish church embedded in glass paperweights.

So far Norton Abbas was putting on an excellent show for her.

We reached the gatehouse. Now was the moment of truth. Anna-Maria paused, and her sharp eye took in the building: she nodded with obvious approval at its handsome stonework and the grandeur of the central arch. Then I saw her peer upwards at the twin carvings on either side. The female figure on the left seemed at that moment to be more naked than ever, while the hand modesetly covering her genitals suddenly made it appear as though she were masturbating. I held my breath. I heard Anna-Maria sigh, and her eyes moved to the second figure, of the rampant satyr with the lopped-off penis. The silence was now interminable, and the longer she looked the more the absent penis seemed to recreate itself in air, huge and throbbing. Finally Anna-Maria gave another and much longer sigh.

'Darling, how your thoughts must rise to God with such beauty all around you.'

And she embraced me with further tears.

After this I began to feel that just possibly everything might be all right. I led her indoors, and she gazed about her. Finally she looked at me approvingly. She loved the gatehouse, she announced; what was more she understood perfectly that I should have been awarded a dwelling separate from those intending to take holy vows. That was only right and proper. At this point I chipped in. How unfortunate, I said, that the nunnery itself was uncomfortably far to walk, so far, in fact, that it was not even visible from here, I added, pointing confidently towards the distant woods and tidal marsh in order to demonstrate that there was no nunnery in sight. Besides, I went on, gaining in confidence by now, the nuns' privacy was something I'd come to respect, and it *was* Easter.

Anna-Maria nodded gravely, and said of course she quite understood; and in spite of having her stout shoes, per-haps it would also prove to be rather far. She was not as young as she used to be, and her varicose veins might not enjoy it.

At this moment, on cue, a coachload of Easter pilgrims from Saintly Tours announced their arrival, and I left Anna-Maria contentedly sipping her morning coffee while I prepared to join them. I explained that in a few minutes we would all of us be offering prayers to the blessed St Cuthburga. This seemed to please her.

Before I left I carefully locked the bedroom door.

How Fergus would have adored to witness this whole scene,

I thought, with a thump of pain, as I walked out to greet the party of pilgrims.

That evening I took Anna-Maria to Mamma Gina's. I'd carefully arranged not to be working that day. This was one more detail I preferred my mother not to know, and Mamma Gina had promised to treat me just as a friend, and to order Carlo to do the same. My whole life at the moment seemed curtained by secrets I daren't confess: there were so many of them, and they were all bursting in on me at once. Altogether it promised to be an evening of suffocating artificiality. I was dreading it.

Then, in my darkest hour, a small miracle occurred. The instant we entered the restaurant Anna-Maria and Mamma Gina took to one another like long-lost sisters. They embraced. They gabbled away in Italian. They laughed with much heaving of flesh. They raised their glasses to each other and to me. The evening never looked back. Even when I slipped away for a few moments to arrange the bill discreetly with Carlo, they scarcely seemed to notice. And when I returned neither of them even turned her head. Italian endearments continued to flow with the wine, and the restaurant was filled with their joy. I looked on in astonishment, transfixed by the sight of two enormous bosoms on either side of me which seemed to swell out towards one another across the table like the meeting of mighty oceans.

And as I sat there the strangest experience came over me. It was a sensation of belonging, of being massively protected. I wasn't alone. I would never again be alone. Everything would be all right. For the first time in my life I understood the meaning of 'family'.

'She wonderful woman, your mother,' Mamma Gina announced as Anna-Maria made her way purposefully towards the Ladies. 'I tell you, she just like me. She love you. And I love you.'

Perhaps it was the misery of the past week that made her words overwhelm me. I put my head in my hands and closed my eyes. I didn't dare open them for fear of bursting into tears, and Mamma Gina's hand on my arm only made it worse. Suddenly I knew I had no choice; I needed to tell

Mamma Gina about the baby, and it had to be done right now, in the five minutes or so it would take for Anna-Maria to disengage herself from all that infrastructure of clothing in the Ladies, and then reassemble it again.

The first minute passed, and I managed to open my eyes without crying.

'I want you to know something,' I said quietly. 'I'm having Fergus's child. I haven't told Anna-Maria.'

Mamma Gina squeezed my arm as if I had just made the most normal announcement in the world. Then she smiled.

'But she knows, my darling. We both know. Of course. Is very good.'

I gave a start. I was appalled.

'What d'you mean, "you know"?'

Mamma Gina was looking horribly wise.

'Is obvious,' she said. 'Mamma Gina can tell. Your mother can tell. Italian women, they know.' She tapped her face with her fingers. 'The face. The skin. The look in the eye. The breasts – a little bigger. Is very good thing.'

I felt even more appalled.

'But it's not a very good thing at all. It's bloody awful.'

Mamma Gina was shaking her head.

'No, no, no. Is good. You 'ave 'usband no good cook, no *bambini*. Now Mr Fergoose very good cook, you 'ave *bambini*. Like I told you. Is very good. Your mother she think very good.'

'She what?' I started to say.

But Anna-Maria was returning to the table. There was another burst of Italian as Mamma Gina explained our conversation. Then to my astonishment Anna-Maria threw her arms round me.

'*Mia cara! Carissima!*'

And so it went on. Embraces. Tears. Kisses. Sobs. Everyone else in the restaurant stopped eating. They smiled. Some raised their glasses. There were cries of '*Bravo!*'

This was dreadful. I couldn't believe it. And yet I was happy. I felt safe. I felt like a heroine. I was being squeezed between the vast twin bosoms of my extended family.

*   *   *

Anna-Maria departed two days after Easter, and by the time I waved her off on the London train it was as though thirty-two years of my life as a daughter had been rewritten.

She had been in her element helping me with the Easter pilgrims. Though she spoke extremely limited English, she'd found this no handicap whatsoever as she presided over my trestle-tables laden with herbs, calling out in voluble Italian as though this were a stall in Bologna market. Far from language being a barrier, her gabble of incomprehensible words acted as a magnet, and it was a brave pilgrim who dared head for the coach without burdening herself with armfuls of 'Herbs of Italy', 'Herbs of Greece', 'Herbs of the Old Testament', plus at least one copy of *St Cuthburga's Cookbook*.

In fact Anna-Maria proved to be a priceless commercial asset, and if she'd stayed much longer I'd have had nothing to sell for the remainder of the summer. The flame-throwers, to whom she chatted away unceasingly all day, held her in mystified awe.

The first evening we spent together she was in a truthful mood, which came as a shock. I'd never known her to tell the truth about anything before, but yesterday's encounter with Mamma Gina had clearly opened the flood-gates. Suddenly the official version of my conception and birth, which had been holy writ all my life, was discarded like yesterday's newspaper. Gone was the magnificently handsome English gentleman whom she'd met while improving her culture in the National Gallery. Instead my father was the lecherous stockbroker who'd favoured his Italian au pair girl with a few quick fucks before conveniently bundling her back home to bear the child he never once set eyes on.

'It wasn't easy in Bologna,' she explained quietly. 'I was supposed to be a virgin, not an unmarried mother. I had to pretend.'

And the pretence, I realised, soon became a kind of reality. It was what was needed, for her sake, and for my sake. Bologna was like that: it was the only way to survive.

We talked late every evening. I surprised myself by telling her everything; and what she chose to pick up surprised me just as much. I expected her to be horrified when I told her about Fergus, and how I'd decided not to see him. But far from begging me to marry him as soon as possible, Anna-Maria took the grand romantic view that mine was the love-match she'd never had, and I must cherish that love for ever, even if I never saw him again. A few tears followed this declaration, accompanied by the avowal that in any case I was far too good for any sausage-maker in Bologna, Lamborghini or no Lamborghini. She begged only one thing of me, that I should give the child the name Foscari. It was women who ruled in our family, she said fiercely. I thought immediately of Caroline, and her pride in being descended from a long line of mistresses. The idea of Anna-Maria and Caroline as twin priestesses of a new feminist church came as something of a shock. I went to bed that night reeling at the thought.

Our last evening together found her in a prophetic mood. It would be best for me to stay in England, she felt sure. Italy was no place for a single woman, least of all with a child. I had friends here who would shield me: Mamma Gina – 'wonderful Mamma Gina' – would find a place for me, she was quite certain. I wondered how she could be so certain, but there was a look in Anna-Maria's eye which hinted at something she knew and I didn't.

And then she left, dressed once again as if for Sunday Mass. It was only after I could no longer see her hand waving from the train window that I realised we had never talked about the convent I was supposed to be attending, or the 'good nuns' who were supposed to be taking such care of me.

I realised then that she hadn't believe a single word of it: that, because she lied, she assumed everyone else did too.

On my own again I kept asking myself, 'Am I being incredibly brave?' During the long hours when I missed Fergus quite terribly I knew the answer was no. But there were other times when I felt strong and resolute, and told myself confidently, 'Yes, I am being brave.' I was proud not to be falling apart. I was proud to be having the child. I was proud of forcing myself to be independent of Fergus.

None the less I couldn't help thinking about him all the time. I needed to do this. It was a way of keeping him at a necessary distance: if I let him slip out of my mind it frightened me that he might sneak up on me when I had no defences, and then I might crumble. It was better to keep all the memories of him clearly in focus, however much they knifed me, rather than dismiss them only to find myself bereft. I made myself think about our love-making, our laughter, our gentle evenings together, the cottage on the cliffs, the sleigh-ride across the frozen lake, the wonderful absurdity of his theories about the history of this place. They were all gone, yet they were all still there like beautiful memories framed on my walls. And they always would be. I must never let them go.

And where was Fergus? I didn't know. He had slipped away, just as I asked him to. There had been only the one plea, with a note of stunned unhappiness in his voice which had cut me to pieces, and then nothing. Part of me expected him to be haunting me – wasn't that what lovers were supposed to do? Yet I was proud that he didn't: there was a dignity about that which I admired.

But – oh God – how I would love to have seen him. Everywhere I went I looked for his face. Every phone call I wondered if it would be his voice. How long would the ache go on like this?

Mamma Gina had given me time off for Easter week. Everyone was on holiday anyway, she said, so the restaurant would be half-empty: Carlo would cope, though he'd miss not having my cleavage to peer down, 'the feelthy bugger'. She laughed, and said she looked forward to having me back: there was something she wanted to ask me.

It must have been the second or third evening after my return when she finally told me what was on her mind. As the last customers left the restaurant around eleven-thirty, Mamma Gina beckoned me over to the small table near the kitchen where we'd so often sat. It was a familiar ceremony, except that this time it wasn't grappa she placed in front of me, it was a glass of champagne.

She rested her elbows and her bosom on the table and peered at me.

'Anna-Maria she tell me you no see Mr Fergoose no more,' she said, frowning. 'Why you do that? He beautiful man. Very good man. Very good cook. He make baby. You foolish woman. Why you not marry him lickety-split?'

She sipped her grappa and continued to gaze at me challengingly.

I tried to explain that Fergus was absolutely not a family man. That he'd never wanted children – it was the reason his first marriage had broken up. That to draw him into marrying me because I was pregnant would ruin everything we had: it was better simply not to see him. I preferred it that way: it was my choice. Couldn't she understand?

Mamma Gina gave a deep sigh, and her bosom shifted several inches across the table.

'Then what you goin' do for cook?'

I laughed and said I'd just have to do without 'cook', wouldn't I?

She shook her head.

'Is no good no cook. You like nun growing beard.' She leant forward, reaching round her bosom to fold her large red hands. 'And what you goin' do for money? What you goin' do for place to live?'

I explained that when my divorce came through I'd get a small settlement from David which I thought I might put towards a flat. Then I'd let out a room free in return for babysitting so I could go on working here in the restaurant in the evenings, if Mamma Gina would have me.

A knowing smile came over her face, and she took another sip of her grappa.

'Now I tell you plan. You like my daughter. You family. Italian family very good. Business here very good. I want make bigger. Next-door shop, ee close. I buy. We make bigger Mamma Gina restaurant. You come with me partner. We share cook.'

I did a familiar double-take: I realised she meant 'share the cooking'.

Having grasped this I felt overwhelmed. I was being offered a partnership in this restaurant. An income. Security. I was 'family'. And my child would have a family.

I threw my arms round Mamma Gina's neck and gushed my thanks at her in Italian.

But she hadn't finished.

'But you no buy flat, Claudia. You keep settlement. You stay gatehouse and no grow things for pilgrims no more. You grow for restaurant. Then we make plenty money and you home with baby all day. Is good, huh? Mamma Gina lotsa good ideas.'

It *was* a good idea. It was a marvellous idea. I couldn't help admiring the way Mamma Gina combined a warm heart with a wonderfully sharp business nose.

'And when you want holiday,' she went on, 'you stay Mamma Gina bunkaloo.' I was puzzled for a moment until I realised she meant 'bungalow'. It was the first time she'd ever mentioned it. 'Is by sea. You teach baby piddle.' I assumed she meant 'paddle'. 'You stay weekend see, very soon.'

I thanked her once again. I was feeling even more overwhelmed. It was only a matter of weeks since I'd found out I was pregnant, and already a whole new life was unfolding. It was all going to work. It was going to be wonderful.

That night I lay in bed thinking of Fergus, wanting him, longing for him, full of sadness but full of certainty. I was going to be all right. And maybe one day . . . and I fell asleep on that most tender of hopes.

The letter from David, in his careful handwriting, informed me that his appointment as environment secretary would be official by the time I read this. He thought I might like to know, which was a strange way of putting it, as if I were some junior in his department rather than his wife.

It was more than ten months since I'd left him, and the letter brought home to me how distant from one another the tides had swept us in that time. Ten months apart after ten years together, a month for every year, and each month had been more intensely filled than any of those previous years. With David's impersonal letter in front of me, I thought of all those changes within me. I felt ten years older in experience, and ten years younger in myself. I'd discovered joy, love, pain, resolve, things that I'd only known existed in others. And I'd discovered friends, friends I needed, and who needed me. I was a new woman, and – 'Good Lord,' I said to myself as I felt the tautening of my belly – very soon there'd be two of us.

I was pleased for David: ever since I'd first known him it was what he'd wanted above all things, certainly more than me. He was in the Cabinet. Wow. Think of that. I'd phone him this evening and say 'Congrats' as if he were an old friend, praying he wouldn't backtrack and start rambling on about how nice it would be if we could get together again, how he missed me, how he still loved me. I was in no mood for any of that.

My less charitable thought after I'd re-read the letter was that I could now ring my lawyer and tell him to press ahead with the divorce. I'd fulfilled my part of the bargain; it was just tough if the new squeaky-clean environment secretary had to face snide questions about his non-sex-life at his first press conference. What went wrong at home, Mr Hazlitt? What price family values, Mr Hazlitt? Was your wife having an affair, Mr Hazlitt? At least they wouldn't ask him if anything was wrong with his cook.

The thought made me laugh.

I went out and bought a paper, and there indeed it was, the government reshuffle, a fairly well-worn pack of cards by and large. Even David, the only new member of the Cabinet, was so grindingly familiar to the public from his television sermons that the reporter could summon up nothing new to say. 'Hazlitt makes it' was the ironic headline: elsewhere the gossip columnist suggested more pointedly that it was a 'limp appointment', with a photo of David in bathing gear as if to emphasise it. If only he could manage a rampant affair with someone starry, I thought; it would do his political rating a power of good. A touch of the Alan Clarks.

This gave me a vision of David's political memoirs in twenty years' time, gathering dust on some 'remaindered' shelf in Weston-super-Mare, its author by then gathering more kindly dust in the House of Lords. Good God. To think, if I'd stuck it out I'd have been Lady Hazlitt one day. Instead I was destined to be Claudia Foscari, unmarried mother.

I'd kept my pregnancy deliberately quiet for more than a month now. Apart from Joan and Geoff, who were sworn to secrecy, and of course Anna-Maria, only Mamma Gina knew about my condition. I'd needed all those weeks to get used to the idea. But now the time to spread the word had come, before people started to gaze with prurient curiosity at my belly. Today would be the day.

I wished I could just pin up a short announcement by the gatehouse arch, and go away for a while. But no, it had to be done – one by one. The same little speech. I dreaded it.

And obviously I had to begin with Caroline.

A wave of cowardice overtook me halfway through tapping out her number. I replaced the receiver and phoned Megan instead.

It rang and rang. I imagined she was in her studio, and waited. Eventually a breathless voice said, 'Yes, hello?'

There seemed little point beating about the bush.

'Megan,' I said, trying to sound composed. 'I'm pregnant.'

There was silence for a moment, then a faint splutter.

'I beg your pardon?'

I imagined Megan to be in a state of shock. Her voice sounded strange.

'I'm PREGNANT!' I repeated loudly.

There was another silence.

'Excuse me,' said the voice. 'This is the South-Western Gas Board.'

Flustered and angry, I slammed down the phone. Once I'd regained some composure I tried again, pausing carefully before pressing each button.

The line was engaged.

I cursed, and walked round the room. I glared at the phone for a minute or two, then pressed the Repeat button. It rang.

This time Megan's voice was unmistakable.

I told her as calmly as I could.

'But that's wonderful,' she exclaimed without a moment's pause. 'Is it Fergus's?'

I was rather thrown by this. I said of course it was, but that he didn't know, and wouldn't know. That I'd decided not to see him.

The tone of voice changed abruptly.

'Oh dear,' she said. 'Really? Goodness me. But I suppose you must know what you're doing.'

I hate people saying things like that. Immediately I felt deeply uncertain that I did know what I was doing. I wanted unqualified understanding and compassion: anything less made me feel fragile and on the verge of panic.

'Yes,' I said firmly, 'I do.'

Then she made things better.

'My dear, can we help in any way? We'd love to, you know. Glyn and I are deeply fond of you.'

It was such a simple thing to say, and I wanted to reach out and hug her. Instead I laughed.

'Yes, you can take the baby off my hands as often as you like, Megan. And if Caroline asks you to paint another cherub in the clouds, you'll know where to look for one.'

I could hear chuckling sounds on the other end of the phone. I'd never given much thought to needing the support of friends before. And I'd never really experienced the feeling of gratitude when it was offered. I was learning so much – sometimes I felt I hardly knew how to take it all in.

Then Megan became practical.

'Come to dinner tomorrow. And when you start getting morning sickness, ring me and I'll tell you how to deal with it. When's the brat due?'

My mouth puckered.

'About Christmas-time. Brilliant timing, wasn't it?'

Megan chuckled again.

'Well, there's certainly a precedent there.'

After a few moments I rang off, feeling warmed.

And now it was Caroline's turn: I couldn't put it off any longer. I'd been dreading this day after day. She was capable of saying anything, and I was feeling far too vulnerable for her special brand of honesty.

I stared at the phone, trying to pluck up courage, willing Caroline to be kind. And then suddenly it rang. I jumped, and without thinking picked it up. A blast of Caroline struck my ear.

'Christ, you've been on the phone for bloody hours. Now listen. It's all happening. They're here, digging up the skeletons.

The drainage people. Bones all over the place. I've told them to stop; that it's sacrilege. I've phoned the Legover woman. And I've rung the bishop. He's coming over to pronounce it sacred ground, or whatever it is they do. Bless it or something. Tomorrow, he says. Isn't he sweet? I don't need to sleep with him, Claudia, do I? I could, I suppose: he was rather good at it fifteen years ago, and it's not the sort of thing you forget just because you become a bishop, is it? The trouble is, Patrick's here, and all the children. How are you, by the way?'

'I'm pregnant.'

As I said it there was a confusion of noises, then the muffled sound of Caroline's voice bawling at the children to get the hell out of the room. I didn't even know if she'd heard me.

Then there was complete silence. I was about to put the phone down when I heard sounds of breathing, followed by a muttered exclamation.

'Jesus.' Then, 'Claudia, I don't know what to say. Is it good news, bad news? Tell me.' There was another pause, and suddenly a laugh. 'Oh yes, I do know what to say. Can I be godmother?'

I suppose I might have expected the unexpected from Caroline. Somehow it managed to cut through all the awkwardness and anxiety within me, and I found myself telling her with perfect ease what had happened, exactly what I felt about it, and what I intended to do. And as I talked and talked I was aware how Caroline, who never normally bothered to listen to anybody if she could help it, was awarding me a rare silence.

'Well,' she exclaimed when I'd finished, 'I think you're totally amazing – and I've never heard such absolute balls in my life.'

I felt shaken.

'What d'you mean?' I said crossly.

Caroline gave a snort.

'Exactly that. Absolute balls. All that stuff about not wanting to trap Fergus into marrying you. Pure romantic rubbish. What books have you been reading? The idea that you want to keep your beautiful affair in a glass case and gaze at it for the rest of your life like a cup you won at school. And the kid's really going to love you for it, isn't he? Or she? Or both of them. I can just hear its little voice: "Oh, thank-you, Mum, how right you were not to give me a dad." Fucking ridiculous, Claudia. Marriage is something you can make as you like, for God's sake. You can make a mess of it, as I have, or you can make it wonderful.' She laughed. 'At least, so I'm told. But at least it has to be a bloody sight better than never seeing the guy at all. That's just . . . well, it's just lunatic. It's barking. You're off your trolley.'

And Caroline gave another snort of irritation down the phone.

I took a deep breath.

'OK, Caroline,' I said, smarting, 'of course you can be godmother. After all, you've had plenty of practice at being God.'

Caroline's blessing was like a rod to beat me with. I could grasp perfectly well what she meant; it was her grasp of my needs that was questionable. Caroline's view of all men was that they existed in order to be pushed around and pulled into place – usually bed – until she grew bored; then she'd treat them so contemptuously that they made for the hills, whereupon she'd complain bitterly of being abandoned. Patrick had managed to survive this raw treatment, partly because he was the father of her children, and partly because he blunted her insults by never taking them seriously. He danced away from them like Mohammed Ali: he was a master at ducking and weaving. Also, he was almost never there: when things grew rough he retreated to the comfort of his bimbos.

So there was no way Caroline could possibly understand Fergus. She'd fancied him the first moment she caught sight of him – upside-down in my sitting-room last summer. And she'd pestered me ever since. What he was like in bed? How many other mistresses did he have? How long did I think it would last? Could she please be first in the queue after me? Tactful enquiries like that.

But the idea of a man being a free spirit was far beyond the range of her experience. The only free spirit Caroline understood was someone's else's vodka-and-tonic.

Over the next few weeks I avoided talking to her about my pregnancy as much as possible, swiftly diverting the conversation whenever she asked challengingly if I'd come to my senses yet. Frowning, she'd then accost Joan or Megan, and harangue them instead. Couldn't they do something about me, for Christ's sake? Why was I so stubborn? And what did I imagine I was going to live on. Selling herbs to pious fruitcakes and serving 'spag bol' to spotty insurance salesmen wasn't going to provide for a growing child, was it? (Megan laughed as she told me this, and suggested that Caroline probably meant it wouldn't pay the fees at Eton or Benenden.)

Mercifully, Caroline's energies were now mostly taken up with preparations for her medical conference, and as this fearful event loomed I decided to take up Mamma Gina's invitation to borrow her 'bunkaloo'. The prospect of another of Caroline's astonishing conferences on my very doorstep was altogether too much, particularly as I'd now begun to suffer from morning sickness.

Megan loaded me with suitable pills and potions, Mamma Gina gave me incomprehensible directions, and off I drove for a long weekend in the general direction of the sea, trusting that somehow I'd manage to find the 'bunkaloo'.

It was May. It was fresh and green. I felt strong. Mamma Gina's directions were less helpful than the map presented to me by Glyn, and after several pauses to consult signposts half-buried in flowering hedgerows I drove my little Fiat past numerous caravan sites towards a stretch of empty bungalows which were neatly ranked beside an equally empty sea.

This was Suburbia-super-Mare, I realised; not quite what I'd expected of an expansive Italian lady from Lucca, though I wasn't at all sure what I had expected. Something more eccentric, perhaps: more of a love-nest where she could enjoy a good cook.

That afternoon I settled myself amid the pink-upholstered G-plan furniture and tried to imagine Mamma Gina passing her windswept summer holidays here, seated on the little wooden terrace with her stockings rolled down to her ankles, large red arms folded across her bosom, eyes occasionally crinkling at the sight of someone she fancied emerging from the waves.

Well, this would soon be my life too, I thought: I'd be joining the clusters of young mothers bravely huddling behind windbreaks, watching the tide dissolve elaborate sandcastles and – I remembered with a smile – holding the small hand of my infant while he learnt to 'piddle' in the shallows.

All that weekend I found myself contemplating this new life, laying it over all the other lives which might have been mine. Supposing I'd stayed with David, I thought: holidays would have continued as they had always been, the obligatory fortnight during the summer recess when we'd pretend to share the beauty of the Italian lakes, a half-bottle of Soave filling the silence between us as David contemplated the phone calls he ought to be making, and I more furtively contemplated the men I might dream of spending the night with.

Or supposing I'd given in to Anna-Maria and gone back home to Bologna: the young Signora Vespucci would be taking her dutiful place at the long dining-table amid regiments of uncles and great-aunts, cousins and in-laws, and everyone's children, including God knows how many of my own.

Or if this had never happened, and I were still with Fergus, what then? We'd be away somewhere, anywhere, the wind in my hair as the Alfa-Romeo meandered along empty French by-roads heading south; and I'd catch his eye, undo a button of my blouse, and know that we were both thinking of a long dinner and a large bed. Naked bodies in the warm night. Free spirits.

Instead, this.

If there'd been a phone I knew I'd have rung Fergus that evening. And the next. The pain was almost unbearable.

Driving home after my weekend I told myself firmly that I was bound to have moments like that; they were all part of the testing process, weren't they? And if I survived them I'd be all the stronger. I wasn't sure I was entirely convinced that this was so, but at least I could congratulate myself that I'd experienced a taste of the future, and survived. Summer at the 'bunkaloo' wouldn't be all that bad, and with a child I'd be grateful for all it had to offer.

But Jesus, what the hell *did* it have to offer?

I pursed my lips and drove on. It was Sunday evening, and at least the Devon countryside was beautiful, I told myself resolutely. Claudia, go on. Enjoy it.

Caroline's medical conference would be over by now, I suddenly remembered. Would she have pulled off another miraculous triumph? I could hear the bells of the parish church ringing out across the town as I drove alongside the old priory wall towards the gatehouse. The whole place seemed surprisingly empty: I'd imagined there would be a gradual spilling-out of earnest delegates still wearing conference name-tags attached to their lapels, and carrying sheaves of literature under their arms. But there was nobody at all. The street was empty. Not even a car.

I parked mine in the usual place, and walked through the gatehouse arch. Still there was nobody around. The medieval barn stood there as though it had remained unused ever since the nuns departed. The meadow was fresh and uncut, though there were signs that people had trampled across it. But the only indication of life was Jehoshaphat, munching lugubriously at the end of his tether, just where I'd left him.

The goat raised his head as he saw me and began to amble purposefully in my direction, a large sheet of paper dangling half-chewed from his mouth. This rather puzzled me. I crossed the open meadow towards him, and as I did so I noticed that the grass around him was littered with more sheets of paper, dozens of them, some already chewed, others just lying there.

Even more puzzled, I bent down and picked one up. It was a photograph. I gave a start. It was a photograph of a young girl, entirely naked. The pose could hardly have been more provocative.

I looked around me. All the sheets of paper were photographs, and all of them were of young girls. My meadow was littered with Lolitas. Some were embracing pot-bellied men, some were . . . Christ, I could hardly believe it: I felt appalled. Indignant. I'd only ever read about such things. What on earth were they doing here? Maybe, I thought, some pervert had wandered into the grounds in the guise of a pilgrim, and had enjoyed a leering afternoon in the sun with his revolting fantasies.

But then why had the photographs just been left here?

I hurried round the meadow picking them all up, removing one particularly nasty one from Jehoshaphat's mouth, which displeased him. But what was I supposed to do with them now? I could hardly put the whole lot in the dustbin. Perhaps I should make a bonfire, but then supposing the wind were to carry some vivid scene of fellatio over the convent wall into the churchyard, or down the High Street.

I hurried indoors, dumped the offensive photos on the floor, and phoned Joan.

'Oh, thank God you're back,' she exclaimed the moment she heard my voice. 'Hang on, I'm coming round.'

She appeared a few minutes later, somewhat breathless. She glanced at the litter of pornographic photos on the floor, looked up at me, and burst out laughing.

'Oh Claudia, I shouldn't laugh. I really shouldn't,' she said. 'But . . .'

She swept her red hair back from her eyes, and stood there shaking her head.

'Well, explain, for Christ's sake, will you?' I pleaded. 'What happened to the conference?'

'Oh, that was fine,' she said. 'Except for one thing. Caroline decided to put a last-minute ad in the local paper in case not enough people turned up. Well, you know how she sometimes gets things wrong, especially when she'd had a few drinks. Anyway, apparently she phoned over the ad, but instead of "Paediatricians' Conference" she must have said "Paedophiliacs' Conference". The police raided it this afternoon: Caroline's at the station right now, answering some rather difficult questions, I imagine.'

I gazed at Joan in disbelief.

'Oh, it's quite all right,' she went on. 'She's got an uncle who's a QC: she rang him straight away and he told her to blame it all on the paper for getting it wrong, and sue them. The likelihood is she'll get enough damages to pay the cost of running Priory Hall for years.'

Joan looked at me quizzically, then cast her eyes back over the litter of photographs on the floor.

'You know, Claudia, from the look on her face as the police whisked her off I wouldn't mind betting she set the whole thing up quite deliberately.'

Twelve

It felt extraordinary to be living for something inside myself which I couldn't actually see. The external world no longer seemed real by comparison: it was merely stage scenery that was forever changing, but without greatly affecting my life or the smaller life that was growing within me.

This 'thing' – I felt I really should give it a name, but what? – was now more than three months old. No real danger of a miscarriage now, Geoff had assured me. He was becoming positively paternal towards me: he seemed quietly pleased to be cherishing a love-child.

'Not too many of those in Norton Abbas,' Joan had commented a little acidly as I left the doctor's surgery.

'Get plenty of rest,' Geoff called after me. 'Not too much heavy work in that garden of yours.'

'I'll send the flame-throwers along to hump the pots around for you,' Joan suggested. 'At least it'll get the smell of them out of the house, and spare me their bloody music for a few hours.'

Everyone was being wonderfully protective, even Caroline, which was a disarming experience. She'd taken to turning up with little gifts, things she remembered having a craving for when she'd been pregnant. Sometimes it would be Turkish Delight, at other times a bottle of Giorgio perfume, once to my surprise a book of John Donne's love poetry.

'I used to read them aloud to myself,' she announced, 'dreaming of all the men I'd so much rather be pregnant by than Patrick.'

But most often she brought champagne.

'*Real* champagne of course,' she'd insist, handing it to me. 'None of your Aussie fizz.'

I was touched and grateful, particularly for the champagne, which I could never have afforded myself. Caroline's own finances appeared to be extremely volatile at present. The money from the London house had finally been swallowed up by Lloyd's ('that bloody idiot Patrick'): on the other hand Caroline herself had just received a generous shot in the arm from damages paid her by the local newspaper for the 'paedophiliac' catastrophe, exactly as her QC uncle had predicted. The unwonted intrusion had disrupted an otherwise brilliantly successful medical conference, she claimed. She carefully refused to divulge whether or not she had plotted the whole disgraceful business herself, though the look of self-satisfaction on her face left no one in any real doubt. The £40,000 she had received – enough to cover expenses on the house for two years – was for 'injury to her professional reputation', as the newspaper had grovellingly put it. This had brought a guffaw from Joan, followed by a glance of furious indignation from Caroline.

Today she seemed to have forgotten Joan's insult, and had just come from bullying her into helping with her next enterprise, the Summer Fête. Judging by Caroline's mood, she had got what she wanted. She was humming to herself.

'Doesn't it make you feel incredibly sexy, being pregnant?' she asked suddenly.

We were strolling across the meadow on a limpid June evening, Caroline having parked the champagne in my fridge to await our return.

'It wouldn't help all that much if I did, would it?' I said.

She shot me a scornful look.

'You mean you're still playing the holy martyr? For God's sake, Claudia.'

I deliberately made no comment. Caroline continued her swinging gait through the long grass, swishing idly at the thistles with a stick as she passed. She was looking very pretty, her blonde hair flowing, her tight jeans emphasising what extremely good legs she had.

'Yes, I never felt sexier than when I was having Chloe,' she mused. 'It was the best part of it really. I had these huge breasts. And wonderful skin. And no periods to worry about. Heigh-ho.' And she gave a sigh. 'Just as well. After that it all falls apart, of course.'

Thank-you, Caroline, I thought. That's just what I need to hear right now.

'The boobs droop.'

(Great.)

'Belly sags.'

(Thanks again.)

'Stretch-marks everywhere.'

(Wonderful.)

'Varicose veins.'

(Yes, I'm looking forward to those.)

'Bags under the eyes because you never get a proper night's sleep.'

(Anything else you can think of, Caroline?)

'Trouble with the water-works.'

(That was one I hadn't thought of.)

Thank heavens at this point she became distracted. She paused and gazed about her.

'God, it's beautiful here. Why don't I come here more often?'

'You could,' I said. 'You own it.'

She frowned.

'No, I don't. The National fucking Trust owns it. But I will, I will. You wait. I'm not beaten yet. What on earth are *those* things?'

We'd reached the edge of the beech-wood, and there among the thin grass rose hundreds of the curious pink and green flowers with reddish leaves I remembered noticing when I'd first arrived here almost exactly a year ago. I'd quite forgotten about them.

'I believe they're wild orchids of some sort,' I said. 'I forget what they're called, but Glyn knows all about them. They're incredibly rare apparently. They should live only in Turkey, or somewhere like that, he says.'

But Caroline was already bored.

'How's your divorce coming along?'

'Slowly,' I said. 'I should get the *nisi* before the end of the summer.'

'And lots of money with it?'

I explained that David didn't have lots of money, and that in any case *I'd* left *him*.

She turned on me.

'What the hell's that got to do with it?' she said crossly. 'He couldn't get it up, so you got up and left him. That sounds perfectly fair to me.' Then she laughed. 'Mind you, when Patrick gets it up you wouldn't notice. I only knew he had when I fell pregnant.'

We were back on familiar ground, and I didn't answer.

Caroline gave a sigh.

'The lab test on the bones has come through, by the way,' she said gloomily. 'They're all male apparently; so I can't go on claiming it was the nuns' burial-ground, bugger it. I've tried the police, told them they might care to investigate a mass murder. But they just laughed, the bastards. They had the cheek to say it sounded like a practical joke to them. How dare they? I've written to the Commissioner. Meanwhile Howl's planting rare grasses round the house: I nicked them from the botanical gardens in Exeter. That should hold up the National Trust for a while.'

She gave another sigh.

'Well, don't you think that champagne should be cool enough by now?'

Caroline's visits were good for my spirits. Even though she entirely failed to understand my resolution not to see Fergus, she never for one moment treated my situation as anything unusual, or to be pitied, or to get anxious about. She always had the gift of casting a veil of normality over any event that took place, no matter how calamitous or improbable it might be. She would rage and shout just long enough for everyone to rush around wringing their hands in sympathy, then calmly and efficiently deal with it herself as if we were all of us fools not to have thought of it ourselves. This was her great power, as well as her power of great comfort. She made our own disasters seem manageable by making them appear entirely unimportant, and often rather funny.

I needed every bit of that reassurance. My thoughts were so often with Fergus that sometimes, when I couldn't bear it, I would rush helplessly to Megan or to Mamma Gina, just to feel the strength of them and to be allowed to cry. Joan I tended to avoid: the ambivalence of her feelings about my whole relationship with Fergus made me uneasy. I even wondered if perhaps she still saw him, and there were moments when I experienced pangs of quite irrational jealousy. Maybe he had sought her out for comfort; and maybe she was only too happy to offer that comfort in the way she had always dreamed of doing.

And when I wasn't jealous of Joan I was jealous of the entire female sex under the age of at least fifty. Fergus was so entirely gorgeous, and in absence seemed more gorgeous than ever. Even if he hadn't already seduced every woman in Devon by the time I met him, he surely had by now. Every time I caught sight of a red sports car I looked first of all to see if some edible blonde was in the passenger seat before I even noticed who was driving it. But it was never Fergus.

I assumed he must be keeping deliberately away. I was grateful for that, but – oh God – I longed to see him.

These were the moments when I told myself that perhaps Caroline was right after all, and that I was being a fool to be clinging to my absurd resolve. A romantic and self-destructive fool.

And yet something always stopped me from ringing him; and an hour later I felt a profound relief that I hadn't.

One morning I woke up and realised it was Midsummer's Day. I was feeling dreadful: the malevolent gods had seen to it that morning sickness should be hitting me particularly badly on the anniversary of my arrival here – when I'd been free as the wind, free at last of David, free to make of my life whatever I chose.

And look what I *had* made of it. I passed my hand across my belly and grimaced in the mirror. I hadn't counted on the curse of St Cuthburga, I decided.

Except for my stomach I looked thin. A scrawny mess. I hadn't eaten anything properly for days. Mamma Gina had tut-tutted, and tried to press plates of steaming pasta on me, accompanied by my favourite pesto sauce, which she'd made specially for me, she announced. 'See, I give you good cook.'

I hadn't even been able to laugh at that, or to eat the pasta.

Stirring myself, I rang Geoff. In that flat doctor's voice of his he explained that I really must try to feed myself sensibly, and if I didn't then of course the morning sickness would be worse. I was just making life difficult for myself. He'd find something to stimulate my appetite, he promised. Joan would drop it in later in the morning when she came to tend her bees.

She arrived about midday looking unusually frisky. She was wearing a skirt and a cotton blouse, which was most unlike Joan. Her hair was loose and she had no bra on, which was even more unlike her. Her nipples showed sharply through the blouse, and there was a red mark on her neck which looked suspiciously like a love-bite.

It didn't matter how unlikely it was, the idea that Fergus might be having an affair with Joan when with a click of his fingers he could have just about any woman he wanted. It didn't matter what my brain told me, I couldn't help feeling sick with jealousy.

'Here you are,' she announced breezily, setting a pot of something on the table beside me. 'Doctor's orders. Lots of sugar in it. Eat it with bread, or by itself if you want to.'

'What is it?' I said weakly.

She gave a shrug.

'He didn't say. Just gave it to me. I'd better go now; the bees are calling. It's the lime-flow season.'

And she skipped away, skirt billowing around her as she crossed the meadow, blouse loose and hair streaming. How pretty she looked, I thought, and how young. Something had happened to her, and I hated her for it.

The last thing I wanted to do was to eat this disgusting-looking muck Geoff had prescribed for me. It reminded me of a wet cow-pat which someone had put in a jar. There was no label to say what it was, which was perhaps just as well. But I made myself believe that my doctor knew best, cut myself a couple of slices of fresh granary bread, and spread the glutinous stuff generously over one of them. Then I swallowed hard to clear my throat of nausea, and took a large bite with my eyes closed.

It was surprisingly good. I felt relieved, and took another bite. It tasted like a mixture of honey and jam, heavily perfumed as though it contained cinnamon. I decided to wash it down with a glass of white wine (thank heaven my taste for it had returned).

No doubt it was all in the mind, but already I felt a whole lot better, and took my bread, wine and whatever-it-was out on to the terrace in the sun. It was deliciously warm and peaceful, and I began to feel almost happy. Life really wasn't all that bad. One of my honey buzzards was on his usual perch, watching me beadily, and swallows were dipping across the open meadow. Bright sails on the far estuary caught the sun, and everywhere there was a humming of Joan's bees. Even Jehoshaphat looked as if he might have a smile on his face.

I spread the second slice of bread, and sipped my wine. Yes, I could do a lot worse than live here, couldn't I? All this space to do as I liked in. Space for the child to play. Friends nearby. Herbs and vegetables to grow for the restaurant, in which I'd soon be a partner after all. Then the occasional weekend at the 'bunkaloo' when I wanted to teach the infant to 'piddle'. Perhaps even some 'good cook'. I found myself laughing.

I was still hungry: I could hardly believe it. I went indoors and came back with a third slice of granary bread, covering it with the last of Geoff's concoction. He'd be proud of me, I thought. What was more, it was working. I felt a new woman. I even poured myself a second glass of wine.

The honey buzzard took off in the direction of Joan's bees, its head predatory and wingtips flared. Such a beautiful creature for a killer. I remembered Glyn explaining how the birds must have been coming here to breed every year since the nuns starting keeping bees in this place. That was more than a thousand years. I felt very insignificant and very temporary, and suddenly very tired.

I carried the remains of my peculiar lunch into the kitchen and, leaving the French windows wide open, stretched myself out on the sofa. I wasn't sure if I wanted to sleep, but I did feel wonderfully relaxed, far more so than I had for weeks. It was obviously the wine: I was simply no longer used to it. But there was something else besides: I was aware of a curious sensation in my body, as if I was weightless, floating, my head floating, and strange things floating about in my head.

I closed my eyes in order to picture what the strange things might be, and suddenly it was like being in the midst of a firework display, except that the fireworks were recognisable shapes all around me; they were human shapes, and I was one of them, naked. I could scarcely believe what was happening, and Christ, it was sexy. I had no idea whether I was already asleep – I suppose I must have been – but I no longer had the least idea where I was. I was nowhere and everywhere. I was floating amid this cosmos of colours and limbs which were cascading around me. Hands were stroking my arms, breasts, thighs. I thought it would never stop, and I hoped it never would. And yet all this time my mind seemed to remain detached from everything that was going on. I was even laughing: 'Jesus, Claudia.' I could hear myself call out. 'I'm about to have a cosmic fuck. This is the ultimate, what people are always writing about, and no one's ever actually experienced. I'm going to make history.' And as I said this, everything around me turned red, a blazing red that poured down all over me.

Somehow I found myself opening my eyes, and the blaze of red was still there. It was the sun in my face. I blinked, and I blinked a second time. Standing motionless by the open French windows was Fergus.

I can only have been half-awake. All I knew was that it seemed natural that he should be standing there, just as he always did, and that I should be lying here waiting for him. The sun was directly behind him as if he'd emerged out of it that very moment, exactly as he had the very first time, when I'd been lying daydreaming in the summer meadow. It was as though we were beginning all over again. He walked over to me. My body wanted his. We were two magnets.

And as he came close I remembered the smell of him. I touched him. We kissed. We undressed in seconds; then without a word I took him inside me. And it was like going back into my dream.

It seemed hours before I dared let my arms fall away from around him in case my cosmic fuck might not be real after all, but only a dream, and I would suddenly wake in the grey ashes of some terrible dawn. When I opened my eyes he *was* there: his hair was across my face, and I took some of it in my mouth. It tasted salty. His face was rough.

I just lay there, exhausted and confused. How had this happened? That extraordinary dream; then Fergus just standing there as if I'd summoned him to enter the dream. I didn't understand anything. What was he doing here? What was *I* doing here? It was incredible, and it was appalling. I would have to tell him. How was I to tell him? And then what? I closed my eyes again to try and shut out the confusion. I just lay there.

One of his hands was resting on my belly, circling it. Then the hand moved up my body on to my breasts. My nipples were swollen and tender as he touched them. I still couldn't bring myself to speak, yet it was very strange, as though the hand touching me already knew. I looked up at him.

Fergus raised himself on one elbow and gazed down at me. He looked older, almost gaunt. Then very gently his hand returned to my belly, stroking the swelling of it. And he smiled: that private smile.

'I'm glad,' he said.

That was all. I was dumbfounded.

'You are?' I murmured.

'Of course.'

There was a long silence. I went on looking at him. His eyes were smiling. And then I cried. I thought it would never stop. Months of tears, an ocean of them. I desperately wanted to turn them off because there was so much I needed to say, so much I needed to ask. And now Fergus was laughing, and that made it even worse. He kept kissing me, kissing my face, my breasts, my belly. And I kept crying.

'It's all right,' he said very softly. 'It's all right.'

I pulled him down to me and held him close with all my strength.

'Fergus, stay, won't you?' I managed to say. 'Just stay. I want to tell you everything, and I want you to tell me everything. Oh Jesus, I'm a mess. And I can't even ask you for a handkerchief. Find me one, please. No, no, don't. Just stay here, very close. And hold me. Don't let go. Don't ever let go.'

He kissed my eyes, and my tears, and said nothing. We just

lay there. There was the smell of his hair, the smell of sweat, the smell of sex.

Gradually I began to feel calmer. I lifted his head away from mine, and gazed up at him.

'You know?' I whispered.

He just nodded.

I went on gazing at him.

'Then tell me, why are you glad?'

His eyes crinkled, and he gave me another of his private smiles.

'Because it's you.'

It was as though my whole body responded to those three words. It was such a simple thing to say, and it meant everything.

'I never thought . . .' I began, and then I couldn't go on.

And suddenly he laughed again, and ran his fingers through my hair.

'You never thought what?' he said. 'That I wanted children. Is that it?' He sat up on the edge of the sofa and looked down on me, smiling. 'And you were right, of course. Horrible little leaking things. Keep you awake all night. Scream when you put them down. Vomit on your shoulder when you pick them up. Throw their food on the floor. Eat earwigs. Torture the cat.'

Now I was laughing too. I hugged him.

'Go on.'

'Well, are you surprised I never wanted children?'

'And . . . ?'

'There's no "and". They're dreadful . . . Except ours.'

I hugged him again, then sat up next to him and grasped his hand.

'But Fergus, it *will* scream all night. It *will* vomit on your shoulder. It *will* eat earwigs and torture the cat.'

He was shaking his head.

'Oh, that's quite different.'

'Why is it different?'

'Because it'll be ours.'

It was such a lovely thing to say, and I wondered if I could ever be happier than I was at that moment.

'I love you, Fergus,' I said. 'And I'm sorry. Terribly sorry.'

Then I looked at him fiercely. 'But it's all your bloody fault. All that stuff you gave me about being a free spirit, about your first wife and how she wanted kids and you didn't. Why did you tell me all that?'

He raised an eyebrow.

'Because it was true.'

'So, what's the difference?' I said.

'I hadn't met you then, had I?'

What on earth could I say? I was on air, and I wanted to beat him with my fists.

'I don't know why I love you,' I said, clasping his head in my hands. 'You're dreadful.'

He pushed me down on the sofa, and kissed me.

'I know. I'd get somebody else if I were you.'

I kissed him back, and ran my hand down his body.

'A bit late for that. Thank God.'

It was growing chilly. I sat up again on the edge of the sofa. Through the open French windows I could see the sun already low behind the beech-wood, and the thought came to me that perhaps a party from Saintly Tours might have trooped past while we were making love all afternoon. Would there be outraged letters to the National Trust? Would I be evicted? Then I realised, 'Bugger it. It doesn't matter now, does it?' I was with Fergus. I would always be with Fergus. He was my man – my beautiful man – my god of the sun. And I wanted to hug the whole world.

'Tell me, Fergus, how did you know?'

He emerged from the bathroom, hair dripping, and a towel draped round him. I pulled the towel away to gaze at him standing there naked. God, I loved his body. His prick looked so neat and shrivelled, and I took it in my hands.

'The little devil,' I said, laughing. 'It did the real devil's work, didn't it? But go on, tell me, how did you know I was pregnant? Or did you just guess?'

Fergus retrieved the towel and began to dry himself.

'Who would you say was your most tactless friend?' he said nonchalantly.

I felt my eyes widen.

'Oh no.'

Fergus nodded.

'The baggage,' I said. 'How dare she?'

'She just let it slip by mistake. I rang her out of the blue yesterday: I couldn't bear not knowing what was happening to you any longer. Does that surprise you? I needed to know if you'd gone back to your husband yet, and whether you were enjoying being the wife of the new environment secretary. Well, Caroline just bellowed with laughter down the phone. "What the fuck are you talking about?" she said. "As if she'd go back to him. Can you imagine *him* making her pregnant?" Then she went "Oops! I shouldn't have said that, should I?" That was all.'

I put my arms round Fergus's neck.

'Was it an awful shock? Oh God, was it?'

He stroked my cheek very gently. And then he smiled.

'In a word, yes.'

'And did you hate me for it?'

'In a word, no.'

'Promise?'

'I felt shattered, and terribly happy.'

'So what did you do?'

'I leapt straight in the car and drove from Exeter in about ten minutes – got stopped for speeding twice on the way. I was determined to get Caroline to tell me the whole story. And she did. She also gave me absolute hell, I have to say.'

I held Fergus tighter.

'Oh darling . . .'

Fergus made a face, then gave a chuckle.

'Joan was there too when I turned up: they'd been planning some kind of Summer Fête. And she wasn't a lot kinder, I can tell you.'

I felt myself give a jolt.

'Joan,' I said. '*She* was there?'

It was like an electric shock in my brain. A sudden flash. A revelation. I was struggling to put things together in my head. Could it really be just a chain of coincidences, Joan being there at Caroline's house, her visit to me this morning, the concoction she brought from Geoff (or so she claimed)? And then those dreams, those incredible erotic dreams. Then Fergus turning up. Could it possibly be?

I was still gazing hard at Fergus.

'What on earth's the matter?' he was saying. 'What is it?'

I took both his hands in mine very firmly.

'Fergus, tell me one thing, will you, please? Joan knows about your recipe, doesn't she? The quince honey. The manuscript you found.'

He seemed startled. Then he nodded.

'Well, yes, she does. Yes.' He looked uncomfortable. 'I showed it to her a long time ago. Then, when I couldn't come here any more I decided to send her a copy of it, to see what she could make of it. I'd lost all interest in the whole thing at that moment because I'd lost you. I just wanted to forget it.' I felt a rush of pure love when I heard him say that. It was all a nightmare, and the nightmare had passed. 'I explained to Joan what I thought "satur rote" meant,' he went on, 'that it was the missing ingredient which I believed might still grow here somewhere, and maybe she'd be able to find it since I no longer had a chance to. That's all. Why?'

'Fergus,' I said, still holding his hands extremely tightly, 'did Joan say anything else to you when you saw her yesterday? Anything about me?'

He raised his eyebrows.

'No, not really. She just said you were away till this afternoon, which is why I didn't come before. Otherwise I'd have been here last night, wouldn't I? As it was I didn't get an awful lot of sleep.'

Suddenly everything had fallen into place. So it *was* true. It had to be true. God Almighty. And Joan had plotted the whole thing.

'Fergus,' I said, feeling extremely shaky, 'I *wasn't* away yesterday. I was here. And Joan knew I was here. In fact she visited me this morning.'

A even more puzzled look settled on Fergus's face.

'Yes,' I added. 'As a matter of fact she brought me a present. Wasn't that kind of her?' I laughed. Then I reached out and touched Fergus's lips very gently with my fingertips.

'Just one other thing, darling,' I said. 'Did you enjoy making love this afternoon?'

It was hard to tell from Fergus's face whether he believed my story. He merely looked dazed. We stared at one another. It was a chain of events so wildly unlikely that I found it hard to imagine anyone believing a word of it should I ever need to explain what had taken place. To be reunited with the man I loved through the agency of some mythical aphrodisiac sounded like an episode in a gothic romance that not even Anna-Maria might be tempted to read. Yet here I was, stunned by an afternoon and evening of incredible love-making induced by a magic concoction I'd always assumed to exist only in Fergus's rich imagination, a piece of pure fiction which he indulged in simply for the sake of this book he claimed to be writing, *The Devil's Work*.

It was an elaborate game we'd both enjoyed playing, and I'd always imagined it would end just as I'd imagined that our affair would end. It would be part of the golden and torn fabric of my year of freedom.

Yet here I was, aware that the sun had just set on the most beautiful evening of my life.

Joan had come hurrying over the moment I phoned. And now the three of us – Joan, Fergus and myself – were standing in my living-room on this warm summer night, the French windows open to the moonlight and the owls. Fergus shook his head, still looking thoroughly mystified. In one hand he held the piece of paper on which he had transcribed the ancient recipe.

'Go on,' Joan said. 'Since I brought it with me, read it out. It sounds such nonsense when I try and read it, God knows how I managed to make anything of it at all.'

Fergus held the sheet of paper under the light and rather theatrically began to declaim the lines written on it. He made it sound like a church litany.

> Take quynces ripe and pare and heue hem smal,
> And al for smal, but kest away the core.
> In honey thene upboile hem, lese and more

De pepur with yt boyling, smalest grounds.
This is the first mannere, the seconds
Is to boil with honey till well thicke,
Thene largelich for meruelles the satur rote.

Fergus gazed across at me, and then at Joan.

'So you found the 'satur rote' then. Don't you think it's time you told us what it is?'

Joan was looking mischievously pleased with herself.

'If you insist,' she said coyly. 'But first wouldn't you like to know how I was so certain it would work?'

We nodded.

'Well,' she went on brightly. 'I decided to try it out on Geoff: I'd just made it, so I gave him some yesterday for his afternoon tea. Then I thought I might as well eat some myself, just for fun. And Jesus, I haven't had so much fun in five years. I tell you, Geoff walked out of the surgery at six o'clock with an erection I could have hung the washing on. I couldn't believe it. We fell on one another. We made love on the kitchen table, just for starters. Then on the stairs. In the bath. And finally in bed. I dread to think what the flame-throwers must have made of it.'

'So that's why you looked so perky this morning, is it?' I said.

Joan suddenly looked embarrassed.

'Ah well, yes. I confess I made a substitution,' she explained with a nervous giggle. 'It was simply too good an opportunity to miss, Claudia, and I'd been wondering how the hell to get the stuff to you without arousing your suspicions. I haven't dared tell Geoff. Will you forgive me?'

By this time we'd already started on the second bottle of champagne. Fergus had dashed out earlier to buy them from the off-licence while I phoned Joan.

'So you took some too,' I said, growing more and more curious. 'Tell me, what was it like? Did you have visions?'

There was a snort from behind Joan's champagne glass.

'Did I have *visions*?' she exclaimed. 'Holy Moses, I could have made love to a lamp-post when I came to. It was incredible. If Geoff hadn't been there I think I'd have rushed out and grabbed the first man I saw.'

Fergus had been gazing first at one of us, then at the other, looking deeply intrigued.

'Well, I don't know,' he said quietly. 'I discover the recipe for the stuff, and I'm the only one who hasn't been allowed to try it.'

I walked over and put my arms round him.

'My darling, you're about the only person I know who doesn't need to. But if you do ever try I'm going to lock you up.'

Fergus kissed me, and I caught a glimpse of Joan's face. She looked pleased and extremely wicked.

And yet Joan had done all this for me. She might so easily have slipped Fergus some of her quince honey ('Do try some, Dr Corrigan. I've just made it') and waited for the result. That tight little body of hers would have relished it. But she hadn't, and I wondered why. I would ask her when the right time came.

'Don't you think it's time you showed us your magic plant, Joan?' Fergus said, walking towards the open French windows. 'A full moon. Is that enough light?'

Joan gave him another mischievous look, and the three of us stepped out on to the terrace. An owl hooted in the far wood, and a soft breeze rippled the long grass caught in the beam of light from the house. In the half-dark I could make out the static form of Jehoshaphat, and imagined his evil marble eyes staring at us. As we set out across the meadow he started moving purposefully towards us, shaking his beard.

'This way,' Joan said briskly.

We followed her. Fergus slipped his arm round me as we stepped through the cool grass, and his hand slid under my blouse on to my breast. My nipple felt hot and tender as he touched it.

'I love you,' he whispered. Then he chuckled. 'Both of you.'

Joan glanced back and said, 'Huh.'

I suddenly had a vision of her making love with Geoff on the kitchen table.

After a while she stopped. We'd reached the edge of the beech-wood. Its dark shapes hung over us, and between its

shadows the moonlight silvered the grass in broad blades.
Across one of them a small creature scurried away. A ferret?

Joan gazed about her. And then she pointed.

There was no colour anywhere in the grass, but in an instant
I knew exactly what she was pointing at. It was as if I'd known
all the time, without realising it. Of course. The orchids. I bent
down, and there they were. Fergus had never seen them before,
and peered at me enquiringly. But *I* had seen them, last year
and this year, sheets of them. It all came back to me, that
conversation with Glyn. A great rarity, he had said. 'God
knows how they got here.' I remembered that. I'd been in
his shop, and he'd pulled down a book from his wild-flower
shelves to show me an illustration of them. Those curious,
stubby little flower heads, reddish-pink mixed with green, the
stem and slender leaves the same reddish-pink.

Tonight in the moonlight they were just a carpet of grey
ghosts. I could barely pick them out from the grass they
grew in.

'There you are,' Joan said with a note of triumph in her voice.
'There's your secret, Fergus. By the hundred. I only used three
or four, just the root, as your recipe said.'

Fergus bent down to look more closely, saying nothing. I
wondered what was going on in his head, and longed to ask
him. But his silence was too intense; it was almost frightening,
as if he couldn't quite believe what he as looking at.

After a while he rose to his feet. I saw him shake his head,
and half under his breath he began to murmur 'satur rote,
satur rote', several times. He let out a deep breath. And then
suddenly he gave a laugh.

'God damn it,' he exclaimed. 'God damn it. And will
somebody now tell me what they are?'

'Some kind of orchid,' I said. 'Go on, Joan, how did you find
out about them? How the hell did you know?'

Even in the moonlight I could make out the look of triumph
on her face.

'Well,' she said, giving her hair a little toss as she enjoyed
keeping us waiting. 'I'd love to be able to say it was brilliant
detective work. But I'm afraid it wasn't: it was a pure accident.
I was with Glyn one afternoon. You weren't around. I'd been

checking on my bees, seeing how much honey there was from the lime-flow. And I saw him wandering around the edge of the meadow gazing at the flowers. So I went over to him. And he was peering down at these funny-looking things. "Aren't they extraordinary?" he said. And did I know what they were? Well, of course I didn't, how could I? So he proceeded to tell me the name of them in a terribly hushed voice as though it was a great secret. "Hooded Orchis," he said, which meant nothing to me at all. Then very solemnly he gave me its Latin name – he would, wouldn't he? You know what Glyn's like about scholarship. And he held up his forefinger as he said it, very precisely, "*Steveniella satyrioides*". That was what did it. The "satyr" bit. That's when I knew.' She gave a giggle. 'So when Glyn had gone I dug up a bit. Then I just followed the recipe you gave me. I already had the quinces and the honey. Simple.'

I heard Fergus give out a sound like a long growl in his throat. Then he reached for my hand, and squeezed it.

'I . . . don't . . . believe . . . it,' he muttered very slowly. '*Satyrioides*. The satyr plant. It actually exists.'

He let out another deep breath, and ran his fingers through his hair. He said nothing for a moment; then with one arm round my waist he reached out and placed his other arm round Joan, pulling her towards him.

'Joan,' he said, and there was that note of irony in his voice which I always loved, 'heaven knows what dangerous star you were born under, but you've managed in one day to revolutionise my life *twice*.'

We laughed.

'It's true,' he added, hugging us both to him. 'Perfectly true. And it's absolutely wonderful.'

And he kissed first Joan, and then me.

A cloud was sliding across the face of the moon, and everything had grown blurred and grey. There was only the far light from the house, and the three of us walked slowly back across the dark meadow, Fergus's arms round both of us.

'You realise, of course,' he said lightly, 'that between us we could change the world.'

*   *   *

It was hot. We were lying in the grass. My head was on Fergus's bare chest, and his hand on my breast. Caroline was right; my boobs were swelling hugely. Jesus, this was after only three and a half months; by eight and a half months I'd be toppling over.

Fergus seemed to approve. His fingers were circling my swollen nipples very tenderly.

'Do you love me?' I said.

'I told you. Both of you.'

He moved his hand down to my stomach, and I placed mine on his.

'When does it start kicking?' he asked.

'God knows. All too soon . . . Fergus?'

'Mmm?'

'Are you sure you won't feel trapped?'

I raised myself on one elbow and gazed at him lying there with his eyes closed against the sun.

'It's a good kind of trap,' he said, reaching up to run his fingers through my hair. 'Listen,' he went on, opening one eye. 'I love you, and that changes everything, doesn't it?'

'Are you sure? You're not going to race off with some little blonde while I'm sitting at home feeding the baby?'

'Probably not.'

I gave a sharp tug at the hairs on his chest.

'Because if you do I'll cut it off; then no amount of Joan's love-potion will do you any good.'

'OK,' he said, settling himself more comfortably in the grass. 'I'll remember that.'

We'd been talking non-stop for days, it seemed, except when we were making love. Fergus's university term had ended for the summer, and we had time, oceans of it. I bathed in it. It was as if we were starting everything from the beginning: all the things we'd never mentioned, had kept hidden; all the things I'd never wanted to know about him in case the dream vanished. It was like reading a new chapter of him every day, and reading him a chapter of my own.

The principal difference was that the chapters of my past tended to feature a succession of Tory party rallies, whereas most of Fergus's featured a succession of large double beds.

'Well, I don't know,' I said as we sat in the dusk one evening. 'I married a man who never wanted to go to bed. Whereas you spent half your life in bed with women you never wanted to marry. What does that tell you about us, Fergus?'

'That we got it right in the end.'

Then there were the unwritten chapters, the ones we were about to write. What would our life be like? Should I still take up Mamma Gina's offer of a partnership? Should we get married once my divorce came through? Where were we going to live?

'It's all very well you having a romantic cliff-top house, Fergus,' I said, 'but the moment the baby starts to crawl it'll tumble straight into the sea.'

We agreed that we'd start by living in his house in Exeter – which I'd yet to set eyes on – and meanwhile he'd do something about making the coastguard's cottage less of a suicide leap. And if Mamma Gina still wanted me to go into partnership with her once the child was old enough to be left, then I'd commute to Norton Abbas from wherever we happened to be. I'd already told her with much regret that I wouldn't be able to serve in the restaurant any more. She patted my belly. She understood, she said.

I'd taken Fergus to meet her. She went all coy and plumped up her bosom at him.

'Mr Fergoose, he beautiful man,' she whispered to me loudly as we left the restaurant.

'She's got some odd ideas about me,' Fergus said as we walked home. 'While you were in the loo she assured me I was a very good cook, but that your husband was a lousy one. How's she supposed to know all that?'

I laughed and gave him a hug.

'I'll demonstrate what she meant later,' I said.

It astonished me how much energy I now had. There were my herbs to look after. There were the endless parties of pilgrims (who had to be kept well away from the phallic tree). There were all the preparations for the baby. And there were Caroline's ceaseless demands for help with her Summer Fête in a few weeks' time.

And there was our new life.

I felt supercharged. I whizzed about the place, humming.

Fergus responded to my cheerfulness with a knowing smile.

'Unhappy people only have a small part of themselves to give to anything,' he said, looking up from his book. 'Unhappiness mops up all the rest.'

While I bustled about he was spending part of each day working. Books now lay piled around my living-room, and reams of paper kept spewing out of his printer. I'd never talked to Fergus about his work before: academic life was an entirely foreign world to me. And when I suggested that it seemed to me mostly holidays interspersed with conferences in glamorous places abroad – hence the disgraceful suntan – he just smiled.

'History is my playground. I enjoy it,' he said.

'I bet you do. All those adoring students.'

'And back-biting colleagues. And lousy pay. If I hadn't had the luck to write a best-seller life would be pretty grey, I can tell you.'

'What about *The Devil's Work*?' I asked. 'How's that going?'

He gave me a wry look. The trouble was, he said, the book had been intended as a historical fantasy – all that stuff about King Henry VIII and Norton Priory. And yet suddenly it was proving to be true: there really *was* a magic about this place. The 'satur rote' existed. It had completely thrown him. He felt like some mad scientist who'd made an absurd guess about molecular structure or DNA, only for laboratory tests to prove him right.

The problem was, what was to be done about it? He was now thinking of rewriting *The Devil's Work* as a piece of serious historical research, which would probably get him hounded out of the university, he felt sure, but might also make him world-famous and magnificently rich.

'And then what do we do about this place?' he said, looking perplexed. 'The moment the book's published everyone with a failing libido is going to descend on Norton Abbas with their little trowels, and within two days there's won't be a single magic orchid left. And the *News of the World* will be sponsoring botanical expeditions to Turkey to strip the Anatolian mountains of the last remaining specimens in the wild. There'll be bacchanalian orgies from Katmandu to California, and then it'll be all over. And who'll be held responsible? Me. I'll get lynched, or burnt at the stake, or something.' He laughed. 'It's not easy being a medieval historian, I can tell you.'

In a less fanciful mood Fergus had decided to go off next week to do some more research on the subject. Now that he could identify the plant, he was anxious to plunder the computer records of the university to see what references to it might exist among the Greek and Latin authors.

'Some grey spinster in the Classics Department is bound to have made an entry, "Aphrodisiacs".'

I rounded on him.

'That's thoroughly sexist.'

'I know.'

Fergus said it so unapologetically that I had to laugh.

'Well, at least we now know the reason for the carvings around the church,' he went on. 'And for your poor mutilated satyr here on the gatehouse. And of course for the phallic yew-tree which I pruned so carefully. The truth is, my darling, this nunnery was God's love factory, and St Cuthburga was its founding high priestess: that's why they made her a saint.' He chuckled. 'I wonder what your friends at Saintly Tours would make of that if they knew?'

Now, lying in the sun with Fergus's hand on my breast, Saintly Tours were uncomfortably prominent in my thoughts. I glanced at my watch. It was three-thirty.

'Fergus,' I said, sitting up and reaching for my blouse. 'We have to make ourselves respectable. A coachload of pilgrims is due here at four.' Fergus gave a grunt, without opening his eyes. 'A rather special coachload. They've particularly asked to see your tree.'

His eyes shot open.

'What d'you mean, *my* tree?'

'You pruned the bloody thing. You said it was all in the cause of historical truth.'

'Then I'm off.'

'No, you're not.'

'Then I'll disguise myself as a pilgrim and listen to what you have to say.'

'I'll shop you.'

The promised visit this afternoon had been the one dark cloud in my week. As the official guardian of the place there was simply no way I could avoid it. The breathless voice on the phone had been that of the secretary of Saintly Tours herself, Judith Burroughs. I remembered her only too well from last summer. She was accompanying this pilgrimage personally, she announced, a party from California. They'd been to Lourdes, Rocamadour, Walsingham; and Norton Priory was to be their finale. 'Oh, what joy,' she'd announced excitedly, 'to see your holy tree again.'

The last time Judith Burroughs had been here, I remembered, she'd assembled her pilgrims around the phallic yew and to my intense relief had pronounced it to be the Tree of Jesse, quoting from the Book of Isaiah. But that was before Fergus had pruned it: the phallus had still been decently clothed within its ancient branches. But now . . .

Half an hour later I was waiting apprehensively by the gatehouse arch. Some distance away I could make out the pallid figure of the Rev Jonathan Pype standing by the open door of the parish church. Suddenly he was joined by a large lady in clerical garb, whom I recognised as the new curate. The vicar's body seemed to flinch as she approached, and he gave a shudder as if to free himself of some evil garment which had settled on his shoulders. At that moment the coach bearing a large banner 'Saintly Tours, European Pilgrimage' came into view, making its way steadily up the High Street towards the gatehouse. Jonathan Pype promptly turned on his heel and I heard the heavy sound of the church door as it slammed behind him. The curate bowed her head and turned away.

Judith Burroughs' smile looked as though it had remained stapled to her face ever since our last meeting nearly a year ago. Her party of Californians, heavy with cameras, disgorged themselves wearily from the coach, many of them sporting hats acquired at previous shrines. (Why hadn't I thought of offering St Cuthburga hats to accompany St Cuthburga's herbs? I'd missed a trick there.)

I'd already commissioned the flame-throwers to stand on duty by the trestle-tables. I didn't imagine Californians would be too anxious to acquire armfuls of biblical herbs, only to have them confiscated by the health authorities in San Francisco; but I had high hopes of St Cuthburga's Cookbook, Second Edition, and had made a specially large display of them, grateful once again that Resurrection Pudding had fallen by the wayside.

Fergus, having agreed to stay on pain of death, lingered at a discreet distance throughout the lengthy genuflections at the shrine of the saint, and at an even more discreet distance when Judith Burroughs began to shepherd her flock towards the topiary garden. The bastard, I thought; he's leaving it all to me. This might be grounds for divorce even before my first divorce came through.

The pilgrims were making heavy weather of the gravel path. Americans are unaccustomed to walking, I reminded myself, especially elderly Californians. Even so, a few more paces and the tree would be in full view. I prayed for a sudden thunderstorm. If only Jehoshaphat would break free and run amok. Couldn't someone have a heart attack? Perhaps I could feign one.

I was still plucking up courage to do this when I heard Judith Burroughs' excited voice.

'Pilgrims,' she cried out, 'I do believe . . . Yes. Oh what marvellous good fortune. We are truly blessed.' And she flung out an arm enthusiastically. Thirty pairs of Californian eyes followed the direction of Judith Burroughs' outstretched hand. And there, behind a tree too small to hide him, stood Fergus. She turned back to her waiting flock. 'Pilgrims,' she announced in a voice trembling with pride, 'by the most wonderful coincidence we have with us a scholar of the greatest distinction, whose knowledge of the early church is unparalleled. Dr Corrigan, please will you join us?' Fergus had no choice, and ambled slowly towards them. 'Now,' she went on, 'we shall have the privilege of hearing from the expert himself the true meaning of the wonder we are about to witness. Come this way, please, all of us.'

And with bold strides she led the way.

I was far too relieved to feel remotely sorry for Fergus. Serves him bloody well right, I thought. At the same time I couldn't help admiring the dignity with which he calmly walked through the party of pilgrims, acknowledging their awestruck faces with the gentlest of smiles and a nod or two. Thirty pair of eyes gazed at him, and then above him at the twenty-foot phallus. I longed to know what they were thinking.

I held my breath waiting to hear what Fergus would say.

He took his time and looked about him; then at the tree.

'Since I'm quite unprepared to address you,' he began with charming modesty, the Irish lilt in his voice emphasised for effect, 'it would be wise for me to remain cautious. This remarkable symbol you see behind me has of course been the subject of intense theological debate for many years,' he went on. 'As a historian, of course I have my own views, which I shall commit to print in due course. Meanwhile, being neither a Roman Catholic nor a theologian, I feel uneasy about pronouncing on matters of Church doctrine. Your estimable guide, Miss Burroughs, being of the Catholic faith herself as well as intimately familiar with holy places, should I think give us the benefit of her opinion before I offer any uninformed comment of my own.'

(Cunning bastard, I thought.)

Then with the same gentle smile he turned to Judith Burroughs, who looked surprised and flattered.

'Well,' she said, reddening a little, 'if Dr Corrigan really feels this to be the case I can only say I'm most honoured. Truly honoured.'

And she gazed up at the tree for a moment before turning to her followers. Her face was radiant.

'Pilgrims,' she went on, 'now that the neglect of centuries has been remedied, and we are able to see this proof of our former sisters' devotion so nakedly revealed' – I felt myself wince – 'it must be clear to you all what it is that stands so boldly before us.' She gave a brief pause, and a further rapid glance at the tree which I could swear was growing more phallic by the minute. 'It is a rod, is it not?' (I saw Fergus close his eyes.) 'Yes, a mighty rod. The very rod with which, as we know from the Book of Exodus, Chapter 17, Verses 1–7, Moses in the desert struck the rock so that the children of Israel and their flocks should have water.'

With that she made a triumphant gesture towards the yew-tree before turning once again to face her audience.

'Isn't that what you see, Dr Corrigan?' (I saw Fergus swallow hard, and his face muscles tauten.) 'Isn't that what all of us see? The rod of Moses?'

There was total silence. I wondered by what miracle the Tree of Jesse had suddenly become the Rod of Moses. Fergus said nothing. Those around him were looking anywhere but at each other. Eventually a robust lady at the rear of the group raised her hand confidently. All eyes turned towards her.

'I beg your pardon, ma'am,' she said in a slow drawl, 'but all I see is a goddam great cock.'

They'd gone. They bought no herbs. They bought no cookbooks. All they took with them was their look of shock. I thought it extremely unlikely that there would be further visits from Judith Burroughs and Saintly Tours. I also imagined that tomorrow morning the telephone lines to the National Trust would be hot, and that the Furies would shortly descend on me in the well-corseted person of Pamela Leggatt.

'I think we may have to leave this place rather hurriedly,' I said.

Fergus looked bemused.

'But if it's true – and it *is* true – what can they do?'

'Sack you for a start. You and your historical truths, Fergus. Who wants to know all that? Can you imagine it? The whole story of this place would cause a public outcry if it got out, don't you see? God's love factory. We may have to emigrate.'

'That sounds a good idea. Where?'

'Fergus, can't you take this seriously?'

He looked infuriatingly calm, reclining on the sofa with a glass of wine in his hand and a bright look in his eye.

'All right then, I'll go over the Trust's head. Appeal directly to the ministry.'

'But that's David.'

'From what you've told me, it sounds as though he could do with this place.'

I threw a book at him, and missed. Then the phone went.
It was Caroline. I had no chance to say a word.

'Claudia, listen,' she yelled. 'The last battle's on. Come over
– now!'

Thirteen

Caroline was standing by the fireplace at the far end of the drawing-room. Apart from the vodka-and-tonic in one hand, the cigarette in the other, the designer jeans and the blouse unbuttoned to the waist, her manner was that of the lady of the manor graciously receiving guests.

Judging by the open blouse I imagined that she'd guessed Fergus would be with me. She awarded him the scowl she invariably reserved for men she fancied: she was happy to let her body do the work.

I could see Fergus making an effort not to look startled, not so much by the torso on offer as by those on display all round the room. It had been transformed since I was last here. All Megan's carefully tailored paintings which had disguised those of the admiral's mistresses had vanished: the originals were once again nakedly on view.

'I told you this was the last battle,' Caroline said. She hadn't bothered to greet us or offer us a drink. 'Well, I've decided that if I go down it's going to be with all guns blazing. And screw that Legover woman. I've put an ad in all the West Country papers announcing that the Hall of the Mystresses will be open to the public again from next week, in time for the Summer Fête *and* my birthday. Oh, and Megan's found another portrait, unfinished, she says, but it's of Daddy's last mistress apparently. She's bringing it along at the weekend, and Patrick's going to be here to help me hang it. Will you come too? How's the baby?'

Carmen appeared timidly at that moment, which reminded Caroline that her glass was empty. As an afterthought she asked us what we might like.

'The girl's in love with Patrick,' she said sourly after Carmen had departed. 'All he did was tell her she was pretty, the bloody liar. Isn't it nauseating? I thought of warning her he'd only got

four inches, but then I realised she wouldn't understand unless
I converted it into centimetres, and that's beyond me.'

Fergus laughed. Caroline glanced at him disapprovingly.

'It's all very well for you two,' she growled. 'It's quite
sickening. When's your divorce coming through, Claudia?'

Carmen returned with two glasses of wine and Caroline's
vodka. She glowered at the girl, who lowered her eyes.

'I hate virgins,' she said crossly as Carmen hurried away. She
stared at my belly. 'Well, at least no one's going to mistake you
for one.'

Caroline was not in one of her better moods. Then, remembering that she'd dressed for Fergus's benefit, she threw him
an unexpected smile and steered us out into the garden.

'So, let me tell you the worst,' she said wearily, settling
into one of the chairs near the swimming-pool. 'And it really
couldn't *be* much worse. Fuck the lot of them.'

And she began to unburden. The first lament was over the
rare grasses she'd stolen from the Exeter botanical garden, and
which Howl had duly planted all round the house and the
rose-beds.

'Well, I assumed they were rare since they were in a
botanical garden. You'd expect that, wouldn't you?' she said
aggressively. 'It turns out they're not. The Trust sent an expert
down. I tried to tell him that Kew were frightfully excited, and
they really ought to know, oughtn't they? But he gave me a
very old-fashioned look and said he *was* from Kew, and what
we were looking at was couch-grass. There wasn't a lot I could
say after that.'

She managed a self-deprecating laugh, at the same time
leaning forward to offer Fergus a clearer view of her bosom.

'So, what else can I do?' she went on.

There was suppressed anger in Caroline's voice. She'd
fought a rearguard action for almost a year now, and had
run out of resources. I tried to imagine what I would do
in her position. There didn't seem to be much choice: either
get out or give in gracefully. Neither sounded like Caroline at
all.

'The builders are moving in the moment we've cleared up
from the Summer Fête, actually *on* my birthday. Can you

believe it? The bastards. It's bad enough being forty without having my own house torn apart around my ears.'

I thought for a moment she was going to burst into tears. But tears were seldom Caroline's currency. I should have known that her response to disaster was always dramatic.

She rose from her chair, calmly peeled off every stitch of clothing, and dived into the pool.

I was glad for Caroline's sake that the letter from the Trust came directly to me. I read it, grimaced, and handed it to Fergus.

'Dear Mrs Hazlitt,' the letter began. 'It has been brought to my notice that a joke of an indecent nature has been practised in the sacred grounds of Norton Priory during your tenure as guardian. Since this outrage can scarcely have been committed without your knowledge we have no option but to hold you personally responsible. Accordingly the Trust insists that the offending tree be cut down and removed forthwith at your expense. Regretfully your occupancy of the gatehouse, as well as your position as an employee of the Trust, is likewise terminated as from July 31st. Kindly confirm your willingness to conform with all of the above. Yours sincerely, P. Leggatt (Mrs).'

'Well, now we know, don't we?' I said. 'At least by the skin of my teeth I'm not going to be homeless. So, what now, Fergus?'

Maybe it was just the sun, but Fergus's blue eyes seemed more piercing than usual at that moment, and the private smile began to flicker on his lips. He tossed the letter on to the table, stretched his arms upwards, then folded them carefully behind his head, gazing at me.

'Oh, this is going to be fun,' he said.

I wasn't sure if I ought to be anxious or excited. I could see that Fergus was revelling in all this. He loved rocking the boat. It was part of his huge attractiveness that his self-confidence thrived on breaking rules which he'd decided were made only to be broken. I thought of David, who always did everything safely: conventions cocooned him. They throttled Fergus.

'What are you going to do?' I asked a little nervously.

He didn't answer for a moment. He seemed to be smiling

at something invisible, far away. Finally he turned to me with an expression of deep satisfaction on his face.

'Something I'm pretty sure no historian has ever done before: obtain a preservation order for a twenty-foot phallus!'

He laughed, and re-folded his hands behind his head.

'How?' I said.

'Well, I happen to be the Trust's historical adviser: that's a good beginning. I'll write to them on university notepaper insisting that the tree be preserved, and we'll see what they say.'

'And if they don't accept your advice?'

'Then I'll go higher.'

I didn't say any more. The gentle anarchist in Fergus was having a field day. I could see how he loved the idea that in the interests of historical truth there should be a national monument which could do nothing but horrify every Christian in the land, a monument to a nunnery that had been God's love factory.

'I suppose I'm lucky the Church of England doesn't issue *fatwas*', he said.

'More to the point, what d'you imagine they'll say at the university?'

Fergus still looked quite unperturbed.

'Oh, it's the summer vacation. They won't know till the autumn, and by that time the battle will have been won.'

'And will you win?'

'Of course.'

'And then?'

He gave a shrug.

'A few stuffy old farts will howl for my dismissal, the same ones who blackballed me over *Cardinal Error* when I applied for a professorship. I might even resign: I've been thinking of doing that anyway.'

I was beginning to feel uneasy.

'What will we live on if you do?'

'Our wits.' Then he laughed. 'The very best thing would be if I could get sacked. That always doubles your credit in the eyes of other universities, particularly American universities.

I'd become a visiting professor, hugely in demand, and earn a fortune travelling around giving lectures.'

'And acquiring even more adoring students.'

Fergus leaned forward and took both my hands in his.

'Nonsense. You'd come too. Both of you. And when the child's old enough to go to school we'll settle down in this little offshore island, and buy a place for the summer in another offshore island that's a bit warmer, like Crete. How's that for a life-plan?'

How could I not love this man? I loved his audacity and his confidence, his humour and warmth, his view of the world as a public stage on which you played whatever part you chose, provided you had the courage to do so.

It was a time for celebrations. All the same, I couldn't help feeling guilty whenever I thought of Caroline and what was about to happen to her. She'd brought me here so that I might share her good life: now her life was black, and mine was golden. What was more, I was leaving. Fergus was insistent that the Trust had no legal right to kick me out of the gatehouse without at least a month's notice. But I no longer cared. I'd had my time here. I'd already over-stayed my year, and I was longing for a fresh chapter to begin. Each time I walked round my borrowed acres I felt myself saying good-bye, to the distant estuary now freckled with bright sails, to the medieval barn, the topiary garden, the ruined priory with its solitary arch; good-bye to my herbs, to Joan's bees, the honey buzzards, the quince orchard; and good-bye most gratefully of all to my harmless-looking orchids, beginning to fade now, ready to wither back beneath the ground where the secret of the "satur rote" would remain for yet another year, just as it had remained for more than a thousand years.

'And what are we going to do about Jehoshaphat?' I said.

Fergus and I were strolling towards the gatehouse arch on our way to dinner with Megan and Glyn, another celebration. The goat greeted our departure by pissing steamily into his water-trough.

'We could always take him to the coastguard's cottage,'

Fergus suggested. 'Let him roam free. He's a goat: he'd love the cliffs. And we could find him a mate, then it won't be just us who breed.'

I hugged his arm to mine.

'When are you going away to do your aphrodisiac research?' I said, laughing.

'In a couple of days.'

'For how long?'

'Inside a week.'

'You *will* come back?'

'Oh, I shouldn't think so.'

I kicked his shin.

'Glyn is thrilled at having you to dinner,' I explained. 'It's thoroughly embarrassing. Megan says he keeps referring to you as "the great Dr Corrigan".'

Fergus made an effort to look modest.

'Oh God.'

'Rubbish. You love it. Adulation. You've had it all your life. And now you've got it from me.'

'Oh, that's all right then.'

I loved the touch of self-mockery in Fergus: it allowed him to get away with being quite so vain.

'Here we are,' I said, and pressed the doorbell. 'Remember Glyn's a church warden, so tread warily about love factories and giant phalluses.'

'I promise.'

The door was flung open by Megan, dressed like a schooner in full sail.

'In your honour, my darlings. Mind you don't trip over the bloody painting.'

We stepped into the narrow hallway, made even narrower by a large canvas propped against the wall; even in the half-light I could see it was a nude of exorbitantly generous proportions. The flesh-tones gave way to mere charcoal outlines just below the rib-cage.

'Yes, there she is, the last one. The admiral popped his clogs and she immediately took off before I could do any more. I stuck the thing in the garage and forgot all about it till the other day.'

'Certainly a large girl,' Fergus was saying admiringly. 'Where did he find her, I wonder?'

'Nobody knows where the admiral found half his women. But from the way she shed her clothes for me to paint her I got the feeling she did it quite often.'

We were ushered into the sitting-room where Megan's flower-paintings formed a demure contrast to the buxom nude in the hallway. She bustled about pouring drinks and offering nibbles.

'Glyn's in a bit of a tizz,' she confided. 'He's cooking some special medieval dish for you, with ale. God help us all.'

I laughed.

'So long as it doesn't have quince honey in it too.'

Megan's deep chuckle rearranged a good deal of flesh. And at that moment Glyn appeared, a chef's apron tied volumi-nously round him. He hurried over to shake Fergus's hand with touching shyness, and then kissed me on the cheek.

'I'm so happy for you,' he announced breathlessly. 'Both of you.'

I corrected him with a smile.

'All three of us, you mean.'

Glyn nodded, looking slightly embarrassed, and wiped his hands nervously on his apron.

'Yes, of course.' Then he turned busily to Megan. 'Dinner is ready, my dear, if you are.'

We trooped into the small dining-room, the table beautifully laid, linen napkins by each place, a forest of wine-glasses, and handsome silver candlesticks on either side of a central bowl of fresh fruit. Glyn served the hors-d'oeuvre, then poured the wine – carefully from the correct side, breathing heavily through his nose like an ageing butler. Megan sat heavily in her colourful spinnaker of a dress, clearly uncomfortable at such formality, her expression suggesting she wished Glyn would manage to relax.

It wasn't until the great medieval dish was served – a steaming stew of some kind in which parsnips and small turnips floated darkly – that Megan found her voice.

'Claudia was hoping you hadn't put any of Joan's magic concoction in the dinner, darling.'

Glyn looked embarrassed for a moment, and then laughed uneasily.

'Oh no, no, no, I assure you not.' He looked across the table to Fergus who was already tucking hungrily into the medieval stew. 'I do hope, Dr Corrigan, that our friend Joan isn't uprooting too many of the orchids. They're so very rare.'

Fergus gently asked Glyn if he would please call him by his first name, then reassured him that as far as he could see there was little danger of the plants being decimated.

'There are many hundreds of them still,' he said. 'You may have noticed.'

Glyn was nodding earnestly.

'Yes, indeed. Certainly so.' He wiped his lips on the linen napkin and leaned forward across the table with a confidential look on his face.

'You see, I'm so wary of showing people those orchids: I thought afterwards that perhaps I ought not to have done so with Joan, even though she's a good friend and I trust her of course. It's just that I remember once being less prudent, and I've always regretted it.'

'When was that, Glyn?' Megan asked, looking bored and clearly anticipating being even more bored by the answer.

'Don't you remember, my dear?' Glyn went on. 'It must have been two years ago. Or three. I told you at the time, or maybe I didn't. I meant to. Come to think of it, you may have been away. It doesn't matter now, but I was most upset.' Megan's eyes closed wearily, and took some time to re-open. 'There was this lady,' Glyn went on. 'A grey-haired lady, rather handsome. She came into the bookshop one afternoon. She was from the National Trust, she explained, and please might I be willing to give her a tour of the priory grounds? She understood I was something of an expert on plants. Well, I'm not of course, but I felt flattered.' Glyn gave a nervous laugh and wiped his lips again. 'Anyway I agreed. It was almost time to close, so I accompanied her. And my goodness, she wanted to know everything, even the Latin names. Extraordinary. She seemed very serious. But when I told her the name of the orchids she suddenly became quite silent, and didn't want to be shown anything more. Well, I thought no more about it until about a week later, when I was again wandering about, and saw to my horror that quite a number of the orchids had been dug up. There were great holes in the ground. I felt terrible about that. They're so rare, those orchids, and plant-hunters are so unscrupulous: I don't believe for one moment she can have been from the National Trust.'

Glyn had been too absorbed in his tale to notice the expression on Megan's face, and on mine. Fergus merely looked puzzled, glancing first at one of us, then the other. I was aware that my eyes were as wide as saucers, and there was a humming sound in my head. My heart was like a drumbeat, and spluttering noises came from my mouth.

I looked across at Megan, who seemed shellshocked, her mouth opening and closing like a large fish.

After a few moments I managed to clear my throat.

'Glyn,' I said, my voice quavering, 'she very probably *was* from the National Trust. And I think her name may have been Pamela Leggatt.'

There was already a pallor of dawn across the summer meadow before Fergus and I finally collapsed into bed that night.

For hour after hour, and with frequent cups of coffee, we tried to put together all the possible scenarios which might explain the extraordinary piece of information Glyn had innocently let slip. It was like trying to solve a jigsaw puzzle without any idea of the finished picture, but with two substantial areas on either side already complete. The huge problem was, what in God's name was in the middle?

At one edge of the puzzle was the scene we'd known about all along: Caroline discovering to her horror that her family house was no longer hers at all, but had been left by her late father in his will to the nation, allowing her no more than a discretionary right to go on living there.

Now, quite unexpectedly, Glyn had put together a number of pieces at the opposite edge of the puzzle. Here was a picture of a grey-haired lady, claiming to be from the National Trust, taking a surprising interest in a cluster of rare orchids in the grounds of Norton Priory, orchids which Fergus and I knew to possess amazing hallucinogenic properties, but which we'd imagined no one else knew about except Joan and Megan. And yet a few days after the lady's visit a number of orchids were found to have been dug up.

'Can we assume the woman *was* Pamela Leggatt?' I asked.

Fergus had a large sheet of paper spread out in front of him on the table, on which he'd been jotting down all kinds of possible motives and outcomes, and endeavouring to shape them into a flow-plan.

He looked up at me sharply.

'How would I know? I've never met the woman,' he said. And then he grinned. 'Academics like to be pompous on these occasions, I have to tell you. We use phrases like *ex hypothesi*. In other words we base arguments on what we hope is an inspired guess. So I think that's what we need to do here, don't you? Let's just assume it was her, and see where that leads us.'

It was like working with a lawyer. I'd never seen Fergus in his academic mode before, the scholar weighing up evidence and moving cautiously towards conclusions. Historians were the Scotland Yard of the past, he'd said to me once, the only difference being that historians know the verdict already and have to work backwards to discover if it was the right one.

'The most promising connection,' he went on, ringing one of his jottings with a biro and linking it with a bold stroke to another jotting, 'has to be between the erotic powers of our plant and the erotic appetite of Caroline's father. That's the line I think we should pursue. It gives us a number of motives on both sides which could explain quite a lot. The question is, how do we find out?'

I peered at Fergus hopefully.

'What d'you suggest?'

He looked thoughtfully out into the night.

'Well,' he said, 'I'm going off to do some research anyway. So perhaps I'll try to do a little more. *Human* research. There are such things as personal records, after all, if one can get access to them. Worth trying. The Trust hasn't sacked me yet.'

For what was left of that night I don't believe I did more than dip in and out of sleep – I felt rather like Caroline diving into her pool. Too much was happening all at once, and my mind was racing. Jesus. In what seemed a matter of days I'd become pregnant, I'd laid plans for being a single mother, I'd been blown sky-high on some weird love-potion, I'd regained my lover, I'd been booted out of my home, and now there was this sinister story of a grey-haired lady making off with magic orchids. Wasn't this supposed to be my year of peace?

It was eight o'clock on a grey morning. Fergus was in the shower, singing an old Beatles song as though his life depended on it. From his performance I was glad it didn't. He'd decided to get moving today, he'd announced, swinging himself out of bed. Sleep could wait. Research couldn't. This was urgent. He'd woken up absolutely convinced that his hunch was right. ('I was spot on about the "satur rote", so why not this too?') He was sure there must be a connection between the theft of the orchids and the admiral's carnal appetites. After the missing ingredient, now the missing clue.

He emerged from the bathroom in a flurry of towel and bare flesh, and gave me a damp embrace.

'It's Caroline we're doing this for, isn't it?' he said, his towel doing battle with his hair. 'She's dreadful and she's splendid. Thank God I'm not married to her. No wonder Patrick's only got four inches; she probably bit off the rest.'

He laughed, and made a dive for his clothes.

I suddenly felt uneasy. I wasn't looking forward to being alone. All those weeks when I'd planned so resolutely to live my life on my own. Then I'd felt miserable and strong. Now I felt happy and weak. How vulnerable it was to be in love. It made me understand why so many people avoid it.

'I'll be staying with my brother in London,' Fergus announced, hopping up and down on one leg trying to steer the other into his jeans. 'I'll ring you when I get there. Then tomorrow it's muck-raking time, at least I sincerely hope it is.'

Half an hour later I watched the red Alfa-Romeo disappear down the High Street. The roof was down, and the last thing I saw was Fergus's arm waving as he pulled away from the traffic-lights.

The sun was breaking through the clouds, and I sat for a while on the terrace in my dressing-gown. I didn't belong here any more: I belonged in that little red car, wherever it was going. And yet there was something peaceful about being alone, at last having time to ponder, take stock, feel all the events of the past weeks settle into place in my brain. I felt like an adventurer waiting by the harbour for my ship to call.

Then Megan rang. Should we tell Caroline? she asked. I said I thought not: we had so little to go on, and it might all come to nothing. I explained about Fergus, and what we'd decided to do.

'I'm glad for you,' she said warmly. 'Whatever comes of all this you'll be all right, the two of you, won't you? It's Caroline I fear for. Everything's going down all around her, and she was never trained for survival.'

'D'you want to bet on it?' I said.

There was a snort down the phone.

'Perhaps not. In the meantime I've got to get this bloody painting up there. So I'll see you at the weekend: we'll have a hanging ceremony. Let me know if you hear anything before then.'

The morning passed aimlessly. I sat down and wrote a long letter to Anna-Maria, telling her that my love-child *would* have a father after all. I wondered as I wrote it if she might be disappointed after all. Her romantic soul had been so touched by my story, and the sudden exodus of the Bolognese sausage-maker from her plans for me had left me thoroughly bewildered. What did she really want?

That evening I called to see Mamma Gina.

'Claudia, you too long away from Eetaly,' she said after I'd been telling her about Anna-Maria. 'Your mamma, she want *bambini*. Your *bambini*. Plenty *bambini*. All Eetalian mammas want *bambini*. You no understand that? She love Mr Fergoose because he good cook, and good cook make plenty *bambini*. She only care about sausage-maker because maybe he good cook too, but Mr Fergoose he better because he beautiful as well as good cook. You lucky girl. And he lucky man. "You no fuck about no more," I tell him. "You finish – what-you-say? – sow wild goats."' (I tried to hide a smile.) '"You make Claudia plenty *bambini* lickety-split."'

This time I didn't refuse the grappa, though I did yawn into it.

'Later you come partner Mamma Gina restaurant,' she

went on enthusiastically, placing her red hands firmly on the table on either side of her bosom. 'And when I old you plenty *bambini* work 'ere, open two-three-four Mamma Gina restaurants, many bunkaloos by seaside, and I sit deckchair very fat and lots-an-lots *piccoli bambini* you teaching piddle in sea. Is good, no?'

I nodded, almost nodding off to sleep.

'OK, Mamma Gina,' I promised. 'I'll try.'

The next few days were a hiatus in my life, waiting for Fergus, waiting for my time here to come to an end, waiting to hear about Glyn's mysterious grey-haired lady. A few coachloads of pilgrims came and went, none of them venturing as far as the phallic tree. I dutifully laid out my pots of herbs on the trestle-tables, and displayed piles of *St Cuthburga's Cookbook* next to them, mainly because otherwise I was in danger of being left with five hundred of them unsold, and short of feeding them to Jehoshaphat I couldn't imagine what I could possibly do with them.

Fergus telephoned each day around bedtime, which made the trudge upstairs afterwards even more dispiriting, and the sight of my *Kama Sutra* bedhead an irritating mockery.

Then on the third evening he sounded excited. He'd wheedled himself access to Pamela Leggatt's *curriculum vitae* – I didn't like to ask how – and tomorrow he should know whether it threw any light on the mystery of the grey-haired lady. Meanwhile would I care to hear what he'd discovered about our orchid?

'Of course I would,' I said. 'Tell me. Tell me everything.'

There was a note of self-congratulation in Fergus's voice as he explained what he'd uncovered. The professor of classical studies at King's College was an old friend, he said, and he'd gone to see him at his home in Dulwich just as he was packing to go on holiday with his family. 'What do you know about classical aphrodisiacs?' Fergus had asked him straight out. The man looked amazed, and then overjoyed. 'Oh, lots,' he'd said. 'I've been waiting for someone to ask me that question for years. Which one?' Fergus mentioned the Hooded Orchis, and gave its Latin name, *Steveniella satyrioides*. The professor clapped his hands with delight – 'Legendary, legendary,' he exclaimed – and then proceeded to reel off a mass of data straight out of his head.

Fergus paused, and I could hear the sound of him flicking through sheets of paper.

'I scribbled it all down. Pages of it. Fascinating. I won't bore you with all of it, but apparently the root of the orchid is known historically as *satyrion*. All sorts of Greek and Roman writers – Dioscorides, Plutarch, Galen, dozens of others – mention it as the most powerful love-potion of them all. In Ancient Greece it was an essential part of their bacchanalian orgies. The Romans drank it in wine and then retired to bed with a succession of mistresses for three days. Then he showed me a passage by an early scholar called Wecker, which he photocopied for me. Want to hear it?'

'Of course.'

'Right, here we go. This is what the guy wrote. "If any man desire to be a strong soldier in the camp of Venus let him be armed chiefly with its bulbous roots, for they all provoke Venery. Satyrion moves exceedingly, and stands most forcibly in this business, and provokes women's desire." Well, it certainly seemed to do that all right, Claudia.'

'Leaving that aside for a moment, my darling,' I said a little archly, 'tell me one thing more. If this plant is so incredibly powerful, why has nobody nowadays heard about it?'

There was a knowing grunt on the other end of the phone.

'I asked him that,' Fergus went on, 'and he gave me a perfectly simple answer: the plant was so sought-after that it became practically extinct centuries and centuries ago. It was probably a great rarity even in Cuthburga's day, which was why she was given some of the roots of it in Rome as a special honour. Then by some freak of nature it managed to flourish at Norton Priory; and because of that freak she found herself canonised. An act of God, or an act of the Devil, take your pick – I don't believe the early Church always drew a distinction between the two: it was Divine Power that mattered. And as for Divine Sexual Power, well, *Olé*!' Fergus gave a laugh, then suddenly became serious. 'It always intrigues me how the Spaniards say "Olé!" They're such good Catholics, and yet the word means "Allah!" I can't tell you how they hate it when you point that out, just as the Scots hate it when you tell them they were the last people in Europe to get the bagpipes.'

It was my turn to laugh.

'Just the sort of thing you *would* know Fergus,' I said. 'I don't think you'll ever be a candidate for being canonised.'

'Not once I've published *The Devil's Work*, certainly. But listen, my darling,' he added, 'that's all just historians' fun-and-games. Tomorrow's the real thing. If I find out anything vital I may just drive straight back. I'll phone you first, then leap in the car.'

'Take care, please,' I said.

'I promise. I love you. Good-night.'

Fergus telephoned at noon. He was in a phone-box, and his voice sounded urgent.

'I'm on to something,' he said. 'And it could be hot, very hot. I'll explain everything when I see you. But alert Caroline, would you? I'll come straight to the big house. Give me twenty minutes to find a pub sandwich and I'll be on my way. Say four hours, OK?'

And he rang off.

My mind was spinning. What could he possibly have found out? The suspense of not knowing was infuriating: I'd have to wait four hours. I kept seeing that jigsaw puzzle in front of me, with its huge empty space in the middle; and I began to speculate, and speculate again. And between each new version of the missing picture I tried Caroline's phone number, once, twice, three, four times. But it was constantly engaged.

In frustration I rang Megan, and then Joan. Megan was up to her armpits in oil-paint, but she promised that of course she'd be up at the house well before Fergus arrived. 'So it's the war council again, is it?' she said cheerfully. 'Well, maybe this time we'll even win. Wouldn't that be terrific?'

Joan let out a whoop and said she'd be round at the gatehouse in two minutes: to hell with the bloody phone, why didn't we just drive up to Caroline's house together? Might we have time for a quick drink first?

Joan *always* had time for a quick drink.

We sat for a few minutes on the terrace in the sun. The

beech-trees had already darkened into the deep green of summer, and the long grass was turning golden. One of the honey buzzards took off from its perch on the priory arch and began to glide low over the meadow. Joan gave a snort.

'Fucking thing. After my bees again.' She watched the graceful bird dip out of sight beyond the orchard. 'You know,' she went on, 'I often think of those creatures as the spirit of this place, as though they've always been here to guard its secret.' Joan laughed. 'And that makes me a kind of traitor, I suppose, breaking the secret.' She turned to gaze at me over the top of her wine-glass. 'Are you glad I did, Claudia?' she added.

I didn't think that needed answering.

'But why did you?' I asked.

Joan drained her glass and said nothing for a moment. Then she looked at me with a strange smile.

'Because I thought it was about time both of us stopped playing games. They were too destructive. You thought I fancied Fergus, which I did. I thought you were being ridiculous, which you were. In fact your dreams were even more stupid than mine. Fergus loved you: that was bloody obvious – to everyone but you apparently. There was no way he was going to stop loving you just because you were pregnant, for God's sake. That was simply ludicrous.' She went on gazing at me very intently. 'He phoned me once,' she went on. 'Wanted to know about you. He sounded so miserable. I almost told him about the baby there and then, and later I wished to hell I had. If I'd known his number I'd have rung him back. Then all of a sudden this magic *thing* came up, and it seemed the perfect answer: that's all.' She laughed. 'I'm a witch, you see. A red-headed witch.'

She gave her hair a quick toss, and got up.

'Come on, we'd better go.'

We walked through the gatehouse arch towards my little Fiat parked under the old priory wall. As she opened the passenger door Joan looked across at me.

'You know I'm really not a particularly nice person,' she said firmly. 'It's just that sometimes I'm less nasty than I think I am. And anyway I'm too old for sex games.'

I smiled at her.

'Nasty or not, thank-you,' I said.

We followed the ancient wall until we reached the gates of Priory Hall, and I turned the car down the long avenue of lime-trees towards the house. Caroline's dark-blue Mercedes was parked by the front door as usual, one wheel sunk in the flower-bed. The bodywork carried a few more dents and bruises each time I saw it: rather like Caroline, I thought.

'Thank God I wasn't brought up this rich,' Joan said, gazing around her. 'You're so vulnerable up on a pinnacle, aren't you? So far to fall. And no safety-net.'

'Patrick?'

Joan looked at me with astonishment, and laughed.

'Patrick a safety-net? He's more a little boy with a shrimping-net and a rubber duck.'

'I'm not so sure,' I said. 'They play games too, both of them.'

Joan didn't answer. Everything that amused me about Patrick, she loathed. All that foppish self-pity.

We walked round the side of the house, expecting to find Caroline either in the swimming-pool or sitting by the side of it with a vodka-and-tonic in her hand. We were half-right: she was in the pool *with* a vodka-and-tonic. She was floating on her back, toes neatly peeping above the surface, hair spread around her on the water like a blonde veil, and the tumbler of vodka balanced precariously between her naked breasts.

'Christ, she's decadent,' muttered Joan.

'Just eccentric,' I said.

Caroline caught sight of us, and turned her head.

'Hello,' she called out cheerfully. And she raised her glass in greeting. 'As you can see, I'm getting my muscles in trim for being forty. Buoyancy exercises. Get Carmen to bring you a drink. No good asking you to join me, you're both far too prudish. What are you doing here anyway? I suppose you want to stay for lunch.'

'Don't worry about that,' I said. 'It's just that there's some news, and Fergus says it's hot. He's coming down this afternoon, and he wanted me to warn you.'

Caroline rolled over, skilfully keeping her vodka glass above the water, and began to do a sidestroke towards the edge of the pool with the aid of her free arm.

'News about what?' she grumbled, clambering out of the water and putting her glass down on the table. She grabbed a towel. 'All news is bad news as far as I'm concerned.'

'This may not be bad news,' I said. 'Fergus has found something out about Pamela Leggatt: that's all I know.'

Caroline looked sour, and pulled a face.

'Huh! The less I find out about that cow the better. The fucking bitch.'

I made a placatory gesture.

'Just *be* here, that's all, Caroline. Around four-thirty. Fergus is coming straight here.'

With her towel round her, hair streaming, suddenly she looked so vulnerable. She blinked some water from her eyes and stood there, saying nothing. The face was tired, strained, the mouth set in a grim sulk of defeat. Yet for a brief moment I caught a glimmer of hope in that face as she gazed at me – until she quickly looked away as if trying to hide it, not daring to admit there could be any hope.

'All right,' she said quietly, 'I'll be here. Come back, won't you? Both of you.' Then hesitantly she added, 'Please.'

I tried to remember when I'd ever heard Caroline use that word before.

All afternoon I tried to imagine what it must be like to lose everything you owned, to fight against that loss until there was no strength left in you, and then as the clock was already beginning to strike midnight – so to speak – to be offered just the faintest hint of a reprieve. Perhaps this was the very worst of moments for Caroline, and a distant hope was more painful than no hope at all.

And I thought of Fergus. Right now he'd be in the fast lane amid the Friday afternoon traffic. I had terrifying visions of a multiple pile-up, the little open car a jagged splinter of red slammed between two juggernauts, body unidentifiable. Oh, be here safe, my lover. Whatever news you have to bring is a million times less important to me than you are.

Black humour comes to my rescue at moments like this. A

single mother one month, a widow the next. Jesus Christ, and this was supposed to be my year of peace.

We all of us heard the Alfa-Romeo coming fast up the long drive, and the spurt of the engine as it stopped.

I flung myself at Fergus, half in the car and half out. I wanted him never, never to go away again. My most precious man on earth – stay. Just stay.

He was tanned by the wind and the sun, his fair hair long and tangled, eyes still crinkled against the glare. He had that surprised look of strain and tiredness.

I heard Joan's voice.

'For God's sake, you two.'

Megan was laughing.

'We could just leave you if you like. There are at least a dozen bedrooms in this house: take your pick. See you later.'

Fergus released me and got out of the car.

'So where is she? Caroline?'

And he gazed about him.

'In the garden,' I said.

Caroline had gathered up her dignity when she heard the sound of the car. 'I'll just wait,' she'd said, looking very serene. 'And if it turns it to be bad news I promise I won't shoot the messenger.'

We walked round to the terrace, all four of us. Caroline had a small hand-bell by her, and she rang it as we approached. She didn't look up, but waited until Carmen appeared.

'Bring out some tea, would you?' she called out. 'Earl Grey, I think. For five. And some Bourbon biscuits. Thank you.'

Only then did she gaze up at us. On any other occasion I suspected Fergus would have fluttered his hands mockingly as he knelt before her, and kissed her fingertips. This time he just seated himself easily in a garden chair and looked across at her with a slight smile.

Caroline lit a cigarette, blew the smoke upwards, then leant forward towards him with her chin resting in the cup of her hand. She pursed her lips and raised her eyes.

'Well. What?'

Fergus took a long breath and cleared his throat.

'Caroline,' he said, leaning back and placing his hands

behind his head, 'I can't promise you anything. I'm not a lawyer – you'll certainly need one. But I'll tell you what I found out this morning.'

I looked at Fergus's face. He never took his eyes off Caroline. I loved that face. And I loved his voice; the softness of it, and the measured way he spoke. It was like watching a man walk a very careful path, step by step.

'Two things: that's all I know,' he went on. 'First of all, before she joined the National Trust six years ago Pamela Leggatt worked as a librarian in the Bodleian Library in Oxford. The last job she did there was to put certain rare manuscripts on microfilm. Now I happen to know – because I've consulted it – that one of the manuscripts put on microfilm at that time contains a number of entries relating to Norton Priory. It's called "Ashmole 61". Claudia knows what I'm talking about: I've described it to her. And one of these entries is the recipe for quince honey which I gave to Joan, and which has had some effect on our lives.' I could see Fergus struggling to keep a straight face as he said that. 'This recipe seems to have been translated from the Greek by someone at Norton Priory in about the twelfth century, though the original Greek recipe was certainly here long before that, in my view probably brought from the Mediterranean by St Cuthburga herself. But that's another story.'

Fergus looked at us, and then at Caroline. She was frowning. The tea arrived, and she went on frowning while she poured it out, and I busied myself handing round the biscuits. My mind was buzzing. We munched in silence for a few moments. Caroline sipped her tea noisily.

'Well,' she said eventually, 'and what's all that supposed to mean?'

I wasn't sure whether she was being deliberately dim. Joan was looking impatient.

'For Christ's sake, Caroline,' she blurted out, 'it means that your Legover lady knew all about the quince honey, *and* the secret ingredient, which is why she got so excited when Glyn identified it for her. Don't you see?'

Caroline was now looking sulky.

'So what?' she said.

Joan gave a groan. Megan was raising her eyebrows. Fergus had a patient expression on his face.

'So, she might well have used it, mightn't she?' I suggested, trying to steer Caroline's mind towards the obvious.

But Caroline merely clicked her tongue, and gazed at me crossly.

'Don't be ridiculous, Claudia. Used it on whom? Who on earth would want to fuck that Legover bitch anyway?'

I closed my eyes in despair.

'Caroline,' I heard Fergus say very gently, 'it didn't have to be for her. It could have been for someone else, someone who liked making love very much, but couldn't any more.'

I opened my eyes and looked across at Caroline. Her face was transformed by shock.

'You mean . . . ·You don't mean . . . You mean . . . My father?'

Fergus just kept gazing at her, letting her take everything in. Then he leant forward.

'The second thing I discovered,' he went on, 'was that within a week of your father's death something rather interesting happened to Mrs Pamela Leggatt. She got an extremely rapid promotion.'

From the bedroom window it looked as if the whole town had hung out its bunting to celebrate my divorce. The document was in my hand, having arrived in the early-morning post. It was an extraordinary thought. I was no longer Mrs Hazlitt. I'd refused a settlement: I'd refused everything. I wanted the slate to be clean. No ties. No recriminations. David was free, and so was I.

I longed to phone Fergus, but I knew he was on some dreary examination board all morning, conducting students' 'vivas' and no doubt appraising their legs a great deal more keenly than their degree papers. How the world flattered him. We all did. I did. I wanted to. And he returned it every day with love and roses. What more could I ask?

I stopped daydreaming. The bunting had arrived apparently from nowhere. It looped prettily between the trees, and from the far window I could see how it zigzagged across the High

Street, past the church, past Glyn's bookshop and Mamma Gina's restaurant, right down as far as the traffic-lights at the bottom of the hill. Caroline might be preparing for her last battle, but there was no lessening of her gift for organisaion.

The area allocated for the Summer Fête was to the right of my meadow, around and beyond the quince orchard and along the stretch of the old priory wall as far as the eye could see. There were marquees already set up, with pennants flying; trestle-tables by the battalion stacked neatly against the trees; a car-park area ribboned off far away to the left; and umpteen notice-boards and painted wooden arrows all clustered in a pile waiting to be distributed around the place, no doubt by some minion Caroline had already taken hostage.

I shook my head in amazement. How on earth did she conjure all this stuff out of nowhere when she never appeared to do anything except drink vodka and bask in the pool? And immediately after the Summer Fête there was her birthday party, or 'wake' as she preferred to describe it. 'Forty, and the fucking builders move in,' she had said bitterly when we last spoke. 'The wrecking-gang. Might as well be the undertakers.'

Jehoshaphat was gazing mournfully at the Fête paraphernalia, having established that the furthest stretch of his rope still left him yards short of anything he could devour. He turned his back and pissed massively in disgust.

There was such a crowd of things on my mind, quite apart from my divorce, my new life, my lover, and our child to come. The phallic yew-tree was still under sentence of death in spite of Fergus's efforts to get a preservation order slapped on it. The Trust, he explained with a frown, were more concerned about the sensibilities of tearful pilgrims than they were about historical truth. He had no intention of letting the matter rest there, he added menacingly.

The fate of the tree concerned me a good deal less than it did Fergus, one phallus in my life being quite enough to satisfy me. What intrigued me more was the future of Joan's miraculous quince honey. Having proved its astonishing effectiveness on herself and on me, she'd become strangely reticent on the subject. How much of the stuff had she actually made? What did she intend to do with it? Joan answered me only with a sly look. Even when I pointed out that it was like being in secret possession of a nuclear weapon, she did no more than shrug. Something was going on in that mischievous head of hers, and I longed to know what.

But what weighed most heavily on my mind was the strange story of Pamela Leggatt which Fergus had succeeded in unearthing. Suddenly the jigsaw puzzle we'd been poring over had an intriguing picture right in the centre of it. Yet this still didn't connect with what was on either side of it, and there seemed no way we could find the all-important missing pieces.

Caroline took a fatalistic line.

'OK, so my father fucked the bitch. What's new? Show me a woman he didn't fuck.'

Both Megan and Joan put up their hands. But Caroline was in no mood for humour.

'My lawyer's absolutely clear about it,' she went on. 'Unless we can come up with proof of dirty dealing, there's nothing we can do. The fact remains that my bloody father left this house to the nation of his own free will, whatever the inducement may have been.'

Even Fergus was left fishing hopefully.

'Was there no correspondence about it among the admiral's papers?'

Caroline shook her head vaguely.

'What about *his* lawyer? What does he have to say?'

'Just a ga-ga old solicitor he was at school with. He knows nothing. Never did.'

'Weren't there any servants in the house at the time?'

'They never stayed more than five minutes. He used to feel them up, and they'd walk out. The house just got filthy, like he did.'

'And his mistress, the resident one?'

'Vanished.'

'Where?'

'God knows.'

There seemed nothing much more to be said, and the gathering broke up in a frustrated silence.

'I can't believe there isn't some way of finding out what went on,' Fergus insisted when we were back at the gatehouse. 'I may just have to do a Watergate on the Trust's headquarters. There must be files there which would blow the whole story.'

I had looked at him uneasily. Having just divorced one husband, the last thing I wanted was to be compelled to visit my next one in jail.

And right now my burglar-detective-lover was posing as an academic, sitting comfortably in the history faculty pretending to ask long-legged students questions about the Domesday Book. Oh Fergus, my lovely maverick.

But at least this evening there would be a light-hearted diversion from the toils and troubles of Priory Hall. Caroline's final act of defiance was about to be performed, the ceremonial hanging of Megan's portrait of Admiral Romsey's very last mistress the unfinished masterpiece she'd shoved in the garage and forgotten.

'God, it's dreadful,' Megan confessed when she called in for a cup of coffee on her way up to the big house. 'I've left the car unlocked in the hope that someone may steal the bloody thing. I really should stick to painting flowers.' She laughed, and her flesh heaved. 'The trouble was, once I'd accepted the first commission it became impossible to refuse the others. How was I to know there was going to be quite such a turnover? After all, we live a quiet life here in Norton Abbas. Jesus, the paint was hardly dry on one portrait before, bingo, there was another one to do. What I don't know about women's tits isn't worth knowing.'

I had an uncomortable feeling that probably applied to Fergus too.

We were all to assemble at six – Caroline's orders. Patrick had driven down that morning, and was already in deep trouble, she didn't specify what. In mid-afternoon Fergus returned from reviewing his students' legs, with a self-satisfied look on his face. Megan and Joan agreed to make their way to Priory Hall separately on the grounds that should the evening prove entirely unbearable each had her own escape-hatch.

As we arrived a procession of cars already lined the drive in front of the big house. Carmen showed us in: a rare spark of animation lit up her face, which I attributed to Patrick's charms – also the reason why he was in deep trouble, I felt sure. I could hear his voice raised in the drawing-room, vigorously denying whatever it was Caroline was charging him with, and enjoying every minute of it. Through the open door I caught sight of Megan and Joan standing at a safe distance from the two combatants.

The first sign that we were to expect the full scope of Caroline's imagination struck us even before we entered the drawing-room. Fergus suddenly stopped, and pointed. I turned my head, and there on the wall just by the door hung a photograph of the admiral. I'd seen it before, but not quite like this. Someone – I assumed it must be Caroline – had cut out the head from the rest of the photograph, and had fixed it carefully on to a large oil-painting of a Turkish harem which I remembered her saying was a family heirloom reputed to be by Ingres.

But it wasn't only the admiral's head which had been fixed to the painting. Carefully arranged below it was the naked torso of one of the Chippendales, to which a large flesh-coloured loofah had been attached in the appropriate place, with two wire pan-scrubbers suspended beneath it. The loofah was pointing enthusiastically towards the door of the drawing-room, and on its tip, secured by means of a pink bow, was hung a printed notice with an accompanying arrow, which read 'To the Hall of the Mystresses – £2'.

It was revolting, and it was clearly meant to be.

'She doesn't intend to give in quietly, does she?' Fergus muttered as we walked in.

The drawing-room had been rearranged specially for next week's public re-opening. House-plants rose exotically from Grecian urns in front of each window and between the portraits. The paintings themselves, I noticed, were now numbered, and a notice by the door identified each number with the name of the particular sitter. For the benefit of those keen to know more about the admiral's mistresses, typed information sheets had been laid out on the large table in the centre of the room. These were in several languages, including what I took to be Japanese, and each was mounted on a wooden board with a handle, which looked suspiciously as though it had been nicked from the parish church. In this way, Caroline explained, visitors would be able to walk round the gallery and learn more about the ladies concerned, their origin, their habits and interests, their period of tenure at Priory Hall, and so on.

She was especially proud of these information sheets, she added. They'd required a great deal of work, particularly getting the translations done in time. She'd made it all up, naturally, including their names. She hadn't the faintest idea who these women were, and Megan certainly couldn't remember; so what enormous fun it had been to invent. After all, visitors to the National Gallery or the Louvre liked to be told about the masterpieces they'd come such a long way to see, didn't they? In fact one was rarely told enough in her view, and never the really interesting things. This was why she'd taken trouble to explain which mistress liked the missionary position, or fellatio, or dressing up in leather or as a nun ('I thought that was rather appropriate here,' she said), so that one would begin to get a feeling of what the house was like in its heyday, as well as an appreciation of her father's wide-ranging tastes – a welcome sense of variety. ('Otherwise all nudes look much the same, don't they?')

Caroline rattled on in this vein. She was a genius at keeping a straight face. Fergus and I were less successful. Megan and Joan were still keeping their distance, exchanging stunned looks. Patrick was clearly longing to be anywhere but here.

'Well now, this is the great moment,' Caroline announced. And with a dramatic gesture of the hand she indicated the large space on the far wall, against which the wrapped package containing Megan's final portrait now rested. A step-ladder stood nearby.

'Patrick, this is what you're here for,' she went on. 'You're good at hammering in small nails. So go to it. Then we'll have the last of my father's champagne to celebrate.'

A resigned look came over Patrick's face as he walked slowly across the room and began to peel away the sheets of brown paper which covered the painting. There were yards and yards of it, and the Sellotape kept sticking to his fingers. He tried to tread it away with his feet, so that it stuck to his shoes. Caroline's tongue kept clicking in irritation.

'For Christ's sake Patrick, you're useless,' she growled.

'Patience, darling, patience. All will be revealed,' he replied calmly. 'She won't run away.' And he wrenched the last swathe of paper from the canvas.

The unfinished nude now gazed out at us. Megan gave a shudder. Fergus cleared his throat. Joan giggled. 'Jesus,' Caroline exclaimed, 'what a ghastly-looking tart. She's deformed . . . Well, go on, Patrick. Hang the wretched thing. What the hell's the matter with you?'

Patrick had his back to us. He didn't seem to be doing anything at all. He just stood there, not moving.

'Perhaps he's contemplating great things,' Joan suggested in a low voice, with another giggle. 'Both of them.'

Caroline shot her an angry look.

'This is ridiculous.' she hissed. 'Patrick!'

Still nothing happened. Then, very slowly, he turned round. There was a shocked expression on his face, and his mouth gave a little twitch. His eyes carefully avoided ours, and his hands flapped awkwardly as if he wished they weren't there. Finally he made an effort to compose himself, and gave an embarrassed laugh.

'It's just that . . . I sort of . . . know her,' he said.

It was Fergus who eventually thrust his way into the screaming-match. I don't believe I'd ever seen him angry before.

'For Christ's sake, both of you, shut up!' he yelled. 'It doesn't matter a damn whether Patrick's sleeping with the woman or not. And it matters even less what *you* feel about it, Caroline. Don't you see what this could mean? Patrick, just get into your bloody car and go and see her. Today. You must know what strip-club she works in. Bribe her, threaten her, wring her neck if necessary, do whatever you like, but *get something out of her*. Find out what went on in this place before she left. Now, go, go, go!'

And Patrick went. More than a little relieved to have avoided the firing-squad, he hit the BMW's accelerator as though his life depended on it. And judging by Caroline's face, it might well have done.

She was still refusing to understand. She stood by the front door glaring furiously at the car as it speeded away down the drive.

'How could Patrick screw a tart like that? It's disgusting. A stripper!'

'Your father didn't seem to mind,' Joan suggested.

Caroline took a sharp intake of breath, and surprisingly said nothing.

'Quite a lot to strip for,' was Fergus's first comment once the two of us were back in the peace of the gatehouse. 'Like father, like son-in-law,' he added with a glint in his eye. 'Darling, I could do with a drink.'

We both could. I produced a bottle of Frascati from the fridge, and handed it to him.

As he opened it Fergus explained that he'd managed to have a quick word with Patrick before he drove off. Assuming he found the girl and got something out of her, however little, it would be best if he rang *here* rather than the big house, Fergus had insisted. Patrick, looking like a whipped puppy, had gratefully agreed.

'He won't phone tonight: it'll be far too late. At least I hope he won't. I could do with a peaceful night, with you.'

Fergus reached over and gently unbuttoned my blouse.

'I love your breasts,' he said, running his hands over them.

'Not as large as the stripper's, I'm afraid.'

'Thank God. I'd get lost in Silicone Valley.'

I laughed.

We sat watching the sun gradually sink behind the beech-wood. Beyond the marquees I caught sight of both honey buzzards gliding low over the quince orchard, and for the first time I noticed their brood of three young making ungainly sorties from tree to tree. Joan's bees were in for a major assault.

Fergus had closed his eyes.

'What are you thinking?' I asked.

He opened one eye.

'I was thinking about living with you. And before that I

was thinking about Caroline.' He sat up, and suddenly looked earnest. 'It's only a hunch,' he said, 'but I bet that stripper knows something. She must do, surely. Megan says she was here for the best part of six months. In other words she was living here – in the gatehouse – at exactly the time when the old bastard made his last will, which was three months before he died. So she *must* have something to tell us.'

I cobbled an omelette together and we ate it on the terrace in the last of the light. There were long silences, and I knew that neither of us could get the business of Patrick and the stripper out of our minds.

'D'you suppose Patrick really had no idea he was screwing his late father-in-law's mistress? God, doesn't it sound ludicrous put like that?' I said.

Fergus smiled, and gave a shrug.

'No, why ever should he? What's more, she almost certainly had no idea who Patrick was either. It should make for a lively meeting, assuming he can find her.'

We retired to bed early. I lay there for a while listening to the owl, and to the soft puttering sounds of Fergus sleeping. Then I must have drifted off.

The phone woke us at two o'clock. Fergus and I both made a blind grab for it. I won. It was Caroline to say she couldn't sleep. That was just what I needed. Fergus groaned and rolled over. I lied and said, 'It's you she wants to speak to, Fergus,' and passed him the phone. He was too fuddled to be rude. There were lots of grunts, then, 'Yes, I'm sure Patrick'll ring in the morning, Caroline. Good-night.'

'Bloody woman,' he muttered. 'We should never have got into this.'

'You love it,' I said.

There was a grumble from the pillow. Then silence. Gradually I felt myself drifting off again, until through the mist of half-sleep a voice boomed in my ear.

'What are we going to call the baby?'

'Oh, for God's sake, Fergus,' I groaned.

'I can't sleep. Bloody Caroline.'

'Nor can I now. Thanks.'

There was another pause.

'Then let's make love.'

Tired sex lingers. He was huge, and I was a little dry which made him feel even more huge. I could feel him deliberately not coming, withdrawing, then entering me again as I shuddered.

Heaven knows how long we floated through the erotic night, in and out of sleep, but I was aware of the dawn unveiling around us. At last I could feel all his muscles tauten as he was about to climax inside me. Then as he came, I came.

And the phone rang.

Even if an H-bomb had dropped I wasn't going to answer it.

After eight rings Fergus rolled off me and I heard a breathless groan which sounded almost like 'Yes'. I could make out only a twitter of a voice on the other end, interspersed with further groans from Fergus. Then suddenly the groans became sharper, and he heaved himself on to one elbow. In the half-light I could see his face shake itself alert. He ran his fingers through his hair and heaved himself to his feet. And still the twittering sound continued.

By now I was fully alert too, alert enough to be aware that the damp patch in the bed was unpleasantly cold. I kicked my legs from under the duvet and rolled over until I was standing by the side of the bed next to Fergus. I tried to hear what was being said, but I could only pick up this infuriating gabble. Then suddenly he seized my hand tightly, and began to pump it up and down as though he were ringing a hand-bell. He was nodding his head vigorously. His face was radiant.

'Lunchtime, OK,' he said. 'You have no idea what it is? . . . And she doesn't know either? . . . Just bring it with you then. We'll be waiting . . . Yes, of course I'll tell her.'

At last he put the phone down. It was light enough now to see his excited expression.

'Well, go on. Tell me, tell me,' I said impatiently.

Fergus sat down heavily on the bed and gazed at me with those intense blue eyes.

'Right. D'you want the lot? Here's the story.' And he took my hand, sliding his fingers gently between mine. 'It's quite a plateful. Not all that easy to grasp – Patrick sounded rather pissed. He's been with the girl most of the night apparently. Only just got back. Her name's Marisa: she's South American. Well, the moment he asked her about Priory Hall she had hysterics: she was absolutely terrified. So he filled her with champagne, told her she was perfectly safe, and she began to talk. And how. For a start, we were absolutely right about the Leggatt woman. Marisa told Patrick there was this grey-haired woman who kept turning up at the house: into alternative medicine of some kind, the girl was given to understand. She didn't know more than that. But now here's the real nugget, Claudia.' Fergus leant forward and placed his other hand on my arm. 'It seems the old boy had been impotent for months, and then suddenly he wasn't! He became an old goat. Unfortunately that was also the end of him. A heart attack. Patrick, I have to say, made a frightful joke about it. The admiral was screwing the girl at the time apparently; and he called out, "I'm coming." "Instead of which, he went," Patrick said. Hardly the way to talk about your father-in-law, is it?'

I just looked at Fergus.

'For God's sake, let's have some coffee,' I said.

I got up off the bed, and quickly washed and dressed. Then I made the coffee. Fergus pulled on a dressing-gown, and we carried our cups out on to the terrace. The sun was just rising above the old priory ruins, and the air was fresh. I was beginning to feel almost human.

'So, what else did Patrick say? Anything?' I asked.

Fergus stroked his unshaven face and looked at me strangely. Then he gave me a knowing smile.

'I've been saving this bit for the coffee,' he said. 'Patrick's got something. A letter. Addressed to Caroline. He thinks he recognises her father's handwriting. Marisa suddenly thrust it at him apparently. Unopened. She's had it all this time: something about having swept it up by mistake with a lot of her own stuff when she left in a panic, and then being too scared to do anything about it because of the police. The girl's an illegal immigrant, I assume. Or into drugs maybe. Or both. Anyway he's bringing it down.'

Fergus drank his coffee and leant back in the garden chair.

'I wonder. I wonder. What d'you think?'

I didn't think. I didn't know. I looked across at Fergus. At that moment all I wanted – burningly – was to start a real life with this unshaven man, a life far away from dead men's mistresses, predatory matrons, phallic yew-trees, medieval love-potions, miracle-hunting pilgrims and dead-of-night phone calls from drunken lechers. Whatever this letter of Patrick's might contain, it would be the absolutely final episode of my life here, I decided.

By midday we were all waiting in the drawing-room of Priory Hall. Caroline was entirely subdued. She looked frightened. I couldn't help remembering how she'd always loved her father, had always been the one to drop everything and hurry down the motorway the moment anything was wrong; which was why she was so devastated when he simply gave the house away, the house where she was born and brought up. She couldn't forgive him for that. It was a betrayal beyond anything she could have imagined.

And now there was this letter. She stood tensely in the middle of the room listening for the sound of Patrick's car.

Megan and Joan were gazing out of the window at the garden, saying nothing. Fergus was pretending to look at a book. Since it was one of Patrick's racing almanacs, I wondered where his thoughts lay. Perhaps in that detached way of his he was busy plotting what might be the final chapter of the book he'd still not shown me, though he'd promised he would do so just as soon as we left this place. 'How do I know how to end it?' he'd said only this morning. And then he'd laughed. 'You see, the Devil's work is never done.'

Would I ever know all the darker layers of this man? And yet I trusted him – I trusted his heart.

We heard a car drawing up.

'Here he is.' Caroline's voice was shaky. But she didn't move; she stood there in the middle of the room, upright as a guardsman, waiting. She folded her arms and looked at no one.

Patrick hesitated at the door when he saw her. The envelope in his hand was long and thin. It was as though he didn't quite know what to do.

'Give it to me,' she said sharply.

He hurried over to where she stood, and she snatched it from him. Tore it open. Pulled out the contents. A letter fell to the floor, but she took no notice of it.

She was holding a larger document in her hand. And as she unfolded it I could see what it was. It was a will.

Those few seconds remain blurred in my mind. I stared at Caroline. We all of us stared at her, at that document she was unfolding. I remember her hands were shaking. I remember seeing tears form in her eyes. I remember what she said, though it was scarcely more than a whisper.

'It's mine, the house. It's mine.'

None of us moved, and none of us said a word. There would be time for that. This was Caroline's moment.

Without looking at any of us she very slowly bent down and picked up the piece of paper from the floor at her feet. She read it. She seemed to read it several times. Then without even the hint of an expression on her face she simply handed it to me.

'Read it, Claudia,' she said softly. 'Read it aloud.'

I took the letter from her. It wasn't long. The handwriting was laboured, and some of the letters were smudged. The notepaper was headed 'Priory Hall, Norton Abbas, Devon'. I noticed the date: it must have been only a week or two before he died.

Then I read it out.

'"My darling Caroline, Being in lousy health this is in case I'm unable to see you before I kick the bucket, and to make some explanation of my muddled affairs. This is my final will, witnessed yesterday by a new solicitor you don't know, the former one being a total ass, as I have been, and for which I hope you'll find it in you to forgive me. Let me only say that I have not been entirely myself recently, and have done things I now bitterly regret. Blame it on the Old Adam if you wish: he was always just a little too fond of Eves. But I have always loved you, and am happy to think that you may live here in this lovely house, where I have been happy, and where

I hope that sometimes you have too, in spite of everything. My blessings on you, and on the children. Your impossible and loving father."'

He'd signed it 'Daddy', but I couldn't bring myself to read that out. Caroline was already holding her head in her hands.

Fourteen

It looked like a party for the whole of the West Country. Could there be anyone within a radius of a hundred miles who made jams, cakes, pots, portraits, tea-cosies, willy-warmers; who knitted, carved, quilted, told fortunes; who had budgerigars to sell, white elephants to peddle, second-hand books to flog; who wasn't here? Caroline's Summer Fête was a carnival, and she was out there somewhere in the midst of it. I caught sight of her from time to time, bullying people she didn't know into buying things they didn't want.

Fergus and I were strolling aimlessly among the stalls, with me endeavouring not to look too conspicuously pregnant, and Fergus doing his best to look as though it was nothing to do with him in any case. We chatted warily, keeping a sharp eye open for people we had no wish to encounter.

At first I didn't notice his change of expression. I was conscious only of an unusual silence. Then he gave a cough, and mumbled, 'Oh my God.'

I glanced at Fergus. There was a horrified expression on his face.

'I didn't arrange this, I promise you,' he said quietly.

I looked hurriedly in the direction he was gazing. And there, crossing the open meadow towards us with a couple of lackeys in tow, was David.

He'd seen us, and was smiling. I wasn't.

'I promise you,' Fergus said again, speaking quickly before David came too close. 'When I wrote to the Ministry about that tree, they promised to send someone. It never occurred to me David would come himself.'

I looked daggers at him. But it was too late to say anything. I set myself to smile and folded my hands across my belly, wishing they were a great deal larger. Jesus, this was going to be awful.

My smile felt hideous. My stomach felt enormous.

He came up to me and kissed me on both cheeks.

'My dear,' he said gently. (I was now a 'dear', was I?) 'I thought I'd come myself, hoping you'd be here. I wanted to see how you were keeping.'

Oh, these courtesies, I thought. And what on earth do I say?

'Thank-you, David.' I turned awkwardly to Fergus. 'By the way, this is Dr Corrigan.'

David gave Fergus a little nod of recognition, and the two of them shook hands.

'I know your face from the box of course,' David said politely.

Fergus awarded him a similar nod of recognition, and produced a smile.

After this little exercise in television flattery David turned back to me, and Fergus tactfully withdrew a few paces. This was getting worse. David looked disconcertingly calm, as if he were some visiting royal with his attendant footmen hovering like dark-suited shadows.

'Before Dr Corrigan and I conduct our piece of business,' he said quietly, 'I felt I had to reassure myself that all was well with you. You'd refused any settlement, after all, and I was concerned, a little anxious. But you do look well, as far as I can see.'

What exactly had he seen? It felt as though my belly was sending out frantic signals to be noticed. I was too flustered to say anything; I just held on to this ridiculous smile.

'Thank-you, David,' I managed to blurt out. 'Yes, every-thing's fine. Perfectly fine.'

There was silence. I was so confused that I wasn't sure if his eyes had wandered to my stomach or not. Then David gave another little nod.

'Yes, I can see,' he said again.

Had he noticed? How could he *not* have noticed? Except that, David being David, he might well not have. Perhaps he thought it was too much pasta. I tried not to smile at the thought.

There was a longer pause. David gave me a long look; and

somehow I knew it was the last look he would ever give me. Even David's good-byes were silent. All the really important things between us had always remained unsaid, right up to the end.

He turned to Fergus.

'Well, Dr Corrigan,' he said lightly, 'shall we make our little inspection?'

I watched the two of them walk away across the meadow towards the topiary garden, the minions picking their way cautiously through the long grass behind them.

I felt numbed. Could this really be happening? There, strolling together, were my ex-husband and my future husband, David in his immaculate dark-blue suit, hands behind his back in the Duke of Edinburgh fashion, Fergus casually dressed as usual and gesturing in the direction of the topiary garden. They seemed deep in conversation. Suddenly I longed to know what was being said, and whether David was talking about me – and indeed whether Fergus was saying anything about me. Might David have guessed? And I found myself smiling. This really was ridiculous: the idea of the two of them discussing the woman they had in common in front of a giant phallus. What in God's name would they find to say?

The moment they were out of sight I hurried back to the privacy of the gatehouse.

Still I couldn't resist peering discreetly out of the bedroom window. Everything looked wonderfully normal. Far over on the right, gesticulating by one of the cake-stalls, I could make out the abundant figure of Mamma Gina, with Carlo lingering behind, his head turning as Caroline's eldest, Chloe, minced past in the briefest of mini-skirts. She'd returned from school only this morning, I remembered.

A few stalls beyond I picked out Joan's blaze of red hair, with two more beacons – the flame-throwers – in close attendance.

I scanned the drifting mass of humanity for others I might recognise. Glyn I could see, poring over second-hand books. And there was Megan, adopting a critical pose a few yards from a woman drawing a portrait of some child. Then I noticed the stooped figure of the Reverend Pype, in relentless black, moving judgmentally among the stalls, buying nothing.

Not to be out there any longer began to seem sadly appropriate. I was leaving this place. I didn't even have anything I could have sold: the sudden rush of summer pilgrims had cleaned me out of herb-baskets, even of *St Cuthburga's Cookbook*. There was nothing left. The greenhouse stood empty. This, too, seemed appropriate: a chapter of my life was closing.

After a while I noticed Fergus and David making their way back along the edge of the beech-wood towards the marquees and stalls. And there was Jehoshaphat heading purposefully towards them, dragging his tether and shaking his beard. I saw David pluck a tuft of grass and hold it out towards him. Oh, big mistake, I thought: there goes another Turnbull & Asser shirt. Perhaps a finger or two. No, I really mustn't be unkind. And I felt a twinge of guilt.

It was just that he looked so clean and neat. David always had: he'd never smelt of anything but soap. To think I'd spent ten whole years of my life with Mr Hygiene. Fergus always smelt of body, and that made me aware of mine. I'd never realised that smell could stand for so much.

Out of the back window I caught sight of the ministerial car, with a uniformed chauffeur waiting. The car was black – it would be, wouldn't it? The secretary of state's official hearse. Fergus's red Alfa-Romeo was parked only a short distance away.

I made myself some tea. Then a little while later I peered out of the back window again to see if the official car was still there. And right below me, walking towards it, was David. No sign of Fergus. The chauffeur hurried round to open one of the rear doors. He saluted as David clambered in, and I noticed he had a carrier-bag with him. But then ministers would be expected to make some token purchase, wouldn't they? I bet it wasn't a willy-warmer, I thought: it would need more than a knitted garment to warm that willy.

I watched him being driven away down the High Street under the skeins of bright bunting. Good-bye David. And this time it really was good-bye. Again I wondered if he'd made any connection between Fergus and me. Quite possibly not: David's powers of detachment had never been in doubt. His wounds had always healed quickly, and I would leave only a small scar. The Box Hill constituency would prove so much more compliant a bride.

Just as I was about to go out and rejoin the Fête, Fergus walked in.

'Sorry about that,' he said, not looking particularly sorry.

I thought about being angry. Instead I laughed. I had to. Fergus looked relieved.

'Well,' he said with that half-smile, 'we had a most agreeable conversation, and he said yes. So the tree's saved.'

I gazed at him very solemnly, trying hard to keep a straight face.

'I'm extremely glad, darling,' I said. 'But did it occur to you that he may possibly not have recognised what it was?'

Fergus looked quite shocked.

'What an appalling thing to say.'

'I know. David always brings out the worst in me. But it could still be true. After all, a rampant penis was an endangered species in our marriage. Tell me, did he mention me?'

Fergus shook his head.

'No.'

'Did you?'

'Of course not.'

I had to laugh. So discretion had ruled. I stepped forward and kissed Fergus, and stroked his face.

'You know, I've learnt two things this afternoon,' I said, running my fingers through his hair. 'That you can be a total louse, and that I can be almost as vain as you are.'

Fergus looked surprised.

'I hoped you were going to say you'd discovered you loved me.'

I gazed at him, and shook my head.

'Good God, no.' And I gave his hair a tug. 'I knew that long ago.'

It was the morning after Caroline's birthday party. The wind had got up, and we lay half-awake listening to it rattling the windows. Outside I could hear the sound of heavy vehicles: presumably the contractors were removing the marquees and the stalls, and all the rest of the paraphernalia from the Summer

Fête. It had been a total triumph, Caroline had declared. Local radio had said so. Everyone had said so. God knows how much money had changed hands: she'd decided to waive her percentage, she said grandly, because the Hall of the Mystresses had attracted more than five thousand visitors over the weekend, which meant ten thousand quid – in cash. And now that the house was hers, that was going to be the end of it; Megan could take all her paintings back where they came from. All scurrilous references to her father were to be removed forthwith.

Megan, who had just placed her birthday present in front of Caroline, looked rather put out.

'Why not hang on to them till Guy Fawkes night, then burn the lot,' Joan suggested. 'You always hated them anyway, Megan. You said so.'

Megan had looked even more put out.

The birthday party improved after that, aided by the final case of Admiral Romsey's champagne. Caroline gleefully waved a fax from her lawyer confirming that an injunction had been slapped on all further activities by the National Trust relating to Priory Hall pending receipt of the admiral's newly discovered will. A similar fax, he assured her, had been sent to the Trust 'attention Mrs Pamela Leggatt'.

'Here's to the Legover bitch, sod her,' Caroline announced, raising her glass.

We'd left the party some time after midnight, seen to the door by an ebullient Patrick, still overwhelmed at finding himself suddenly a hero in Caroline's eyes, and his tryst with the busty Marisa graciously forgiven.

'After all that, I think we could do with a quiet day,' I said.

Fergus replied with a grunt, pulling the duvet higher round his ears.

I got up to make coffee. Outside I could see the contractors struggling to prevent the last of the marquees being torn away in the wind.

And then the phone went.

That, I thought, has to be one of two people. Either it's Anna-Maria with some Monday morning advice on being pregnant, or it's Caroline.

It was Caroline.

'Claudia.' The voice sounded unusually subdued, and I wondered for a moment if she were still drunk from yesterday evening. 'Claudia,' she said again, 'I'm forty, and I can't bear it. My boobs have dropped an inch over night. And I found a grey hair this morning. I'm middle-aged. What am I going to do?'

I suppose I should have realised that, having finally won her battle with the National Trust, Caroline would discover some other tragedy to plague her life.

'Can I come round?' she went on. 'I need company.'

It was the last thing Fergus and I needed, but I said yes. Fergus guessed what was in store, and disappeared muttering into the bathroom. I caught the sound of his electric razor, and the occasional curse.

If Caroline needed company, it had better be diluted, I decided. I rang Joan, and then Megan.

'Help,' I said to each of them. 'Caroline's in a middle-age crisis. Please come and lighten our morning. A few jokes would be welcome.'

Not for the first time I misjudged Caroline. Having spilt out her miseries over the telephone, she arrived around drinks time looking remarkably pretty and buoyant. Megan and Joan, who had dragged themselves here unwillingly at least an hour earlier, looking windswept, gazed at her sourly. Fergus made an unsuccessful effort to smile.

Caroline gazed around her for a drink, found one, and stretched herself elegantly on the sofa.

'Now, Claudia,' she said purposefully, 'what I need to ask you is this. Tell me, that stuff of Joan's, did it make you as randy as hell? I mean *really* randy?'

I was taken aback. Both Megan and Joan looked surprised. Fergus had an intrigued expression on his face.

'Yes, it did rather,' I answered cautiously, trying to imagine what revelations were about to follow.

'Well,' she said. She pursed her lips and looked at me sharply. 'All I can say is I'm horrified. When I said I wanted to hit forty with a bang, I certainly never intended it to be with my husband. It's absolutely disgusting.'

She held a straight face for a moment, then burst out laughing.

We glanced at each other. The idea that Caroline, having regained her house, had also regained a husband, seemed altogether too much. Then, as if by telepathy, another thought seemed to enter our minds at the same time. I looked at Fergus. He looked at Megan. She looked at me. Finally we all looked at Joan.

Only Caroline appeared quite unaware of what each of us was thinking.

'Joan,' I said, 'you gave Caroline some of your quince honey for her birthday. Is that it?'

Joan looked across at me brightly.

'Oh no,' she answered brightly. 'She bought it from my stall.'

There was another silence. Again we looked at one another. I think until that moment I'd never fully taken in what Joan had done, and what it could mean. Her mysterious quince honey had seemed little more than a wonderful joke. OK, so the stuff had worked on Joan and Geoff, and on me. But perhaps this was merely a happy accident. Joan and Geoff hadn't made love for years; they were both of them sunk deep in frustration. I'd been in an appalling state, facing the prospect of living alone as an unmarried mother. So it made perfect sense. The mind, after all, was capable of surprising things: one always underestimated its power over the body. All it needed was a little outside help; and maybe if I'd eaten lots of oysters the result would have been precisely the same. In any case everyone knew that aphrodisiacs didn't really exist: they were just old wives' tales, or at most a trick, like self-hypnosis. We all had fertile imaginations. As for Fergus, he always loved letting his imagination run free – that was why he was writing this book, *The Devil's Work*. It was a ludicrous idea, that you could boil up the root of some orchid, and it would blow your mind. Whatever Fergus might pretend, he didn't actually believe in it.

But now, as I glanced at him standing casually behind the sofa and gazing at us, I knew for certain that he really did believe it. And that I did too. It was no longer just Joan and me;

it was Caroline too. What was more, not only Caroline: Who the hell else had bought quince honey from that innocent little stall of hers at the Summer Fête? What further mischief had Joan caused? And when, and how, might that mischief erupt?

I had visions of an epidemic, with half the nation passionately in rut.

'Joan,' I said uneasily, 'exactly who else did you sell it to?'

She looked coy for a moment and shrugged her shoulders, as if she couldn't quite remember.

'Oh well, let me think now,' she said, smiling and pouring herself another glass of wine. 'I don't know who most of them were of course.' She paused and looked thoughtful. 'But there was one man who said he was a high-court judge – I remember him.' I noticed Megan wince. 'Then there was a rather jolly bishop, Bath and Wells I think. Very fond of quinces, he assured me. Oh yes, and that rather beautiful actress you see on TV a lot, what's her name? Joan something-or-other. Then who was that vaguely royal person *you* knew, Caroline? A cousin of the Queen I think you said she was. She bought quite a lot; said they'd be wonderful presents for the family.' Joan giggled. 'I suppose she must have meant the Royal Family, come to think of it.'

She paused and sipped her wine, not appearing to notice the expressions on our faces. Fergus gave a meaningful cough and threw me an amazed look.

'Who else now?' Joan went on. 'Nobody very interesting, I think. Unless you include our vicar, that is. He bought some. "Supporting local produce," he said rather pompously. Went away looking very pleased with himself. Oh, now wait a minute, there *was* somebody else; a rather grand politician, a minister of some sort; I didn't catch his name, but he did say he was here on official business, he didn't say what.'

I closed my eyes. My vision of a nation in rut had never until that moment included my ex-husband.

Only Caroline seemed to take all this entirely in her stride. She yawned and lit a cigarette.

'It seems to me, Joan,' she said languidly, 'that you've managed to set up what the French call the "*Bonk Nationale*".'

Joan smiled appreciatively.

'And why not? Everyone's so bloody stodgy and complaisant in this country, don't you think? Do a lot of good to shake them up a bit. A bit of raunch, that's what we all need.'

I could see from Fergus's face that he had quite different thoughts. He walked over to the far window, and I joined him. The wind had whipped up into a gale outside, so there was no risk of being overheard.

'She's gone mad, that woman,' he said in a low voice. 'Raving mad. She hasn't thought about anything except making mischief. This is bound to reverberate. You can't go distributing powerful aphrodisiacs round the country and expect nothing to happen. Something's bound to. Then it'll be bedlam, sheer bedlam; and the press will leap on it. And the moment's it's traced to this place, just imagine. "Love potion traced to former nunnery"' – Fergus spelt out the headline with his hands. '"Doctor's wife peddles aphrodisiac." Claudia, there'll be mass hysteria. Your little pilgrimages to St Cuthburga will be nothing by comparison. It'll be like the Second Coming.' He winced and gave a wry smile. 'Perhaps I should rephrase that.'

'So what d'you think we should do?' I asked, feeling increasingly uneasy.

Fergus glanced over to where Joan was still calmly sipping her wine. Her face was that of a little girl who has just gleefully tossed a fire-cracker into the school assembly.

'Well,' he said, looking at me wistfully, 'there are two things we can do, my darling. We either stay here and prepare for a siege by the entire international press corps. Or we get the hell out of it quick.'

'How quick?'

'Tomorrow?'

'And the others?'

'Caroline had better do the same: we need to tell her. Megan's all right, she can lie low. And that leaves Joan.' He threw another glance across the room to where Joan was happily pouring herself yet another glass of wine. 'It's up to her, isn't it? She's made her lovers' bed: maybe she'll just have to lie in it.'

*   *   *

I could never have anticipated my year of peace would end quite like this. We packed hurriedly that afternoon, filling suitcases with whatever we might conceivably need while we took refuge in the coastguard's cottage. My few bits of furniture and kitchen stuff could stay. I might just leave them for good, small mementoes of the strangest and richest time of my life. I'd leave them in memory of the Blessed St Cuthburga and of the admiral's mistresses, whose spirits so powerfully inhabited this place. I'd come to think of it as haunted. My own life would never have been remotely the same without them; yet I suspected that the moment of exorcism was very close, and I had absolutely no wish to be around when it happened.

In fact, even as I pondered on these things, I knew that I was never going to come back.

'We could always slip abroad if things become too hot,' Fergus suggested. 'I don't have to be at the university till the autumn. A quiet summer somewhere in France, how does that grab you? We could rent a place.'

It sounded perfect. A quiet summer far away from tearful pilgrims and dangerous orchids. Oh yes.

'And what would you do there?' I asked.

Fergus laughed, and ran a hand over my bare shoulder.

'Be with you. Shouldn't that be enough?'

What could I say after that? I just hugged him.

'And *The Devil's Work*?' I said. 'Might you finish that?'

He gave a shrug.

'If I can think how to end it. Perhaps I never will: it's all become a bit too real, and it was never meant to be.'

'Not even the heroine?'

There was another laugh. The intense blue eyes were gazing at me.

'Yes, she became real too. Author's perk, I think that was.'

We were standing in the living-room surrounded by loaded boxes and suitcases. It was six o'clock. We'd planned to go and see Caroline, then have a farewell dinner at Mamma Gina's, a last taste of 'good cook'. I should miss her.

I should also have liked to take a last walk round my borrowed acres, but the rain was now flailing across the meadow. The beech-trees were bending like reeds, and I felt sorry for Jehoshaphat standing there stoically in the midst of the gale. Megan had promised to come and move his stake while we were away. I should miss him too, the miserable bugger.

I was leaving a lot of friends.

We drove up to Caroline's. Her voice could be heard the moment we got out of the car. Wandering round the side of the house, we found her in the swimming-pool, laughing in the cascading rain. To my astonishment Patrick was in the pool with her.

'Join us,' she called out cheerfully to Fergus. 'I haven't swum with two naked men since the last General Synod.'

'You dare!' I whispered, gripping him closer under the umbrella.

We watched them clamber out and make a dash for the house. Fergus gave a chuckle.

'Well, if he's only got four inches, all I can say is it must shrink when it's erect. D'you think they may actually be all right, at last?'

'Till the next time,' I said. 'Or till the quince honey runs out.'

Fergus shook his head.

'A restless lady.' He squeezed my arm. 'Are you?'

'No.'

'Thank God.'

When we were indoors, much to my surprise Caroline explained that she'd already planned to leave the next day. She'd had quite enough invasions recently without the press, she announced, standing wrapped in a towel in the middle of the drawing-room, making sure Fergus was in a position to admire her legs. All Megan's paintings had disappeared: there was only a formal portrait of her father in full dress uniform, hanging in the place of honour above the fireplace. Yes, there was a villa somewhere, she said vaguely, rearranging the towel so that Fergus could admire rather more of her: not far from Rome – it belonged to the Vatican actually, but the Pope never used it until the end of August. They were all of them flying out there tomorrow. Why didn't we join her? It was wonderfully private if one didn't mind the papal guard turning up from time to time.

Caroline did a little more rearranging of her towel for Fergus's benefit.

I firmly said thank-you but I was afraid we had other plans. Besides, I added, I was sure that she and Patrick would like time on their own.

She shot me a disapproving look.

'So, what d'you think you'll do when you come back, now the house is yours?' I asked, anxious to change the subject.

Caroline just shrugged.

'God knows.' Then she smiled.

'Perhaps I'll be content for a while to raise a toast to the wonderful absence of the Legover woman.' She turned to Fergus. 'What d'you suppose will happen to the bitch?'

Fergus laughed.

'I imagine her illustrious career will go downhill even faster than it went up. Downhill and out the exit door on the end of a boot.'

Caroline looked thoroughly pleased.

'That has to be the best thing I've ever heard about the National Trust. You know, I might even join. D'you think they'd have me after all this? I could give them some great fundraising ideas.'

I had visions of half the stately homes of England being hung with portraits of noble mistresses, and galleries of Van Dycks and Rubens subtly improved by the addition of loofahs.

'I'm sure they'd welcome them, Caroline,' I said.

Soon afterwards we left for Mamma Gina's. By ten-thirty, bruised by hugs and warmed by many grappas, we were fighting our way through the gale towards the gatehouse, clothes drenched, hair lashing across our faces, our umbrellas hopelessly blown inside-out.

On the radio they announced that winds were now reaching hurricane force in the West Country.

'Christ, what a last night,' I said as we stood dripping among the suitcases. 'Did somebody invite Wagner?'

We made love in the *Kama Sutra* bed for the last time.

'There's one position I never quite mastered,' Fergus murmured, raising his head from between my breasts. 'I put it down to you being pregnant, so I had to be careful.'

'If you'd been a bit more careful I wouldn't *be* pregnant,' I said.

'Are you sorry?'

I shook my head, and pulled his head down on to my breast again. He ran his hand over my belly.

'When am I going to be able to feel it kick?'

'All too soon.'

'What time is it?'

'Christ knows. Why are you so horribly wide awake?'

'Because we're leaving. And the gale's stopped. The sun seems to be shining.'

God knows where my watch was. I reached out and turned on the bedside radio. I liked rolling news programmes; they always gave me the feeling that Norton Abbas wasn't quite as isolated as I'd imagined. An interview with some earnest ecologist was just coming to an end. There followed a lot of banter about the 'silly season' – 'nothing ever happens' – 'everyone's off on holiday' – 'why don't we just close down the news station and join them?' Then one of the presenters let out a laugh. 'Hang on a minute, there *is* something here just come in, reports of some very strange happenings in the West Country, people behaving . . . Well, how shall I put it? . . . Most oddly. In public too, in broad daylight.' He gave another laugh. 'Well, well. A high-court judge has been charged with an indecent act in a Marks & Spencer's car-park in Exeter. With his wife, what's more. And here's another. A vicar in Norton Abbas has been caught *in flagrante* with his woman curate. Goodness me. D'you suppose they've been putting something in the water down there in Devon? And here's yet another report just in, from the Home Counties this time – getting closer. Amazing goings on at Tory Party headquarters in Box Hill, Surrey. That's the environment secretary's constituency. Police called in. No details yet. We'll keep you informed. Ah well, that's woken us all up, hasn't it?'

It had woken me up too. A vicar and his curate: that could only be Jonathan Pype. And Box Hill. Might that conceivably

be David? 'Police called in. We'll keep you informed,' the man
had said.

I didn't think I wanted to be kept informed. I wanted to get
as far away as possible.

Fergus had already made hurriedly for the bathroom: I could
hear him sluicing water over his face. Then he emerged, tossed
his sponge-bag into one of the suitcases, and grabbed his
clothes.

'Well, it's certainly all happening, isn't it? How long before
the press home in on this place? A couple of hours, not
more. And we're absolutely *not* going to be here. I'll make
the coffee.'

I dressed and hastily finished the last of my packing. It was
like a countdown. Two hours, Fergus thought.

He handed me a cup of coffee.

'Have I got time for a last look round?' I asked. 'I'd love to.
You know, in spite of all this I feel quite sad.'

It was true, I did feel sad. There was so much I would miss.
The strange beauty of this place. Memories. And so many
unexpected things I would never find again.

'I'll come with you,' Fergus said. 'It means a lot to me too.
Remember the meadow, the first time?'

I wrapped my arms round him.

'You were very wicked – thank God.'

He smiled, and kissed me.

'Let's go, then,' he said.

We walked out into the sun. The gale had blown itself out
in the night, and there was scarcely a breath of wind. It was
hot already. The golden grass in the meadow lay drenched and
glistening, flattened by the wind. Over to the left I caught sight
of one of my honey buzzards keeping sentinel as always on the
old priory arch, fluffing out his damp feathers in the sun.

We took the path towards the quince orchard. Everything
looked peaceful, as if the gale had never been. Joan's bees
would soon be out foraging as usual. I'd loved them being
here. I'd miss them too.

It was a moment or two before I realised something was
wrong. The bee-hives. They were there, but . . . they were
scattered. As though someone had tossed them about the

orchard. Not a single one was left standing. Frames of honey-comb lay littered across the grass.

I grabbed Fergus's arm. And as we gazed at the desolation four honey buzzards flew up from the wreckage of the hives, and flapped heavily away with harsh cries past the beech-wood towards the tidal marsh.

I turned to Fergus.

'It's awful. Terrible. Poor Joan. The gale – it must have been.'

There was a strange look on Fergus's face. He didn't say anything for a moment. And then he nodded.

'Maybe.'

I wasn't sure what he meant. We walked away in silence. The whole place seemed blighted now. We skirted the beech-wood and stopped to gaze out over the estuary. The water was still choppy, and there were no coloured sails. It looked suddenly bleak.

Torn branches littered the ground as we made our way round the far side of the wood towards the topiary garden. The tall stockade of ancient yew-trees seemed quite untouched by the gale, and we took one of the narrow entrances into the inner garden. There were the sculpted urns, chalices, mitres, pyramids, strange beasts, all of which Fergus and I had so carefully clipped last winter from a jungle of disuse.

This time it was Fergus who stopped abruptly. He had been walking ahead of me while I took my last look at the urns and the beasts.

'Claudia,' he called out. There was a note of urgency in his voice. 'Come here.'

I hurried towards where he was standing. For a moment I didn't recognise where we were. A mountain of earth and roots rose up before me: I couldn't even see beyond it. Fergus walked round the other side, and I heard him give a long gasp.

'The tree,' was all he said.

And there it was. It lay like a fallen giant across the open space, its head buried in the yew-hedge beyond, its vast trunk cushioned on a tangle of tiny branches.

We stood there gazing at it for a long time. I felt shocked. At the same time I wanted to burst out laughing at the idea that this huge tree-phallus had stood erect for centuries and centuries until the day my ex-husband arrived to give it his blessing – whereupon it collapsed. Oh David, I thought, how you always did like power.

'You still think that was the gale?' Fergus asked.

'Well, what else?'

He turned his head to look at me, and there was that mysterious expression on his face.

'If it was, it certainly picked its targets,' he said quietly. '*If it was.*'

We turned away and walked back towards the gatehouse along the edge of the meadow. This place was beginning to feel even more eerie. I looked across the acres of flattened grass. Only then did I notice that something was missing. The meadow was empty. There was no Jehoshaphat.

I hurried over to where I knew the goat's stake had been. But there was merely a gash in the ground, and a streak in the long grass where the stake had been dragged. There was no sign of the animal whatever.

'Claudia,' I heard Fergus call out.

He was standing some distance away on the edge of the beech-wood, gazing at the ground. He was shaking his head.

'I can't believe it,' he said as I hurried over to join him. 'I just can't believe it.'

I looked around me. It was as if the whole area along the fringe of the wood had been lightly ploughed. And there strewn across the middle of the wreckage lay Jehoshaphat's tether.

There was an astonished look on Fergus's face.

'They've gone, the orchids,' he was saying. 'Every single one of them.'

I was too horrified to say anything. First the bees. Then the tree. And now the orchids.

Fergus was on his knees, running his fingers through the bare earth. He was still shaking his head.

'I feel terrible.' He turned to gaze up at me. 'D'you realise, that's a thousand years of history gone in one night?' He looked around him, and there was a perplexed expression on his face. 'And now no one, except us, will ever know the truth about

Norton Priory, thanks to your goat.' He rose to his feet. 'And if I were to write a learned paper about it, people would simply say I'd lost my marbles, wouldn't they? I can just hear it: "Always was a bit crazy, that Dr Corrigan. Most unsound."'

He made a sour face. And then I noticed a shadow of that familiar half-smile.

'On the other hand, my darling,' he said, dusting the earth from his hands, 'when the world's press turn up here in an hour or so, which they certainly will, there'll be nothing – absolutely nothing – for them to see. It'll have been just a fantasy. Another old wives' tale. There'll be a few jokes about midsummer madness. And that'll be it. End of story.'

Suddenly his face brightened.

'And as for that book of mine, well, it has the perfect ending now, doesn't it? And what's more, no one will ever feel the need to believe it. Pure fiction.' He paused, and gazed at the devastation around him. 'You see, Claudia, the Devil's done his work.' Then he gave a chuckle. 'Or maybe it was the opposition this time.'

I wasn't sure whether to laugh or not.

'Fergus,' I said, slipping my arm through his, 'you may be concerned about God, the Devil and your bloody book, but let me tell you, right now what concerns me is that I'm the one who's just let loose the randiest goat in England.'

A look of pure delight came over Fergus's face.

We'd loaded both cars. I was taking a last look round and was about to close the door, when the phone rang.

'If it's the press, just hang up,' Fergus called out from the terrace.

'Claudia,' came the familiar languid voice. 'You *are* leaving today, aren't you?'

Had Caroline already forgotten the fond farewells of yesterday evening?

'Yes,' I said. 'Right now, in fact.'

'Oh, good. Because I've got someone for the gatehouse right away.'

'Who?' I asked, trying not to sound put out.

'It's Howl. You know, my gardener.' There was a moment's

silence, followed by the muffled sound of Caroline yelling at one of the children. 'You remember asking me what I was going to do when I'm back from Italy?' she went on. 'Well, I've decided.'

I glanced at Fergus, and raised my eyes to the ceiling.

'Really? What, Caroline?'

'Oh, it's a brilliant idea, darling, though it's Joan's actually. She brought a whole lot of them round a few days ago: I meant to tell you. I'm going to grow orchids. In a big way.'

Author's Footnote

The powerful aphrodisiac known as Satyrion is mentioned by numerous classical writers in Greece and Rome. Doubtless its source-plant (the Hooded Orchid) was keenly sought after by early plant-hunters, thereby contributing to its scarcity and ultimately, one may assume, to its relative neglect by authors and alchemists alike in more recent centuries.

The Hooded Orchis (*Steveniella satyrioides*).
'Orchid of extreme rarity, known from the Crimea and Pontus in eastern Turkey where it occurs in mountain pastures and open woodlands.'
(*A Field Guide to the Orchids of Britain and Europe* [Collins])

'Satyrion is used as an aphrodisiac.'
(Valmont de Bomare, French naturalist, 1731–1807)

'Satyrion. From Greek *Saturion*, from *saturos* – a satyr. Owes its name to the power, attributed to it in earlier times, of arousing amorous feelings. Satyrions, like nearly all the terrestial orchids, have two, generally ovoid, tubercles which, because of their shape and disposition, bear a fairly close resemblance to testicles, whence their common name in French of "*testicules de chien*" ("dog's testicles") as well as other less refined names by which they used to be known, and are still known in country districts. Since Antiquity their distinctive appearance has also been responsible for the belief in their powerful aphrodisiac qualities. Their tubercles used to be dried, ground and infused in good wine to make a potion which was employed to fortify the sexual organs, promote the secretion of sperm and facilitate conception. They were also made into a preserve. Even today Satyrion enjoys a certain popularity in some Oriental countries. It is a fact that the tubercles have restorative properties and can, to a certain extent, reinvigorate flagging strength. In the pastures these plants are particularly sought after by cows and goats, on whose milk yields they appear to have a significant effect.'
(*La Grande Larousse*, encyclopaedia [trans])